THE BOOKS OF JOHN DICKSON CARR

It Walks by Night, 1930
The Lost Gallows, 1931
Castle Skull, 1931
The Corpse in the Waxworks, 1932
Poison in Jest, 1932
Hag's Nook, 1933
The Mad Hatter Mystery, 1933
The Eight of Swords, 1934
The Blind Barber, 1934
Death-Watch, 1935
The Three Coffins, 1935
The Arabian Nights Murder, 1936
The Murder of Sir Edmund Godfrey, 1936
The Burning Court, 1937
The Four Flase Weapons, 1937
To Wake the Dead 1937
The Crooked Hinge, 1938
The Problem of the Green Capsule, 1939
The Problem of the Wire Cage, 1939
The Man Who Could Not Shudder, 1940
The Case of the Constant Suicides, 1941
Death Turns the Tables, 1941
The Emperor's Snuff-Box, 1942
Till Death Do Us Part, 1944
He Who Whispers, 1946
The Sleeping Sphinx, 1947
The Life of Sir Arthur Conan Doyle, 1949
Below Suspicion, 1949
The Bride of Newgate, 1950
The Devil in Velvet, 1951
The 9 Wrong Answers, 1952
Captain Cut-Throat, 1955
Patrick Butler for the Defence, 1956
Fire, Burn!, 1957
The Dead Man's Knock, 1958
Scandal at High Chimneys, 1959
In Spite of Thunder, 1960
The Witch of the Low-Tide, 1961
The Demoniacs, 1962
The Grandest Game in the World, 1963 (limited-edition pamphlet)
Most Secret, 1964
The House at Satan's Elbow, 1965
Panic in Box C, 1966
Dark of the Moon, 1967
Papa La-Bas, 1968

The Ghosts' High Noon, 1969
Deadly Hall, 1971
The Hungry Goblin, 1972
Crime on the Coast, 1984 (by Carr and others)

WRITING AS CARTER DICKSON
The Plague Court Murders, 1934
The White Priory Murders, 1934
The Red Widow Murders, 1935
The Unicorn Murders, 1935
The Punch and Judy Murders, 1936
The Peacock Feather Murders, 1937
The Third Bullet, 1937
The Judas Window, 1938
Death in Five Boxes, 1938
The Reader is Warned, 1939
Fatal Descent, 1939 (with John Rhode)
And So to Murder, 1940
Nine-and Death Makes Ten, 1940
Seeing Is Believing, 1941
The Gilded Man, 1942
She Died a Lady, 1943
He Wouldn't Kill Patience, 1944
The Curse of the Bronze Lamp, 1945
My Late Wives, 1946
The Skeleton in the Clock, 1948
A Graveyard to Let, 1949
Night at the Mocking Widow, 1950
Behind the Crimson Blind, 1952
The Cavalier's Cup, 1953
Fear Is the Same, 1956

WRITING AS CARR DICKSON
The Bowstring Murders, 1933

WRITING AS ROGER FAIRBAIRN
Devil Kinsmere, 1934

SHORT-STORY AND RADIO-PLAY COLLECTIONS
The Department of Queer Complaints, 1940 (as by Carter Dickson)
Dr. Fell, Detective, and Other Stories, 1947
The Exploits of Sherlock Holmes, 1954 (with Adrian Conan Doyle)
The Third Bullet and Other Stories, 1954
The Men Who Explained Miracles, 1963
The Door to Doom and Other Detections, 1980
The Dead Sleep Lightly, 1983
Fell and Foul Play, 1991
Merrivale, March and Murder, 1991

John Dickson Carr

MERRIVALE, MARCH AND MURDER

Edited with an Introduction by
Douglas G. Greene

LIBRARY OF CRIME CLASSICS®

MISTER E'S™

INTERNATIONAL POLYGONICS, LTD.
NEW YORK CITY

ACKNOWLEDGMENTS

So many enthusiasts, scholars, and collectors of John Dickson Carr's works have helped with the publishing of *Merrivale, March and Murder* that in naming any of them I run the risk of slighting others. Nonetheless, I do want specifically to acknowledge the assistance of Robert Adey, Jack Adrian, Jim Keirans, Barry Pike, Douglas Waugh, Johan Wopenka, and Geoff Webster. Tony Medawar continues to amaze with his sleuthing ability and his generosity in sharing his discoveries, and it is to Tony that we owe the unearthing of the previously unrecorded Carr story "The Diamond Pentacle." John Young's encouragement continues to be instrumental in my Carrian research. To these people and to unnamed others, I extend warmest thanks.

MERRIVALE, MARCH AND MURDER

Copyright © 1991 by Clarice M. Carr, Bonita Cron, Julia McNiven and Mary Howes.

Introductions: Copyright © 1991 by Douglas G. Greene
Published by arrangement with Harold Ober Associates Incorporated, 425 Madison Ave., NY, NY 10017
Library of Congress Card Catalog No. 91-57932
ISBN: 1-55882-101-5

Library of Congress Cataloging-in-Publication Data

Carr, John Dickson, 1906-1977.
  Merrivale, march and murder / John Dickson Carr.
    p. cm.
  ISBN 1-55882-101-5 : $22.95
  1. Detective and mystery stories, American. I. Title.
PS3505.A763M47   1991
813'.52—dc20   91-57932 CIP

Printed and manufactured in the United States of America.
First IPL printing September 1991.
10 9 8 7 6 5 4 3 2 1

CONTENTS

INTRODUCTORY NOTE

John Dickson Carr invented larger-than-life detectives to solve extraordinary cases. He was uninterested in sleuths who can be described as "ordinary" and in mysteries whose main attraction is that they are "believable." The role of a storyteller, he believed, is not to imitate life: fiction really should be (and in his stories really is) stranger than truth. Let ordinary coppers and private eyes investigate dull muggings on mean streets; it takes no lesser mortal than a Great Detective to solve ingenious puzzles about disappearances from locked rooms, guns fired by disembodied hands, footprints on the tops of hedges, and bodies surrounded by unmarked sand.

In collecting John Dickson Carr's short stories, we have organized the volumes around his detectives. *Fell and Foul Play* (1991) contains nine short cases of Dr. Gideon Fell, as well as a selection of other stories. The earlier posthumous collection, *The Door to Doom*, originally published in 1980, will be reprinted soon. It contains all the short stories about Carr's first detective, the satanic Monsieur Henri Bencolin of the Sûreté, and other material. *Merrivale, March and Murder* is based on the two short tales of Sir Henry Merrivale and the nine cases of Colonel March of Scotland Yard's Department of Queer Complaints. As with the other volumes, this book also contains a number of non-series stories, including three nearly unknown tales that have never previously been published in a Carr book. In prefaces to each section of this book, I shall intrude on you again with descriptions of Sir Henry Merrivale and Colonel March, a few notes on early publication of the stories, and some miscellaneous observations.

Douglas G. Greene
Norfolk, Virginia
January 1991

THE ADVENTURES OF
SIR HENRY MERRIVALE

INTRODUCTION

Sir Henry Merrivale, whose cases were chronicled under Carr's pseudonym of "Carter Dickson," is one of fiction's greatest comic detectives. His entry into his cases is usually a marvelous slapstick pratfall: "with a rush and a crash, heels in the air," as Carr described it in a letter. The Old Man (or H. M., as his friends call him) is holder of one of the oldest baronetcies in England. During the First World War, he was head of Great Britain's counterespionage department against Germany, and in his first novels, beginning with *The Plague Court Murders* (1934), he is still head of the Military Intelligence Department. He occupies a room in the War Office with a portrait of Fouché on the wall, a bottle of whiskey in the safe (labeled "Important State Documents" in five languages), and a secretary named Lollypop Ffolliot. There he grouses about the ingratitude of the world as represented by "that reptile," Inspector Humphrey Masters, who is "always trying to do me in the eye." Although first described as a socialist, H. M. eventually succumbs to Carr's dislike of Britain's Labour Party and ends up a member of the Senior Conservatives' Club.

Although secret-service activity plays a role in three of H. M.'s early cases, *The Unicorn Murders* (1935) and *The Punch and Judy Murders* (1936), and *And So To Murder* (1940) Sir Henry Merrivale is primarily a detective specializing in impossible crimes and other events produced by what he calls "the blinkin' awful cussedness of things in general."

His own belief to the contrary, Sir Henry Merrivale is wildly undignified. His cleanest epithets are "Burn me" and "Lord love a duck"; he thinks that he is being polite when he calls a young woman "my dolly" or "my wench"; he addresses a jury as "fatheads"; he describes the Prime Min-

ister as "Horseface," the Commissioner of Police as "old
Boko," and a member of the government as "Squiffy"; when
he gobbles down his favorite drink, whiskey punch, his toast
is "honk, honk" or "mud in your eye." During his investiga-
tive career, he drives a train and hits a cow, launches a ship
by bonking the mayor on the head with a champagne bottle,
disguises himself as a Muslim holy man, causes a riot in the
New York subway, dictates scurrilous memoirs, and takes
singing lessons with disastrous effects on the ears of everyone in the vicinity. But despite all this, the Old Man is not
a buffoon. He has a "childlike, deadly brain" and, while "sittin' and thinkin'," can sort out the facts of the case, discover
how the impossible situation was created, and nab the murderer. Carr often uses the comedy of the H. M. stories to
conceal the clues. "Once we think an author is only skylark-
ing," he said, "a whole bandwagon of clues can go past
unnoticed."

There are only two short cases of Sir Henry Merrivale.
Carr wrote "The House in Goblin Wood" in 1946 at the
request of his friend Frederic Dannay (who, with his cousin,
collaborated on the writings of "Ellery Queen") to enter in
the second annual short story contest sponsored by *Ellery
Queen's Mystery Magazine.* The story received the Special
Award of Merit, though Dannay later admitted that most
readers thought it should instead have been awarded the first
prize. "The House in Goblin Wood" was published simultaneously in the November 1947 issues of *Ellery Queen's Mystery Magazine* in the United States and *The Strand Magazine*
in Britain.

H. M.'s second short case, a novelette originally called
"Ministry of Miracles," was published serially in the British
magazine, *The Housewife,* January through March 1956.
Meanwhile, Carr's agents sold the American rights to *Ellery
Queen's Mystery Magazine,* but Dannay did not like Carr's

title; the word *ministry* might sound too churchly to American readers. Therefore when the story appeared in *Ellery Queen's Mystery Magazine*, March 1956, it was called "The Man Who Explained Miracles." Carr liked Dannay's title and used it, almost without change, for his short-story collection, *The Men Who Explained Miracles* (1963); for that book Carr retitled the story "All in a Maze," and it is under that title that it appears in *Merrivale, March and Murder*.

THE HOUSE IN GOBLIN WOOD

In Pall Mall, that hot July afternoon three years before the war, an open saloon car was drawn up to the curb just opposite the Senior Conservatives' Club.

And in the car sat two conspirators.

It was the drowsy post-lunch hour among the clubs, where only the sun remained brilliant. The Rag lay somnolent; the Atheneum slept outright. But these two conspirators, a dark-haired young man in his early thirties and a fair-haired girl perhaps half a dozen years younger, never moved. They stared intently at the Gothic-like front of the Senior Conservatives'.

"Look here, Eve," muttered the young man, and punched at the steering wheel, "Do you think this is going to work?"

"I don't know," the fair-haired girl confessed. "He absolutely *loathes* picnics."

"Anyway, we've probably missed him."

"Why so?"

"He can't have taken as long over lunch as that!" her companion protested, looking at a wrist watch. The young man was rather shocked. "It's a quarter to four! Even if . . ."

"Bill! There! Look there!"

Their patience was rewarded by an inspiring sight.

Out of the portals of the Senior Conservatives' Club, in awful majesty, marched a large, stout, barrel-shaped gentleman in a white linen suit.

His corporation preceded him like the figurehead of a man-of-war. His shell-rimmed spectacles were pulled down on a broad nose, all being shared by a Panama hat. At the top of the stone steps he surveyed the street with a lordly sneer.

"Sir Henry!" called the girl.

"Hey?" said Sir Henry Merrivale.

"I'm Eve Drayton. Don't you remember me? You knew my father!"

"Oh, ah," said the great man.

"We've been waiting here a terribly long time," Eve pleaded. "Couldn't you see us for just five minutes?—The thing to do," she whispered to her companion, "is to keep him in a good humor. Just keep him in a good humor!"

As a matter of fact, H. M. was in a good humor, having just triumphed over the Home Secretary in an argument. But not even his own mother could have guessed it. Majestically, with the same lordly sneer, he began in grandeur to descend the steps of the Senior Conservatives'. He did this, in fact, until his foot encountered an unnoticed object lying some three feet from the bottom.

It was a banana skin.

"Oh, dear!" said the girl.

Now it must be stated with regret that in the old days certain urchins, of what were then called the "lower orders," had a habit of placing such objects on the steps in the hope that some eminent statesman would take a toss on his way to Whitehall. This was a venial but deplorable practice, probably accounting for what Mr. Gladstone said in 1882.

In any case, it accounted for what Sir Henry Merrivale said now.

From the pavement, where H. M. landed in a seated position, arose in H. M.'s bellowing voice such a torrent of profanity, such a flood of invective and vile obscenities, as has seldom before blasted the holy calm of Pall Mall. It brought the hall porter hurrying down the steps, and Eve Drayton flying out of the car.

Heads were now appearing at the windows of the Atheneum across the street.

"Is it all right?" cried the girl, with concern in her blue eyes. "Are you hurt?"

H. M. merely looked at her. His hat had fallen off, disclosing a large bald head; and he merely sat on the pavement and looked at her.

"Anyway, H. M., get up! Please get up!"

"Yes, sir," begged the hall porter, "for heaven's sake get up!"

"Get up?" bellowed H. M., in a voice audible as far as St. James's Street. "Burn it all, how *can* I get up?"

"But why not?"

"My behind's out of joint," said H. M. simply. "I'm hurt awful bad. I'm probably goin' to have spinal dislocation for the rest of my life."

"But, sir, people are looking!"

H. M. explained what these people could do. He eyed Eve Drayton with a glare of indescribable malignancy over his spectacles.

"I suppose, my wench, *you're* responsible for this?"

Eve regarded him in consternation.

"You don't mean the banana skin?" she cried.

"Oh, yes, I do," said H. M., folding his arms like a prosecuting counsel.

"But we—we only wanted to invite you to a picnic!"

H. M. closed his eyes.

"That's fine," he said in a hollow voice. "All the same, don't you think it'd have been a subtler kind of hint just to pour mayonnaise over my head or shove ants down the back of my neck? Oh, lord love a duck!"

"I didn't mean that! I meant . . ."

"Let me help you up, sir," interposed the calm, reassuring voice of the dark-haired and blue-chinned young man who had been with Eve in the car.

"So you want to help too, hey? And who are *you*?"

"I'm awfully sorry!" said Eve. "I should have introduced you! This is my fiancé. Dr. William Sage."

H. M.'s face turned purple.

"I'm glad to see," he observed, "you had the uncommon decency to bring along a doctor. I appreciate that, I do. And the car's there, I suppose, to assist with the examination when I take off my pants?"

The hall porter uttered a cry of horror.

Bill Sage, either from jumpiness and nerves or from sheer inability to keep a straight face, laughed loudly.

"I keep telling Eve a dozen times a day," he said, "that I'm not to be called 'doctor.' I happen to be a surgeon—"

(Here H. M. really did look alarmed.)

"—but I don't think we need operate. Nor, in my opinion," Bill gravely addressed the hall porter, "will it be necessary to remove Sir Henry's trousers in front of the Senior Conservatives' Club."

"Thank you very much, sir."

"We had an infernal nerve to come here," the young man confessed to H. M. "But I honestly think, Sir Henry, you'd be more comfortable in the car. What about it? Let me give you a hand up?"

Yet even ten minutes later, when H. M. sat glowering in the back of the car and two heads were craned round toward him, peace was not restored.

"All right!" said Eve. Her pretty, rather stolid face was flushed; her mouth looked miserable. "If you won't come to the picnic, you won't. But I did believe you might do it to oblige me."

"Well . . . now!" muttered the great man uncomfortably.

"And I did think, too, you'd be interested in the other person who was coming with us. But Vicky's—difficult. She won't come either, if you don't."

"Oh? And who's this other guest?"

"Vicky Adams."

H. M.'s hand, which had been lifted for an oratorical gesture, dropped to his side.

"Vicky Adams? That's not the gal who . . . ?"

"Yes!" Eve nodded. "They say it was one of the great mysteries, twenty years ago, that the police failed to solve."

"It was, my wench," H. M. agreed somberly. "It was."

"And now Vicky's grown up. And we thought if you of all people went along, and spoke to her nicely, she'd tell us what really happened on that night."

H. M.'s small, sharp eyes fixed disconcertingly on Eve.

"I say, my wench. What's your interest in all this?"

"Oh, reasons." Eve glanced quickly at Bill Sage, who was again punching moodily at the steering wheel, and checked herself. "Anyway, what difference does it make now? If you won't go with us . . ."

H. M. assumed a martyred air.

"I never said I *wasn't* goin' with you, did I?" he demanded. (This was inaccurate, but no matter.) "Even after you practically made a cripple of me, I never said I *wasn't* goin'?" His manner grew flurried and hasty. "But I got to leave now," he added apologetically. "I got to get back to my office."

"We'll drive you there, H. M."

"No, no, no," said the practical cripple, getting out of the car with surprising celerity. "Walkin' is good for my stomach if it's not so good for my behind. I'm a forgivin' man. You pick me up at my house tomorrow morning. G'bye."

And he lumbered off in the direction of the Haymarket.

It needed no close observer to see that H. M. was deeply abstracted. He remained so abstracted, indeed, as to be nearly murdered by a taxi at the Admiralty Arch; and he was halfway down Whitehall before a familiar voice stopped him.

"Afternoon, Sir Henry!"

Burly, urbane, buttoned up in blue serge, with his bowler hat and his boiled blue eye, stood Chief Inspector Masters.

"Bit odd," the Chief Inspector remarked affably, "to see you taking a constitutional on a day like this. And how are you, sir?"

"Awful," said H. M. instantly. "But that's not the point. Masters, you crawlin' snake! You're the very man I wanted to see."

Few things startled the Chief Inspector. This one did.

"You," he repeated, "wanted to see *me*?"

"Uh-huh."

"And what about?"

"Masters, do you remember the Victoria Adams case about twenty years ago?"

The Chief Inspector's manner suddenly changed and grew wary.

"Victoria Adams case?" he ruminated. "No, sir, I can't say I do."

"Son, you're lyin'! You were sergeant to old Chief Inspector Rutherford in those days, and well I remember it!"

Masters stood on his dignity.

"That's as may be, sir. But twenty years ago . . ."

"A little girl of twelve or thirteen, the child of very wealthy parents, disappeared one night out of a country cottage with all the doors and windows locked on the inside. A week later, while everybody was havin' screaming hysterics, the child reappeared again: through the locks and bolts, tucked up in her bed as usual. And to this day nobody's ever known what really happened."

There was a silence, while Masters shut his jaws hard.

"This family, the Adamses," persisted H. M., "owned the cottage, down Aylesbury way, on the edge of Goblin Wood, opposite the lake. Or was it?"

"Oh, ah," growled Masters. "It was."

H. M. looked at him curiously.

"They used the cottage as a base for bathin' in summer, and ice skatin' in winter. It was black winter when the child vanished, and the place was all locked up inside against drafts. They say her old man nearly went loopy when he found her there a week later, lying asleep under the lamp. But all she'd say, when they asked her where she'd been, was, '*I don't know.*'"

Again there was a silence, while red buses thundered through the traffic press of Whitehall.

"You've got to admit, Masters, there was a flaming public rumpus. I say: did you ever read Barrie's *Mary Rose?*"

"No."

"Well, it was a situation straight out of Barrie. Some people, y'see, said that Vicky Adams was a child of faërie who'd been spirited away by the pixies . . ."

Whereupon Masters exploded.

He removed his bowler hat and made remarks about pixies, in detail, which could not have been bettered by H. M. himself.

"I know, son, I know." H. M. was soothing. Then his big voice sharpened. "Now tell me. Was all this talk strictly true?"

"What talk?"

"Locked windows? Bolted doors? No attic trap? No cellar? Solid walls and floor?"

"Yes, sir," answered Masters, regaining his dignity with a powerful effort, "I'm bound to admit it *was* true."

"Then there wasn't any jiggery-pokery about the cottage?"

"In your eye there wasn't," said Masters.

"How d'ye mean?"

"Listen, sir." Masters lowered his voice. "Before the Adamses took over that place, it was a hideout for Chuck

Randall. At that time he was the swellest of the swell mob; we lagged him a couple of years later. Do you think Chuck wouldn't have rigged up some gadget for a getaway? Just so! Only . . ."

"Well? Hey?"

"We couldn't find it," grunted Masters.

"And I'll bet that pleased old Chief Inspector Rutherford?"

"I tell you straight: he was fair up the pole. Especially as the kid herself was a pretty kid, all big eyes and dark hair. You couldn't help trusting her story."

"Yes," said H. M. "That's what worries me."

"Worries you?"

"Oh, my son!" said H. M. dismally. "Here's Vicky Adams, the spoiled daughter of dotin' parents. She's supposed to be 'odd' and 'fey.' She's even encouraged to be. During her adolescence, the most impressionable time of her life, she gets wrapped round with the gauze of a mystery that people talk about even yet. What's that woman like now, Masters? What's that woman like now?"

"Dear Sir Henry!" murmured Miss Vicky Adams in her softest voice.

She said this just as William Sage's car, with Bill and Eve Drayton in the front seat, and Vicky and H. M. in the back seat, turned off the main road. Behind them lay the smoky-red roofs of Aylesbury, against a brightness of late afternoon. The car turned down a side road, a damp tunnel of greenery, and into another road which was little more than a lane between hedgerows.

H. M.—though cheered by three good-sized picnic hampers from Fortnum & Mason, their wickerwork lids bulging with a feast—did not seem happy. Nobody in that car was happy, with the possible exception of Miss Adams herself.

Vicky, unlike Eve, was small and dark and vivacious. Her large light-brown eyes, with very black lashes, could be arch and coy; or they could be dreamily intense. The late Sir James Barrie might have called her a sprite. Those of more sober views would have recognized a different quality: she had an inordinate sex appeal, which was as palpable as a physical touch to any male within yards. And despite her smallness, Vicky had a full voice like Eve's. All these qualities she used even in so simple a matter as giving traffic directions.

"First right," she would say, leaning forward to put her hands on Bill Sage's shoulders. "Then straight on until the next traffic light. Ah, clever boy!"

"Not at all, not at all!" Bill would disclaim, with red ears and rather an erratic style of driving.

"Oh, yes, you are!" And Vicky would twist the lobe of his ear, playfully, before sitting back again.

(Eve Drayton did not say anything. She did not even turn round. Yet the atmosphere, even of that quiet English picnic party, had already become a trifle hysterical.)

"Dear Sir Henry!" murmured Vicky, as they turned down into the deep lane between the hedgerows. "I do wish you wouldn't be so materialistic! I do, really. Haven't you the tiniest bit of spirituality in your nature?"

"Me?" said H. M. in astonishment. "I got a very lofty spiritual nature. But what I want just now, my wench, is grub.—Oi!"

Bill Sage glanced round.

"By that speedometer," H. M. pointed "we've now come forty-six miles and a bit. We didn't even leave town until people of decency and sanity were having their tea. Where are we *going*?"

"But didn't you know?" asked Vicky, with wide-open

eyes. "We're going to the cottage where I had such a dreadful experience when I was a child."

"Was it such a dreadful experience, Vicky dear?" inquired Eve.

Vicky's eyes seemed far away.

"I don't remember, really. I was only a child, you see. I didn't understand. I hadn't developed the power for myself then."

"What power?" H. M. asked sharply.

"To dematerialize," said Vicky. "Of course."

In that warm sun-dusted lane, between the hawthorn hedges, the car jolted over a rut. Crockery rattled.

"Uh-huh. I see," observed H. M. without inflection. "And where do you go, my wench, when you dematerialize?"

"Into a strange country. Through a little door. You wouldn't understand. Oh, you *are* such Philistines!" moaned Vicky. Then, with a sudden change of mood, she leaned forward and her whole physical allurement flowed again toward Bill Sage. "*You* wouldn't like me to disappear, would you, Bill?"

(Easy! Easy!)

"Only," said Bill, with a sort of wild gallantry, "if you promised to reappear again straightaway."

"Oh, I should have to do that." Vicky sat back. She was trembling. "The power wouldn't be strong enough. But even a poor little thing like me might be able to teach you a lesson. Look there!"

And she pointed ahead.

On their left, as the lane widened, stretched the ten-acre gloom of what is fancifully known as Goblin Wood. On their right lay a small lake, on private property and therefore deserted.

The cottage—set well back into a clearing of the wood so as to face the road, screened from it by a line of beeches—

was in fact a bungalow of rough-hewn stone, with a slate roof. Across the front of it ran a wooden porch. It had a seedy air, like the long yellow-green grass of its front lawn. Bill parked the car at the side of the road, since there was no driveway.

"It's a bit lonely, ain't it?" demanded H. M. His voice boomed out against that utter stillness, under the hot sun.

"Oh, yes!" breathed Vicky. She jumped out of the car in a whirl of skirts. "That's why *they* were able to come and take me. When I was a child."

"They?"

"Dear Sir Henry! Do I need to explain?"

Then Vicky looked at Bill.

"I must apologize," she said, "for the state the house is in. I haven't been out here for months and months. There's a modern bathroom, I'm glad to say. Only kerosene lamps, of course. But then," a dreamy smile flashed across her face, "you won't need lamps, will you? Unless . . ."

"You mean," said Bill, who was taking a black case out of the car, "unless you disappear again?"

"Yes, Bill. And promise me you won't be frightened when I do."

The young man uttered a ringing oath which was shushed by Sir Henry Merrivale, who austerely said he disapproved of profanity. Eve Drayton was very quiet.

"But in the meantime," Vicky said wistfully, "let's forget it all, shall we? Let's laugh and dance and sing and pretend we're children! And surely our guest must be even more hungry by this time?"

It was in this emotional state that they sat down to their picnic.

H. M., if the truth must be told, did not fare too badly. Instead of sitting on some hummock of ground, they dragged a table and chairs to the shaded porch. All spoke in strained voices. But no word of controversy was said. It was only afterward, when the cloth was cleared, the furniture and hampers pushed indoors, the empty bottles flung away, that danger tapped a warning.

From under the porch Vicky fished out two half-rotted deck chairs, which she set up in the long grass of the lawn. These were to be occupied by Eve and H. M., while Vicky took Bill Sage to inspect a plum tree of some remarkable quality she did not specify.

Eve sat down without comment. H. M., who was smoking a black cigar opposite her, waited some time before he spoke.

"Y' know," he said, taking the cigar out of his mouth, "you're behaving remarkably well."

"Yes." Eve laughed. "Aren't I?"

"Are you pretty well acquainted with this Adams gal?"

"I'm her first cousin," Eve answered simply. "Now that her parents are dead, I'm the only relative she's got. I know *all* about her."

From far across the lawn floated two voices saying something about wild strawberries. Eve, her fair hair and fair complexion vivid against the dark line of Goblin Wood, clenched her hands on her knees.

"You see, H. M.," she hesitated, "there was another reason why I invited you here. I—I don't quite know how to approach it."

"I'm the old man," said H. M., tapping himself impressively on the chest. "You tell me."

"Eve, darling!" interposed Vicky's voice, crying across the ragged lawn. "Coo-ee! Eve!"

"Yes, dear?"

"I've just remembered," cried Vicky, "that I haven't shown Bill over the cottage! You don't mind if I steal him away from you for a little while?"

"No, dear! Of course not!"

It was H. M., sitting so as to face the bungalow, who saw Vicky and Bill go in. He saw Vicky's wistful smile as she closed the door after them. Eve did not even look round. The sun was declining, making fiery chinks through the thickness of Goblin Wood behind the cottage.

"I won't let her have him," Eve suddenly cried. "I won't! I won't! I won't!"

"Does she want him, my wench? Or, which is more to the point, does he want her?"

"He never has," Eve said with emphasis. "Not really. And he never will."

H. M., motionless, puffed out cigar smoke.

"Vicky's a faker," said Eve. "Does that sound catty?"

"Not necessarily. I was just thinkin' the same thing myself."

"I'm patient," said Eve. Her blue eyes were fixed. "I'm terribly, terribly patient. I can wait years for what I want. Bill's not making much money now, and I haven't got a bean. But Bill's got great talent under that easygoing manner of his. He *must* have the right girl to help him. If only . . ."

"If only the elfin sprite would let him alone. Hey?"

"Vicky acts like that," said Eve, "toward practically every man she ever meets. That's why she never married. She says it leaves her soul free to commune with other souls. This occultism—"

Then it all poured out, the family story of the Adamses. This repressed girl spoke at length, spoke as perhaps she had never spoken before. Vicky Adams, the child who wanted to attract attention, her father Uncle Fred and her mother Aunt Margaret seemed to walk in vividness as the shadows gathered.

"I was too young to know her at the time of the 'disappearance,' of course. But, oh, I knew her afterward! And I thought . . ."

"Well?"

"If I could get *you* here," said Eve, "I thought she'd try to show off with some game. And then you'd expose her. And Bill would see what an awful faker she is. But it's hopeless! It's hopeless!"

"Looky here," observed H. M., who was smoking his third cigar. He sat up. "Doesn't it strike you those two are being a rummy-awful long time just in lookin' through a little bungalow?"

Eve, roused out of a dream, stared back at him. She sprang to her feet. She was not now, you could guess, thinking of any disappearance.

"Excuse me a moment," she said curtly.

Eve hurried across to the cottage, went up on the porch, and opened the front door. H. M. heard her heels rap down the length of the small passage inside. She marched straight back again, closed the front door, and rejoined H. M.

"All the doors of the rooms are shut," she announced in a high voice. "I really don't think I ought to disturb them."

"Easy, my wench!"

"I have absolutely no interest," declared Eve, with the tears coming into her eyes, "in what happens to either of them now. Shall we take the car and go back to town without them?"

H. M. threw away his cigar, got up, and seized her by the shoulders.

"I'm the old man," he said, leering like an ogre. "Will you listen to me?"

"No!"

"If I'm any reader of the human dial," persisted H. M., "that young feller's no more gone on Vicky Adams than I am. He was scared, my wench. Scared." Doubt, indecision crossed H. M.'s face. "I dunno what he's scared of. Burn me, I don't! But . . ."

"Hoy!" called the voice of Bill Sage.

It did not come from the direction of the cottage.

They were surrounded on three sides by Goblin Wood, now blurred with twilight. From the north side the voice bawled at them, followed by crackling in dry undergrowth. Bill, his hair and sports coat and flannels more than a little dirty, regarded them with a face of bitterness.

"Here are her blasted wild strawberries," he announced, extending his hand. "Three of 'em. The fruitful (excuse me) result of three quarters of an hour's hard labor. I absolutely refuse to chase 'em in the dark."

For a moment Eve Drayton's mouth moved without speech.

"Then you weren't . . . in the cottage all this time?"

"In the cottage?" Bill glanced at it. "I was in that cottage," he said, "about five minutes. Vicky had a woman's whim. She wanted some wild strawberries out of what she called the 'forest.'"

"Wait a minute, son!" said H. M. very sharply. "You didn't come out that front door. Nobody did."

"No! I went out the back door! It opens straight on the wood."

"Yes. And what happened then?"

"Well, I went to look for these damned . . ."

"No, no! What did *she* do?"

"Vicky? She locked and bolted the back door on the inside. I remember her grinning at me through the glass panel. She—"

Bill stopped short. His eyes widened, and then narrowed, as though at the impact of an idea. All three of them turned to look at the rough-stone cottage.

"By the way," said Bill. He cleared his throat vigorously. "By the way, have you seen Vicky since then?"

"No."

"This couldn't be . . . ?"

"It could be, son," said H. M. "We'd all better go in there and have a look."

They hesitated for a moment on the porch. A warm, moist fragrance breathed up from the ground after sunset. In half an hour it would be completely dark.

Bill Sage threw open the front door and shouted Vicky's name. That sound seemed to penetrate, reverberating, through every room. The intense heat and stuffiness of the cottage, where no window had been raised in months, blew out at them. But nobody answered.

"Get inside," snapped H. M. "And stop yowlin'." The old maestro was nervous. "I'm dead sure she didn't get out by the front door; but we'll just make certain there's no slippin' out now."

Stumbling over the table and chairs they had used on the porch, he fastened the front door. They were in a narrow passage, once handsome with parquet floor and pine-paneled walls, leading to a door with a glass panel at the rear. H. M. lumbered forward to inspect this door and found it locked and bolted, as Bill had said.

Goblin Wood grew darker.

Keeping well together, they searched the cottage. It was not large, having two good-sized rooms on one side of the passage, and two small rooms on the other side, so as to make space for bathroom and kitchenette. H. M., raising fogs of dust, ransacked every inch where a person could possibly hide.

And all the windows were locked on the inside. And the chimney flues were too narrow to admit anybody.

And Vicky Adams wasn't there.

"Oh, my eye!" breathed Sir Henry Merrivale.

They had gathered, by what idiotic impulse not even H. M. could have said, just outside the open door of the bathroom. A bath tap dripped monotonously. The last light through a frosted-glass window showed three faces hung there as though disembodied.

"Bill," said Eve in an unsteady voice, "this is a trick. Oh, I've longed for her to be exposed! This is a trick!"

"Then where is she?"

"H. M. can tell us! Can't you, H. M.?"

"Well . . . now," muttered the great man.

Across H. M.'s Panama hat was a large black handprint, made there when he had pressed down the hat after investigating a chimney. He glowered under it.

"Son," he said to Bill, "there's just one question I want you to answer in all this hokey-pokey. When you went out pickin' wild strawberries, will you swear Vicky Adams didn't go with you?"

"As God is my judge, she didn't," returned Bill, with fervency and obvious truth. "Besides, how the devil could she? Look at the lock and bolt on the back door!"

H. M. made two more violent black handprints on his hat.

He lumbered forward, his head down, two or three paces in the narrow passage. His foot half-skidded on something that had been lying there unnoticed, and he picked it up. It was a large, square section of thin, waterproof oilskin, jagged at one corner.

"Have you found anything?" demanded Bill in a strained voice.

"No. Not to make any sense, that is. But just a minute!"

At the rear of the passage, on the left-hand side, was the bedroom from which Vicky Adams had vanished as a child. Though H. M. had searched this room once before, he opened the door again.

It was now almost dark in Goblin Wood.

He saw dimly a room of twenty years before: a room of flounces, of lace curtains, of once-polished mahogany, its mirrors glimmering against white-papered walls. H. M. seemed especially interested in the windows.

He ran his hands carefully round the frame of each, even climbing laboriously up on a chair to examine the tops. He borrowed a box of matches from Bill; and the little spurts of light, following the rasp of the match, rasped against nerves as well. The hope died out of his face, and his companions saw it.

"H. M.," Bill said for the dozenth time, "where is she?"

"Son," replied H. M. despondently, "I don't know."

"Let's get out of here," Eve said abruptly. Her voice was a small scream. "I kn-know it's all a trick! I know Vicky's a faker! But let's get out of here. For God's sake let's get out of here!"

"As a matter of fact," Bill cleared his throat, "I agree. Anyway, we won't hear from Vicky until tomorrow morning."

"*Oh, yes, you will*," whispered Vicky's voice out of the darkness.

Eve screamed.

They lighted a lamp.

But there was nobody there.

Their retreat from the cottage, it must be admitted, was not very dignified.

How they stumbled down that ragged lawn in the dark, how they piled rugs and picnic hampers into the car, how they eventually found the main road again, is best left undescribed.

Sir Henry Merrivale has since sneered at this—"a bit of a goosy feeling; nothin' much"—and it is true that he has no nerves to speak of. But he can be worried, badly worried; and that he was worried on this occasion may be deduced from what happened later.

H. M., after dropping in at Claridge's for a modest late supper of lobster and *pêche Melba*, returned to his house in Brook Street and slept a hideous sleep. It was three o'clock in the morning, even before the summer dawn, when the ringing of the bedside telephone roused him.

What he heard sent his blood pressure soaring.

"Dear Sir Henry!" crooned a familiar and sprite-like voice.

H. M. was himself again, full of gall and bile. He switched on the bedside lamp and put on his spectacles with care, so as adequately to address the phone.

"Have I got the honor," he said with dangerous politeness, "of addressin' Miss Vicky Adams?"

"Oh, yes!"

"I sincerely trust," said H. M., "you've been havin' a good time? Are you materialized yet?"

"Oh, yes!"

"Where are you now?"

"I'm afraid," there was coy laughter in the voice, "that must be a little secret for a day or two. I want to teach you a really *good* lesson. Blessings, dear."

And she hung up the receiver.

H. M. did not say anything. He climbed out of bed. He stalked up and down the room, his corporation majestic under an old-fashioned nightshirt stretching to his heels. Then, since he himself had been waked up at three o'clock in the morning, the obvious course was to wake up somebody else; so he dialed the home number of Chief Inspector Masters.

"No, sir," retorted Masters grimly, after coughing the frog out of his throat, "I do *not* mind you ringing up. Not a bit of it!" He spoke with a certain pleasure. "Because I've got a bit of news for you."

H. M. eyed the phone suspiciously.

"Masters, are you trying to do me in the eye again?"

"It's what you always try to do to me, isn't it?"

"All right, all right!" growled H. M. "What's the news?"

"Do you remember mentioning the Vicky Adams case yesterday?"

"Sort of. Yes."

"Oh, ah! Well, I had a word or two round among our people. I was tipped the wink to go and see a certain solicitor. He was old Mr. Fred Adams's solicitor before Mr. Adams died about six or seven years ago."

Here Master's voice grew triumphant.

"I always said, Sir Henry, that Chuck Randall had planted some gadget in that cottage for a quick getaway. And I was right. The gadget was . . ."

"You were quite right, Masters. The gadget was a trick window."

The telephone, so to speak, gave a start.

"What's that?"

"A trick window." H. M. spoke patiently. "You press a spring. And the whole frame of the window, two leaves locked together, slides down between the walls far enough so you can climb over. Then you push it back up again."

"How in lum's name do you know that?"

"Oh, my son! They used to build windows like it in country houses during the persecution of Catholic priests. It was a good enough *second* guess. Only . . . it won't work."

Masters seemed annoyed. "It won't work now," Masters agreed. "And do you know why?"

"I can guess. Tell me."

"Because, just before Mr. Adams died, he discovered how his darling daughter had flummoxed him. He never told anybody except his lawyer. He took a handful of four-inch nails, and sealed up the top of that frame so tight an orangutang couldn't move it, and painted 'em over so they wouldn't be noticed."

"Uh-huh. You can notice 'em now."

"I doubt if the young lady herself ever knew. But, by George!" Masters said savagely. "I'd like to see anybody try the same game now!"

"You would, hey? Then will it interest you to know that the same gal has just disappeared out of the same house *again?*"

H. M. began a long narrative of the facts, but he had to break off because the telephone was raving.

"Honest, Masters," H. M. said seriously, "I'm not joking. She didn't get out through that window. But she did get out. You'd better meet me," he gave directions, "tomorrow morning. In the meantime, son, sleep well."

It was, therefore, a worn-faced Masters who went into the Visitors' Room at the Senior Conservatives' Club just before lunch on the following day.

The Visitors' Room is a dark sepulchral place, opening on an air well, where the visitor is surrounded by pictures of dyspeptic-looking gentlemen with beards. It has a pervading mustiness of wood and leather. Though whisky and soda stood on the table, H. M. sat in a leather chair far away from it, ruffling his hands across his bald head.

"Now, Masters, keep your shirt on!" he warned. "This business may be rummy. But it's not a police matter—yet."

"I know it's not a police matter," Masters said grimly. "All the same, I've had a word with the Superintendent at Aylesbury."

"Fowler?"

"You know him?"

"Sure. I know everybody. Is he goin' to keep an eye out?"

"He's going to have a look at that ruddy cottage. I've asked for any telephone calls to be put through here. In the mean-time, sir—"

It was at this point, as though diabolically inspired, that the telephone rang. H. M. reached it before Masters.

"It's the old man," he said, unconsciously assuming a stance of grandeur. "Yes, yes! Masters is here, but he's drunk. You tell me first. What's that?"

The telephone talked thinly.

"Sure I looked in the kitchen cupboard," bellowed H. M. "Though I didn't honestly expect to find Vicky Adams hidin' there. What's that? Say it again! Cups that had been . . ."

An almost frightening change had come over H. M.'s expression. He stood motionless. All the posturing went out of him. He was not even listening to the voice that still talked thinly, while his eyes and his brain moved to put together facts. At length (though the voice still talked) he hung up the receiver.

H. M. blundered back to the center table, where he drew out a chair and sat down.

"Masters," he said very quietly, "I've come close to makin' the silliest mistake of my life."

Here he cleared his throat.

"I shouldn't have made it, son. I really shouldn't. But don't yell at me for cuttin' off Fowler. I can tell you now how Vicky Adams disappeared. And she said one true thing when she said she was going into a strange country."

"How do you mean?"

"She's dead," answered H. M.

The word fell with heavy weight into that dingy room, where the bearded faces looked down.

"Y'see," H. M. went on blankly, "a lot of us were right when we thought Vicky Adams was a faker. She was. To attract attention to herself, she played that trick on her family, with the hocused window. She's lived and traded on it ever since. That's what sent me straight in the wrong direction. I was on the alert for some *trick* Vicky Adams might play. So it never occurred to me that this elegant pair of beauties, Miss Eve Drayton and Mr. William Sage, were deliberately conspirin' to murder *her.*"

Masters got slowly to his feet.

"Did you say . . . murder?"

"Oh, yes."

Again H. M. cleared his throat.

"It was all arranged beforehand for me to be a witness. They knew Vicky Adams couldn't resist a challenge to disappear, especially as Vicky always believed she could get out by the trick window. They wanted Vicky to *say* she was goin' to disappear. They never knew anything about the trick window, Masters. But they knew their own plan very well.

"Eve Drayton even told me the motive. She hated Vicky, of course. But that wasn't the main point. She was Vicky Adams's only relative; she'd inherit an awful big scoopful of money. Eve said she could be patient. (And, burn me, how her eyes meant it when she said that!) Rather than risk any slightest suspicion of murder, she was willing to wait seven years until a disappeared person can be presumed dead.

"Our Eve, I think, was the fiery drivin' force of that conspiracy. She was only scared part of the time. Sage was scared all of the time. But it was Sage who did the real dirty work. He lured Vicky Adams into that cottage, while Eve kept me in close conversation on the lawn . . ."

H. M. paused.

Intolerably vivid in the mind of Chief Inspector Masters, who had seen it years before, rose the picture of the rough-stone bungalow against the darkling wood.

"Masters," said H. M., "why should a bath tap be dripping in a house that hadn't been occupied for months?"

"Well?"

"Sage, y'see, is a surgeon. I saw him take his black case of instruments out of the car. He took Vicky Adams into that house. In the bathroom he stabbed her, he stripped her, and *he dismembered her body in the bathtub.*—Easy, son!"

"Go on," said Masters without moving.

"The head, the torso, the folded arms and legs, were wrapped up in three large square pieces of thin transparent oilskin. Each was sewed up with coarse thread so the blood wouldn't drip. Last night I found one of the oilskin pieces he'd ruined when his needle slipped at the corner. Then he walked out of the house, with the back door still standin' unlocked, to get his wild-strawberry alibi."

"Sage went out of there," shouted Masters, "leaving the body in the house?"

"Oh, yes," agreed H. M.

"But where did he leave it?"

H. M. ignored this.

"In the meantime, son, what about Eve Drayton? At the end of the arranged three quarters of an hour, she indicated there was hanky-panky between her fiancé and Vicky Adams. She flew into the house. But what did she do?

"She walked to the back of the passage. I heard her. *There she simply locked and bolted the back door.* And then she marched out to join me with tears in her eyes. And these two beauties were ready for investigation."

"Investigation?" said Masters. "*With that body still in the house?*"

"Oh, yes."

Masters lifted both fists.

"It must have given young Sage a shock," said H. M., "when I found that piece of waterproof oilskin he'd washed but dropped. Anyway, these two had only two more bits of hokey-pokey. The 'vanished' gal had to speak—to show she was still alive. If you'd been there, son, you'd have noticed that Eve Drayton's got a voice just like Vicky Adams's. If somebody speaks in a dark room, carefully imitatin' a coy tone she never uses herself, the illusion's goin' to be pretty good. The same goes for a telephone.

"It was finished, Masters. All that had to be done was remove the body from the house, and get it far away from there . . ."

"But that's just what I'm asking you, sir! Where was the body all this time? And who in blazes *did* remove the body from the house?"

"All of us did," answered H. M.

"What's that?"

"Masters," said H. M., "aren't you forgettin' the picnic hampers?"

And now, the Chief Inspector saw, H. M. was as white as a ghost. His next words took Masters like a blow between the eyes.

"Three good-sized wickerwork hampers, with lids. After our big meal on the porch, those hampers were shoved inside the house where Sage could get at 'em. He had to leave most of the used crockery behind, in the kitchen cupboard. But three wickerwork hampers from a picnic, and three butcher's parcels to go inside 'em. I carried one down to the car myself. It felt a bit funny . . ."

H. M. stretched out his hand, not steadily, toward the whisky.

"Y'know," he said. "I'll always wonder if I was carrying the—head."

ALL IN A MAZE

When Tom Lockwood first saw her, she was running down the stairs in terror. Behind her stretched the great sweep of stairs up to the portico of St. Paul's; above, Paul's Dome almost shut out the gray spring sky. A pigeon fluttered its wings. But there were very few people to see what happened.

The girl glanced over her shoulder. She was still so badly frightened that Tom's first thought was instinctive: she might stumble and pitch headlong. So he ran towards her.

His next thought, born of his journalistic work, was the grotesqueness of this whole scene, as the bell boomed out the stroke of four: a very pretty girl, with dark hair and wide-spaced gray eyes, fleeing in blind panic from the House of God.

Then she did stumble.

Tom caught her before she fell, and lifted her up gently by the elbows.

"Steady does it, you know," he said, and smiled down at her. "There's nothing to be afraid of, really."

Instantly she recoiled; then she saw his expression, and hesitated. Tom Lockwood's own mother could not have called him handsome. But he had such an engaging and easy-going expression, especially in his smile, that almost any woman would have trusted him on sight—and would have been right.

"*Nothing* to be afraid of," he repeated.

"Isn't there?" the girl blurted out. "When last night, by some miracle no one can understand, they try to kill me? And now, just now, a voice speaks where no voice could have spoken? And tells me again I am going to die?"

Taxis hooted up Ludgate Hill. A rather sinister-looking policeman stood at the left-hand side of St. Paul's church-

32

yard. Tom had a topsy-turvy sense that he did not really hear the words she was speaking.

She spoke with passion, in a beautiful voice with—was it?—some very faint tinge of accent. Her hair really was black and shining, worn in a long bob; the gray eyes, their pupils dilated with fear, had long black lashes. Tom was so conscious of her physical presence that he hastily let go her elbows.

"You don't believe me!" she cried. "Very well! I must go."

"No! Wait!"

The girl hesitated, looking at the pavement.

And Tom Lockwood was inspired almost to eloquence.

"You're alone," he said. "Oh, there may have been people with you in the Cathedral! But you're alone in yourself; you feel lost; you don't trust anybody. Will you trust a perfect stranger, if I tell you I only want to help you?"

To his intense embarrassment, tears came into her eyes.

"What you need—" he began. It was on the tip of his tongue to say "a couple of whiskies," but, in his present exalted mood, he decided this was unromantic. "Across the road," he said, "there's a tea shop of sorts. What you need is to drink tea and tell me your troubles. After all, hang it, I'm a reasonably respectable bloke! You see that policeman over there?"

"Yes?"

"*He* knows me," said Tom. "No, no, not because I'm an old lag just out of jail! As a matter of fact, I'm a crime reporter for the *Daily Record*. Here's my press-card."

"You are journalist?"

Her eyes flashed up; she pronounced the word almost as *journaliste*.

"Not where you are concerned. Please believe that! And you—are you by any chance French?"

"I am English," she retorted proudly, and drew herself up

to her full height of five feet one. "Ah, bah! I am named Jenny. Jenny Holden. That is English enough, surely?"

"Of course. And I'm Tom Lockwood."

"But, you see," Jenny continued, "I have lived most of my life in France. When they brought me here for a visit, things seemed all funny but very nice, until—"

Jenny glanced back over her shoulder. Fear struck again, as though some terrifying presence lurked inside the Cathedral.

"Mr. Lockwood," she said, "of course I will go with you. And we need not be introduced by a policeman." Then her passionate voice rose. "But let us hurry, hurry, hurry!"

They dodged across through the skittish traffic to the tea shop at the corner of Paternoster Row. They passed the policeman in question, who seemed to fascinate Jenny. He was one of the Old Brigade: bulky and almost seven feet tall, just what any foreign visitor would expect to see.

Tom waved at him by way of greeting. The law saluted gravely but, when Jenny's head turned away, gave her companion a wink of such outrageous knowingness that Tom's ears went red.

At the door of the tea shop, however, Tom hesitated and turned round.

"Stop a bit! Was there somebody with you at St. Paul's?"

"Yes, yes! My Aunt Hester and my Cousin Margot."

"*They* didn't frighten you?"

"No, of course not!" Jenny's lips became mutinous. "I do not like my Aunt Hester. She behaves like a duchess, with a lorgnette, and you can hear her talking all over a restaurant. You know what I mean?"

"Bitterly well."

"My Cousin Margot, she is young and I like her. But I wish to get away from them. Please!"

"Right," said Tom, opening the door. "In you go."

He allowed the door to close very briefly behind her so that she should not hear him when his voice carried clearly across to the policeman.

"Dawson! You haven't seen us. Understand?"

The law did. His wink was more portentous than ever.

In the tea shop, more properly a tea bar, two girls chattered and banged tins behind the counter. But the place was deserted, including the two booths at the back. When the newcomers sat opposite each other in the farther booth, over thick mugs of a beverage which was at least hot, Jenny's terror was decreasing. She accepted a cigarette, had it lighted for her, and hesitated. Then she burst out: "You see, it is so difficult to say! I don't wish you to think I am silly, or have fancies, or am off my head. That is what *they* think."

"'They'?"

"Aunt Hester. And others."

"Aunt Hester," said Tom, "shall be hung out on the clothes-line, preferably upside down, at the first opportunity. Meanwhile . . ."

He broke off, because Jenny bubbled with that laughter he came to know so well.

"You are nice!" she declared, like a magistrate imposing sentence. "Oh, how it is pleasant to meet people who make you laugh! Instead of—"

Jenny stopped, and disquiet settled on her again.

"It is silly," she insisted, "but I must say it. Can you explain miracles?"

"No. But I know a man who can. Did you ever hear of Sir Henry Merrivale?"

"Sir Henry *Merrivale?*"

"Yes."

"But he is awful!" cried Jenny. "He is fat and bald, and he swear and carry on and throw people out of windows."

"He is not, perhaps," Tom admitted, "quite the ladies'

man he thinks he is. But he can explain miracles, Jenny. That's his purpose in life nowadays."

"You mean this?"

"Yes, I mean it."

"Then I had better explain from the beginning. My name—"

"I know your name," said Tom, looking at the table. "I am likely to remember it for a very long time."

There was a pause, while both of them hastily swallowed tea.

"Well!" said Jenny. "My father and mother went to live in France, at Cannes, before I was born. What with the war, and everything else, I had never been to England. My mother died during the war. My father died two years ago. My guardian is my father's old friend Général de Senneville. And I am now twenty-five: in France, I am what you would call in England an old maid."

"Are you, now?" breathed Tom, almost with awe. "Oh, crikey! Have you ever seen yourself in a mirror?"

Jenny looked at him, and then went on very quickly.

"It was always my father's wish I should come to England. I should see all the sights like any tourist: Westminster Abbey, the Tower of London, St. Paul's—"

"Steady, now!"

"Yes, I am steady. Général de Senneville, my guardian, said this plan was a good one, and did much honor to everyone. So he sent me, in charge of my Aunt Hester, just before I get married."

"Before you—!" Tom blurted out, and then stopped.

Jenny's face went pink. Tom, in the act of lighting a cigarette for himself, held the match for so long that it burned his fingers. He cursed, dropped both match and cigarette into the mug of tea; then, to hide his expression, he shoved the mug of tea down on the floor under the seat.

"But what else could I do?" Jenny asked defensively. "It was arranged many years ago, between my father and the général. At twenty-five, and an old maid, surely that was best?"

The damage had been done. They could not look at each other's eyes.

"And who's the bloke you're marrying?" he asked casually.

"Armand de Senneville. The général's son."

"Do you love him?"

All Jenny's English feelings warred with her strict French upbringing.

"But you are not practical!" she exclaimed, the more vehemently because her feelings won every time. "An arranged marriage always turns out best, as the général says. It is understood that I do not love Armand, and Armand does not love me. I marry him because—well! it must be done, at twenty-five. He marries me because he wishes to obtain my dowry, which is very large."

"Does he, by God!"

"How dare you!"

"These old French customs." Tom folded his arms moodily. "You hear about 'em, you know they exist, but they're still hard to believe. What about this Armand de Senneville? He has oily black hair, I suppose, and sidewhiskers down his cheeks?"

"You must not speak so of my fiancé, and you know it!"

"All right, all right!"

"He has dark hair, yes, but none of the rest of it. He is charming. Also, he is one of the best businessmen in France. Armand is only thirty-five, but already he owns three newspapers, two in Paris and one in Bordeaux."

"Whereas I . . ."

"You said?"

"Nothing. He's with you, I suppose?"

"No, no! He was bitterly opposed to this holiday. He could not get away from business; he speaks no English and does not like the English. He has to consent, because his father wishes it. But he warns Aunt Hester to keep a sharp eye on me, in case I should be silly and fall in love with some dull, stupid Englishman—"

Abruptly Jenny paused. Her own cigarette, unnoticed, was burning her fingers; she threw it on the floor.

Tom looked straight at her.

"Which you might do, mightn't you?"

"No! Never! Besides, Aunt Hester and the de Sennevilles would never let me."

While Stella and Dolly clattered tins and banged cups behind the counter of the prosaic tea bar, Tom Lockwood took a great and secret and mighty resolve. But he did not show it in his brisk tone.

"Now, then! Let's get down to cases. What has frightened you so much?"

"Last night," answered Jenny, "someone tried to kill me. Someone turned on the tap of the gas heater in my bedroom. It was impossible for this to be done, because all the doors and windows were locked on the inside. But it was done. Already I had a note saying I was going to die."

Jenny's eyes seemed to turn inwards.

"By good luck, they save me. But I don't wish to speak of last night! This morning I am very—sick is not a nice word, is it?—no! I am ill. But Aunt Hester said this was nonsense, and it would revive me to go sightseeing again. That is why we went to St. Paul's. Do you know St. Paul's?"

"I'm afraid I haven't ever been inside the place for a long time."

"It happened," said Jenny, "in the whispering gallery."

Whispering gallery.

The eerie sibilance tapped against the nerves even in this commonplace tea bar, with traffic rushing outside.

"You climb up stairs," said Jenny. "Spiral stairs. Stairs and stairs, until you are breathless and think you will never get to the top. Then there is a tiny little door, and you go out into the gallery."

Then Tom remembered—how vividly this whispering gallery had impressed him. It was dizzily high up, just under the curve of the dome: circular, some two hundred feet across, and with only an iron railing to keep you from pitching down interminably to the acres of folding chairs on the ground floor below.

Noises struck in with brittle sharpness. Gray light filtered in on the tall marble statues of saints round the vast circle. It was solemn, and it was lonely. Only one verger, black-clad, stood guard there.

More than ever Tom was conscious of Jenny's presence, of her parted lips and quick breathing.

"I am not a coward," she insisted. "But I did not like this place. If you sit on the stone bench round the wall, and someone—even two hundred feet away—whispers near the wall, that whisper comes round in a soft little gurgly voice out of nowhere.

"Please attend to me!" Jenny added, with deep sincerity. "I was not well—I admit it. But I was not unbalanced either. Ever since I have received that first note saying I would die, I have watch everyone. I trust nobody—you were right. But I trust you. And, on my oath, this happened as I tell it.

"There were only five persons in all that dusky gallery. You could see. My Aunt Hester and my Cousin Margot. A fat red-faced countryman who is come to see the sights with a packet of sandwiches and a thermos flask of tea. The verger, in a dark robe, who tells you about the gallery.

"That is all!

"First the verger showed us how the whispering gallery is worked. He leans against the wall to the left—you do not even have to be against the wall. He says something that we, on the right of the door, hardly hear at all. But it goes slipping and sliding and horrible round the dome. Something about 'This Cathedral, begun by Sir Christopher Wren—' and it jumps up in your ear from the other side.

"After that we separated, but only a little. I was nervous—yes, I admit that too! I sat down on the stone bench, all prim. Aunt Hester and Margot went to the railing round the open space, and looked over. Margot giggles and says, 'Mama, would it not be dreadful if I jumped over?'

"Meanwhile, the fat countryman has sat down fifty feet away from me. Calmly he opens the grease-proof paper and takes out a sandwich. He pours out tea from the thermos into the cup; he is taking a deep drink when the verger, who is outraged at sandwiches in St. Paul's, rushes toward him from ten feet away.

"Mr. Lockwood, I know what I saw! The countryman could not have spoken; he is really and truly gulping down tea. The verger could not have spoken—I could see his mouth—and anyway he is too far away from the wall. As for Aunt Hester or Margot, that is nonsense! And, anyway, they are much too far away from the wall, and leaning over the railing.

"But someone spoke in my ear just then.

"It was in English, and horrible. It said: 'I failed the first time, Jennifer. But I shall not fail the second time.' And it gloated. *And there was nobody there!*"

Jenny paused.

With all the nervousness of the past days, there were shadows under her eyes, and she was more than pale. But a passion of appeal met Tom across the table.

"No, I did not say anything!" she told him. "If I had, Aunt

Hester would only say I was imagining things. Just as she said I was imagining things last night, and must have turned on the gas-tap myself, because the room was all locked up inside.

"No, no, no! I jumped up and ran out. I ran down those stairs so fast no one could have caught me. I did not know where I was going or what I should do. If I prayed anything, I think I prayed to meet . . ."

"To meet whom?" prompted Tom.

"Well! To meet someone like you."

After saying this, defiantly, Jenny drank stone-cold tea.

"But what am I to do?" she demanded, with tears on her eyelashes. "I know Aunt Hester means me no harm—how could she? But I can't face her—I won't! Where am I to go?"

"I will tell you exactly," said Tom, reaching across and taking her hands. "You are going with me to see old H. M., otherwise Sir Henry Merrivale, at an office which nowadays is humorously called The Ministry of Miracles. Afterwards—"

Bang!

The door of the tea bar flew open with a crash which half shattered its glass panel. Tom, sitting with his back to the door, first craned round and then leaped to his feet.

Outside the door, but not yet looking into the tea bar, stood an imperious and stately lady who was addressing someone beyond her.

"I am well acquainted, constable," she was saying, "with Sir Richard Tringham, the Commissioner of Police. Your deliberate falsehoods will not help you when I report you to him personally. You have denied you saw any young lady run down the steps of the Cathedral. You have denied she met a young man in sports coat and gray flannels. Finally, you have denied they went into any of the shops or other disgusting places along here. Is this so, or is it not?"

"'S right, marm," stolidly answered Police-Constable Dawson.

Whereupon Aunt Hester made her entrance like Lady Macbeth.

"I am Mrs. Hester Harpenden," she announced to the walls at large. "And I have *distinctly* different information from a newspaper seller. I have—"

Here she saw Tom, who was standing in the middle of the floor.

"That's the man," she said.

Up to this time Stella (rather bucktoothed) and Dolly (distinctly pretty) had remained stupefied and silent behind the counter. Now both of them gave tongue.

"Disgusting place, eh?" cried Dolly. "I like that!"

"Busted the door, officer," screamed Stella. "Busted the door, that's what she done!"

"Busted the door, did she?" repeated Police-Constable Dawson, in a sinister voice. "Oh, ah. I see." And he reached for his notebook.

Meanwhile, as Aunt Hester calmly advanced, Tom glanced back towards Jenny.

But Jenny was not there. She was gone; she was not anywhere in the place.

The sharp pang this gave him was not his only feeling. For an instant he believed he had strayed from St. Paul's churchyard into a world of monsters and twilight, where anything might happen; and, in a sense, he was not far wrong.

"Young man," Aunt Hester asked quietly, "where is my niece?"

"Do you see her here, madam?"

"No. But that does not mean . . . A back entrance! Ah, yes! Where is the back entrance here?"

"Just a moment," said Tom, stepping in front of her. "Have you a warrant to search these premises?"

"Do I need a warrant to find my own niece?"

"Yes, yer do and all!" screamed Stella. "Either yer orders tea and cakes, which is wot we're 'ere for, or out yer go straightaway. 'S right, officer?"

"'S right, miss," agreed the law.

Aunt Hester was not fooled for a moment.

Seen close at hand, she was—or seemed—less formidable than bitter and bony, with a high-bridge nose and washed-out blue eyes, as though she had suffered some disappointment in youth and never forgotten it. Tom could tell her clothes were fashionable, as Jenny's were fashionable, without knowing why he knew.

"Then you are all against me, it seems," she smiled. "Well! This will indeed make a budget of news for my friend the Commissioner of Police!"

"By the way," Tom said casually, "*who* did you say is the Commissioner of Police?"

"But Sir Richard Tringham, of course!"

"Oh, put a sock in it," said Tom. "Sir Richard Tringham has been dead for seven years. The present Commissioner is Colonel Thomas Lockwood. And I ought to know—he's my father."

"Cor!" whispered Dolly.

"'S right, marm," agreed Police-Constable Dawson.

Aunt Hester, not in the least impressed, merely raised her shoulders.

"Ah, well!" she smiled. "If police-officers are bribed to tell untruths, then I had better be off."

Majestically she strolled towards the front of the shop. With a gesture of contempt she opened her purse, took out a couple of pound notes, and murmured something about paying for the glass door as she tossed the notes towards Stella.

Then, when she was within a step of the door, she whirled round and screamed at Tom like a harpy.

"*Where is my niece?*"

And Tom's temper crashed over too, like the glass platform of cakes which Dolly had been nervously handling.

"In a place where you'll never find her," he yelled back, only hoping he was telling the truth.

"If I prefer charges of abduction—"

"When she goes away of her own free will? Don't talk rot! And shall I tell you something else, Mrs. Harpenden?"

"By all means. If you can."

"That girl is of age," said Tom, advancing towards her. "Even under French law, her guardian no longer has any authority over her. But she doesn't seem to know that. She's being pushed and bullied and hounded into a marriage she doesn't want, by a lot of ghouls who are only interested in her money. And I tell you straight: I mean to stop it."

"Ah, I see. You want her money."

The steamy room was dead quiet, with fragments of shattered glass and coloured cakes all over the counter and floor. Both Stella and Dolly had cowered back.

"Yes, that hurt," said Tom. "You knew it would hurt. All right: if you want open war, it's war from this time on. Agreed?"

"Oh, agreed," replied Aunt Hester, her head high. "And I have a feeling, dear Mr. Lockwood, that you are not going to win. *Good* day."

With all the honors she marched out, closed the door, and turned right toward Paternoster Row. They had time to see a brown-haired girl of seventeen or eighteen, with slanting eyes and a mischievous look, run after her. It could only have been Jenny's Cousin Margot.

Tom, exasperated to see those two pound notes lying on the counter, flung down another two to match them.

"That's for the smashed container and the cakes," he said.

"But, reolly, now!" protested Dolly, in an ultra-refined

voice. "This is too much money. And is the Commissioner of Police reolly your father?"

"'S right, miss," said Police-Constable Dawson, and stolidly marched out.

"Ducks, ducks, ducks!" cried Stella, addressing Tom. Being not very pretty, she was more inclined to sympathize with his bedevilments. "You needn't worry about your young lady. 'Course there's another way out of 'ere!"

"There is?"

"'Course there is. At the back, and turn sideways. I saw your young lady run out as soon as we heard the old witch's voice outside. Either the young lady's still hiding in the passage past the washroom, or she's gorn out into Paternoster Row."

"My deepest thanks!" said Tom.

He turned and plunged towards the back—only to be stopped short by another figure materializing in this extraordinary tea shop.

This was a shortish, wiry man with his light-brown hair cropped close to the head after a prevailing American fashion. He was perhaps in his middle thirties; he wore loose-fitting clothes, and his tie could be seen at sixty paces in any crowd.

"Now hold it, brother!" he urged. "Don't go busting out of there or you'll louse up the whole deal."

Tom blinked at him.

"The old lady," continued the stranger, evidently referring to Aunt Hester, "left her car—it would be a limousine—parked in Paternoster Row. It's not there now. She'll be screaming for the cops again, and you'll run smack into her. Besides, the kid is safe now."

"The kid? You mean Jenny? Where is she?"

Something like a self-satisfied smile crept across the newcomer's face.

"I told the chauffeur," he said, "to drive her straight to a guy named Sir Henry Merrivale, at an address he seemed to know. Sit down for a minute, until the old dame stops yelling about her stolen car."

Tom Lockwood extended his hand.

"Maybe you won't want to shake hands," retorted the newcomer almost evilly, and put his hands behind his back, "when you hear what I am."

There was about him something distinctly foreign, in a way that no American is ever foreign. Though Tom could not analyze it, his companion enlightened him.

"Get it?" he asked. "I'm a Canadian. Lamoreux's the name—Steve Lamoreux. I was born in Montreal; I can speak French as well as I speak English. In Paris they say my accent is terrible; but they understand me. I'm a newsman for *L'Oeil*. Been in France for six months. Don't you get it *now*?"

"Well, I . . ."

Steve Lamoreux's shrewd brown eyes, in the hard yet sympathetic face, were almost glaring at him. And Lamoreux spoke bitterly.

"I'm the stooge," he said. "I'm the tail. In other words, I'm Armand de Senneville's hired spy to keep out of the way, never let the girl see me, but make sure she doesn't meet any boy friends. If she does . . ."

Tom, aware that both Stella and Dolly were listening with all their ears, raised his voice.

"Could we have two more teas, please?" he called. Then, to Lamoreux: "Into the booth here. And keep your voice low."

They sat down opposite each other.

"What the hell?" said Lamoreux. "I'm only human. That girl's too innocent; I won't see her pushed around. What's more, I can't take this miracle stuff any longer—not for a hundred bucks a week or anything else. Do you realize that, but for a thousand-to-one chance, she'd be lying dead at the mortuary this very minute?"

It was a cold and ugly statement, just as the great bell of St. Paul's boomed out the hour of five.

"She didn't tell you how bad it was last night, did she?" asked Lamoreux.

"Not the details, no."

"No, you bet she didn't! The girl has guts—I'll say that for her."

"But how do you know she didn't tell me?"

"Because I overheard every word you two said in here! Look!" persisted Lamoreux, tapping a finger into his palm. "When they started out today, in their grand limousine, I followed in a taxi. Aunt Hester knows me, and knows all about me. Her husband, Uncle Fred, and young Margot—well, they've seen me once, here in England. I couldn't help that, but they'd never seen me before, and it doesn't matter. Jenny doesn't, and mustn't, even suspect.

"Those were my orders from young de Senneville. He didn't dare send a Frenchman as a tail—it might be too conspicuous. But Jenny's seen this map of mine more than once at the newspaper office; if she spotted me, it might shake her faith in good old Armand."

"Quiet!" Tom warned softly.

It was Dolly who appeared, demurely, setting down two mugs of tea already sugared. Though she seemed inclined to linger, Lamoreux's glance sent her away miffed.

"Armand de Senneville," Tom said between his teeth. "What I should like to do to that . . . !"

"Easy, now, brother! You're talking about my boss."

"He may not be your boss much longer. You may get a better one."

"How's that? Say it again."

"Never mind; get on with the story."

"Well! Aunt Hester and Margot and Jenny had their car parked in Paternoster Row. They told the chauffeur to wait there. I ditched my taxi, and sat in the car with the chauffeur. We could see the whole front of St. Paul's. We knew we could see 'em come out."

"And then?"

"You know what happened. About thirty-five minutes later, she comes tearing down the steps. You grab her. I think to myself, 'Steve, this is your job; this is where the balloon goes up.' Over you come to this place. I sneak in the back way, and I'm practically against a matchboard partition behind you. When I heard about a voice speaking in the whispering gallery, when no voice could have spoken, I damn near fainted. And there's another thing."

"Yes?"

Uneasily Lamoreux drew out a packet of Yellow French cigarettes. He struck an old-fashioned sulphur match; he brooded while holding the match until the sulphur burned away. Then, still lost in thought, he lit the cigarette and flicked away the match.

"When I first got a gander at you, see—" Lamoreux stopped.

"Well? What is it?"

"I thought it was an ordinary pick-up. Then, when I heard you two talking, I thought you were a right guy. And I still think so."

They glared at each other, because no man pays a compliment to another's face. Then, after an embarrassed pause:

"That's why I stuck my neck out. I could see Aunt Hester charging for this joint before either of you two did. I knew Jenny would duck for a way out. And *she* knew the car was parked just beside here. So I rushed out and told Pearson— that's the chauffeur—to drive her straight to this guy H. M.

I'd heard of the old—the old gentleman; and I knew *he* was all right."

Lamoreux pointed his cigarette at Tom with grimacing emphasis.

"But get this!" he added. "I'm no guardian angel or *preux chevalier.* The hell with that stuff. Somebody in dead earnest tried to bump off that kid. Somebody'll try again, and I want no part of it. All I'd like to know, for the sweet suffering Moses's sake, is who's doing this and why?"

Lamoreux's voice rose up piercingly until he remembered they were in public.

Then it sank to a whisper. They sat and thought and worried.

"Armand de Senneville—" Tom began.

"Look," the other said wearily. "You've got that guy on the brain. De Senneville wants to marry her for her money. What good is it to him if she's knocked off here in England?"

"Yes. I suppose that's true."

"But take it the other way round!" argued Lamoreux. "Take that gang in their country house near Hampton Court. I don't doubt Aunt Hester, at least, will get a large slice of dough when this marriage comes off. She's been in France dozens of times—she's cheering for matrimony like nobody's business. All right! Then what motive has she, or any of 'em, to kill Jenny and lose the money themselves?"

Steve Lamoreux at last took a sip of tea, which so disgusted him he did not speak for thirty seconds.

"It's nuts!" he said. "It makes no sense however you look at it."

"On the contrary," said Tom, "it's got to make sense! That's why you and I are going to see H. M. as fast as a taxi can take us."

"But I can't go there!"

"Why not?"

"Because Jenny's there, and she might spot me. All the same, if you want to reach me at any time before seven this evening, call me up at this number. If you want me any time after that, here's the number of my hotel near their house."

With a little gold pencil he scribbled two telephone numbers on a sheet torn from a notebook, and handed it to Tom.

"Locked rooms!" said Lamoreux. "Whispering voices! No motives! Brother, I'd give my last dime to go with you! What's the old—what's Sir Henry going to say about this one?"

In a little more than twenty minutes, Tom Lockwood found out.

"Y'see," said Sir Henry Merrivale, with surprising meekness, "I'm sort of in trouble with the government."

"How do you mean?" asked Tom.

"Well, sort of," said H. M.

The old sinner, all sixteen stone of him, sat behind the desk in the familiar office, twiddling his thumbs over his corporation. His shell-rimmed spectacles were pulled down on his broad nose, and light from the windows behind him glistened on his bald head. On his face was the look of such martyrdom that it had won Jenny's complete sympathy and only enraged Tom.

"Well, y'see," H. M. pursued, "I've been abroad for maybe two or three years . . ."

"Ah, yes!" said Tom. "It was in New York, wasn't it, that you wrecked the subway at Grand Central Station and nabbed the right murderer on the wrong evidence?"

"Oh, son! I dunno what you're talkin' about," said H. M., giving him an austere look.

"And in Tangier, I think, you blew up a ship and let the real criminal escape just because you happened to like him?"

"Y'see how they treat me?" H. M. demanded, his powerful voice rising as he addressed Jenny. "They've got no respect for me, not a bit."

"Poor man!" Jenny said warmly.

"Oh, Lord," moaned Tom. Like most people, he could never resist the temptation to make fun of the great man; and then, to his astonishment, he found women sympathizing with H. M.'s most outrageous exploits.

"But why," he persisted, "are you in trouble with the government?"

"It seems I spent more money than I should have, or burn me, than I can account for. It also seems—would you believe it?—I shouldn't have had banking accounts in New York, Paris, Tangier, and Milan."

"You didn't know, of course, you weren't allowed to have those banking accounts?"

"*Me?*"

"Never mind," said Tom, smiting his forehead. "What happened to you?"

"Oh, Lord love a duck!" said H. M. "When I got back to England, you'd have thought I was Guy Fawkes and the Cato Street conspirators all rolled into one. They hoicked me up on the carpet before an old friend of mine. I won't say who this louse is, except to tell you he's the Attorney-General."

"No," said Tom. "By all means don't breathe a word."

"'Henry,' he says to me, 'I've got you over a barrel.'"

"Did the Attorney-General actually use those words?"

"Well . . . now!" said the great man, making a broad gesture and giving Tom a withering look. "I'm tellin' you the gist of it, that's all. 'Henry,' he said, 'on the evidence I have here I could have you fined a hundred thousand pounds or stuck in jail for practically a century.'" Here H. M. broke off and appealed to Jenny. "Was this just?" he demanded.

"Of course it wasn't!" cried Jenny.

"'However,' he says, 'you pay up in full, with a fine, and we'll forget it. *Provided*,' he says—"

"Provided what?"

"I'm to go back to my own office here, d'ye see? It used to be part of the War Office, before they messed everything about in the war. And I'm to be in charge of Central Office Eight of the Metropolitan Police."

"Please," said Jenny in her soft voice, "but what is Central Office Eight?"

"It's me," H. M. replied simply. "Anybody who calls it The Ministry of Miracles is going to get a thick ear. They had enough fun, curse 'em, with the late Ministry of Information. If anything rummy turns up at Scotland Yard—any loony case that doesn't make sense—they chuck it at my head."

Here H. M.'s expression changed.

"Y'know," he said, "strictly among ourselves, I don't mind so much. I'm gettin' old and mellow now—"

"I'll bet you are," Tom muttered sardonically under his breath.

"—and it's comfortable here, sort of. Well!" said H. M., sitting up briskly and rubbing his hands together. "The old man's in business again. You got any miracles you want explained?"

"Have we!" said Tom. "Jenny! Haven't you told him?"

He himself had just arrived, hurrying in to find H. M. pouring out his woes and tribulations. In the old dusty office, high above Whitehall, Tom and Jenny looked at each other.

That office, as H. M. had said, was comfortable. Above the fireplace still hung the satanic portrait of Fouché, Minister of Police under Napoleon. There was a very impressive-looking safe, inscribed IMPORTANT STATE DOCUMENTS: *DO NOT TOUCH!*—but containing only a bottle of whiskey. The office had seen many strange things happen—it would see many more.

"I told him about what happened in the whispering gallery, yes!" said Jenny. "But I do not even know how I have come here at all! I hated to leave you in the tea shop, but Aunt Hester was so furious I could only run. Then, at the car, the chauffeur says that some Canadian gentleman—"

"That's all right. I can explain later."

"Some Canadian gentleman, who has been sitting with him in the car when we went into St. Paul's, told him to drive me straight to this H. M. of yours. You have said so too, so I go." Jenny's brow wrinkled. "And I was so, so wrong about your H. M.!"

"Oh?" enquired Tom.

"Yes, yes! He does not swear or carry on or throw people out of windows. He is what you call a poppet."

"Hem!" said the great man modestly.

"Frankly," said Tom, eyeing the stuffed owl across the desk, "I shouldn't call it a well-chosen word to apply to him. You'll find out. However! When I'd chucked out Aunt Hester, with the aid of two counter-girls and a friendly cop, I thought I'd never get here. I was afraid some infernal thing or other had happened to you, and I might never see you again."

"You may see me," said Jenny, and stretched out her hands, "whenever you wish."

"*Oi!*" interposed a thunderous voice.

The alleged poppet was now glaring at them with a malignancy which raised Jenny's hair.

"There's not goin' to be any canoodling in this office, is there?" he demanded. "All my life I've tripped over young people with no idea except to canoodle. Now listen to me, my dolly."

His big voice altered and sharpened. The whole atmosphere of the office changed as his small eyes narrowed behind the spectacles. He might be irascible, unreasonable, and childish, but he was still the Old Maestro—and you trifled with him at your own risk.

So H. M. spoke gently.

"You understand, my dolly, what I've already told you? That neither Général de Senneville nor Armand de Senneville has any hold over you? And neither have Aunt Hester and Company? That you're a perfectly free woman?"

Jenny pressed her hands against her cheeks.

"Yes," she said. "I suppose I always knew that, really. But . . ."

"But what?"

"People are so *determined*. They don't yield a bit. And it's always gone on like that. So you say to yourself, 'Oh, what's the use?'"

"Yes, I know," nodded H. M. "But that's what causes so much unhappiness in this world, especially for gals. Well, what's your feeling now? Do you want to fight 'em and beat 'em hands down?"

"Yes!"

"Do you still want to go on staying at your Aunt Hester's house? What's-its'-name? New Hampton Court?"

"It's called Broadacres, on the river. Tomorrow, they tell me, they will save the best of the sights for last—they say they will take me to see Hampton Court Palace in the afternoon."

"They say that, hey?" H. M. muttered thoughtfully. Something flickered behind his glasses and was gone. "Never mind! Do you still want to stay at your Aunt Hester's?"

"No. But what else can I do, except return to Paris?"

"Well," glowered H. M., scratching the back of his neck, "I've got a house, and a wife, and two daughters, and two good-for-nothing sons-in-law I've had to support for eighteen years. So I expect you'd better move in too."

"You mean this?" cried Jenny, and sprang to her feet. "You would really want me?" she asked incredulously.

"Bah," said H. M.

"Sir H. M.! How to thank you I do not know . . . !"

"Shut up," said the great man austerely.

Jenny sat down again.

"Then there's your clothes," he mused. "That's a very fetchin' outfit you've got on now, and I expect you brought a whole trunkful?"

"Yes, my clothes! I forget!"

"Don't worry," said H. M. with a suggestion of ghoulish mirth. "I'll send a police-officer to fetch 'em. If that doesn't put the breeze up Aunt Hester to a howlin' gale, I don't know her kind. But understand this, my dolly!"

Again his tone sharpened and struck.

"Aunt Hester'll hit back. Don't think she won't. Also, you're likely to have the whole de Senneville tribe here and on your neck." H. M. blinked at Tom. "I say, son. Shall you and I handle 'em?"

"With pleasure!" said Tom. "And definitely without gloves."

"In the meantime," H. M. went on, looking very hard at Jenny, "I've heard about this rummy business in the whispering gallery, yes. But there's something else you've got to tell me, and very clearly, before I can help you at all."

"Just a minute!" interrupted Tom.

"Oh, for the love of Esau," howled H. M. "What's wrong *now?*"

"A voice spoke where no voice could possibly have spoken," said Tom. "Do you believe that?"

"Certainly."

"Then how was it done?"

"Oh, my son!" groaned H. M., with a pitying glance. "You don't mean to say that trick fooled you?"

"Do you know how it was done?"

"Sure I do."

"Then what's the explanation?"

"I'm not goin' to tell you."

Tom got up and did a little dance round his chair. H. M. sternly ordered him back into it.

"I'm not goin' to tell you," he went on with dignity, "because very shortly I'm goin' to *show* you. You can see with your own eyes. That's fair enough, hey?"

Whereupon his own eyes narrowed as he looked at Jenny.

"Stop a bit! We don't want Aunt Hester to pick up the trail too soon. You said you came here in a car, with a chauffeur. Is the car still waiting? Or did you send it back?"

"I have sent it back," retorted Jenny. "But I *know* I can trust Pearson—he is the chauffeur. I have told him to say I have gone off on my own, alone, to have tea at Lyons'."

"Which Lyons'?"

Jenny's gray eyes opened wide.

"I am English, I keep telling you!" she insisted. "But how can I know much of England if I am never here? Is there more than one Lyons'? The only London restaurants of which I have heard are Lyons' and the Caprice and the Ivy."

"Those three grand old restaurants!" exclaimed Tom, and resisted an impulse to put his arms round her. "H. M., Aunt Hester will think Jenny is giving her the raspberry, which is exactly what you'd do yourself."

"Uh-huh. That'll do. Now then: about this first miracle—of a gas-tap being turned on in a locked room."

When H. M. produced his ancient black pipe, and began to load it with tobacco looking (and tasting) like the steel wool used on kitchen sinks, Tom knew he must brace himself for more trouble.

"My dolly," said H. M., "a lot of bits and pieces have come flyin' out of your story. I can see this aunt of yours. I can see her daughter, Margot, who's eighteen years old and up to mischief. I can see your Uncle Fred, who's tall and red-faced and looks like a retired major. I can see this white Georgian house, with long windows, set back from the river. But burn me if I can see the details!"

"How do you mean?"

"For instance. D'ye usually sleep with the windows closed, to say nothin' of being locked? Is that an old French custom?"

"No, no, of course not!"

"Well, then?"

"It is the details," said Jenny, biting her lip, "I have not wished to talk about. They are—bad. I feel the gas strangle me again. But never mind! First, Aunt Hester put me into a bedroom on the ground floor."

"Why?"

"And why not?" Jenny exclaimed reasonably. "It is a very nice room. But it has two windows stretching to the ground. Aunt Hester is frightened of burglars, and asks me please to keep the windows tight-locked. By the time I am ready for bed, I am so scared that I put both bolts on the door as well—on the inside. You see, it was at dinner I received the note."

"What note?"

"It was a little note, folded up in my napkin at the table. I thought—"

"Yes, my dolly?"

"At first," Jenny explained, peeping sideways at Tom, "I thought it was from a young man I met at a tea party they gave. He has made what you call the eyes at me. So—"

"*That's* an old French custom, if you like," Tom said

politely. "You thought the note was from him, and you didn't want anybody else to know?"

Jenny turned on him flaming.

"I do not like this young man at the tea party! I do not wish to see him again! But if he has written a note to me, can I give the poor man away?"

"No. Sorry, Jenny. Shouldn't have said that."

"But it is not from him at all, or anything like that. I read it under the table. It was only one line, in a handwriting I never saw before. It said, *'You will die tonight, Jennifer.'*"

Jenny moistened her lips. H. M. had lighted the pipe, and an oily cloud of smoke crept over the desk.

"At first I thought it was a joke. What else can I think? Then I looked at the rest of them, all so normal, with the candles burning on the dinner table. And I know I am alone. I am a stranger, even if I am in my own country—and I am frightened!

"I did not even dare ask if the note was a joke. So I hid it, and afterwards I lost it. At eleven o'clock, when it was time to go to bed . . ."

"Yes, my dolly? Go on!"

"I sleep badly," said Jenny. "Always I have. No matter how late I go to bed, I always wake up at 5 or 5:30 in the morning. There was a custom I had in France, first when I lived with my parents and afterwards at the house of Général de Senneville. A maid brought me a cup of chocolate at six in the morning.

"When Aunt Hester asked if she could do anything more, I asked if I might have the chocolate, or else tea, at that time. I had been there several days, but it was the first time I venture to ask. Aunt Hester lifts her eyebrows and said, 'Do you think, Jennifer my dear, that is quite fair to the servants?'

"I said no, no, please to forget it. But Margot, who has green eyes and is nice, she is always up before six, she says, and will be glad to bring me a cup of tea then. Very well! I go to my room. I turn on the light. I fasten the bolts both at the top and bottom of the door. Then I turn round. And one of the windows, which I have left locked, is wide open."

Jenny paused.

H. M., wrapped in his cloud of nauseous smoke, was as expressionless as an idol.

"I rush across," continued Jenny, her voice rising. "I close and lock the window again. Then I think, 'Suppose someone is hiding in the room?' But I must not be stupid and rouse the whole house. And so—well! I search the room myself. Nobody is hiding there. I think perhaps some servant has opened the window to air the room, and I feel better.

"It is a warm night—very warm, they tell me, for an English spring. So I do not need to turn on the gas heater in the fireplace when I undress. I close the window curtains almost shut. But I smoke a cigarette or two, you can bet, before I have the nerve to turn out the light. But I do turn out the light, finally. And soon I am asleep. Then—"

"Hold on!" interposed H. M. softly, and took the pipe out of his mouth.

"Y-yes?"

"What time did you turn in? Do you remember?"

"Yes. I see my wrist watch. It is ten minutes past twelve."

"Did any of this family know beforehand about your habit of takin' chocolate at six in the morning?"

"N-no, I do not think so. How could they? I—"

Again Jenny was trembling; and, worst sign of all, she was again glancing over her shoulder. Tom got up and put his hands on her shoulders.

"Hadn't we better stop this, H. M.?" he demanded.

"We can't stop it, son, and you know we can't. That gal really was in a locked room. It's practically impossible to tamper with bolts when they're at the top and bottom of the door. Those Georgian window-locks are dead sure for safety. Unless I can get a hint about this, the old man's dished."

"I am very well, thank you," said Jenny. "I can go on, if you wish."

"Well?" said H. M., putting the pipe back in his mouth.

"First there was a dream. It was horrible, but I don't remember it now. Then I knew I was awake, and being strangled so I could not breathe. This part is hard to describe. But—when you are dying, or even losing consciousness, you can still hear sounds clearly even though you can barely see?"

"Yes, my dolly. That's right."

"I could tell it was just growing daylight, no more. But somebody was pounding on the outside of the door. And I hear Margot's voice crying my name. I tried to scream back, but there is no breath, and already—this is not pretty—I had been sick.

"Next, which is all confused, I heard a man's voice outside with Margot. It was an American voice I have never heard before. It said, 'What's wrong, kid? Isn't she okay?' Margot screams that the room is full of gas, and can't he smell it from under the door? He says, 'You won't break down that door. Where's the window?'

"Still I am just conscious. I can hear everything, though it must be like being hanged. I hear them run away, and someone else join them. Then I see—all blurry, because my eyes have nearly gone—I see someone's fist, wrapped in a coat, punch through the glass of the far window.

"This is my Uncle Fred, who has been roused too. He unlocks the window and pushes it all the way up. Someone runs to turn off the gas-tap at the heater. I think this is the American. I cannot see, but I hear him say a wicked word, and say, 'So-and-so, but it's turned full on!' He turns it off.

Margot rushes towards me, spilling a tea tray on the carpet. That is all I remember, until the doctor is there."

Jenny lifted her hands, and let them fall on the handbag in her lap. As the oily smoke from H. M.'s pipe reached her at last, she began to cough.

H. M. put down the pipe and knocked it out.

"The doctor, hey?" he repeated. "And what did the doctor say?"

"It was not the doctor who spoke to me. It was Aunt Hester. She said, 'This is not very considerate of you, Jennifer. To try to kill yourself because you are not happy about your future husband.'"

Tom Lockwood's grip tightened on her shoulders. "Your Aunt Hester said that?"

"Yes! And it is not true! But they ask how anyone could have tried to kill me, when the room is all locked up inside?"

"Anything else, Jenny?"

"I say, 'Where is the American?' They say, 'What American?' and claim he is a delusion of mine. They stand round my bed, all big-eyed—Aunt Hester and Cousin Margot and even poor old Uncle Fred—and look down at me. They say it is a mercy the doctor is their family doctor, and will not report this to the police. Dear God, do you wonder I am afraid of them?"

"H. M.!" Tom said sharply, after a pause.

"Well?"

"You may have been wondering about this mysterious American . . ."

"Frankly, son, I have. I don't see where he fits in."

"He isn't an American," said Tom, "but he isn't a delusion either. That gang made a bad slip when they claimed he was. I'll tell you all about him at the proper time. Meanwhile, do you see any clue at all?"

H. M., who had been sitting with his eyes closed and a

very mulish look on his face, now opened his eyes slowly and inspected Jenny.

"My dolly," he said, "I've got only one more question to ask now. But I want you to be awful careful how you answer it. You could hear all these voices clearly when you were nearly unconscious. You could hear the pounding on the door, the footsteps running away, and the rest of it. *Did you hear any other sound besides that?*"

"What—what kind of sound?"

"Any kind!"

"No, I don't think so."

"You're sure of that, now?"

"Yes, positive!"

"Oh, Lord love a duck," observed Sir Henry Merrivale, with his mouth falling open. "So *that's* how the locked room was worked!"

"How?" shouted Tom.

"I'm the old man," said H. M., tapping himself impressively on the chest. "You let me deal with this in my own way. I'm goin' into action at once."

H. M. reached for the telephone at his elbow. He dialed for an outside exchange, and then dialed the number. During a long pause, while they could hear the ringing tone go on interminably, Tom Lockwood listened to an air-vent which hummed and hummed in the ceiling, and at intervals he studied H. M.'s face, now as malignant as the Evil One's.

The ringing tone broke off. There ensued, from H. M.'s side, the following weird and wonderful conversation.

"Looky here, my wench. I want to speak to Sam. . . . Oh, yes, I can! This is the old man. You just tell him I squared it when he was givin' a beautiful party for sixteen beautiful gals without any clothes on, and the silly-ass coppers broke in. Yes, the old man! . . ."

A grateful note crept into H. M.'s big voice.

"That you, Sam? How are you . . . ? Never better, Sam! There's a question I want to ask you. . . . Thank'ee, Sam. How many vents are working now? . . ."

Tom Lockwood looked up wildly at the air-ventilator humming and whacking above his head. He looked at an equally bewildered Jenny.

"Only three? You're sure of that? Right, Sam. Gimme their names and descriptions. Yes, I said descriptions! Uh-huh. . . . No, the first one's no good. Try the second. . . . Lord love a duck, that sounds like the one we want! But try the third, just for luck. . . . No, he's no good either. It's Charley Johnson. Gimme the address. It's nearly six o'clock—he's bound to be at home now. . . . Thanks a million, Sam. And try to keep to one woman next time, hey? All right, all right!"

Ringing off with the handsome air of one who has made all things clear, Sir Henry Merrivale spun the dial once again.

"Sergeant? I want a squad car, to hold three people and a driver, as quick as kiss-your-hand. Two minutes? Outside the Horse Guards Avenue entrance? Right!"

Lumbering to his feet, H. M. took down from a rack an ancient Panama hat and thrust it on. This hat, which had a band of startling colors and whose brim was turned down all round like a bowl, gave an even more sinister look to the great man's unmentionable face.

"Sir!" protested Tom. "What in the name of sense is all this business of air-vents, and how can it help us?"

"You wanted a miracle explained, didn't you?" demanded the great man. "All right. Are you comin' with me, or not?"

Within the promised two minutes, and in the police car— Jenny and Tom sitting in the back seat, H. M. piled in front with the chauffeur—they whipped out of Horse Guards Avenue, turned left, and shot down Whitehall. H. M., who himself has never driven a car without landing through a shop window or against a lamppost, made caustic comments about driving skill to a red-eared police driver.

Far beyond the towers of Westminster, behind its stately terraces and flats, lies a region of dingy, almost unknown streets. The red-brick houses in these streets, by a show of brass knobs and letter-slots, try to keep up a brave pretense that they are private homes and not lodging homes.

But gritty winds make discarded newspapers dance along their gutters; children scream; there is an over-riding clatter of dustbins. Before one such dingy house, which did look like a private home and really was, the car stopped.

"Come on, you two," grunted H. M.

He impelled Jenny and Tom out of the car and up a flight of stone steps to the front door. There he jabbed his finger at the bell.

"For the last time," said the desperate Tom, "will you tell what an air-vent—" H. M. pulled down the brim of his hat even harder.

"Who said anything about an air-vent?" he howled. "*I* didn't. I said 'vent.' That's the theatrical and professional term for a ventriloquist. Didn't you ever hear a ventriloquist?"

Jenny's hands flew to her open mouth.

"According to your story," pursued H. M., "there were only four persons in the whispering gallery with you. This time we can acquit both your Aunt Hester and your Cousin Margot—they were leaning over the railing, much too far away from the wall.

"We can acquit the outraged verger in charge of the place. But who else was there? According to you, a fat and red-faced countryman—a little too thoroughly dressed up as a countryman, wasn't he?—who carried a packet of sandwiches and a thermos flask.

"When you heard the words, he was sitting against the walls and plainly drinking tea. All right, my fatheads! Who's the only man alive who can make his dummy speak clearly while he himself is walloping down a full glass of water? You know the answer.

"I rang up the king of all impresarios and found out the names and descriptions of the only three vents working in London. This Charley Johnson won't know much about the case. Somebody handed him a fiver to play what he thought, and probably still thinks, was a joke. But *he*, when we see him, can tell us who bribed him to—"

The front door was hurled open.

There is no other word for it—the door crashed against the wall and all but rebounded.

In the doorway there stood, swaying slightly, that same fat man Jenny recognized from the whispering gallery. His face was now less professionally red; he was bald, and wore no wig. Instead of his countryman's clothes, he was wrapped round in a somewhat grubby dressing gown of black and orange stripes. In one hand he held a whiskey-and-soda, in the other a half-eaten sandwich.

But what held them was the expression of his face. His eyes were so horribly wide open that a ring of white showed all the way round the iris.

"*Look out, you two!*" snapped H. M.

Tom dragged Jenny back just in time.

Charles Johnson, making a bubbling noise, took one step forward. Then he pitched headlong down the stone steps, turning over twice before he lay face down on the pavement.

The smashed glass, the half-eaten sandwich, had flown wide and fallen. Because of the man's tiger-striped dressing gown, it was a moment or two before any of them saw the black handle of the knife driven into his back just under the left shoulder blade.

Nobody moved until the police driver sprang out of the car. It did not need the driver's nod, looking up, to tell them Johnson was dead.

Children's roller skates crashed past on the opposite side of the street, amid shouting. A few windows banged up; a few women's heads were thrust out. That was all.

H. M.'s face was white.

"Easy, my dolly," he said, putting his hand on Jenny's arm and speaking with surprising gentleness. "Is that the man you saw at the whispering gallery?"

The shock was too great. Jenny could only nod.

"Then that means," said H. M., "this is no straight business of frightening a gal out of her wits. It means there's somebody who's dead-determined, crazy-mad, to get what he or she wants. Somebody got here before us and shut Johnson's mouth. Murder with a knife is all in the day's work. And that means . . ."

He brooded so long, ruffling his fingers at his temples, that Tom could not remain quiet.

"H. M.!" he said. "What is it?"

"It means there's been a slight change of plans," he answered.

"How?"

"You, my dolly," said H. M., "aren't going to spend the night at my house after all. If you've got the nerve, you're goin' straight back to spend the night at Aunt Hester's."

A golden sky was becoming tinged with purple over the thin Tudor chimneys of Hampton Court Palace.

Sir Henry Merrivale, in his most maddening mood, sat on an upended wheelbarrow, in one of the few remaining Tudor quadrangles: of dark red brick, with its white stone lions uprearing from the walls beside sly little windows. H. M.

was again smoking his black pipe, and looked up at Tom without favour.

"Well," he asked querulously, "where's the whole party *now?*"

"As far as I know, they're still tramping through miles and miles of picture galleries."

"But looky here, son!" protested the great man. "According to my watch, and the notices posted up, this place should have been closed for a long time. Shouldn't they all have been flung out of here hours ago?"

"Yes. But it seems Uncle Fred has a lot of influence with the director or the curator or whatever they call him. They're being taken over the whole show at their leisure, particularly since Jenny's keen to see the maze; and that's a long way from here."

"Maze, hey?" H. M. repeated thoughtfully.

"Now listen to me!" roared Tom, assuming an oratorical posture. "Since a few minutes past six yesterday afternoon, when you got rid of us all, until half an hour ago, when I set eyes on your ugly dial again, you've asked questions by the bucket. But you won't answer a single question yourself. Why?"

"'Cause I'm the old man."

"And you thank that's a good enough reason?"

"Sure it is. I say, son. How is . . . I mean, how is . . . ?"

Tom regarded him bitterly.

"How is Jenny taking this?" he asked. "What the devil do you expect, after that asinine order she was to go back to Aunt Hester's last night? She's taking it badly, of course! But she won't let any of 'em see for a minute she's afraid."

Here the old sinner had at least the grace to look discomfited.

"Well . . . now!" he growled. "I had my reasons, hadn't I? Burn me," and H. M.'s voice rose up passionately, "people are always sayin', 'What an old cloth-head he is; stick him upside down in the dustbin.' Then they see what I mean. And they yell, 'Why, Henry; pull him out and dust him off; we should never have guessed it.' And of course they wouldn't have guessed it, the star-gazin' goops! Only—"

H. M.'s eloquence was interrupted only by a back-wash taste from his own black pipe. Then he simply sat and looked evil.

"All right, all right!" he said. "What did you do last night?"

"Steve Lamoreux and I stood guard outside Jenny's windows all night—"

"Stop a bit, son. Does the gal know who Lamoreux is?"

"She doesn't know he's Armand de Senneville's spy, naturally! And she can't meet him. But, for all practical purposes, he *isn't* a spy. He won't stand for violence—"

"Uh-huh. I know. I talked to him in my office today. You were sayin'?"

"Well, while the rest of 'em were at dinner, Steve and I sneaked into her bedroom and dismantled the gas heater . . ."

Tom paused in even more exasperation. H. M., with a silent and ghoulish mirth, was rocking in ecstasy.

"Oh, son! You didn't think the murderer would try *that* simple little trick again?"

"*Simple* little trick?"

"Easy as shellin' peas."

"Will you acknowledge to me," demanded Tom, after a hard-breathing pause, "that the door of the room really was tightly bolted on the inside and couldn't have been tampered with?"

"Sure."

"Will you acknowledge that both windows were securely

locked on the inside and that they weren't tampered with in any way?"

"Agreed without a struggle."

"Will you finally acknowledge that, with no funny business about outside gas meters or the like, somebody— *somebody actually in that room*—turned on the gas-tap?"

"That's right, son."

"Then how in hell did the murderer get in and out of that room?"

"I'm not goin' to tell you. Now wait!" said H. M., and pointed with the stem of his pipe. "Yesterday you raved and danced about the 'miracle' of the ventriloquist, didn't you? But that was easy. And this is just as easy, maybe easier, if you think about it. I want you to think about it. Meanwhile, you'd better think of something and somebody you've rather neglected."

"Oh? Who's that?"

"Armand de Senneville himself. You hated him from instinct and from jealousy. But maybe your instincts were right. *I* had him investigated today."

"Well?"

"He's tough, son." H. M. said somberly. "He's tougher than you think. He's an outstanding businessman, a first-class journalist, a mechanical expert, and he was liaison officer with the Yanks for four years during the war. Finally, he's as conceited as the devil; he swears, in private, there's *nothing* he ever wanted that he hasn't got."

"But Armand de Senneville's in Paris!"

"He doesn't have to be here, don't you see?" H. M. asked patiently. "Now listen. You, and the gal Jenny, and even Steve Lamoreux, have all thought there was a whole conspiracy of the Harpenden family—Uncle Fred, young Margot, and Aunt Hester—against Jenny Holden."

"And isn't there?"

"No! Coincidence has mixed you up. There's only one, one of those three, who has any knowledge of it. One of them, bribed by Armand de Senneville, would pay any price to have Jenny Holden frightened out of her wits. I give you three: which one?"

It was growing darker in the ancient quadrangle. Tom paced up and down the paving stones, his footfalls stirring back ghostly echoes from the walls.

H. M. knocked out his pipe and replaced it.

"Burn me," he said in a worried voice, "where's that whole family now? You were supposed to be keepin' track of 'em, weren't you?"

"I couldn't! Aunt Hester knows me too well, from that bang-up row in the tea shop! But Steve is trailing 'em, and giving me signals from windows whenever he can."

"But they can't stay in there forever! It'll be pitch dark! I'd give my ears to know where they've gone!"

It was unnecessary to sacrifice H. M.'s ears.

From under the archway to a second quadrangle the sound of "*S-s-t!*" hissed at them in a way which made H. M. leap up from the overturned wheelbarrow.

Steve Lamoreux approached as warily as a red Indian. Tom, not without difficulty, had persuaded him to put on a dark suit and an inconspicuous necktie. But his short brown hair stood up as wirily as ever, and he infuriated H. M. by addressing the great man as Pop.

"They're outside," he said, "at the back of the joint. They're going along that broad path, at the back of the palace, that runs a long way to the left between the palace and the gardens. They've got the oldest guide here, who's deaf and practically blind. And for the love of Pete, Pop, get a wiggle on or they'll close the inner gates and *we'll* be locked in!"

H. M., not without much ruffling of his dignity, was

hauled and impelled through the archway, across another quadrangle, and then through a very long archway at whose end they could see the last gleam of daylight.

They stopped at the outer edge of the arch. Just ahead lay the immense gardens, their straight-ruled lines of flower beds draining of colour in twilight. Peering round the edge of the arch to the left, Tom saw the very broad, sanded path beside ancient walls.

Five persons, their backs to the conspirators in the archway, strolled along this path about a hundred yards ahead. Though it was too dark to discern faces at that distance, Tom knew who they were as they walked abreast.

First, on the extreme left, doddered an old guide in uniform. Next, marching briskly, strode Aunt Hester. Jenny walked nervously between the giggling Margot, who danced with short steps, and the firm military stride of Uncle Fred on the extreme right.

"All right," whispered Tom. "What do we do now?"

"I know what we *could* do," said Lamoreux.

"You do, hey?" sneered H. M.

"Yes! They can't recognize us in this light. If we just strolled after 'em, three abreast but keeping back, they'd take us for another privileged tourist party like themselves. That is, if somebody could do a little spiel like a guide."

The role of guide caught Sir Henry Merrivale's fancy at once.

"Hem!" he said, tapping himself on the chest. "Me."

Lamoreux looked doubtful.

"Okay, Pop, you're the boss. But are you sure you know enough about the history of this joint?"

"*Me?*" said the outraged H. M. "The palace of Hampton Court," he bellowed, "begun by Cardinal Wolsey in the year 1515, was in 1526 pinched from this worthy prelate by that howlin' old ram King Henry the Eighth, whose wives I shall now proceed to—"

"Pop! Quiet!"

"Am I a guide," H. M. asked loftily, "or ain't I?"

"You are," snapped Tom. "And if the balloon goes up, it goes up. Anyway, I can *see* Jenny. They can't hurt her now. Let's go."

Out they marched, trying to tread softly, with Lamoreux on the inner side, Tom in the middle, and H. M. on the outer side.

It was quiet, so intense that they could hear the footsteps of those far ahead of them as well as their own. Peace lay in the hollow of a warm spring night, with the fragrance of grass and trees. You would never have guessed that death was walking with them along the broad white path—and moving closer at every pace.

Tom Lockwood did not know this, of course. But he sensed danger-fangs everywhere. He kept his eyes fixed on Jenny as though she might disappear, and his nerves were twitching like a landed fish.

So he quite literally jumped as a mighty voice smote through his thoughts.

"On our right," it thundered, "we got the famous Hampton Court gardens, forty-four acres of elegant spinach, first laid out by King William the Third and completed in 1734."

"For God's sake be careful," whispered Tom. "William the Third died in 1702."

H. M. swung round, fists on hips.

"And d'ye think I don't know that?" he bellowed. "I didn't say the old sour-puss finished 'em, did I? I just said he laid 'em out—which is what I'm goin' to do to you, young man, if you don't shut up and stop interruptin' my lecture."

"Pop! The soft pedal! Give it the old soft pedal! Holy cats, they'll hear you as far as Thames Ditton!"

But, whatever devilment H. M. had meditated—and Tom knew he had planned it in advance—the damage was done. Five persons, mere shapes in the twilight, turned round and looked back.

Out from the group, head high, marched Aunt Hester. She strode along the full distance that separated them, and looked straight at H. M.

"You, I fancy," she said coolly, "must be the man Merrivale?"

"On our left," bellowed H. M., "we see the celebrated tennis court. The game of tennis, originally played with a wooden ball, was designed with the laudable purpose of knockin' somebody's eye out—which it generally did. One famous match—"

"Answer me, please!" said Aunt Hester. "On whose authority, may I ask, are you in these grounds after official visiting hours?"

H. M. gave her a wicked look.

"On Sir Hugh Rossiter's," he said. "The same as yours. Want to ring him and find out?"

Since H. M. knew everybody, this might possibly be true. Aunt Hester did not dare risk the challenge. Besides, she was more interested in someone else.

"One of you, I believe," she stated crisply, "I have already met. Indeed, Mr. Lockwood, I wish to have a word with you."

"Fire away," said Tom.

"Ever since you abducted my niece yesterday, and afterwards returned her in—I *hope*—a condition suitable to a bride, poor Jennifer has been talking nonsense which I propose to stamp out here and now."

"Oh?"

"Yes. Absurdly enough, the girl believes she is in love with you . . ."

"Is she, by God!" exclaimed Tom.

Whereupon he completely lost his head. Raising his voice, he shouted clearly and loudly through the twilight.

"*Jenny!*" he called. "*Jenny! Do you love me?*"

Jenny spun round in the broad white path.

"*Yes!*" she shouted back.

"*Will you marry me?*"

"*Yes!*"

Dead silence.

"Well . . . now!" observed Sir Henry Merrivale, with much complacence. "Since that's all settled and finished—"

"Oh, cripes!" breathed Steve Lamoreux, in a voice Tom had never heard him use. "If that's how people propose to each other in England, maybe it's true you're kind of casual. Do you just get married on the telephone, or what?"

But Aunt Hester was not amused. The paint stood out against her pale face; she was alert, smiling—and dangerous.

"How interesting!" She laughed. "It surely will interest her dear guardian and," Aunt Hester's eyes slid sideways, "the *fiancé* to whom she is pledged. Tell me, Mr. Lockwood, what is your yearly income?"

Tom stared at the ground.

"Well! I didn't want to . . ."

"Come, Mr. Lockwood!" said Aunt Hester, with honeyed sweetness. "You are a reporter on the *Record*, we know. Just what *is* your yearly income?"

"Tell her, son," growled H. M.

"All right!" said Tom, raising his head. "When death duties are subtracted, it'll be about twelve thousand pounds a year."

"*Twelve—thou—*"

"I didn't earn it," snapped Tom. "My mother left it to me. I've published just one unsuccessful novel. When I walked up Ludgate Hill yesterday, I was thinking about chucking my job and trying full-time writing. That's what I'll do, when Jenny marries me. It's why I told you, Steve, you might get a better boss; you can have my job, and they'll hand it to you on a plate. But I've never given two hoots about Jenny's money, and I'd rather prefer it if she didn't have a penny to her name."

"This is the most fantastic—" Aunt Hester was beginning, when she stopped dead.

H. M. slowly extended his neck, and gave her such a look as could not have been matched by Satan himself.

"Madam," he said, "you've got no business with us. Sling your hook."

"I absolutely refuse—"

H. M. extended his finger until it almost touched Aunt Hester's nose.

"Madam," he said, "are you goin' to hop it? Or do you prefer to find yourself, sittin' down, in the middle of King William's spinach?"

Aunt Hester hopped it. Before that glare, which would have caused the Angels of Light themselves to retire to prepared positions, she could have done nothing else.

She ran hard towards the group ahead, and appeared to be talking rapidly. The whole group faced round and began hurrying, at a faster pace, in their original direction. Jenny seemed violently to object, but Margot gripped her arm and hastened her on.

Tom Lockwood, a powerfully built young man, was all for charging forward and starting a fight at once. His companions held him back.

"Easy, son!" said H. M. "Not just yet, I tell you! We've got 'em in sight. They can't get away."

"Pop," declared Lamoreux, whose face was pale and pinched, "you're a so-and-so. You're a so-and-so and a this-

and-that. You deliberately yelled all that guff about spinach and tennis balls, just so the old dame would come tearing back here. Why did you do it?"

"Well . . . now!" said H. M. with a modest look. "I rather wanted to know, d'ye see, if some person would meet some other person. Am I making myself clear?"

"No. You're not."

"Never mind, son," soothed H. M. "I haven't been so much worried about that gal as about another person. Besides, I repeat, they can't get away. We've got 'em in sight."

Lamoreux stopped in his tracks.

"Oh, no, we haven't!" he said in a high voice. "Where are they now? They've disappeared!"

It was true.

Once past the gardens and the long line of the palace, the road was closed in by tall trees, dusky and spectral against a windless night, with an occasional bench on either side. Five persons had vanished from the road.

"H. M.," said Tom, seizing his companion's arm, "you seem to be the expert on Hampton Court. Where does this road lead?"

"Steady, son! It leads to one of the main entrances—the Lion Gate. But, if you turn to the left before you reach the gate, you'll soon get to the open space where they've got the maze—"

"The maze!" said Tom, and every nameless fear boiled up inside him. "Run, you blighters! *Run!*"

That H. M. himself did run, despite his large corporation and his dislike of any pedestrian exercise, can only be stated as a fact. Lifting his chin so as to cleave the air, he belted along that road as fast as his younger companions.

Some hundred and twenty yards farther on, they saw the dim gleam of a light past an avenue of trees branching to the left. Into this they flew abreast, found themselves in a large open space, and stopped.

For the first time they heard the wheezing, rusty voice of the old guide.

"Now, miss," he was pleading, "you don't really want to go into the maze, do you? 'Tisn't very difficult, not what we like to pretend it is. But that's in the daytime. You don't want to go in at night, miss."

"But I do!" Jenny insisted firmly. "All my life I've been reading about the Hampton Court maze, and I'll die if I don't explore it. Won't you lend me your electric torch?"

In the clearing, a hut or small pavilion had been set well back, evidently used as somebody's living quarters; on a pole against the side of the hut burned a sickly electric bulb.

The famous maze was set well out from the hut. It was roughly oval in shape, a little higher than a man's head, of green hedge raggedly trimmed. Illumined in bright green and dead shadow by the sickly light, it loomed up less as a place of comedy than as a secret, malicious trap.

The entrance must be at the far side, because the entire party was assembled there. Slant-eyed Margot was jumping up and down with joy.

"May I go in too, Mama?" she shrilled. "*May* I go?"

"No, you may not," said Aunt Hester sharply. "Afterwards, perhaps, if dear Jennifer—"

"Lot of nonsense, *I* call it," grumbled Uncle Fred from under his gray military moustache.

"*Please* may I have the electric torch?" said Jenny in a voice no man could resist.

"Ah, well," mumbled the guide. "'Ere's the torch. I s'pose I can always climb up on top of the stepladder by the entrance, and give you directions if you get lost. Be nippy, now."

"I will! I will!"

"Jenny!" called Tom. "Jenny, wait! I'm going with you!"

His words did not carry to her. Faintly he heard the creak of a small gate, and the brushing of Jenny's body against the narrow sides of the maze.

Tom sprang forward. Instantly Sir Henry Merrivale locked both his arms from behind, and held him back.

"No, son," said H. M., in so soft and deadly a voice that Tom was startled. "You're not goin' into that maze."

"Why not?"

"Whose life," asked H. M., glancing round him, "d'ye think I've been worried about, as much or more than the little gal's herself? *Yours.*"

"Are you crazy?"

"No. But you're not goin' inside that maze."

Tom, with one sudden heave and jerk, tore loose even from H. M.'s powerful grip.

"I'm sorry, sir. But that's where I'm going, and neither you nor anybody else is going to stop me."

He ran across the sanded space, and round the side to the entrance. He saw the startled face of Uncle Fred, who was swinging a heavy yellow cane. He saw Aunt Hester, with rigid mouth. He saw the pretty, mischievous face of Margot, who was slipping away in another direction.

The guide had already shakily mounted to the top of the stepladder beside the entrance. Tom swung open the little gate, twisted sideways as he plunged into the maze, and attempted to run.

It was impossible.

The hedge-walls were so narrow that tendrils stung his face. Though it was not pitch-dark, just enough light filtered down from the dim bulb outside to distort the eyesight and turn dark shapes into illusions. He might run slap into a hedge-wall at any second, and just saved himself from doing so.

Gently, now!

Stopping at a turn, Tom felt down on his left and found the thin wall, of hard and curved wire, built a little below waist height. In this maze, he remembered it had been said, you must always turn to the left. He did so, and presently turned left again.

That was when he saw, deeper inside these thinnish walls, the firefly glimmer of Jenny's torch. It vanished again—but it was there.

"Jenny!" he called. "Wait for me! It's Tom!"

"Tom! Darling!" Her voice slipped through the walls rather than above them. "Where are you?"

"I don't know. Where are you?"

"Very near the center of the maze, I think."

"Then stop where you are! Wait until I catch up with you!"

"Oh, no!" Jenny retorted demurely. "I'll get to the center and turn off the torch. Then you can find me and tell me how much you love me."

"Jenny, wait!"

But the firefly glimmer danced away. He could hear her brushing and hurrying on. In a moment or two there was a cry of pleasure, as evidently she found the center of the maze. The light of her torch went out.

Tom moved forward, more slowly and carefully. The electric bulb at the hut was now so distant and so dim that it gave scarcely any light. Tom didn't know where he was. Walls loomed up and closed round him. It wasn't pleasant, being shut into a twisting maze where . . .

Then he stopped, listening.

Somebody was following him stealthily through the maze.

Somebody, not much lighter than his own weight, was stalking him—with what intent? Tom ran forward and stopped. The footsteps behind him ran forward and stopped. Tom ran again. But he was not left in doubt long.

A closer footfall, a looming of a shape in near-darkness, made him glance over his shoulder. He saw the upsurge of someone's silhouette. A distant gleam flashed on the blade of the knife as if lifted high—and struck.

All that saved Tom from being stabbed in the back, as Johnson the ventriloquist had been stabbed, was the dim light and the attacker's misjudgment. The blade of the knife ripped through the cloth of the coat over Tom's shoulder. The attacker, plunging forward so hard that he collided with Tom, sent his victim sprawling one way and drove his own head and shoulders, grotesquely, straight into the hedge on the other side.

Somebody screamed one word, nothing more.

With a crackling of branches, the attacker wrenched out his left arm and then withdrew his head. Before he could disengage his knife-hand, Tom landed a vicious right-hander that opened his assailant's cheekbone and drew first blood.

Then they faced each other, two dim shapes, between the narrow walls.

There were no Queensberry Rules here. Neither man was a boxer. But both were enraged and both meant murder.

The attacker held his knife blade out, to leap forward and rip up. Just as he lunged, Tom kicked him in the groin. The attacker, in intense agony, began to double up; his knife fell and tinkled. Tom hit him again.

The attacker, straightening up, flew in with both fists. Tom hit him twice, left and right, in the belly. Then he put all his strength into a right cross to the man's jaw—which, if it had landed, would have broken Tom's hand.

But it did not land on the jaw. Instead it landed, with just as murderous effect, in the soft flesh under the man's left ear. The attacker, brain paralyzed and legs suddenly gone to water, reeled backwards and fell.

"Now where the devil," Tom was thinking, "did we get so much space?"

Then he realized they had been fighting very near the entrance to the center of the maze. For the first time he heard voices, and bodies thrashing about in the maze.

Behind him loomed up the blaze of an electric torch. Above it showed the malignant countenance of Sir Henry Merrivale. Next, cowering away in one side of the maze's center, Jenny switched on her own torch.

Both beams converged on the man who lay on his back in the center of the maze. His eyes were closed; he breathed stertorously; sluggish blood flowed from a cut in his cheek.

Jenny's face grew so white, and she turned her head away so abruptly, that Tom thought she was going to be sick.

But his own feelings were swallowed up in incredulity.

"This is impossible!" he said, pointing to the man on the ground. "That's Steve Lamoreux, the reporter!"

"*Oh, no, it's not,*" said Sir Henry Merrivale. "*That's Armand de Senneville himself.*"

"Explanations?" demanded H. M., in a tone of dismal surprise. "You don't mean to tell me you *need* explanations?"

Jenny and Tom, both seated beside the desk in H. M.'s office at the end of the following day, instantly and vehemently said they did need explanations.

H. M. sighed.

"Y'know, my dolly," he said, "you ought to have seen through your *fiancé*, Armand de Senneville, sooner than you did. He tried to prevent your trip to England. He couldn't prevent it—his father's word was law. But he knew how much you'd been repressed and kept under the thumb in France. He knew, as he casually warned Aunt Hester, you'd probably fall bang for the first presentable, easy-going

Englishman who made you laugh and didn't think correct behavior was everything in life. Which is what you did."

"I did not!" Jenny cried indignantly. "I have fall bang for Tom, yes. But that is a different thing!"

Tom hastily intervened in order to evade the devastating question, "How is it different?"

"Then de Senneville," he said, "had only to crop his hair, have it dyed brown, wear very loud clothes, and pose as a French-Canadian reporter from one of his own papers?"

"But Armand," insisted Jenny, "speaks no English!"

"No?" said H. M. "That's what he told you, my dolly. But as I explained to Tom here, the bloke was attached for four years to the American Army as a liaison officer. So surely he could speak English. In fact, his ear was perfect; his American was perfect. But he had to play the part of a French-Canadian to explain how he spoke both languages."

"And yet," exclaimed Jenny, her eyes clouding, "I still do not understand this Armand! If he wished to keep men away from me, why did he not say he spoke English and go with the whole party of us?"

"You don't understand that, my dolly? Though it's the key to his whole character?"

"No! Why is it the key?"

"Because he was too proud," said H. M., "and he was far too conceited. He wouldn't demean himself in public by showin' he was concerned. He wouldn't admit that any man alive could take you away from the great Armand.

"Listen, my dolly, he never wanted to kill *you!* Neither did Aunt Hester. All they wanted to do was scare you so much that you'd run straight back to France. Don't you remember what you said yourself, in this office? I asked, 'Do you still want to stay at your Aunt Hester's?' And you cried out, 'No, but what else can I do except return to Paris?'—Got it now?"

"Then," Jenny blurted out, "just to get my dowry, this Armand has . . ."

"Oh, he wanted your money," said H. M. somberly. "But, towards the end, I don't think that was all. That murderous fight in the maze wasn't done altogether for money. I expect, in his own queer way, he was a little bit in love with you."

Again, since Jenny's eyes were clouding worse than ever, Tom intervened.

"But the locked room!" he said. "Where the gas-tap was turned on even while windows and door were both locked on the inside!"

"Well . . . now," H. M. sighed wearily. "I'd better tell you about it, because that locked room told me the whole ruddy truth before I even knew who was behind it.

"On the famous Night of Terrors," he added, pointing at Jenny, "you found, in your napkin at dinner, a note readin', 'You will die tonight, Jennifer.' Eh?"

"But who wrote the note?" interrupted Tom.

"Aunt Hester wrote it," snapped H. M. "There's never been much mystery about her. Her words and actions were too plain. She was the dominatin' character of her family, the only one, as I more than hinted, whom de Senneville bribed and prompted.

"After dinner," H. M. continued, still pointing at Jenny, "you went to your room at a little past eleven o'clock. One of the long windows, which you'd left closed, was now wide open. Correct?"

"Yes," said Jenny, and shuddered.

"You closed and locked the window again. You didn't need to touch or go near the gas fire. At shortly past twelve you went to bed, and soon fell asleep. The next thing you knew, Margot was bangin' on the door at six o'clock. A mysterious 'American' voice is asking what's wrong. They ran round to the window, pickin' up Uncle Fred on the way.

Uncle Fred smashes the window. The mysterious 'American,' whom you can't see because you're too far gone, rushes over the the gas fire. He says, 'So-and-so, but it's turned full on!' And, apparently, he turns it off. Correct again?"

"Yes, yes."

"Not to me it isn't," said H. M., shaking his head. "Whoever this mysterious American was, he was the joker behind the trick. He told a flat lie. That gas *couldn't* have been turned full on."

"Why not?"

"Because you'd have been dead," H. M. said simply. "Let's suppose somebody, in the middle of the night, sneaks in and turns on the gas full-strength. Never mind what time it was. Let's even say it was as late, as impossibly late, as five o'clock in the morning. But there's no person in the world, breathing full-strength gas in an unventilated room, who can breathe it for an hour and still live. So I asked you a question to prove it."

"What question?"

"Oh, my dolly! You could describe every small noise you heard even when you were only half conscious. But you *didn't* hear any noise of a gas fire turned on full, which would have roared like a tornado. That's all."

"Oh!" exclaimed Jenny, caught up with a jolt. "Then . . .?"

"Yes! Just before you retired to your room, Armand de Senneville—alias Steve Lamoreux—sneaked in and turned on the gas heater a tiny thread—only a tiny thread, not noticeable at all. He went out, leavin' the window wide open for good ventilation.

"You came in and closed the window. Well! What does happen, in very big rooms like that one, with such a tiny leak of gas? You can't hear it, you can't even smell it, for well over an hour. The bed is too far away. And it's caused tragedy before this. Meanwhile, for nearly six hours, the room is very slowly fillin' up with gas. When they found you, you were in just the condition I'd have expected.

"That's pretty much everything, my dolly. Armand de Senneville was lurkin' close outside, of course. You bet he was! He'd calculated his times, as he always does, but he was damned near too late to bust in himself, as he intended.

"He *had* to meet Margot—he couldn't help it. But that gal's a silly kind of wench, so excited she never wondered what he was doin' there. Uncle Fred barely noticed him. Later, it was easy for Aunt Hester to look 'em straight in the eye and tell 'em both they'd been dreaming. She was the only one who knew our Armand by sight. But, as for the 'miracle' of the locked room . . ."

"And that is all?" cried Jenny.

"Sure. What else did you expect?"

"I am disappoint!" suddenly exclaimed Jenny, hammering her fists on her knees. "I think this is a miracle. I think it cannot be solved. And then you show it is easy as eating sweets. Sir H. M., I hate you!"

The subsequent behavior of Sir Henry Merrivale, his martyrdom and his passionate addresses to the ceiling, is best left undescribed.

"So that's all the thanks I get, hey? They come to me and say, 'It's a miracle.' I say, 'It ain't,' and show 'em how it's done. Then they say, 'Oh, is that all? Silly old dummy! Stick him in the dustbin again.'"

It was fully half an hour before they smoothed him down.

"Very well!" he said, with a dark look at Jenny. "I'll not state what I think of some people. I'll just tell you what happened next and upset the whole apple cart. Aunt Hester had to drag a very sick and scared gal all the way to St. Paul's, so that Armand's hired ventriloquist could perform on time.

"But the apple cart was upset an awful smash. 'Steve

Lamoreux,' sittin' in the car just as he said he did, saw you run down the steps of St. Paul's and literally fall into this young feller's arms. When you went into the tea shop—well, Bob's your uncle. You bet he sneaked in and listened behind the partition. What he heard was just what he'd feared. You two were practically fallin' into each other's arms over the tea."

"I feel like this," Jenny confessed.

"I still feel like it," said Tom.

"Shut up," said the great man. "There were several courses open to 'Steve Lamoreux.' He chose the best, which was winnin' Tom Lockwood's confidence and stayin' close to him. So he deliberately sent this gal to me, supremely and conceitedly thinkin' the old goop would never see through *his* scheme.

"After Aunt Hester's row in the tea shop," here H. M. looked at Tom, 'he went in and told his story. He more than won your confidence, son. He won your friendship."

"Yes," admitted Tom, and looked down at a closed fist. "He did."

"Of course, he couldn't go with you when you came to my office. He admitted the gal mustn't meet him. What he did is easy to guess. He followed you, and hung about in Horse Guards Avenue. D'ye know, I think I can see his face when we three piled downstairs and out to a police car, and I gave the address of his own hired ventriloquist.

"He got to the house about fifty seconds before we did, probably by waving a fiver in under a taxi-driver's nose. He nipped in by the back door, struck faster than a snake, and nipped out the same way while Johnson's body rolled down the front steps.

"And that tore it. As I said, the whole aspect of the business had changed.

"According to what I could deduce about the gas fire and

the whispering gallery, *nobody* was actually trying to kill this gal. Somebody was trying to frighten her so much that she'd take the first plane back to Paris.

"Now who would be interested in doin' that, in conjunction with Aunt Hester? Who? You guess. And what about this odd 'American' or 'Canadian' who kept turning up all over the place without any explanation? Everybody promised to explain him; but nobody did."

H. M. pulled down his spectacles and glowered at Jenny over them.

"You see, my dolly, why I wanted you to go back to your aunt's house that night? You weren't in any real danger. And it wasn't likely somebody would try any games that night. If anything happened at all, it would happen during the expedition to Hampton Court next day—for one thing. Aunt Hester was far too insistent about takin' you there.

"And I could be there to stop it. And yet, burn me, I nearly missed it!"

The somber spectacles were now turned towards Tom.

"Son," observed H. M., "did you see the look on 'Steve Lamoreux's' face when you shouted along the path and asked this gal to marry you? And she said yes?"

"No, but I heard his voice. It was a voice I'd never heard him use before."

"Well! When it turned out you had tons of money and they couldn't accuse you of being a fortune hunter, did you notice him at any time after *that?*"

"Yes! His face was all pinched up and as pale as dough. But I thought—"

"Maybe you did. He had a knife with him, just in case. And that was the time he finally decided you were goin' to die."

Jenny pressed her face in her hands, and turned away.

"Oh, I was the villain!" said H. M. "In my role of guide,

I wanted to see how Aunt Hester would act when she met Steve Lamoreux face to face. She behaved pretty well, but she couldn't keep her eyes from slidin' away when she mentioned the gal's *fiancé*.

"It was a silly-ass thing to do. I admit it. 'Cause I'd already made up my mind. That same day, since Armand de Senneville had been attached to the Yanks, I got his record and saw his photograph. To put the tin hat on it, 'Steve Lamoreux' had the star-gazin' cheek to walk into my office and spin his yarn.

"Even if I hadn't known already, the idiot gave himself away. He *would* smoke Yellow French cigarettes, and use sulphur matches. Even when he was very excited, he automatically held the match away from him until the sulphur had burned off—"

"Yes," interrupted Tom. "I saw him do that. But what about it?"

"Oh, son! He claimed he'd been in France only six months—"

"Yes, that's what he told me too!"

"And no foreigner on earth, after only six months in France, can get used to those sulphur matches. You always forget and swallow a lungful of sulphur. Only a Frenchman native-born automatically holds the match away for a few seconds. There, in my own office, was a Frenchman speakin' the most exquisite Yank.

"But *you* were the one in real danger, son. If I'd known beforehand you'd spent the night before prowlin' round this gal's windows with Armand de Senneville, I'd have had a fit. I repeat: he struck like a snake and killed poor old Johnson. Why? Just because he didn't want this gal to find out that it was *he* who was scaring her, or he'd lose her.

"Finally, last night at Hampton Court, I still don't know what funny business de Senneville, or Aunt Hester, or both of 'em, had planned. There wasn't time—the fireworks went up with a bang. I tried to keep you from goin' into that maze. Didn't you see me look round? Didn't you notice Lamoreux had slipped away? You dashed into the maze. He must have crawled up on top of it—we didn't see him enter—and followed you. But sometimes, for chivalrous young fools like you, there is mercy. You met the tough egg with his knife, and you knocked him flat. And that was the end."

There was a long silence, until Tom cleared his throat.

"H. M., what will they do to him?"

"Oh, they can't prove yet he killed Johnson. Not yet. In the meantime, he'll do a long stretch on two counts of attempted murder: with gas and with a knife. Then the coppers will snaffle him for killing Johnson. And he'll get what he deserves, son—he'll hang."

Jenny stood up suddenly, trembling. Tom put his arms around her, and held her tightly.

"It's all right!" he insisted. "Jenny, dear, it's all right!"

"Yes," said Jenny, holding him just as tightly, "but that is why you must not leave me, ever. It is all right—*now!*"

For once in his life, Sir Henry Merrivale did not roar out about canoodling in his office. Slowly, somberly, he got up from his chair and wandered over to one of the windows. There, his hands folded behind his back, he stood looking out over the river and the mighty curve of London.

THE CASES OF COLONEL MARCH
AND THE DEPARTMENT
OF QUEER COMPLAINTS

INTRODUCTION

The cases featuring Colonel March and the Department of Queer Complaints are the only stories which Carr conceived as a series. The stories are based on a tantalizing concept: that there exists in Scotland Yard a department to handle "complaints which do not seem to bear the light of day or reason." If someone reports a ghost in a garden, or a blue pig that terrorizes London's Borough of Stepney, or an ambulatory corpse, or a thief who steals only green candlesticks, the case is sent to Department D–3, popularly known as "The Department of Queer Complaints." It is headed by Colonel March, whom Carr based on his close friend Major C. J. C. Street, the author of detective novels under the pseudonyms "John Rhode" and "Miles Burton." John Dickson Carr and his wife Clarice frequently visited Street in Kent, and Carr collaborated with him on the 1939 novel, *Fatal Descent*, about an impossible murder in a closed elevator.

Colonel March resembles "a stout colonel in a comic paper," with a speckled face, bland blue eyes, and a cropped sandy mustache. He has a fund of useless information and he is fascinated by puzzles of all sort, from jigsaw puzzles on up. Rather than depending on subtlety, he solves cases because "his mind is so obvious that he hits it every time."

Carr wrote the Queer Complaints series for *The Strand Magazine*, edited by Reeves Shaw. *The Strand* had published Arthur Conan Doyle's short stories about Sherlock Holmes during the 1890s and later, and when Carr began writing for the magazine, it was still the leading fiction periodical in England, printing new tales by such writers as P. G. Wodehouse, Agatha Christie, Margery Allingham, and many others. Carr wrote his first stories about Colonel March in 1937, and they appeared at irregular intervals under the "Carter Dickson" pseudonym between April 1938 and January 1940; a final, slightly belated tale was published in February 1941. Seven of the stories were collected in the 1940 volume, *The Department of Queer Complaints*; the remaining two ("The Empty Flat" and "William Wilson's Racket") appeared in *The Men Who Explained Miracles* in 1963. *Merrivale, March and Murder* marks the first time that the entire series has appeared in a single volume. They are printed here in the original order of publication, rather than their order of appearance in *The Department of Queer Complaints*.

THE NEW INVISIBLE MAN

A taxi brought him to the Derby Street entrance of New Scotland Yard. He was a well-dressed man with somewhat protuberant eyes, an inquiring nose, and a frantic seriousness of manner. And he was so excited that the constable on duty at the entrance could hardly make out a word he was saying.

"Murdered him right in front of me!" gabbled the newcomer, holding to his bowler hat as though it might blow off. "Might have murdered me too, and very nearly did, because the next bullet hit the lamp-shade beside me, and—"

"Now, sir!" urged the law soothingly. "Who did all this?"

"A pair of gloves did," said the newcomer.

"A what?"

"A pair of gloves. Only they hadn't got any hands inside them. Or any arms or body either, for that matter. The fellow was invisible. And mark my words, he'll kill that girl next!"

The constable stood back and studied him. This man did not look demented. His eyes were watery, and he gulped out steamy breaths on the raw air.

"Yes, sir," said the constable. "Straight on; first turning; third door on the left."

He spoke a formula. The door he indicated bore only the words, D–3, COLONEL MARCH, but many stories lay behind it. It is, in fact, the home of queer tales, and exists solely for the purpose of receiving them. To the Metropolitan Police come strangers with complaints which do not seem to bear the light of day or reason. But, unless the complainant is an obvious lunatic, such matters have to be investigated; and Department D–3 is their clearing-house.

D–3 has its own staff, notably Inspector (ex-Captain) Roberts, who served under Colonel March in different days.

It is not governed by the routine organization, and deals direct with the Commissioner's office. Some maintain that Colonel March was put in charge of it because nothing on earth could possibly surprise him. He is also well served by his vast fund of good-for-nothing information, and his absorption in any kind of puzzle from a jigsaw up. Those who get past Inspector Roberts find in the inner office a large, amiable man (weight seventeen stone) with a speckled face, an interested blue eye, and a very short pipe projecting from under a cropped moustache which might be sandy or grey.

On this particular morning, the agitated man in the bowler hat did get past the outer office. Business, as Colonel March pointed out to Inspector Roberts, was bad; and they might as well hear what the man had to say.

"I am aware," said the newcomer, with a certain dignity, "that you must think me mad. Very well. Say that I *am* mad—" His native caution checked him. "Er—no, don't say that; perhaps I am a little upset. But surely my name and standing should be sufficient guarantee that I am telling the truth? My name is Rodman, Horace Rodman. I am the senior partner of Rodman & Hughes, Chartered Accountants and Income Tax Consultants. I have lived for sixteen years at Number 24 St. Nicholas Row, Hampstead. Sir, I saw a murder done; and, Heaven help me, nobody will believe it."

His voice had acquired an asthmatic and passionate note.

"It's quite all right," March assured him. "I knew a fellow once who had the same trouble. Just fire away."

"I'm not sure I know how," said Rodman abruptly, after a pause. He reflected. "It concerns a new block of flats which has just gone up opposite my house in St. Nicholas Row." He reflected again. "A number of houses were torn down to make room for the flats. My friend Mrs. Atchison, of Number 18, told me she was not sorry to see Number 23 go, because it certainly had an unpleasant reputation in her grandfather's time."

"You mean it was supposed to be haunted?" asked March, with slightly greater interest.

"No, no, no!" cried the other. "I did not say so," he added. "And I cannot imagine any—er—'haunt' transferring itself to the modernistic building across the way. I must tell you about the architecture; it has a great deal of bearing on what I saw. You have probably noticed these new Spanish-style buildings, in yellow stucco with green facings: where every corner is rounded, and every room has one long window stretching entirely across it, like the glass door of a book-case? Eh? Yes. That was how I could see so clearly.

"You see, the flats are not yet quite finished. Although there are a number of 'let' signs in the windows, only three or four families have moved in. I am interested in my fellow-man, sir," said Mr. Rodman, rather defiantly. "I am a student of human nature, and I don't care who knows it. Well, I *had* noticed the couple occupying the four-room flat which is directly opposite the second-floor windows of my house. They are (or profess to be) a Mr. and Mrs. James Hartley. The husband is a nondescript young man, who drives a 1936 Hillman coupé, and has an office in the City. The wife is a really beautiful, and, I believe, refined girl."

His sudden lyricism embarrassed him.

"I had several times noticed the young lady going in and out; and once I met her in the street. I have also seen her, with a dust-cloth round her head, cleaning the windows opposite. Mrs. Atchison thought this unbecoming in her. So did Mr. and Miss Paulus, at Number 20. I can only say," declared Mr. Rodman emphatically, "that I don't agree. She has hair the colour of ripe—well, such is the case. This much I can tell you: she is in very terrible fear of something. For God's sake do not think I am imagining things for one reason or another. If you had seen her face, as I did, after it happened . . .

"It happened, you see, only last night, February twelfth, when I was going up to bed. My bedroom is on the second-floor front. I usually retire punctually at eleven; but I was a little later than usual, because I had been fidgety all evening. I don't know why.

"Before turning on the light in my bedroom, I went across to draw the curtains. That was how I came to be looking straight across, not forty feet away, into the dark window opposite. No curtains have been put up there. It is not Mr. and Mrs. Hartley's bedroom or sitting-room. As a matter of fact, it is not yet finished, except for carpets which have been fitted throughout, and one or two odds and ends packed away there. I had seen it by daylight, and knew it for a room hardly more than ten feet square, raw enough, with cream-painted walls, cream-varnished doors, and grey carpeting.

"It was a quiet night, and very cold. In front of the flats there is a double street-lamp, which threw a faint kind of glow up over the yellow-and-green building and high up through the window. Someone, bent low, was moving quickly and stealthily round that room. It might be nothing? Quite. Quite! But the man was carrying an automatic pistol, and wore a big pair of dirty, white-cotton gloves—I saw one of them flatten out against the window like a starfish."

Rodman paused. Colonel March's big sandy-haired head was bent forward with concentration. He glanced sideways at Inspector Roberts, who was now not quite so sure of the visitor's lack of mental balance.

"You could see all this," said March, "from across the street?"

"I fetched a pair of field-glasses," said Rodman, with sudden loftiness. "Kindly do not interrupt me. The man took off his gloves, and put them down with the pistol on a round table in the middle of the room. Then he came towards the window and turned on the light. It was a dusty electric bulb, hanging from an unshaded socket in the ceiling near the window. But it gave a passable light; and I had a good look at the man's face. It was not James Hartley, or any man I had seen in those flats. I tell you I knew he was an old sinner, from the very turn of his neck and hands. He was a wicked-faced old man with a drooping mustache and thick-lensed spectacles which gave him an intensity of stare rather like the pictures of Doctor Crippen. His overcoat had a fur collar, too. And he began to run his hands along the window-ledge, as though he were searching for something.

"Please remember the bareness of that room. I could see all of it. There was nobody else there. It had three cream-painted doors—one in the rear wall, in line with the window, and one in each of the two side walls. I should have noticed if any door had moved an inch. Not one did. The only articles of furniture were an ordinary kitchen chair, near the window; and the bare table in the centre, on which the man had put down his pistol and gloves. A box with three doors and a window. There wasn't a crevice where anyone could have hidden.

"The man began groping along the window-ledge. Finally he opened one big pane of the window and put out his bald head; I remember his shadow from the street-lamp climbing up the yellow stucco wall. He uttered a peculiar kind of whistle, which sounded very loud in the quiet street. Then he drew in his head and turned back to the door at the rear of the room as he was in the act of locking the window.

"If that whistle was a signal, he got an answer. Two shots were fired at him point-blank.

"They were fired, I tell you, from the other side of that table in the middle of the room, between the table and the rear door. They were fired from the heavy automatic which had been lying on the table. I saw them fired. The first bullet struck him in the chest and kicked him back against the window-ledge, where he fell. The second bullet missed him, drilled through his window, smashed my window, and broke the glass shade of the lamp not a foot from my head. I saw the hand that fired the pistol; but there was no other person in that room."

Rodman nodded his head twice.

"I have the bullet, you know," he added with ghoulish hopefulness. "I dug it out of the wall in my bedroom and brought it along."

Colonel March was refreshed. His large face wore a quizzical look which was not disbelief at all; he tapped his fingers on the desk separating him from Rodman, as though he were about to make a move in a game of draughts.

"Just a moment," he interposed, "while I make sure I understand you. You *saw* this pistol fire the shots?"

"I did."

"Where was the pistol, exactly?"

Rodman changed colour. "Held by one of the big gloves, at the back of the room."

"Was it on the table?"

"No; above the table."

"I see. You were actually looking through the place where the murderer must have been standing?"

"I was."

"Excellent! . . . Any comments, Roberts?"

Inspector Roberts smiled. "Well, sir, it's interesting enough; but where's the corpse? People usually complain in the case of a murder, you know. Mr. Rodman says this occurred last night. That would be F Division. I was talking to the Divisional-Inspector only this morning, and he said nothing about it."

"Oh, yes. I am aware of that," snapped Rodman, still a

curious colour. "You see, I haven't told you the worst of it yet. Shall I go on? Thank you.

"I was alarmed. I'm not ashamed to admit that. For a few seconds I quite literally couldn't move. I knew I had to go over there: duty. Besides, I was curious. But I had to find a policeman first. I hurried downstairs, got my hat and coat, and tumbled out. There was no difficulty about finding a policeman; the man on the beat had heard the shots too, and was coming to investigate. The window in the flat was now dark. I told the policeman what I had seen, though I dare say he didn't take it all in, for one reason or another. We entered the flats together.

"There were two lifts, but they didn't work; there was a porter, but we couldn't find him. We were in a great concrete shell of a building, rasping to every echo, and with a few frosted-glass lights. But I knew (Mrs. Atchison had found out) the number of the Hartleys' flat. We went upstairs and knocked. After a minute or two Mrs. Hartley opened the door. Er—her first name is Elizabeth, or Betty. She was wearing a pink dressing-gown, and looked as though she had been roused out of bed. But she was frightened; I could tell that. The trouble was—"

"Well?" prompted Colonel March.

"She swore there was absolutely nothing wrong in the flat; that she had been in bed, and had heard no shots. The constable said quite sensibly: 'Well, ma'am, there were shots, because I heard them myself; and this gentleman says one of them nearly killed him.' She said that the inner walls of the flat were soundproof. It is only fair to admit that this is true.

"We demanded to be shown the unfurnished room. She made no difficulty about this. It opened off the central hall, where odds and ends of lumber were stacked in confusion: a sewing machine, a big box full of framed photographs, sheets of printed paper, a folding Japanese screen through which the constable unfortunately put his foot. We cleared this away, and went in. That was when I began to have a queer sensation that something spongy had got into my head where the brain ought to be.

"For the old man I had seen, alive or dead, was not in the room. And there was no bullet-hole in the window," he repeated.

"Gentlemen, I think that bewildered me more than the absence of the victim. There might have been time for a victim to have been carried away or hidden before we arrived. I say there *might*. But a solid .38-calibre bullet (I have it here) had gone through the glass of this window before it went through the glass of mine; and there was not a scratch here to show where it had passed. Gloves and pistol were also missing.

"The policeman, I admit, looked at me oddly. I went round that room like—I had almost said, like a terrier sniffing. I don't care! Let me assure you that there was no possibility of my having been mistaken about the room, or got the wrong room. There is only one place on a direct line with my bedroom; you must test it as I did then.

"I saw the grey carpeting, the cream walls. Here was the kitchen chair. Here was the table. Here were the three equidistant doors: the rear one opened into the hall, the right-hand one opened into the sitting-room, and the left-hand one into an empty linen-closet. The only thing I had been unable to see from my bedroom was a radiator under the window. The only mark of any kind in the room was a long triangular indentation in the pile of the carpet, where, Mrs. Hartley explained, the folding Japanese screen had stood before they cleared this room of lumber.

"Now, Mrs. Hartley was terrified of something. That I'll swear. She has very expressive hazel eyes, and she did not even seem to hear what I was saying. She stood there with her face flushed, hugging her dressing-gown round her in the cold, but she seemed as much puzzled as terrified. I warned her, for her own good, that if she was having anything to do with thieves and killers she would regret it."

He moved his neck.

"The worst of it occurred when her husband came bursting in, tying on *his* dressing-gown, and alleging that *he* had been roused by our voices 'yelling' in his flat in the middle of the night. I was not yelling. But he was in a vile temper. His hair, which was rumpled, stuck straight out in front like the peak of a cap; and his face, which I should have described as nondescript and rather unpleasant, now looked concretely sinister.

"By this time the constable had grown apologetic, but I would have none of this. 'Never apologize, never explain' is my motto; an aristocratic motto, if I may say so. Hartley, I am afraid, was angry. He denied that he had ever seen or heard of the old man.

"'So,' he said, 'you saw a pair of gloves pick up a gun and shoot somebody who doesn't exist? Blast my ears with lightning! Did you wake me up in the middle of the night just to tell me that? You didn't see a line of cigars hanging in the air and smoking themselves, did you? Look at this flat. It's an ordinary flat, or at least I thought it was. Look at this door. It's a practical door, and no invisible man walked through it. If you want to search the place, go ahead. And then get out.'

"But this did not last. When we went into the sitting-room, where it was warm, something occurred that struck the anger off his face. Up to that time I was at my wits' end. Perhaps I talked sharply, and turned things out of drawers; but I am accustomed to being obeyed unquestioningly, as any clerk of mine will tell you. Then I knew I was right, for I saw it: a photograph, in an old-fashioned frame, brightly lighted by a table-lamp. There was no mistaking those staring spectacled eyes; it was a photograph of the old man who had disappeared.

"Hartley knew that I had seen it, and his expression altered. The whole atmosphere of the room changed, too. He made a quick movement to get in front of the picture, or snatch it away, but I was there ahead of him. His forward movement was so violent that he slipped on the smooth pile of the carpet; he must have twisted his ankle, for he went down with a crash that turned him muddy pale. Mrs. Hartley ran to him, screaming his first name. When she lifted up his shoulders I was rather appalled by the look she gave me; for what had I done?

"A few minutes later I was out in the street, advised by the constable to go home. They showed me proofs of the truth. I could not doubt the truth, and you will sympathize with me when I say I had the horrors all night. But I'm a taxpayer, and a decent citizen, and I insist on knowing the meaning of it. That photograph was a picture of Hartley's grandfather, who died before the war."

At this point, quietly, a constable came into the room with an official form filled up. There was a rattle as Inspector Roberts put coal on the fire. The echo of Rodman's shrill voice still seemed to linger; firelight grew brighter in the big room while Roberts used the poker. And the constable said:

"A Mr. and Mrs. Hartley to see you, sir."

"Ask Mr. and Mrs. Hartley to wait a moment," said Colonel March blandly.

He got up and went over to stand with his back to the fire. He had the military trick of standing as though bent a little forward from the waist, his arms slightly curved at his sides; but this stiffness contrasted with the amusement of his speckled face. A bland blue eye surveyed them, and his short pipe seemed in danger of scorching his nose as he sniffed amusedly at it.

"We must discuss the matter first," he explained. "Mr. Rodman, I rather envy you. Your adventure is what a younger generation would describe as hot stuff."

"If," said Rodman, freezing up, "you prefer to make fun of—"

"Not at all," the other assured him. "I believe every word you say."

Inspector Roberts, though youngish, was well trained. He did not actually drop the poker with which he was stirring the fire, though he looked as if it had been a near thing.

"You think," cried Rodman, "I saw a—?"

"Ghost? Oh, no." Colonel March added, as though consolingly: "Not this time, anyhow."

"Then it was a real crime after all? A real man was shot with a real bullet in that room? Is that what you think?"

"I am quite sure of it."

Rodman seemed as taken aback as though he had never believed this. "But how? I ask you, *how*? There was nobody in the room; there was no corpse, as your friend says; there was no bullet-hole in the window; there was—"

"Wait a bit," urged March. "Never mind your notebook for the moment, Roberts. Before we consider any course of action, I should like to dig a few more gems out of our friend's admirable narrative style. Mr. Rodman, how long have the Hartleys lived in that flat?"

"Two weeks last Monday, I think."

"Previous to last night, had you ever been inside the room where the man was shot?"

"Never."

"That little table in the room, now. You said it was a round table. Was it also a three-legged table?"

"Didn't I tell you it was? But please listen to me," begged

Rodman, as though he had not been able to get in a word edgeways. "If a man was killed there, who was he? I've questioned people till I'm blue in the face, and nobody ever saw him or heard of him. Where's his body? And how was it done? And did Hartley kill him? I ask you, as a public servant, to answer relevant questions, if you can think of any answer. What difference does it make whether the table had three legs or four legs? Or whether the room had one door or two doors or six doors, for that matter?"

"On the contrary," said Colonel March, "the number of doors is very important. If there had been only one door in the room, the criminal would not have been able to act."

"But I tell you nobody went in or out by any of the doors!"

"Oh, that," said Colonel March. "I quite agree with you."

"Then—"

"No, you don't," said the other, with ferocious geniality. He pointed his finger. "You're enjoying yourself immensely. You never got such a thrill in your life as you've had out of this. You came here with the particular purpose of mystifying me, to spread the glad tidings of terror to a wider audience than Mrs. Atchison; and now you're damned well going over the same jumps you set for me . . . Ask Mr. and Mrs. Hartley to come in."

It might be wondered how Rodman's description of this couple coincided with the facts. It is possible that his account of Mrs. Hartley, at least, was coloured by a romantic imagination. Betty Hartley did not seem ethereal or spiritual. She was a good-looking, healthy-looking girl whose grave hazel eyes were redeemed by dimples at the corners of the mouth; a brown velour hat was tilted over her thick yellow hair. Her husband, peering over her shoulder, had rather a strong face with a trace of irony in it. They both stopped dead on the threshold when they saw Rodman.

"Oh, bother!" said the girl explosively.

"Come in," said Colonel March, teetering before the fire. "Come in and sit down. This is Inspector Roberts. The other one I think you know. Mr. Rodman had been telling us a very interesting story—"

"I don't doubt it," observed Hartley with an air of gloom. "Well, what do you think?"

"I think," said Colonel March, "that you were very foolish to come here."

Rodman had been right about one thing, at least: Betty Hartley was afraid.

"He insisted on coming," she said. "I told him not to come. I begged him not to, though not for the reason you may be thinking. We came here to give our version of what happened the other night. But since Mr. Rodman has been good enough to—"

"My dear young lady," said Rodman, as though he were beginning a letter. He tried to soften this. "Please see, try to see, that I am acting in your own interests. Look at you: you're trembling. I have always made my own decisions in this life, and—"

Betty Hartley spoke fretfully. She said: "Oh, dry up!"

"As for me," remarked Hartley with a cheerful air, "I hold by the *corpus delicti*. I wouldn't like to swear how the thing works, but I know it gives a devil of a lot of trouble in detective stories. You can't hang me until you can produce the victim's teeth or whiskers. And I hope, conversely, that I'm not to blame if a ghost walks on the premises." His tone changed, and he looked up. "Why was I foolish to come here?"

Colonel March's voice became sharp.

"Because, if I know your symptoms at all, you ought to be home in bed," March answered. "You must have a nasty bullet-wound in your shoulder where your wife shot you last night."

*   *   *

There was a silence of such bursting quality that they even became aware of dim outer noises in the building: the passing of footsteps or the closing of a door. It took a little time for the words to sink in. Mr. Horace Rodman got to his feet, and sat down again. He has since described (to Mrs. Atchison) that he has seldom been so taken aback in his life—especially at the scared face of Betty Hartley. But he was just as taken aback by the subsequent amusement. Hartley had sat down, looking less ill. And both Hartley and Colonel March were chuckling.

"So you spotted it," said Hartley. "Well, thank the Lord for that."

"Furthermore," insisted the Colonel, with an expression of great pleasure nevertheless, "if you don't put your arm back in that sling again, you'll get into serious trouble with the doctor. Mrs. Hartley, I beg your pardon. I know the shooting wasn't a part of the game, but I hardly think you'll get into any difficulty over—"

"I don't see how you can stand there and laugh," cried the girl. "It was horrible. And you don't understand! I—"

"I hope I understand," said the Colonel. He turned to Hartley. "You're a theatrical producer, aren't you?"

"And doing well," agreed the other with decision. "Two fairly good runs in two years. Not West End, maybe. But wait! So you'd heard of me, eh? Which one did you see, *The Riddle in Red* or *Dead Voices?*"

Colonel March was apologetic.

"As a matter of fact, neither. Mr. Rodman's painstaking account of your talk made it seem likely, and *you* said, 'Look at this door. It's a practical door.' The choice of term was distinctive. A *practical* door or window, meaning a real one, is a word used exclusively in stage terminology. The big box of framed photographs suggested the theatre, as the sheets of printed paper suggested playbills. But when I heard about the long triangular indentation in the pile on the carpet, just as used by your famous predecessor, I felt sure you were trying out a variation of the original illusion. D'you mind telling me what you were up to?"

"Stage version of *The Invisible Man*," replied Hartley with enthusiasm. "Never been done. And I can't do it. Look! If I take—" He broke off. "You know the basis of the trick?"

"It deserves to be mentioned with reverence," said March, in equal enthusiasm. "It is a variation of the first really revolutionary stage-illusion of modern times. The magician and illusionist, Colonel Stodare, presented it first as 'The Sphinx' in 1865. On the same principle the great Maskelyne built his Disappearing Cabinet, and it has been the foundation of nearly every ghost-illusion since.

"This is how 'The Sphinx' was presented. In the middle of three sides of a black-draped stage stood a circular table with three legs. On this table appeared a severed head without a body. It talked, answered questions and so on; yet the audience could see over, under, and through the table to assure themselves there was no person there. Ah, you remember it? Now imagine a square, which is the stage. In the centre of the square imagine a triangle, formed by the three legs of the table, with its apex or point towards the audience. In each of the two long sides of the triangle— towards the audience—is set a looking-glass. You think you are seeing under the table to the back wall. What you actually see is the reflection of the two side walls and floor, similar black curtains and carpeting, coming together to form a perfect whole. The invisible body, of course, is hidden by the two sheets of looking-glass.

"You, Mr. Hartley, made an ingenious improvement on it. Your room had three white-painted doors, exactly the same on three sides. Your Sphinx-table stood in the middle. One of the looking-glasses would reflect half of the under part of the door on the right; the other would reflect half of the under part of the door on the left. The walls were the same; carpet was fitted up to the baseboards. A watcher opposite would apparently see under the table—to the rear wall, carpet, and rear door: which door was really the fitted-together reflection of the doors on either side.

"In your sinister Crippen role, evilly moustached, you had to take certain precautions. You had to wait until you were in the room, until you had put down gloves and pistol on the table and moved to the window, before you could turn on the light. Otherwise you would have been seen smack in the looking-glass. Afterwards a pair of gloves, ably played by your wife and helpmeet, could be made to appear above the table and perform what antics they liked. The invisible man!"

Hartley made a gesture of silent applause. Betty Hartley was almost in tears. But by this time Mr. Horace Rodman had reached a point of hysteria.

"Illusion!" he howled. "Don't tell me I saw an illusion. I won't believe it. I won't have it. A real bullet broke my window. It nearly killed me. But it went through their window without—"

"You play this one," Hartley said politely to Colonel March.

"Thank you," said the Colonel. "Correct me if I am wrong: that was an error; that was not intended, any more than you were intended to be shot." He turned to Rodman. "I rather think that part of it is clear, from your own recital. When you went bursting into their flat that night, it was very cold in the little room. You particularly commented to me on how cold it was. But there was a radiator in that room, and the flat was centrally heated throughout. In the next breath you explained how you went into the sitting-room, where it was quite warm. Am I being deeply subtle if I suggest that it was cold because the window—or one pane of it—had been open for some little time? You pointed out that several panes of those long windows open out like little doors. The terrible moustached figure opened one pane, stuck his head out, and whistled to attract your attention in case he hadn't already done so. He left it a few inches open, and didn't think to lock it again until you broke in with the policeman some time afterwards. I rather think that is how the bullet crept out."

Hartley was nursing his arm and musing.

"My dear old Grandpop," he said, "the most villainous-looking old coot who ever carried a collection-plate in church. I have impersonated him, under the stimulus of his picture, in several repertory-productions where some seedy thug is—"

"I think I must be going mad," Rodman interrupted, staring at Colonel March. "What did I hear you say? 'Whistled to attract my attention?' Attract *my* attention? Why?"

Hartley looked politely at his wife.

"And *you* play this one," he said.

"I will," said Betty, seeming to bristle up inside. She turned on Rodman. "Do you know what you are?"

"My dear young lady—"

"Do you know what you've been doing, you and your precious Mrs. Atchison? Do you deny you've been snooping and spying on us, just as you do on everyone else you can, only worse, ever since we've moved into that flat? You've tried to find out everything about us you can. You've stood up there with a pair of field-glasses and followed me from room to room, making life a perfect misery to me. I'll bet—"

("Better see that the door is closed," Colonel March said to Hartley.)

"—and, since we were going to test the mirror-illusion

anyway, I thought we'd just teach you a jolly good lesson, and scare your hair off. I suppose it's all my fault, really. I thought that was a property-gun, loaded with blanks. Only it wasn't. And I'm glad I broke your beastly old window, anyway. But when we saw what an awful row we'd caused with real shots, we had to pretend it didn't happen, or you'd have had us in the police-court for shooting at you. Jim would have had to explain what he was about, and ruined the play—"

"Light of my life—" began her husband pacifically.

"And, of course, Jim would go on. I had to hold you off while he got rid of the grandfather make-up and slid the mirrors out from the grooves on the table and hid them, and closed the window. Oh, I don't mind anything else; but I can't forgive you for being so virtuous and triumphant when you grabbed that photograph, and saw Jim slip and land with his full weight on the carpet just after he'd g-got a bullet—"

"You'll have to say it another time, Mrs. Hartley," said Colonel March, looking out of the open door. "Mr. Rodman seems to have left us in a hurry."

She grew calmer, and grinned impishly. "That's off my chest, anyhow. I'm terribly sorry, though. Can he prosecute us?"

"Somehow," said Hartley, "I don't think he will. When this story begins to circulate—no, I don't think he will. With regard to his future conduct, too; when the butcher and the candle-stick-maker hear their version of his heroic conduct, he will be—"

Colonel March nodded magnificently, like an emperor.

"Exactly," he said. "The real invisible man."

THE CRIME IN NOBODY'S ROOM

Bands were playing and seven suns were shining; but this took place entirely in the head and heart of Mr. Ronald Denham. He beamed on the car-park attendant at the Regency Club, who assisted him into the taxi. He beamed on the taxi-driver. He beamed on the night porter, and he felt an irresistible urge to hand banknotes to everyone in sight.

Now, Ronald Denham would have denied that he had taken too many drinks. It was true that he had attended an excellent bachelor party, to celebrate Jimmy Bellchester's wedding. But Denham would have maintained that he was upheld by spiritual things; and he had proved his exalted temperance by leaving the party at a time when many of the guests were still present.

As he had pointed out in a speech, it was only a month before his own wedding to Miss Anita Bruce. Anita, in fact, lived in the same block of flats and on the same floor as himself. This fact gave him great pleasure on the way home. Like most of us, Denham in this mood felt a strong urge to wake people up in the middle of the night and talk to them. He wondered whether he ought to wake up Anita. But in his reformed state he decided against it, and felt like a saint. He would not even wake up Tom Evans, who shared the flat with him—though that stern young business man usually worked so late at the office that Denham got in before he did.

At a few minutes short of midnight, then, Denham steered his way into the foyer of Medici Court. Pearson, the night porter, followed him to the automatic lift.

"Everything all right, sir?" inquired Pearson in a stage whisper. Denham assured him that it was, and that he was an excellent fellow.

"You—er—don't feel like singing, do you, sir?" asked Pearson with some anxiety.

"As a matter of fact," said Denham, who had not previously considered this, "I do. You are full of excellent ideas, Pearson. But let us sing nothing improper, Pearson. Let it be something of noble sentiment, like—"

"Honestly, sir," urged Pearson, "if it was me, I wouldn't do it. *He's* upstairs, you know. We thought he was going to Manchester this afternoon, to stay a week, but he changed his mind. He's upstairs now."

This terrible hint referred to the autocrat of Medici Court, Cellini Court, Bourbon Court, and half a dozen other great hives. Sir Rufus Armingdale, high khan of builders, not only filled London with furnished flats which really were the last word in luxury at a low price; he showed his pride in his own merchandise by living in them.

"No special quarters for me," he was quoted as saying, with fist upraised for emphasis. "No castle in Surrey or barracks in Park Lane. Just an ordinary flat; and not the most expensive of 'em either. That's where I'm most comfortable, and that's where you'll find me."

Considering all the good things provided in Armingdale's Furnished Flats, even his autocratic laws were not much resented. Nor could anyone resent the fact that all the flats in a given building were furnished exactly alike, and that the furniture must be kept in the position Rufus Armingdale gave it. Medici Court was 'Renaissance,' as Bourbon Court was 'Louis XV': a tower of rooms like luxurious cells, and only to be distinguished from each other by an ornament on a table or a picture on a wall.

But Sir Rufus's leases even discouraged pictures. Considering that he was something of an art-collector himself, and had often been photographed in his own flat with his favourite Greuze or Corot, some annoyance was felt at this.

Sir Rufus Armingdale did not care. You either leased one of his flats or you didn't. He was that sort of man.

Otherwise, of course, Ronald Denham's adventure could not have happened. He returned from the bachelor party; he took Pearson's advice about the singing; he went up in the automatic lift to the second floor; and he walked into what the champagne told him was his own flat.

That he went to the second floor is certain. Pearson saw him put his finger on the proper button in the lift. But nothing else is certain, since the hall upstairs was dark. Pushing open a door—either his key fitted it or the door was open—Denham congratulated himself on getting home.

Also, he was a little giddy. He found himself in the small foyer, where lights were on. After a short interval he must have moved into the sitting-room, for he found himself sitting back in an armchair and contemplating familiar surroundings through a haze. Lights were turned on here as well: yellow-shaded lamps, one with a pattern like a dragon on the shade.

Something began to trouble him. There was something odd, he thought, about those lamp-shades. After some study, it occurred to him that he and Tom Evans hadn't any lamp-shades like that. They did not own any bronze bookends either. As for the curtains . . .

Then a picture on the wall swam out of oblivion, and he stared at it. It was a small dull-coloured picture over the sideboard. And it penetrated into his mind at last that he had got into the wrong flat.

Everything now showed itself to him as wrong: it was as though a blur had come into focus.

"Here, I'm sorry!" he said aloud, and got up.

There was no reply. The heinousness of his offence partly steadied him. Where in the name of sanity was he? There were only three other flats on the second floor. One of these was Anita Bruce's. Of the others, one was occupied by a brisk young newspaper man named Conyers, and the other by the formidable Sir Rufus Armingdale.

Complete panic caught him. He felt that at any moment a wrathful occupant might descend on him, to call him a thief at worst or a snooper at best. Turning round to scramble for the door, he almost ran into another visitor in the wrong flat.

This visitor sat quietly in a tall chair near the door. He was a thin, oldish, well-dressed man, wearing thick-lensed spectacles, and his head was bent forward as though in meditation. He wore a soft hat and a thin oilskin waterproof coloured green: a jaunty and bilious-looking coat for such a quiet figure. The quiet light made it gleam.

"Please excuse—" Denham began in a rush, and talked for some seconds before he realized that the man had not moved.

Denham stretched out his hand. The coat was one of those smooth, almost seamless American waterproofs, yellowish outside and green inside; and for some reason the man was now wearing it inside out. Denham was in the act of telling him this when the head lolled, the smooth oilskin gleamed again, and he saw that the man was dead.

Tom Evans, stepping out of the lift at a quarter past one, found the hall of the second floor in complete darkness. When he had turned on the lights from a switch beside the life, he stopped short and swore.

Evans, lean and swarthy, with darkish eyebrows merging into a single line across his forehead, looked a little like a Norman baron in a romance. Some might have said a robber baron, for he carried a brief-case and was a stern man of business despite his youth. But what he saw now made him momentarily forget his evening's work. The hall showed four doors, with their microscopic black numbers, set some distance apart. Near the door leading to Anita Bruce's flat, Ronald Denham sat hunched on an oak settle. There was a lump at the base of his skull and he was breathing in a way Evans did not like.

It was five minutes more before Denham had been whacked and pounded into semi-consciousness; and to such a blinding headache that its pain helped to revive him. First he became aware of Tom's lean, hook-nosed face bending over him, and Tom's usual fluency at preaching.

"I don't mind you getting drunk," the voice came to him dimly. "In fact, I expected it. But at least you ought to be able to carry your liquor decently. What the devil have you been up to, anyway? Hoy!"

"He had his raincoat on inside out," was the first thing Denham said. Then memory came back to him like a new headache or a new explosion, and he began to pour out the story.

"—and I tell you there's a dead man in one of those flats! I think he's been murdered. Tom, I'm not drunk; I swear I'm not. Somebody sneaked up behind and bashed me over the back of the head just after I found him."

"Then how did you get out here?"

"Oh, God, how should I know? Don't argue; help me up. I suppose I must have been dragged out here. If you don't believe me, feel the back of my head. Just feel it."

Evans hesitated. He was always practical, and there could be no denying the bruise. He looked uncertainly up and down the hall.

"But who is this dead man?" he demanded. "And whose flat is he in?"

"I don't know. It was an oldish man with thick glasses and a green raincoat. I never saw him before. Looked a bit like an American, somehow."

"Nonsense! Nobody wears a green raincoat."

"I'm telling you, he was wearing it inside out. If you ask me why, I'm going to bat my head against the wall and go to sleep again." He wished he could do this, for he could not see straight and his head felt like a printing-press in full blast. "We ought to be able to identify the flat easily enough. I can give a complete description of it—"

He paused, for two doors had opened simultaneously in the hall. Anita Bruce and Sir Rufus Armingdale came out, in different stages of anger or curiosity at the noise.

If Evans had been more of a psychologist, he might have anticipated the effect this would have on them. As it was, he stood looking from one to the other, thinking whatever thoughts you care to attribute to him. For he was an employee of Sir Rufus, as manager of the Sloane Square office of Armingdale Flats, and he could risk no trouble.

Anita seemed to take in the situation at a glance. She was small, dark, plump, and fluffy-haired. She was wearing a négligé and smoking a cigarette. Seeing the expressions of the other three, she removed the cigarette from her mouth in order to smile. Sir Rufus Armingdale did not look so much formidable as fretful. He had one of those powerful faces whose features seem to have run together like a bull-pup's. But the old dressing-gown, fastened up at the throat as though he were cold, took away the suggestion of an autocrat and made him only a householder.

He breathed through his nose, rather helplessly, until he saw an employee. His confidence returned.

"Good morning, Evans," he said. "What's the meaning of this?"

Evans risked it. "I'm afraid it's trouble, sir. Mr. Denham—well, he's found a dead man in one of the flats."

"Ron!" cried Anita.

"A dead man," repeated Armingdale, without surprise. "Where?"

"In one of the flats. He doesn't know which."

"Oh? Why doesn't he know which?"

"He's got a frightful bump on the back of his head," said Anita, exploring. She looked back over her shoulder and spoke swiftly. "It's quite all right, Tom. Don't get excited. He's d-r-u-n-k."

"I am not drunk," said Denham, with tense and sinister calmness. "May I also point out that I am able to read and write, and that I have not had words spelled out in front of me since I was four years old? Heaven give me s-t-r-e-n-g-t-h! I tell you, I can describe the place."

He did so. Afterwards there was a silence. Anita, her eyes shining curiously, dropped her cigarette on the autocrat's hardwood floor and ground it out. The autocrat seemed too abstracted to notice.

"Ron, old dear," Anita said, going over and sitting down beside him, "I'll believe you if you're as serious as all that. But you ought to know it isn't *my* flat."

"And I can tell you it isn't mine," grunted Armingdale. "There certainly isn't a dead man in it. I've just come from there, and I know."

If they had not known Armingdale's reputation so well, they might have suspected him of trying to make a joke. But his expression belied it as well. It was heavy and lowering, with more than a suggestion of the bull-pup.

"This picture you say you saw," he began. "The one over the sideboard. Could you describe it?"

"Yes, I think so," said Denham desperately. "It was a rather small portrait of a little girl looking sideways over some roses, or flowers of some kind. Done in that greyish-brown stuff; I think they call it sepia."

Armingdale stared at him.

"Then I know it isn't mine," he said. "I never owned a sepia drawing in my life. If this young man is telling the truth, there's only one flat left. I think I shall just take the responsibility of knocking, and—"

His worried gaze moved down towards the door of the flat occupied by Mr. Hubert Conyers, of the *Daily Record*. But it was unnecessary to knock at the door. It opened with such celerity that Denham wondered whether anyone had been looking at them through the slot of the letter-box; and Hubert Conyers stepped out briskly. He was an unobtrusive, sandy-haired little man, very different from Denham's idea of a journalist. His only extravagance was a taste for blended shadings in his clothes, from suit to shirt to necktie; though he usually contrived to look rumpled. He was always obliging, and as busy as a parlour clock. But his manner had a subdued persuasiveness which could worm him through narrower places than you might have imagined.

He came forward drawing on his coat, and with a deft gesture he got into the middle of the group.

"Sorry, sorry, sorry," he began, seeming to propitiate everyone at once. "I couldn't help overhearing, you know. Good evening, Sir Rufus. The fact is, it's not my flat either. Just now, the only ornaments in my sitting-room are a lot of well-filled ashtrays and a bottle of milk. Come and see, if you like."

There was a silence, while Conyers looked anxious.

"But it's got to be somebody's flat!" snapped Sir Rufus Armingdale, with a no-nonsense air. "Stands to reason. A whole confounded sitting-room can't vanish like smoke. Unless—stop a bit—unless Mr. Denham got off at some other floor?"

"I don't know. I may have."

"And I don't mind admitting—" said Armingdale, hesitating as everyone looked at him curiously. The autocrat seemed worried. "Very well. The fact is, *I've* got a picture in my flat something like the one Mr. Denham described. It's

Greuze's 'Young Girl with Primroses.' But mine's an oil painting, of course. Mr. Denham is talking about a sepia drawing. That is, if he really saw anything. Does this dead man exist at all?"

Denham's protestations were cut short by the hum of an ascending lift. But it was not the ordinary lift in front of them; it was the service-life at the end of the hall. The door was opened, and the cage-grating pulled back, to show the frightened face of the night porter.

"Sir," said Pearson, addressing Armingdale as though he were beginning an oration. "I'm glad to see *you*, sir. You always tell us that if something serious happens we're to come straight to you instead of the manager. Well, I'm afraid this is serious. I—the fact is, I found something in this lift."

Denham felt that they were being haunted by that phrase, 'the fact is.' Everybody seemed to use it. He recalled a play in which it was maintained that anyone who began a sentence like this was usually telling a lie. But he had not time to think about this, for they had found the elusive dead man.

The unknown lay on his face in one corner of the lift. A light in the roof of the steel cage shone down on his grey felt hat, on an edge of his thick spectacles, and on his oilskin waterproof. But the coat was no longer green, for he was now wearing it right-side-out in the ordinary way.

Anita, who had come quietly round beside Denham, seized his arm. The night porter restrained Tom Evans as the latter bent forward.

"I shouldn't touch him, sir, if I was you. There's blood."

"Where?"

Pearson indicated a stain on the grey-rubber floor. "And if I'm any judge, sir, he died of a stab through the heart. I—lifted him up a bit. But I don't see any kind of knife that could have done it."

"Is this the man you saw?" Armingdale asked Denham quietly.

Denham nodded. Something tangible, something to weigh and handle, seemed to have brought the force back to Armingdale's personality.

"Except," Denham added, "that he's now wearing his raincoat right-side out. Why?"

"Never mind the raincoat," Anita said close to his ear. "Ron, you don't know him, do you? You'll swear you don't know him?"

He was startled. She had spoken without apparent urgency, and so low that the others might not have heard her. But Denham, who knew her so well, knew that there was urgency behind the unwinking seriousness of her eyes. Unconsciously she was shaking his arm. His wits had begun to clear, despite the pain in his skull; and he wondered.

"No, of course I don't know him. Why should I?"

"Nothing! Nothing at all. Ss-t!"

"Well, I know him," said Hubert Conyers.

Conyers had been squatting down at the edge of the lift, and craning his neck to get a close view of the body without touching it. Now he straightened up. He seemed so excited that he could barely control himself, and his mild eye looked wicked.

"I interviewed him a couple of days ago," said Conyers. "Surely you know him, Sir Rufus?"

"'Surely' is a large word, young man. No, I do not know him. Why?"

"That's Dan Randolph, the American real-estate king," said Conyers, keeping a watchful eye on Armingdale. "All of you will have heard of him: he's the fellow who always deals in spot cash, even if it's a million. I'd know those spectacles anywhere. He's as near-sighted as an owl. Er—am I correctly informed, Sir Rufus, that he was in England to do some business with you?"

Armingdale smiled bleakly. "You have no information, young man," he said. "And so far as I'm concerned you're not getting any. So that's Dan Randolph! I knew he was in England; but he's certainly not made any business proposition to me."

"Maybe he was coming to do it."

"Maybe he was," said Armingdale, with the same air of a parent to a child. He turned to Pearson. "You say you found him in that lift. When did you find him? And how did you come to find him?"

Pearson was voluble. "The lift was on the ground floor, sir. I just happened to glance through the little glass panel, and I see him lying there. So I thought I'd better run the lift up here and get you. As for putting him there—" He pointed to the *Recall* button on the wall outside the lift. "Somebody on any floor, sir, could have shoved him in here, and pressed this button, and sent him downstairs. He certainly wasn't put in on the ground floor. Besides, I saw him come into the building to-night."

"Oh?" put in Conyers softly. "When was this?"

"Might have been eleven o'clock, sir."

"Who was he coming to see?"

Pearson shook his head helplessly and with a certain impatience. "These ain't service-flats, sir, where you telephone up about every visitor. You ought to know we're not to ask visitors anything unless they seem to need help, or unless it's somebody who has no business here. *I* don't know. He went up in the main lift, that's all I can tell you."

"Well, what floor did he go to?"

"I dunno." Pearson ran a finger under a tight collar. "But excuse me, sir, may I ask a question, if you please? What's wrong exactly?"

"We've lost a room," said Ronald Denham, with inspiration. "Maybe you can help. Look here, Pearson: you've been here in these flats a long time. You've been inside most of them—in the sitting-rooms, for instance?"

"I think I can say I've been in all of 'em, sir."

"Good. Then we're looking for a room decorated like this," said Denham. For the third time he described what he had seen, and Pearson's expression grew to one of acute anguish. At the end of it he shook his head.

"It's nobody's room, sir," the porter answered simply. "There's not a sitting-room like that in the whole building."

At three o'clock in the morning, a somber group of people sat in Sir Rufus Armingdale's flat, and did not even look at each other. The police work was nearly done. A brisk divisional detective-inspector, accompanied by a sergeant, a photographer, and a large amiable man in a top-hat, had taken a statement from each of those concerned. But the statements revealed nothing.

Denham, in fact, had received only one more mental jolt. Entering Armingdale's flat, he thought for a second that he had found the missing room. The usual chairs of stamped Spanish leather, the refectory table, the carved gewgaws, greeted him like a familiar nightmare. And over the sideboard hung a familiar picture—that of a small girl looking sideways over an armful of roses.

"That's not it!" said Anita quickly.

"It's the same subject, but it's not the same picture. That's in oils. What sort of game do you suppose is going on in this place?"

Anita glanced over her shoulder. She had dressed before the arrival of the police; and also, he thought, she had put on more make-up than was necessary.

"Quick, Ron; before the others get here. Were you telling the truth?"

"Certainly. You don't think—?"

"Oh, I don't know and I don't care; I just want you to tell me. Ron, you didn't kill him yourself?"

He had not even time to answer before she stopped him. Sir Rufus Armingdale, Conyers, and Evans came through from the foyer; and with them was the large amiable man who had accompanied Divisional-Inspector Davidson. His name, it appeared, was Colonel March.

"You see," he explained, with a broad gesture, "I'm not here officially. I happened to be at the theatre, and I dropped in on Inspector Davidson for a talk, and he asked me to come along. So if you don't like any of my questions, just tell me to shut my head. But I do happen to be attached to the Yard—"

"I know you, Colonel," said Conyers, with a crooked grin. "You're the head of the Ragbag Department, D–3. Some call it the Crazy House."

Colonel March nodded seriously. He wore a dark overcoat, and had a top-hat pushed back on his large head; this, with his florid complexion, sandy moustache, and bland blue eye, gave him something of the look of a stout colonel in a comic paper. He was smoking a large-bowled pipe with the effect of seeming to sniff smoke from the bowl rather than draw it through the stem. He appeared to be enjoying himself.

"It's a compliment," he assured them. "After all, somebody has got to sift all the queer complaints. If somebody comes in and reports (say) that the Borough of Stepney is being terrorized by a blue pig, I've got to decide whether it's a piece of lunacy, or a mistake, or a hoax, or a serious crime. Otherwise good men would only waste their time. You'd be surprised how many such complaints there are. But I was thinking, and so was Inspector Davidson, that you had a very similar situation here. If you wouldn't mind a few extra questions—"

"As many as you like," said Sir Rufus Armingdale." "Provided somebody's got a hope of solving this damned—"

"As a matter of fact," said Colonel March, frowning, "Inspector Davidson has reason to believe that it is already solved. A good man, Davidson."

There was a silence. Something unintentionally sinister seemed to have gathered in Colonel March's affable tone. For a moment nobody dared to ask him what he meant.

"Already solved?" repeated Hubert Conyers.

"Suppose we begin with you, Sir Rufus," said March with great courtesy. "You have told the inspector that you did not know Daniel Randolph personally. But it seems to be common knowledge that he was in England to see you."

Armingdale hesitated. "I don't know his reasons. He may have been here to see me, among other things. Probably was. He wrote to me from America. But he hasn't approached me yet, and I didn't approach him first. It's bad business."

"What was the nature of this business, Sir Rufus?"

"He wanted to buy an option I held on some property in—never mind where. I'll tell you in private, if you insist."

"Was a large sum involved?"

Armingdale seemed to struggle with himself. "Four thousand, more or less."

"So it wasn't a major business deal. Were you going to sell?"

"Probably."

Colonel March's abstracted eye wandered to the picture over the sideboard. "Now, Sir Rufus, that Greuze, 'Young Girl with Primroses.' I think it was recently reproduced, in its natural size, as a full-page illustration in the *Metropolitan Illustrated News?*"

"Yes, it was," said Armingdale. He added: "In—sepia."

Something about this afterthought made them all move forward to look at him. It was like the puzzle of a half-truth: nobody knew what it meant.

"Exactly. Just two more questions. I believe that each of these flats communicates with a fire-escape leading down into the mews behind?"

"Yes. What of it?"

"Will the same key open the front door of each of the flats?"

"No, certainly not. All the lock-patterns are different."

"Thank you. Now, Mr. Conyers—a question for you. Are you married?"

"Married? No."

"And you don't keep a valet?"

"The answer to that, Colonel, is loud and prolonged laughter. Honestly, I don't like your 'social' manner. Beston, our crime news man, knows you. And it's always, 'Blast you, Beston, if you print one hint about the Thing-gummy case I'll have your hide.' What difference does it make whether I'm married or not, or whether I have a valet or not?"

"A great deal," said March seriously. "Now, Miss Bruce. What is your occupation, Miss Bruce?"

"I'm an interior decorator," answered Anita. She began to laugh. It may have been with a tinge of hysteria; but she sat back in a tall chair and laughed until there were tears in her eyes.

"I'm terribly sorry," she went on, holding out her hand as though to stop them, "but don't you see? The murder was done by an interior decorator. That's the whole secret."

Colonel March cut short Armingdale's shocked protest.

"Go on," he said sharply.

"I thought of it first off. Of course there's no 'vanishing

room.' Some sitting-room has just been redecorated. All the actual furnishings, tables and chairs and sideboards, are just the same in every room. The only way you can tell them apart is by small movable things—pictures, lamp-shades, book-ends—which could be changed in a few minutes.

"Ron accidentally walked into the murderer's flat just after the murderer had killed that old man. That put the murderer in a pretty awful position. Unless he killed Ron too, he was caught with the body and Ron could identify his flat. But he thought of a better way. He sent that man's body down in the lift and dragged Ron out into the hall. Then he simply altered the decorations of his flat. Afterwards he could sit down and dare anyone to identify it as the place where the body had been."

Anita's face was flushed with either defiance or fear.

"Warm," said Colonel March. "Unquestionably warm. That is why I was wondering whether you couldn't tell us what really happened."

"I don't understand you."

"Well, there are objections to the redecoration. You've got to suppose that nobody had ever been in the flat before and seen the way it was originally decorated. You've also got to suppose that the murderer could find a new set of lamp-shades, pictures, and book-ends in the middle of the night— Haven't you got it the wrong way round?"

"The wrong way round?"

"Somebody," said March, dropping his courtesy, "prepared a dummy room to begin with. He put in the new lamp-shades, the book-ends, the copy of a well-known picture, even a set of new curtains. He entertained Randolph there. Afterwards, of course, he simply removed the knick-knacks and set the place right again. But it was the dummy room into which Ronald Denham walked. That, Mr. Denham, was why you did not recognize—"

"Recognize what?" roared Denham. "Where was I?"

"In the sitting-room of your own flat," said Colonel March gravely. "If you had been sober you might have made a mistake; but you were so full of champagne that your instinct brought you home after all."

There were two doors in the room, and the blue uniform of a policeman appeared in each. At March's signal, Inspector Davidson stepped forward. He said:

"Thomas Evans, I arrest you for the murder of Daniel Randolph. I have to warn you that anything you say will be taken down in writing and may be used in evidence at your trial."

"Oh, look here," protested Colonel March, when they met in Armingdale's flat next day, "the thing was simple enough. We had twice as much trouble over that kid in Bayswater who pinched all the oranges. And you had all the facts.

"Evans, as one of Sir Rufus's most highly placed and trusted employees, was naturally in a position to know all about the projected business deal with Randolph. And so he planned an ingenious swindle. A swindle, I am certain, was all he intended.

"Now you, Sir Rufus, had intended to go to Manchester yesterday afternoon, and remain there for a week. (Mr. Denham heard that from the night-porter, when he was advised against singing.) That would leave your flat empty. Evans telephoned to Randolph, posing as you. He asked Randolph to come round to your flat at eleven o'clock at night, and settle the deal. He added that you *might* be called away to Manchester; but, in that event, his secretary would have the necessary papers ready and signed.

"It would have been easy. Evans would get into your empty flat by way of the fire-escape and the window. He would pose as your secretary. Randolph—who, remem-

ber, always paid spot cash even if it involved a million—
would hand over a packet of banknotes for a forged doc-
ument.

"Why should Randolph be suspicious of anything? He
knew, as half the newspaper-reading world knows, that Sir
Rufus lived on the second floor of Medici Court. He had
seen photographs of Sir Rufus with his favourite Greuze over
the sideboard. Even if he asked the hall-porter for directions,
he would be sent to the right flat. Even if the hall porter said
Sir Rufus was in Manchester, the ground had been prepared
and Randolph would ask for Sir Rufus's secretary.

"Unfortunately, a hitch occurred. Sir Rufus decided not to
go to Manchester. He decided it yesterday afternoon, after
all Evans's plans had been made and Randolph was due to
arrive. But Evans needed that money; as we have discovered
to-day, he needed it desperately. He wanted that four thousand pounds.

"So he hit on another plan. Sir Rufus would be at home
and his flat could not be used. But, with all the rooms
exactly alike except for decorations, why not an *imitation* of
Sir Rufus's flat? The same plan would hold good, except that
Randolph would be taken to the wrong place. He would come
up in the lift at eleven. Evans would be waiting with the door
of the flat open, and would take him to a place superficially
resembling Sir Rufus's. The numbers on the doors are very
small; and Randolph, as we know, was so near-sighted as to
be almost blind. If Evans adopted some disguise, however
clumsy, he could never afterwards be identified as the man
who swindled Randolph. And he ran no risk in using the flat
he shared with Denham."

Anita interposed. "Of course!" she said. "Ron was at a
bachelor party, and ordinarily it would have kept him there
whooping until two or three o'clock in the morning. But he
reformed, and came home early."

Denham groaned. "But I still can't believe it," he insisted. "Tom Evans? A murderer?"

"He intended no murder," said Colonel March. "But, you see, Randolph suspected something. Randolph showed that he suspected. And Evans, as a practical man, had to kill him. You can guess why Randolph suspected?"

"Well?"

"Because Evans is colour-blind," said Colonel March.

"It's too bad," Colonel March went on sadly, "but the crime was from the first the work of a colour-blind man. Now, none of the rest of you could qualify for that deficiency. As for Sir Rufus, I can think of nothing more improbable than a colour-blind art-collector—unless it is a colour-blind interior decorator. Mr. Conyers here shows by the blended hues of brown or blue in his suits, shirts, and ties that he has a fine eye for colour effect; and he possesses no wife or valet to choose them for him.

But Evans? He is not only partially but wholly colour-blind. You gave us a spirited account of it. Randolph's body was sent up in the lift by Pearson. When Evans stepped forward, Pearson warned him not to touch the body, saying that there was blood. Evans said: 'Where?'—though he was staring straight down in a small, brightly lighted lift at a red bloodstain on a grey-rubber floor. Red on any surface except green or yellow is absolutely invisible to colour-blind men.

"That was also the reason why Randolph's waterproof was put on inside out. Randolph had removed his hat and coat when he first came into the flat. After Evans had stabbed him with a clasp-knife, Evans put the hat and coat back on the body previous to disposing of it. But he could not distinguish between the yellow outside and the green inside of that seamless oilskin.

"You, Mr. Denham, let yourself into the flat with your own key: which in itself told us the location of the 'vanished' room, for no two keys are alike. I also think that Miss Bruce could have told us all along where the 'vanished' room was. I am inclined to suspect she saw Randolph going into your flat, and was afraid you might be concerned in the murder."

"Oh, well," said Anita philosophically.

"Anyway, you spoke to a corpse about his coat being inside out; and Evans rectified the error before he put the body in the lift. He had to knock you out, of course. But he genuinely didn't want to hurt you. He left the building by way of the fire-escape into the mews. He disposed of his stage-properties, though he was foolish enough to keep the money and the clasp-knife on his person, where they were found when we searched him. When he came back here, he used the main lift in the ordinary way as though he were returning from his office. And he was genuinely concerned when he found you still unconscious on the bench in the hall."

There was a silence, broken by Armingdale's snort.

"But colour-blindness! What's that got to do with the solution? How did you come to think the murderer must have been colour-blind to begin with?"

Colonel March turned to stare at him. Then he shook his head, with a slow and dismal smile.

"Don't you see it even yet?" he asked. "That was the starting-point. We suspected it for the same reason Randolph suspected an imposture. Poor old Randolph wasn't an art critic. Any sort of coloured daub, in the ordinary way, he would have swallowed as the original 'Young Girl with Primroses' he expected to see. But Evans didn't allow for the one thing even a near-sighted man does know: colour. In his effort to imitate the decorations of Sir Rufus's flat, the fool hung up as an oil-painting nothing more than a sepia reproduction out of an illustrated weekly."

ERROR AT DAYBREAK

Under the white light of daybreak, the beach seemed deserted for a full half-mile towards the headland. The tide was out, showing a muddy slope at the foot of smooth sand. But it had begun to turn, and flat edges of surf moved snakily back towards the beach.

A narrow lane led down to it, between the high and crooked banks which closed it off from the road. Until you were well out on the sands it was impossible even to see Norman Kane's cottage some distance up towards the right. But one landmark showed in a dark wedge against sand and sea. For several hundred yards out into the water a line of rocks ran in humped formation, curved at the end, in a way that suggested the paw of an animal. It seemed to catch at the incoming tide. Bill Stacey knew it at once for the Lion's Paw, and he set off down the lane towards the beach.

It is to Stacey's credit that he still felt moderately cheerful after having just tramped two miles on an empty stomach, carrying a heavy suitcase. Norman Kane had specified the train he was to take from London, and the wayside station at which it would land him. But Kane had said nothing about a certain lack of transport at that hour of the morning.

The prospect of seeing Marion—Kane's niece and secretary—so cheered him that he forgot the matter. He did not know whether Kane knew he was in love with Marion. Norman Kane had for him the slightly amused tolerance with which Kane would naturally regard an easy-going journalist like Stacey. And Stacey, in turn, had concealed from a hero-worshipping Marion his belief that Norman Kane was an imposing, dignified, and strenuous crook.

For in his way Kane was a great man, a power in the City and a company-juggler of skill. And he was genuinely fond of Marion, as he was of all his dependants. With his theatricalism went tireless energy; it was only at Dr. Hastings's orders, when he had developed signs of a bad heart, that he had been dragged off for the summer to South Wales.

Heart trouble, Stacey knew, was often the case with these ex-athletes who have run to fat. Kane's worried looks, Marion's worried looks, had disturbed him the last time he saw them. But, as he came out on the beach in the morning light, he felt that nothing ever could happen to Kane.

There was the man himself. Even at a distance he recognized Kane's bulky figure, jauntily wrapped in a dark-red bath-robe with white facings, striding along with a towel over his arm, kicking the sand out of his way with rubber slippers. His bath-robe made a spot of colour against that lonely shore, where the Lion's Paw stretched out into the tide.

And Kane strode out briskly along the Paw. He was not going to bathe. He was going out along the rocks to dive.

"Here!" Stacey said aloud. Swimming, in that sea, with a bad heart? The mutter of the surf was growing as it drove in, and the farther end of the Paw was already awash.

"Ahoy there!" he yelled. "Kane! Hoy!"

The cry seemed to linger in emptiness across the sands. But it reached Kane, who turned round. He was some fifty yards out on the ridge, but he lifted his towel and waved it.

"Ahoy, my lad!" he bellowed back. "I didn't expect you so early. Come for a dip! The water's fine. Everything is—"

Then it happened.

Stacey never forgot that big, greyish-haired figure, framed against the sea and the dark crook of the Lion's Paw. He was too far away to catch the expression on Kane's face. But Kane's voice died away in a gulp, a puzzled kind of gulp, and his shoulders drew together. For a moment he stood looking at the beach, swaying a little and pressing his arms as though he were cold. Then he pitched forward on his face like a bag of sand.

It was a second or two before Stacey began to run. As he did so he noticed other figures moving on the beach. From some distance away to the right, in the direction of Kane's cottage, he saw Marion running towards him. There was a gleam on her yellow hair; she wore a bathing-suit and a beach-robe blown out by the wind. Behind her lumbered Dr. Hastings, in a white linen suit.

But Stacey did not wait for them. He knew instinctively that something had happened to Norman Kane, something that was worse than a faint.

Along the top of the Lion's Paw there had been worn a natural sunken path some two feet wide. Picking his way out across this, he found Kane's great bulk wedged into it. Kane's right hand, still clutching the towel, was doubled under him; his left hand lay limply outstretched ahead. Stacey took his pulse, but there was no pulse.

He stood staring down, listening to the slap and swing of the water against the rocks. Heart gone: just like that. At that moment he did not notice the small hole or tear in the back of the dark-red bath-robe, just over the heart. He was too dazed to notice anything more than the fact of death. He hurried back to the beach, where he met Marion and Dr. Hastings.

"Steady," he said, as the girl tried to push past him. "You'd better go out there, doctor. But I'm afraid he's done for."

None of them moved. He could not quite estimate the effect of his words on Kane's niece. He realized, too, that he had never before seen Marion without her glasses which had added a business-like and almost prim touch to her good looks. Over her shoulder towered Dr. Hastings, whose wiry, close-cut hair had a Teutonic look, and his expression a Teutonic heaviness.

"Oh!" said the girl. She was looking at him curiously, and she breathed hard. "Was it—suicide?"

"Suicide?" repeated Stacey, startled. "No. His heart gave out. Why should you think it was suicide?"

"Oh!" said Marion again. She put her hand on his arm and pressed it. "I want to see him. No, I'm quite all right. I hope I can move. I can't think very well."

Dr. Hastings, who seemed about to launch a violent protest, checked himself and pushed past. They went with him to the body, and watched while he made his examination. Then he urged them back towards the beach.

"Look here," Hastings began heavily. He cleared his throat, and tried again. "Yes, he's dead right enough; but possibly not for the reason you think. Do you know if Lionel is up yet, Marion?"

So that fellow was at the cottage, thought Stacey. He had never liked the supercilious and aesthetic Mr. Lionel Pell. Norman Kane had once courted Lionel's mother, in the days before she had married the late Mr. Pell; and this seemed to give Lionel the idea that he had some claim on Kane, particularly with regard to sponging.

"Lionel?" repeated Marion. "I—I haven't seen him. I got up and went out for an early bathe at the other side of the bay. But I shouldn't think he was up yet. Why?"

"Because," replied Dr. Hastings with his usual directness, "he'll have to get out his car and drive to the village and get the police. I'm afraid this is murder."

The surf was driving in now, with deepening thunder. A wave veered against the rocks and flung up a ghostly mane of spray. A cold wind had begun to blow from the south, fluttering Marion's beach-robe. She looked at the doctor with rather blind blue eyes, winking as though to keep back tears.

"We had better go up to the house," Hastings went on heavily, "and get something to use as a stretcher: he's a weight to move. There are some bad cross-currents out at this distance when the tide rises, and we don't want him washed out to sea before the police get here."

Then Stacey found his voice.

"The police? Good God, what do you want with the police? His heart—"

"His heart was as sound as yours or mine," said Hastings.

"So," said Marion, "you knew that."

"I should hope I knew it, my dear girl. I happen to be his doctor. Now keep your chin up and let's face the facts. He's been murdered. What little blood there is doesn't show up well against that dark-red bath-robe; but you probably noticed it. And you may have seen the cut in the back of the bath-robe just over the heart."

Stacey put his arm round Marion, who had begun to tremble. He spoke with restraint.

"Look here, Doctor. I don't like to suggest that you're out of your mind, but you might come aside and talk nonsense to me instead of talking it to her. Murdered? How could he have been murdered? He was all alone in this path. There wasn't anybody within a hundred yards of him. You must have seen that for yourself."

"That's true," put in Marion suddenly. "I was sitting up at the top of the beach, up under the bank, getting dry; and I saw him go past. That *is* true, Doctor."

"Yes. It is true. I saw him from the verandah of the cottage," agreed Hastings.

"Then why all this talk about murder?" asked Stacey. "Hold on! Are you saying he was shot with a long-range rifle, or something of the sort? It would have to be very long range. His back was towards the sea when he was hit, and there were several miles of empty water behind him."

"No, I am not saying that."

"Well?"

"He was killed," answered Dr. Hastings slowly, "with

some kind of steel point like an old-fashioned hatpin. That's what I think, anyhow. I haven't removed it. And I can't swear to the exact nature of the weapon until the post-mortem."

That afternoon, while the grey rain fell, Superintendent Morgan tramped up to the cottage. He had joined the quiet group assembled inside the verandah—Marion, Dr. Hastings, Lionel Pell, and Bill Stacey sat there. Outside, the sea looked oily and dangerous, as though by its restless movements it were about to burst against the cottage. Superintendent Morgan wore a sou'wester and an oilskin cap; the expression of his face was a contrast to his soft voice.

He glared at Dr. Hastings.

"And that's that," he said. "I'm suggesting to you, Doctor, that you did this deliberately."

"You mean," asked Hastings, examining all sides of the matter, "that I killed Mr. Kane?"

"That is not what I mean. I mean, that you deliberately allowed that body to be washed out to sea. Don't worry. We'll find it. Indeed we will. That was an incoming tide, and it's somewhere along the beach." The superintendent's light eyes opened. His sing-song voice was more disturbing than violent. "I say you deliberately let it be carried off so that we shouldn't find out how Mr. Kane was killed."

"Miss Kane and Mr. Stacey," said Hastings shortly, "will tell you I warned them. I wanted to get a stretcher and move him in time. We were too late, that's all. Why shouldn't I want you to find out how he was killed?"

"Because it's an impossible thing you tell us. The man was alone. No one could have touched him. And yet he was stabbed. There was a way of doing that. If we had found the body we should have known how it was done."

"Probably you would have," agreed Hastings.

There was an ominous silence, broken by the flat drizzle

of the rain. Bill Stacey, sitting beside Marion, did not look at the superintendent. He found himself more curious about another person, a man who lounged across the verandah near the doorway.

The stranger weighed some seventeen stone and his waterproof made him seem even larger. From under a sodden tweed cap a bland blue eye surveyed the company; and from under a cropped moustache, which might be sandy or grey, there projected a large-bowled pipe, at which he seemed to be sniffing. Stacey had heard the superintendent address him as Colonel March. Colonel March listened, but so far had said nothing.

"Meantime," said Superintendent Morgan, taking out a notebook, "there are more queernesses here. I want to hear about them, if you please. Miss Kane!"

Marion glanced up briefly. She had been holding herself in well, Stacey thought, and preserving her blank, 'secretarial' manner.

"We've heard a good deal, hereabouts," Morgan went on, "about Mr. Kane and his bad heart. You tell us you knew he didn't have a bad heart at all."

"I guessed it. So did Dr. Jones in the village, I think."

"Then why did he keep on saying he had?" demanded Morgan.

"I—I don't know."

"Then tell me this, miss. When you first heard this morning that Mr. Kane was dead, you asked whether it was suicide. Why did you ask that?"

"I—"

"Truth, miss!"

"I've been worried about him," answered Marion. "He's been threatening suicide, if you must know. And he's been acting queerly."

Lionel Pell intervened. Lionel's way of speaking, which

sometimes made him as unintelligible as a gramophone running down, now became almost clear. His long legs were outthrust; and his usual expression of supreme indifference was now replaced by one almost helpful. He sat back, long of nose and jaw, and laid down his pronouncement.

"The word, I believe, is 'childish,'" he decided. "The poor old boy—Norman, of course—has been playing with toys. Tell them about the cardboard soldiers, Marion. And the air-rifle."

Marion gave him an almost malevolent look.

"There's nothing very funny or childish about the air-rifle. It's a powerful one, hardly a toy at all. You've used it yourself. But I admit I don't understand about the soldiers.

"You see," she appealed to Morgan, "only the night before last my uncle came home with a huge box of cardboard soldiers. He bought them in Cardiff. They were gaudily painted, each of them five or six inches high. In the bottom was a wooden cannon, painted yellow, that fired a hard rubber ball. My uncle went back to his study and unwrapped them, and set them all up on the table."

At this point, Stacey noticed, the man called Colonel March stirred and glanced across with sudden interest. They all saw it; it brought a new atmosphere of tension. The superintendent looked at her with quick suspicion.

"Did he, Miss Kane? Did he seem to be—er—enjoying himself?"

"No," she replied quite seriously. "He looked ill. Once he came out, for no reason at all, and begged my pardon."

"Miss Kane, do you mean your uncle was insane?"

Dr. Hastings interposed. "Norman Kane," he said, "was one of the sanest men I ever met."

"Now I will tell you something myself," said Superintendent Morgan. "He 'begged your pardon,' you say. You talk of suicide. I have heard of your Mr. Kane from my cousin, Morgan David. My cousin tells me that your Mr. Kane was not much better than a swindler. My cousin says his companies are crashing, and that he was going to be prosecuted. Is *that* a reason for suicide? I think it is."

"I know nothing of my uncle's private affairs," said Marion. And yet it was, Stacey felt, the thing she had been fearing. Marion wore a print frock, and she seemed less like a secretary than a nurse—a nurse at the bedside of a patient who she had determined should not die.

"Is that, I ask you, a reason for suicide?"

"It may be a reason for suicide," snapped Dr. Hastings. "But it won't explain how a man could run himself through the back at an angle his hand couldn't possibly reach—and in full sight of three witnesses as well."

"Murder or suicide, it is still impossible!"

"And yet the man is dead."

"One moment," said Colonel March.

It was an easy, comfortable voice, and it soothed tempers frayed by rain and fear. His presence was at once authoritative and comfortable, as though he invited them to a discussion rather than an argument; and his amiable eye moved round the group.

"It's not my place to butt in," he apologized, "but there are one or two things here that are rather in my line. Do you mind, Superintendent, if I ask a question or two?"

"Glad," said Morgan fervently. "This gentleman," he explained, throwing out his chest, "is the head of D-3 Department at Scotland Yard. He is down here—"

"—on not a very exciting errand," said Colonel March sadly. "A matter of a curious thief who steals only green candlesticks, and therefore comes under the head of our special investigation department. Excuse me: Miss Kane, two days before he died your uncle bought a box of cardboard soldiers. Will you get me that box of soldiers now?"

Without a word Marion got up and went into the cottage. Dr. Hastings looked up suddenly, as though on the defensive.

"We have also heard," Colonel March continued presently, "that he bought an air-rifle. I think you used that air-rifle, Mr. Pell?"

Lionel sat up. With the superintendent he had been friendly and helpful. With Colonel March he had adopted his usual indifference, the air of ease and right with which he (at twenty-three) had called Kane 'Norman' and conferred a favour by accepting loans.

"I *have* used it," he said. "It was not my property. Are you under the impression that our late good host was killed by being shot with one of those microscopic pellets out of a toy air-rifle? Or, for that matter, by a little rubber ball out of a toy cannon?"

"Where was the air-rifle kept?"

You could not shake Lionel's placidity.

"I believe I kept it in my room. Until last night, that is. Then I lent it to Marion. Hadn't you better ask her?"

Marion returned in a few moments, with a large and bright-coloured box, which she handed to Colonel March. She seemed to feel that her name had been mentioned; for she looked quickly between Lionel and Bill Stacey. Colonel March opened the box, sniffing at his pipe.

"And yet," he said, with a sharpness which made Stacey uneasy, "the rubber ball is gone. Where, I wonder, is the air-rifle now? You borrowed it, Miss Kane?"

"Look here—" interrupted Dr. Hastings, with an oddly strained expression. He got up from his chair and sat down again.

"Yes, I borrowed it," Marion answered. "Why? Didn't I tell you? I took it out with me when I went to swim this morning, at the other side of the cottage. I shot a few meat tins and things, and then put it down. When I came back to this side of the beach I must have forgotten it."

She stared at them, her eyes widening.

"I'm afraid it'll be ruined, in all this rain. I'm sorry. But what of it? Is it important?"

"Miss Kane," said Colonel March, "do you usually go out for a swim as early in the morning as that?"

"No. Never. Only I was horribly worried about my uncle. I couldn't sleep."

"You were fond of him?"

"Very fond of him," said Marion simply. "He had been very good to me."

Colonel March's expression seemed to darken and withdraw. It was as expressionless as his ancient cap or his ancient pipe; and he said nothing. But he closed the box of soldiers with great care, and beckoned the superintendent to one side. They had not long to wait for the result.

Late that afternoon a body was washed up on the shore two miles below Barry Island. And Marion Kane was detained for questioning at the police-station, as a prelude to formal detention on a charge of murder.

Stacey spent one of the worst nights of his life. He told himself that he must keep calm; that he must resist the impulse to telephone wildly for solicitors, invade the police station, and generally make a nuisance of himself. He realized, wryly, that he was not a strong, silent man like Dr. Hastings. In difficulties he wanted to do something about them, if only to adopt the dubious course of hitting somebody in the eye.

Things would be all right, he assured himself. Kane's own solicitor was coming from London, and the police were fair. But this very feeling that the police were fair disturbed him worst of all. After a sleepless night at the cottage he dozed off at dawn, and came downstairs at ten o'clock. Lionel Pell was coming up the verandah steps with a newspaper. It was still raining, and so dark that Dr. Hastings had lighted the oil-lamps in the living-room.

"Here's their case," said Lionel, holding up the newspaper. "Our superintendent has been talking indiscreetly. It's plastered all over the world."

"Their case? Their case against—?"

Stacey had to admit that his opinion of Lionel had changed. Lionel had no affectations now; under press of trouble he was only lanky and awkward and human.

"Well, they don't mention her name, of course. She's not officially under arrest. It's very carefully worded. But they appear to have found that air-rifle buried in the sand at the top of the beach under the bank. They found it at the exact place where Marion says she was sitting when old Norman fell, and in an almost direct line with the Lion's Paw."

Against the lamplight from one of the living-room windows appeared Dr. Hasting's head. It was only a silhouette with wiry cropped hair, but they saw his knuckles bunch on the window-sill.

"*I* don't know anything about it," Lionel urged hastily. "I was in bed and asleep when it happened. But you recall, Bill, that until you came well out on the beach yesterday morning you couldn't see Marion at all. You were in the little lane. Dr. Hastings couldn't see her either. He was on the verandah here, and this cottage is set well back behind the line of the bank.

"If Norman were shot in the back, particularly with a weapon like that, he wouldn't feel it the moment he was hit. People don't, they say. He would hear a hail from Bill Stacey, and turn round. Then he would fall forward with the weapon in his heart—"

From the window Hastings uttered a kind of growl.

"The weapon?" he said. "As a matter of academic interest, will you tell me just what an air-rifle has to do with this, anyhow?"

"Oh, come! You won't be able to dodge responsibility like that, Doctor," said Lionel, who always dodged responsibility.

"Dodge—?"

"Yes. It's your fault. You were the one who suggested that the wound was made by a point and shaft like an old-fashioned hatpin?"

"Well?"

"Those air-rifles, you know; they're pretty powerful. Hardly like a toy at all. But sometimes the lead pellets stick in the barrel and clog it. So as a rule the makers give you a very thin, light rod to clean the barrel with. If you cut off about three-quarters of the rod, and sharpen the other end to a needle-point, you would have a short missile that could be fired with very damaging force in the ordinary way."

There was a silence, except for the noise of sea and rain. Stacey walked to the end of the verandah.

"I've heard rot before," he said, as though making a measured decision. "But never in my life. . . . Do you realize that there's no air-rifle powerful enough to carry any kind of missile with enough force to kill at a distance of well over fifty yards?"

"Yes, I know," admitted Lionel. "But you see the trouble?"

"No, I don't."

"It's just plausible," said Lionel. "I don't believe it. It only worries me."

"I want my hat," said Dr. Hastings suddenly. "Where's my hat? This can't go on; I won't have it. I'm going down to the police station and tell them what really happened."

Outside the cottage there was a rustle of footsteps, stumbling footsteps in the gloom. It was so dark that they could barely see the two persons who came up the steps, but Dr. Hastings picked up a lamp inside the window and held it so that the light fell on Colonel March and Marion Kane.

Colonel March was wheezing a little, but as bland as ever. Marion's expression could not be read. There was relief in it, and disillusionment, and even peace; despite the signs of recent emotion, she was smiling.

"I should like a cigarette, please, Bill," she said. Then she took his arm. "Thank heavens," she added, "for an ordinary decent human being."

"The superintendent and I," said Colonel March, "have come to apologize. Of course, we did what we did entirely with Miss Kane's consent. We have concocted a fiction and kept on the lee side of libel. We have set a trap and heard it snap. We have given you all, I fear, a bad night. But it was the only way we could bring the corpse back to tell his own story. . . . You had better come up now, Mr. Kane."

It was a very muddy, shamefaced, and glowering corpse who walked up the steps behind Superintendent Morgan. Norman Kane, whose heart had stopped beating more than twenty-four hours ago, was now very much alive; and looked as though he wished he weren't.

Norman Kane's grey-haired dignity did not sustain him. He seemed undecided whether or not to hide behind Superintendent Morgan. For a moment he stood opening and shutting his hands. Then he caught sight of Dr. Hastings standing in the window, holding up the lamp.

"You traitor," he roared, and flung himself at the doctor.

"He was dead," insisted Stacey. "His heart had stopped; I'll swear to that. How did he manage it?"

On a clear, cool morning after the rain, Marion, Stacey,

and Colonel March stood on the beach looking at a new tide. Colonel March frowned.

"You had better hear the story," he said. "Kane was wrong in nearly everything; he was wrong in the way he flared out against Dr. Hastings. Hastings is his friend, and only tried to help him when his pig-headed piece of deception would have been discovered in two minutes.

"You will already have guessed the fact which Miss Kane feared: Norman Kane was heading for a bad financial smash. It might not necessarily mean prison, but it would mean ruin and penury. Kane did not like such embarrassments. So he planned to stage a fake death and disappear, with a good sum laid by. Other financiers have been known to do it, you know," Colonel March added dryly.

Marion shied a pebble at the water and said nothing.

"He was going to 'die' and have his body washed out to sea—never to be found," the colonel went on. "But he did not want either the stigma of suicide or the prying investigation of a murder. So, with the assistance of Dr. Hastings, he arranged to die of heart failure on the Lion's Paw. There had to be an independent witness there to swear to his death: you, Mr. Stacey. You were summoned for that purpose. Hastings had to be there to corroborate you. Then Hastings would shepherd you to the cottage, many hundred yards away, as the tide rose. Kane, a supremely powerful swimmer, could let himself into the water, swim out and round to the headland, and disappear.

"So for a long time he gabbled everywhere about his weak heart. But he would not listen to Hastings, who told him it was very risky. Miss Kane knew that his heart was not weak. Even the village doctor knew it. If Kane, therefore, suddenly dropped dead of a complaint he did not have, there would be a strong suspicion of fraud at the start. It was altogether a foolish plan. Even so it might have gone through if, on the very morning chosen for the 'death' Miss Kane had not decided to get up for an early swim.

"She was not accustomed to getting up early, as she told us. Norman Kane and Dr. Hastings thought they would have the whole beach to themselves at that hour—except for their special witness: a young man of—er—unsuspicious nature."

Stacey looked at him gloomily.

"For 'unsuspicious,'" he said, "read 'imbecile.' Very well; but I was in full command of what faculties I have, Colonel. I know when a man is dead. And I tell you his heart had stopped."

"I beg your pardon," beamed Colonel March. "His heart had not stopped. But his pulse had stopped."

"His pulse?"

"You will recall how he was lying. Flat on his face, with his right hand doubled under him, but his left hand stretched out invitingly. He was also lying wedged in a kind of trough; and you know his enormous weight. To move him and get at his heart would be difficult and awkward. You would never try to do it, with that limp hand stretched out towards you. You would automatically feel the pulse at his wrist. And there was no pulse."

"But how the dickens can you stop a pulse? It's the same as a heart."

"You stop it," said Colonel March, "by means of a small, hard, rubber ball, such as the little one supplied with the toy cannon in the box of soldiers. It is a good trick, which was exhibited before a group of doctors in London some time ago—and it worked. At the same time it is so simple that I suggest you try it for yourself. Kane, of course, got it from Dr. Hastings. The small rubber ball is placed under the armpit. The arm is pressed hard against the side; the flow of blood is cut off; and the man is 'dead.' Kane lay with his upper arm against his side, but with his lower arm from elbow to wrist extended for your inspection. That is all.

"Even so, the whole plan almost crashed, because Miss Kane appeared on the scene. You, Mr. Stacey, had found the body and announced death from heart failure. But Hastings knew that this would never do. Miss Kane strongly suspected that the weak heart was a sham.

"If the body had already been swept out to sea, if she had come on the scene only afterwards, she might have wavered. She might have been uncertain. She might have thought it was suicide, which they tried to conceal from her under a mask of heart failure. But there was the body. If something were not done quickly, she would have insisted on examining it. And it would never do for her to find a living man."

Marion nodded. She was still shaken from the after-effect of a somewhat bitter hoax, but she thrust out her chin.

"I certainly should have!" she said. "Only the doctor—"

"Diverted your attention. Exactly. He is an ingenious fellow, Hastings; and no wonder he was upset that morning. He diverted it in the only possible way, with a sudden clap of violence and murder. He drew you hastily back to the beach, so that Kane should not overhear. He shocked you out of your wits, which made it easy for him to put ideas into your mind.

"Remember you never actually *saw* any trace of a wound or a weapon. All you saw was a very minute tear in the back of the dressing-gown, where it had been skagged on a nail.

"That tear (he admits) put the idea into his mind while he was making his 'examination.' To account for such a very small puncture, and such a complete absence of blood, he had to think of some weapon corresponding to that description; so he postulated something like an old-fashioned hatpin. He could have said it was suicide, of course. But he knew that a man could neither stab himself in the back at that angle, in the presence of witnesses, nor press such a weapon so far into the flesh as to be invisible. Whereas it was just possible that a thin blade might have been projected or fired by a murderer. It was altogether too possible. Dr. Hastings had acted wildly and unwisely on the spur of the moment, to prevent the discovery of his friend's hoax. But he must have grown somewhat ill when he saw the case we spun out of a completely harmless air-rifle."

Colonel March smiled apologetically.

"It was a very weak case, of course," he said, "but we had to bring the corpse back. We had to have something— suggestive, but non-committal and non-libellous—to stare at Kane from the Welsh newspapers. It had to be done before he got away to the Continent, or we might never have caught him. The discovery of a drowned body, washed up at Barry, was very helpful; it aided the illusion with which we might snare Kane. The matter was suggested to Miss Kane, who agreed . . ."

"Agreed?" cried Marion. "Don't you see I had to know whether . . . I have looked up to him all my life. I had to know whether he would cut and run just the same if he thought I might be hanged for his murder."

"Which he did not do," said Colonel March. "Mr. Norman Kane, I think, has had a refreshing shock which will do him no harm. I should like to have seen him when he crept into town last night; when he found that he was not dead of heart failure and washed out to sea, but that his murdered body has been found and his niece was accused of having killed him. No wonder he burst out at Hastings. But what did he do? He must have realized, Miss Kane, that this charge against you would sooner or later be shown as nonsense; and yet he came back. It was a decent thing to do, as decent as the thing you did yourself. I think it likely that, if he faces his difficulties now, he will save himself as he thought he was saving you."

HOT MONEY

Just before closing-time on a Tuesday afternoon in December, a saloon car drew up before the St. James's office of the City and Provincial Bank, and four men got out. Lights were burning inside the bank, but the day was raw and murky. Two of the newcomers went to the counter, where they accosted the cashiers with pistol-muzzles cradled over their arms. The third, who wore no hat or coat, walked behind the counter; and, before anybody knew what he was doing, began quietly drawing the blinds on the windows.

The fourth, who had taken a forty-five-calibre revolver out of his overcoat pocket, spoke with great clearness.

"You know why we're here," he said. "Just keep quiet and nothing will happen to you."

One of the clerks, a youngster, laughed; and was instantly shot through the chest with a silenced gun.

The noise it made was no louder than that of slapping two cupped palms together, a kind of *thock*. The clerk tumbled sideways, rattling against a scales, and they heard his body strike the floor. Then all noise seemed to die away under the bright, hard lights, except the sound of the newcomers' footsteps on the marble floor.

"That's right," said the man who had first spoken. "Just keep quiet and nothing will happen to you."

The thing was incredible; but it was happening. Possibly every man in the bank, now staring in various twisted positions with hands in the air, had seen it happen in a film, and had smiled at it as being confined to another continent. But with great precision the man who had drawn the blinds was now clearing out the safe, transferring what he wanted to a neat leather bag. Outside bustled the traffic of St. James's; passers-by saw a closed bank, and thought nothing of it. By the third minute it had become unbearable. The manager, risking it, ducked under the counter for a gun, and was shot down. Then the leader of the gang leaned close to a young clerk named John Parrish, and said:

"Thanks, kid. You'll get your cut."

Like four well-trained ghosts, the raiders came together and melted out into the street. Their car was away from the kerb before the alarm sounded.

Now the robbery of the City and Provincial Bank failed because of one small but important fact. In England you can rob quite easily; you can even, if you do not mind risking the gallows, rob with violence; but you cannot make a getaway afterwards. 'Skipper' Morgan, late of Cicero, Illinois, might be excused for not realizing this. But Pudge Henderson, Slugger Dean, and Bill Stein, all of whom knew Dartmoor as the rest of us know our own homes, should have realized it. Possibly they expected the very daring of the raid to bring it off for them, and they changed cars three times before, early that evening, two Flying Squad cars cut them off on the road to Southampton.

Skipper Morgan wanted to shoot it out, and was brought down in a flying tackle which broke his arm. But here the police met a snag: of twenty-three thousand pounds in cash and bonds, not one penny was found on the fugitives.

Chief Inspector Ames visited Skipper Morgan that night.

"You're in bad, Skipper," he said pleasantly. "One of those fellows you shot is likely to die. Even if he pulls through, you can reckon on a good long stretch."

The other said nothing, though he looked murderous. It was Ames who had broken his arm.

"I don't say it'd help you," pursued the chief inspector, "if you told us what you did with that money. But it might, Skipper. It *might*. And you might tell us whether that young clerk at the bank, the one you said would get his cut, was in it with you."

"Dirty little rat," said the Skipper, out of pure spite and malice. "Sure he was in it. But I want to see my lawyer; that's what I want."

So they detained John Parrish. To Marjorie Dawson he wrote: "Don't you believe a word of it. Cheer up."

A solicitor for Morgan was speedily produced. This was none other than Mr. Ireton Bowlder, that aloof gentleman with the aristocratic nose and the wide clientèle. Scotland Yard regarded him with disfavour, because he never failed to put their backs up. True, there was little that even Mr. Ireton Bowlder could do for the prisoners; but he contrived to suggest, with a fishy smile and a sad shake of the head, that they would leave the court without a stain on their characters. Still the stolen money was not forthcoming.

"It's one of two things, sir," Chief Inspector Ames told the Assistant Commissioner. "They've hidden it, or they've turned it over to a fence."

"A fence for stolen money?"

"And bonds," said Ames. "Nothing easier. Of course we've got the numbers of the notes, fivers and above. But they can easily be disposed of abroad: people are buying and hoarding English money, and they don't necessarily inquire where it comes from. I know of two fences like that, and I hear there's a third operating who's the biggest in the business. Getting rid of 'hot' money used to be difficult; but it's simple now. It's more than a new kind of racket; it's a new kind of big business. The state of Europe being what it is, thousands of people are trying to get out of there and into England without their authorities knowing they've got any money at all. Hoarding English money is the best way to do it. If we could get a line on who's doing this—"

"Any suspicions?"

"Yes, sir," answered Ames promptly. "Ireton Bowlder."

The Assistant Commissioner whistled. "If it only could be!" he said, with dreamy relish. "Lord, if it only could be! But be careful, Ames; he's got a lot of influence. And what makes you think it's Bowlder, anyway?"

"It's all underground so far," Ames admitted. "But that's what the boys say. Now, we nabbed Morgan and his mob just outside a village called Crawleigh. Bowlder's got a country house only a mile from there. Bowlder was at his country house on Tuesday night, though as a rule he only goes down at week-ends. Skipper Morgan was down there twice in the week before the robbery. It doesn't prove anything. But taken with the rest of the rumours—"

"What about the boy Parrish?"

Ames grinned. "Had nothing to do with it, sir. It was Morgan's temper, that's all, or Morgan's idea of a joke. I'm convinced of it, and so is the bank. But Parrish might be useful."

Just how useful Chief Inspector Ames did not realize until the following day, when Miss Marjorie Dawson came hurrying up to town.

She was a quiet, fair-haired girl, pretty yet unobtrusive, though now strung up to fighting pitch. Her hazel eyes had a directness of gaze which was as good as a handclasp; she had, even in this difficulty, a sense of humour. She told the chief inspector things which made him swear. But, after a half-hour interview, it was not to the Assistant Commissioner that Ames took her. He took her to a door on the ground floor labelled *D-3: Colonel March.*

"Colonel March," he said, "let me introduce Miss Marjorie Dawson. Miss Dawson is engaged to be married to young Parrish. She's now employed as secretary to Ireton Bowlder's aunt—"

"Not any longer," said the girl, smiling faintly. "Sacked yesterday."

"And she says Bowlder's got the City and Provincial Bank money."

Colonel March was a large, amiable man, with a speckled face, a bland eye, and a large-bowled pipe projecting from under a cropped moustache. He rocked on his heels before the fire, and seemed puzzled.

"I am delighted to hear it," he said formally. "But why come to me? This, Miss Dawson, is the Queer Complaints Department. Business has been bad lately; and I should be very glad to tackle the problem of a blue pig or a ghost in the garden. But, if you've landed Ireton, why come to me?"

"Because it's a queer complaint, right enough," said Ames Grimly. "What Miss Dawson tells us is impossible."

"Impossible?"

Marjorie Dawson looked from one to the other of them, and drew a deep breath of relief. Colour had come back into her face.

"I hope you're being frank with me," she said. She appealed to Colonel March. "Inspector Ames tells me that you haven't really got a case against John Parrish, and don't mean to hold him—"

"No, no; you can have him whenever you want him," said Ames with impatience.

"—but I came up here after somebody's blood," the girl admitted. "You see, the local police wouldn't believe me; and yet it's true, every word of it."

"The money vanished in front of their eyes," said Ames.

"One moment," said Colonel March, with an air of refreshed interest. He pushed out chairs for them. "Disappearing money. That is better; that is distinctly better. Tell me about it."

"It was at Greenacres," said the girl, so eager to tell the

story that they had to guide her to the chair. "Greenacres is Mr. Bowlder's country house. As Mr. Ames told you, I'm Miss Bowlder's secretary; she keeps house for her nephew.

"I'm not going to tell you what I felt when I heard about the robbery. The first I knew of it was when I opened the newspaper at the breakfast-table on Wednesday, and saw John's name staring up at me—as though he'd committed a murder or something. I couldn't believe it. I knew it was a mistake of some kind. But I thought Mr. Bowlder might know—"

"Might know?" prompted Colonel March.

She hesitated, her forehead puckered. "Well, not that, exactly. I thought he might be able to help me, being a solicitor. Or at least that he would know what to do.

"It was barely half-past eight in the morning. I was the only one up in the house, except servants; Miss Bowlder doesn't get down until nine. Then I remembered that Mr. Bowlder had come down to Greenacres the afternoon before, and I could go to him straight away.

"That's how it happened. You see, when Mr. Bowlder is at Greenacres he always has nine-o'clock breakfast with his aunt: very dutiful and all that. Any letters that come for him in the morning are always put in his study—which is at the back of the house. Before he goes in to breakfast, he always goes to the study to see if there are any letters. So back I went to the study, to catch him alone before he went to breakfast. I didn't knock; I just opened the door and walked in. And I got such a shock that I thought I must be seeing things.

"The study is a large, rather bare room, with two windows looking out over a terrace. It has recently been painted, by the way, which is rather important. It was a bright, cold, quiet morning; and the sun was pouring in. There is a bust of somebody or other on the mantelpiece, and a big flat-topped desk in the centre of the room. Of course, I hadn't expected to find anybody there. But Mr. Bowlder was sitting at the table, fully dressed. And spread out in rows on the table were at least twenty packets of banknotes of all denominations. Nearly every packet was fastened with a little paper band with *City and Provincial Bank* printed on it.

"I simply stood and stared. My head was full of the City and Provincial Bank. And, anyway, it's not his own bank.

"Then Mr. Bowlder turned round and saw me. The sun was behind his head and I didn't get a good view of his face; but all of a sudden his fingers crisped up as though he were going to scratch with them. Then he got up and ran at me. I jumped aside; he slammed the door, and bolted it on the inside."

She paused.

"Go on, Miss Dawson," said Colonel March in a curious voice.

"It takes a long time to tell," she went on rather blankly, "but in a second or two I put together a whole lot of things. Skipper Morgan's gang had been arrested just outside our village; the paper said so. Morgan's picture was in the paper, and I knew I had seen him at Greenacres the week before. John had been down there to visit me, too. I suppose Morgan saw him there, and that's why Morgan made such very funny jokes about John when the bank was robbed. It was all a kind of whirl in my head; but it came together as a dead certainty.

"There is a telephone in the hall just outside Mr. Bowlder's study. I sat down and rang up the local police."

Here she looked at them with some defiance.

"What I was afraid of was that Mr. Bowlder would come out of the room and take the money away and hide it somewhere before the police arrived. I didn't see how I could stop him if he did. But he didn't even come out of the study. That worried me horribly, because the room was as quiet as a grave and I wondered what he might be up to. I like people to *do* something.

"Then I thought: 'Suppose he got out of a window?' But I remembered something about that. As I told you, the woodwork of that room had been painted only a few days before. It wasn't the best of painting jobs; and as a result both windows were so stuck that it was impossible to open them. Annie had been complaining about it the day before; they were to have been seen to that very day. So, when the police arrived—I could hardly believe my good luck—Mr. Bowlder was still in that room with the money.

"It was an inspector and a sergeant of the local police. They were on hot bricks, because Mr. Bowlder is an important man; but the Morgan gang had been caught near there and they weren't taking any chances. While I was trying to explain, Mr. Bowlder opened the door of the study. He was as pleasant and sad-faced as ever.

"He said: 'Money? What money?'

"I explained all over again, and I'm afraid I got a bit incoherent about it. But I told them the money was still in the study, because Mr. Bowlder hadn't left it.

"He said—and don't I remember it!—'Gentlemen, this young lady is suffering from optical illusions. At nine o'clock in the morning this is a pity. I am aware that you have no search-warrant, Inspector, but you are at liberty to make as thorough a search of this room as you like. How much money was there, Miss Dawson?'

"I said thousands and thousands of pounds: it sounded wrong even as I said it. Mr. Bowlder laughed.

"He said: 'Thousands and thousands of pounds, eh? Gentlemen, if you can find any money in this room—apart from a few shillings on my person—I will donate it all to police charities. But there is no money here.'

"And there wasn't. Enough money to fill a suitcase; and yet it wasn't there."

Colonel March frowned. "You mean the police didn't find it?"

"I mean it wasn't there to be found. It had just vanished."

"That's as true as gospel," declared Chief Inspector Ames with vehemence. "I rang them up half an hour ago and talked to Inspector Daniels. Search? They had the whole place to pieces! Bowlder sat and smoked cigarettes and egged them on. They even got an architect in to make certain there were no secret cavities anywhere in the room."

"And?"

"There weren't any. There wasn't a hiding-place for so much as a pound note, let alone a sackful of the stuff. The point is, what's to be done? I don't think Miss Dawson is lying; but all that money couldn't vanish into thin air. How could it?"

Colonel March was pleased. He relighted his pipe; he rocked on his heels before the fire; then, becoming conscious of the impropriety, he coughed and tried to conceal the fact that he was pleased.

"I beg your pardon," he said. "But this is the best thing I have encountered since the Chevalier C. Auguste Dupin (you recall?) went after the purloined letter. Ahem. Now let us see. We establish that there are no secret panels, cavities, or other flummery. Windows?"

"Just as Miss Dawson said. The windows were so stuck that two men couldn't move 'em. Nothing could have been taken out of the room like that."

"Fireplace?"

"Bricked up. They don't use it, because the room is centrally heated. Bricks solidly cemented and untouched. No possible hiding-place in or round the fireplace."

"Furniture?"

Ames consulted his notebook. "One flat-topped table, one small table, two easy-chairs, one straight chair, one bookcase, one lamp-standard, one standing ash tray. You can take it for granted that not one of those got away without the closest examination; and nothing was hidden in any of them. Anything to add to that, Miss Dawson?"

Marjorie shook her head.

"No. And it wasn't in the carpet or the curtains, or behind the picture, or in the leaves of the books, or even in the bust I mentioned; not that you could put all that money there, anyway. It just wasn't there." She clenched her hands. "But you do believe me, don't you?"

"Miss Dawson," said Ames slowly, "I don't know. You're certain Bowlder didn't leave the study at any time before the police arrived?"

"Positive."

"He couldn't have slipped out?"

"No. I was in front of the door all the time. It's true, Inspector. What reason would I have for lying to you? It's only got me the sack, and it hasn't helped John. I've thought and thought about it. I thought of the trick, too, of hiding a thing by leaving it in plain sight, where nobody notices it. But you certainly couldn't leave the City and Provincial Bank money in plain sight without anybody noticing it."

"Well, it beats me," admitted the chief inspector. "But then that's why we're here. It's impossible! Daniels swears there wasn't an inch of that room they didn't go over with a fine-tooth comb. And yet I believe you, because I've got a feeling Bowlder has been too smart for us somehow. Any ideas, Colonel?"

Colonel March sniffed at his pipe.

"I was just wondering," he muttered; and then a doubtful grin broke over his face. "I am still wondering. Look here,

Miss Dawson; you are sure there was *no* article of furniture
in that room you haven't described to us?"

"If you mean things like ashtrays or desk-ornaments—"

"No, no; I mean quite a large article of furniture."

"I'm certain there wasn't. There couldn't very well be a
large article of furniture that nobody would see."

"I wonder," said Colonel March. "Is Mr. Bowlder still at
Greenacres? Excellent! I very much want to speak to him;
and I want to see his study."

Under a sky heavy with threatening snow, the police left
Scotland Yard early in the afternoon. It contained Chief
Inspector Ames and the plain-clothes man who was driving
in the front seat, with Marjorie Dawson and Colonel March
in the rear seat. To the girl's protests that she wished to
remain in London with Parrish, Colonel March was deaf; he
said there was time enough. At four o'clock they drove into
the grounds of an ugly but highly substantial and highly
respectable country house in Victorian Gothic.

Colonel March stood up as the car stopped in the drive.

"Where," he asked, "are the windows of the study?"

"At the back," said Marjorie. "You take the path round to
the left—"

"Let's take it," said Colonel March.

Dusk was coming on, but no lights showed at Greenacres.
They circled the house under the blast of an east wind, Colonel March stumping ahead with his coat-collar turned up
and an old tweed cap pulled low on his forehead. Climbing
some flagged steps to a terrace, they looked into the nearer
of the study windows; and came face to face with Mr. Ireton
Bowlder looking out at them.

One of Bowlder's hands flattened out against the glass
with white fingers. The other hand, which was wrapped in

a handkerchief, he thrust into his pocket. In the twilight he looked nervous and a trifle greenish of countenance.

"Good afternoon," said Colonel March politely. The wind whipped the words away; and Bowlder inside the glass was as silent as a fish in an aquarium, though his lips moved. Then Bowlder raised the window.

"I said good afternoon," repeated Colonel March. Before Bowlder could move back he had reached out and shaken hands with him through the window. "You know most of us, I think."

"Yes," said Bowlder, looking at Marjorie. "What do you want?"

Colonel March leaned against the ledge of the window.

"I thought you would like to know," he said, "that the manager of the City and Provincial Bank was a little better this morning. That will probably make the charge against five persons something a little less than murder.

"Indeed. The fifth is young Parrish, I suppose?"

"No," said Colonel March. "The fifth is probably your-self."

Again the wind whipped round the corner of the house, ruffling Bowlder's neat hair. But Bowlder himself was not ruffled. He regarded them with a pale and sceptical smile: then he began to close the window.

"Better not," the colonel advised. "We're coming in."

"You have a warrant?"

"Oh, yes. That window is now in working order, I see. Robinson," he looked at the plain-clothes man, "will climb through and stay with you while we go round by the front door."

By the time they reached the study, Bowlder had turned on a standard-lamp by the table, upon which it threw a bright light, though most of the room was left in shadow. The room was exactly as Marjorie Dawson had described.

"Now, then," said Bowlder quietly, "will you explain what you mean by this nonsense about a charge?"

"If," said Colonel March, "the City and Provincial Bank money is found here, you're likely to be charged with Skipper Morgan. That is what I meant."

"Gentlemen—and Miss Dawson—listen to me. How many times have I got to submit to this? You don't really mean you want to make still another search?"

"Yes."

"Look round you," said Bowlder. "Take a long, careful look. Can you think of any place that could have been overlooked the first time?"

Chief Inspector Ames had to admit to himself that he couldn't. But Colonel March, instead of searching for a secret in the room, lowered himself into an easy-chair by the table. Removing his cap and turning down the collar of his coat, he faced them with a kind of sleepy affability.

"In order to show you what I mean," he went on, "I must point out one of the curiously blind spots in the human mind. Has it ever occurred to you, Ames, that there's one piece of furniture in a room that nobody ever notices?"

"No, sir, it hasn't," said Ames. "You mean it's hidden?"

"On the contrary, I mean that it may be right there in front of everyone's eyes. But few people will ever see it."

"Are you trying to tell me," asked the chief inspector, "that there's such a thing as an invisible piece of furniture?"

"A mentally invisible piece of furniture," returned Colonel March. "Would you like proof of it? You have one, my boy, in the sitting-room of your own flat. I imagine there's one in the bedroom as well. It is under your eyes all the time. But suppose I said to you: 'Give me a list of every piece of furniture in your flat.' You would then give a list of things down to the smallest lampshade or ashtray; but I am willing to bet you would omit this whacking great object—"

Chief Inspector Ames looked round rather wildly. But his eye fell on Mr. Ireton Bowlder, and he checked himself. Bowlder, who had been lighting a cigarette, dropped the match on the floor. Under the bright light of the lamp his forehead shone with sweat; and he was not smiling.

Ames stared at him.

"Whether or not I understand you," he said, "by Jupiter, that fellow does!"

"Yes. I thought he would," agreed Colonel March, and got to his feet. "That's where he has hidden the money, you see."

"Oh, what on earth are you talking about?" cried Marjorie Dawson. She could keep herself in hand no longer, and she almost screamed. "What could be invisible? What is there we can't see? What part of the room is it in? What's the size of it? What's the colour of it, even?"

"As for size," replied the Colonel, "it may vary a good deal, but in this case it is about three feet high, two and a half feet long, and three or four inches deep. In colour it is sometimes painted a bright gilt; but in this case the object is painted a modest brown."

"*What?*"

"I mean, said Colonel March, "a steam-radiator. Particularly a dummy radiator like that one in the corner over there."

Ireton Bowlder made a run for the door, but he was tripped and brought down by P.C. Robinson. They were compelled to use hand-cuffs when they took him away.

"The possibilities of a dummy radiator, used for concealing something inside," said Colonel March, when they were on their way home, "deserve the attention of our best crooks. It is very nearly a perfect hiding-place. It is compact. It will hold a great deal of swag. And is is the one thing we never seem to notice, even if we happen to be looking at it.

"Nobody, you see, regards it as a piece of furniture at all; certainly not as a piece of furniture in which anything could possibly be concealed. Inspector Daniels never looked twice at the radiator in Bowlder's study, and it is difficult to blame him. The radiator gave out heat, like an honest radiator; it was of iron; it seemed solid; it was clamped to the floor.

"You can buy one of them easily enough. They are really disguised oil-stoves; portable, with several concealed burners, one under each coil. I have never forgotten the shock I received, sitting comfortably by a steaming radiator in the house of a friend of mine, when it suddenly occurred to me that the house was not centrally heated. Bowlder's radiator, as you saw, was a more elaborate affair, but one that could be constructed without difficulty. Two of the coils contained no burners, were invisibly hinged at the back, and formed a hollow receptacle as large as he could wish. The house was centrally heated, so that a mere radiator aroused no suspicion whatever. It was, in short, a private safe without lock or combination, but so commonplace as to defy suspicion. I have been waiting for somebody to try the trick; and lo, somebody did."

Marjorie Dawson looked at him inquiringly.

"You mean you expected to find one of those things when we went down to Greenacres? she asked.

"I am the Department of Queer Complaints," said Colonel March with apology, "and I was on the look-out for it as soon as central heating was reported in that room. I wasn't sure, of course, until we talked to Bowlder through the study window. The banknotes would get rather warm, you can understand, from being in a compartment next to the oil burner. They wouldn't scorch, any more than our clothes scorch when we put them to dry on top of an ordinary radiator, but they would be tolerably warm; and so would the fastenings when Bowlder opened his safe. That was why he had to wrap a handkerchief round his right hand. And it was Chief Inspector Ames, with unerring intuition, who hit on the real clue long before it ever came to me."

"I did?" demanded Ames.

"Yes," said Colonel March. "You told me, with an accuracy beyond your wildest knowledge, that the money was hot."

DEATH IN THE DRESSING-ROOM

The lights were dimming when Jim Matthews entered the Orient Club. The hot, smoky room swallowed him up as though he were padded into layers of cotton-wool. Following the head waiter, he groped among the tables in a darkness faintly lightened by the white of table-covers, of shirt-fronts, of women's shoulders.

Then the drums began.

They drowned the stir and mutter which never deserts a night club, as though the echo of all the voices in the world were imprisoned there. The drums began with a kind of tom-tom beat, growing deeper and more rapid. A blue spot-light appeared from the other side of the room. It touched the polished dance-floor, it touched the edge of the orchestra from which the drums were now thundering. It allowed Jim Matthews to see that the head waiter was bowing him to a table. True enough, the table was in a very good position on the edge of the dance-floor. But it was occupied.

A girl in a white fur wrap looked round, startled, as they appeared. She was sitting alone at a table for two. The blue spot-light allowed Jim to make out only that she had brown hair and wide-spaced eyes and that by her clothes she was clearly not one of the girls of the house. On the table stood an unopened bottle of champagne, with a placard reading "Reserved."

Not a word was audible under the noise of the drums. To the girl Jim Matthews tried to convey apology; to the head waiter he indicated the 'reserved' placard. That dignitary lifted his shoulders in a broad and hideous shrug, and in pantomime indicated that all the other tables were full. Jim, though he hated making himself conspicuous, argued back in pantomime. The head waiter leaned close.

"Miss Rapport—she *dance*," he hissed.

He stabbed his finger urgently towards a curtained doorway, through which the star of the show was due to appear. He almost pushed Jim down into the chair, and then he disappeared.

What exasperated Jim Matthews was that the head waiter had paid absolutely no attention to what the girl at the table might think about it. He had not even looked at her. The matter wasn't of any importance, maybe; but Jim was already beginning to dislike the manners of the Orient Club. He glanced across at the girl in the white fur wrap.

"Sorry," he shouted.

He thought that she smiled and shook her head. Then they both looked back at the floor again, for Francine Rapport was beginning her Javanese temple dance.

Jingling faintly, a figure in a high, weird head-dress moved into the blue spotlight. "Francine Rapport," though born in Holland and brought up in New York, was purely Oriental in her good looks. Her face was almost unrecognizable in a mask of paint, with lines drawn upwards from the outer corners of the eyes and accentuating them, a stolid mask. She was small, her skin amber in colour; the body well-rounded, but of a muscled litheness. Her costume, of large metal ornaments, glimmered under a light coating of oil. Her hands moved up that costume, grew taut above her head, descended with the palms outspread, and the dance began.

Jim Matthews reminded himself that he was not here to watch Francine Rapport. Yet he probably knew more about her than most of the patrons did. She must be into her forties, after a knockabout career with Tony Caplin; but she did not look it. Jim wondered where Caplin was to-night. He half got up from his chair—and saw Caplin, proprietor of the Orient Club, standing by the orchestra platform on the edge of the spotlight.

This was the moment when the girl in the white fur wrap slipped away from the table.

Well, it was no business of his. He watched her moving away into the darkness between the tables, in the direction of the orchestra platform. He sat down again. The tom-tom beat of the drums had quickened; the string music crept more insistently; and it came to Jim Matthews, as clearly as though he had heard an alarm bell, that something was going to happen.

Francine Rapport was afraid. He had no idea of what she was afraid, though anything was possible at the Orient Club. But it showed even in the rhythm of the dance, in the turn of her fingers or eyes, as though the fine body were really that of a priestess threatened by the temple god. So perhaps it was as well that she finished the dance a second too soon; and, a second too soon, the lights of the Orient Club flashed on.

They showed Jim Matthews that the girl in the white fur wrap was on her way back to his table. She had been moving quietly. But she started a little, caught out by the lights only a few feet away. She was just opening her handbag to slip something inside. She slipped it inside, and the handbag closed with a click, but not before Jim had seen what it was. It was a man's leather pocket-wallet.

Under the roar of applause that went up for Francine Rapport, Jim looked into the other girl's eyes. She was stooping slightly forward, as though to hide both the wallet and her own handbag. Her face was flushed dull red. On the dance-floor, Francine Rapport was bowing to the applause; then Francine turned and ran for the curtained doorway to the dressing-room. Chairs were pushed back. The orchestra, with a preliminary throat-clearing from the saxophone, burst into a lively dance number. And the girl in the white fur wrap, imitating the movement or thrown into a panic by it, lost her head and ran. With a muttered exclamation Jim Matthews got to his feet and followed her. After all, it was what he was there for, wasn't it?

Couples were taking the floor, looking unreal in the thick, smoky haze. The poured out to such an extent that Jim was caught as though in a football rush. From a microphone issued Tony Caplin's rich, hollow voice. "The boys are playing for you—" Jim dodged through, keeping his eye on the white fur wrap. It disappeared through the curtained doorway to the dressing-rooms. He reached the doorway only thirty seconds later; but the girl had gone.

Beyond was a passage in which he saw several doors, all closed. It was badly lighted, dingy, and full of the scent of stale powder. He met nobody. The whole house seemed to shake to a measured stamping over the music; but it might have come from another street. Then a door at the end of the passage opened; the girl in white came out and closed the door softly. She breathed as though she had been running; she adjusted her wrap before she turned round.

And Jim Matthews stepped in front of her.

"Excuse me," he said.

"Yes?"

She spoke coldly, with sudden calmness. Tony Caplin, Jim thought, knew how to choose his employees. This girl was a limb of the Orient Club, probably as skillful in the crafts of blackmail as Francine herself; but she could have passed anywhere. Both her features and her voice had that fine-drawnness which is supposed to indicate breeding; her brown eyes and the arch of the eyebrows showed cold wonder as she looked back at him.

"Would you mind telling me," Jim continued, "what

you were doing with that wallet you put in your handbag a minute ago?"

"Wallet? Really? What wallet?"

"Oh, stow it," said Jim. The way he spoke was caused by mingled anger and disappointment. "I'm a police officer, miss."

This startled her, no less than the stolid tone he had deliberately adopted. He saw in her face incredulity, doubt, fear, and growing underneath them, a certain amusement.

"Really? I see. You're one of those people who have a terribly good time and then arrest the management for selling drinks after hours."

"I have nothing to do with that." He tried not to speak hotly. "I only ask you, would you mind explaining what you were doing with that wallet?"

"So I suppose I shall have to tell you. I picked it up off the floor. Oh, yes, that's quite true. Not being able to appreciate the charms of Miss Francine Rapport, which evidently stagger you men so, I went out to the bar during her dance. On the way I picked up the wallet. Naturally, when the lights went on I wanted to find the proper owner."

"Then why didn't you?"

"What on earth do you think I'm doing here? Miss Rapport, I understand"—she spoke with a degree of quiet hatred—"is part-owner here. I am sorry if the proper procedure is to stand up on a table and shout that you have found a wallet. *I* thought of taking it to Miss Rapport."

"And did you give it to her?"

For the first time the girl's eyes shifted.

"No. She—she isn't here. Evidently she didn't come back here right after her dance. Perhaps you'd be good enough to let me pass so that I could take the wallet to Mr. Caplin? Come with me, if you like. By all means."

Someone was humming dreamily. Along the passage strutted a good-looking maidservant in cap and apron. She was a blonde, but her looks were of such an order that Jim suspected a touch of negro blood. Carrying a dressing-gown over her arm, she gave them a pleasantly impudent look as she wormed past to open the door.

The girl in white made an attempt to get away. Jim saw the intention in her eyes; he closed his fingers round her wrist. Just at that moment the door was opened and, after the fraction of a second, the maid screamed.

"I didn't do it," the girl in white cried. "I swear I didn't do it!"

Even from the doorway they could see it. In an untidy dressing-room of pseudo-Oriental garishness, Francine Rapport sat at a dressing-table before a mirror ringed with lights. She lay forward across the table, her elaborate head-dress awry. Her back was bare except for the fastenings of a broad metal breastplate, which winked and glimmered under a film of oil. The bangles had slid down from her arms like coiled snakes. And she was not a pleasant sight, for she had been stabbed through the back with a pair of long and narrow-bladed scissors.

Still gripping the wrist of the girl in white, Jim went in. Murder! A murder case for the first time in his short police experience. He felt a slight physical queasiness. The woman had died very recently; and, despite the clumsiness of the weapon, from a direct heart-wound. There were no signs of disorder on the dressing-table except that a sandalwood box was open and a fragment of paper was pressed in the dead woman's fingers.

Faintly along the passage from the dance-floor, hollow

and soothing out of a microphone, drifted Tony Caplin's rich voice: "A selection of o-old, old favourites, beginning with the immortal 'Bye-bye, Blackbird.' Let her go-oh, boys."

Jim turned to the maid.

"Who are you?"

"Me? I'm Paula." In an extremity of terror she pressed her hands to the sides of her head and wagged it, an old gesture of her ancestry.

"Her maid?"

"Eh?"

"Miss Rapport's maid?"

"Yes, *sir*. Who wants to know?" She glared at him.

Jim told her. "Were you here when she came back from her dance a few minutes ago?"

"I wasn't! I wasn't, and I can prove I wasn't! She gave me a message to take to Mr. Caplin, to come and see her when she'd finished her dance, and that's what I went and told him. And—"

"Steady. Do you know which is table number sixteen out there? Right, then. At table sixteen you'll find a big, heavy-set man; sandy moustache, short hair, speckled kind of face. His name is Colonel March. Ask him if he can come in here, but don't mention this to anyone else. Got that?"

When the maid was gone, Jim bent closer to the dressing-table. It was easy to make out a few words written on the fragment of paper in Francine Rapport's hand: "*like this. Ever your adoring—Tommy.*" The smooth, clean fingers, with their nails dyed purple, held to this as though they held someone even in death.

Jim Matthews did not touch anything. This was not the concern of Department D–3. He and Colonel March were at the Orient Club in search of a super-pickpocket, and they had evidently found her; but someone has to take charge when a pickpocket tells lies within ten feet of a murdered woman. He led the girl in white to a chair.

"Let me have your name and address, please."

"I'm sorry. I can't tell you that."

Jim shut up his notebook. "That's your privilege," he said. "I also want you to understand that you're not bound to answer any questions I may ask you. But if you'd only realize—"

"I don't mind answering your questions," said the girl, and the tears started into her eyes. "It can't be much worse for me than it is, can it?"

"Then why didn't you tell me you knew she was dead?"

"Do you think I'm insane? You'd only have thought exactly what you did think. But I didn't kill her. I came in here, and found her dead, and came out again. That's all I know. All I wanted to do was get away. I don't expect you to believe that. I probably shouldn't believe it myself if I were in your place; but it's the truth."

She sat back in the chair with an expression of cool despair.

"Then what about that wallet?"

"It's Tony Caplin's wallet. You might as well know that now."

"You stole it?"

"No. Don't worry. I'm not going to assume a pose of injured innocence, or jump up and fly into a tantrum: as she used to do." Her eyes moved towards Francine. "But I really didn't steal it. He dropped it. He dropped it, I tell you!"

"Have you still got the wallet? You'd better let me have it, then."

An expression of cynicism came into her face, a kind of pleasure as though in some ironical secret. If he had not seen her other expression when she was off guard, he could have believed her. Without a word she opened her handbag, took out the wallet, and handed it to him. It was of plain black leather, without name or initials, but its contents were damning enough. This was no ordinary wallet: it contained, neatly folded, a thousand pounds in fifty-pound notes.

They were startled by an exclamation from the doorway. Tony Caplin was staring with a sickly look at the woman sprawled across the dressing-table.

Even those who knew Caplin's crookedness or his innate viciousness were compelled to admit his charm. He went through the world with the manner and the voice of a perpetual radio-announcer. Not bad air or drinks or late hours seemed to impair his alertness. His wiry dark hair, his pleasant light eyes and close-shaven jaw, made him look like an advertisement in a chemist's window. But all this was gone now.

He said: "Who are you?" And then, in a higher key: "My God, what is it?"

"Steady, sir! Don't touch anything!"

Caplin had hurried to Francine. He touched her shoulder, and then he began to beat his fist into his palm with a kind of frenzy.

"She's dead," he said.

"Yes. We—"

"They got her," said Caplin. "She was all I had. Who did it? Tell me who did it and I'll kill him! I mean that." He whirled around towards the girl in white. "Who's that? Who are you?"

All this time Jim Matthews felt that the girl was studying Caplin. He could not interpret her expression. But she appealed to Matthews.

"At least"—she spoke with quiet urgency—"you can

clear up one thing. I mean, about that wallet. Mr. Caplin can clear it up: it's his wallet. I saw him drop it. And he can tell you who I am, too; he can vouch for me."

Jim held it out.

"Is this your wallet, sir?"

"To hell with the wallet," snarled Caplin. Then he blinked, and his bewilderment grew. "What wallet? Where? What are you talking about?"

"Does this belong to you?"

"Certainly not."

"And I suppose you'll say, too," insisted the girl in a soft, steady voice, "that you don't know me either?"

Caplin spoke with a sort of desperate courtesy. "Madam, I don't know what you're talking about. I do know that Francine's dead. I loved Francine. I come in here and find her like this, with a pair of scissors—" He stopped, his face working as though he were going to weep. "—and all you people can do is babble about a wallet, wallet, wallet. No, I don't know who you are. I never saw you before in my life. Did you kill her?"

"Did *you?* asked the girl.

The other had got a grip on himself.

"I've done a lot of things in my life," he answered grimly. "To judge by the number of police in the place to-night, they think I've done a lot more. But there's one thing I didn't do. I didn't kill Francine. I never left that orchestra platform from the time she was dancing until one minute ago."

That was true. Jim admitted it to himself; and so, by the look on her face, did the girl.

"Fifty people will testify to that. For once in my life," muttered Caplin, a savage and surprised look coming into his eyes, "for once in my life I'm in the clear when dirty work's been done. And *this* kind of dirty work. This kind!"

"Quite so," agreed a new voice. "This kind."

It belonged to Colonel March. The seventeen stone of Colonel March filled the doorway. His thumbs were hooked in the pockets of his white waistcoat; he was as bland as ever, but his eye looked wicked.

"Hello, copper," observed Tony Caplin—yet without offence.

"Good evening," said Colonel March.

"Come to run us all in?"

"No," said Colonel March seriously. "I've telephoned the divisional station about this. They will take charge. I really came to break up your newest and, I think, most ingenious racket."

"I don't understand that," said Caplin sharply.

Colonel March studied him. Behind that huge façade there was a kind of admiration.

"My good Anthony," he said, "confound you for a genius! You don't use guns. You don't use knock-out drops. You don't even need a chucker-out. Your weapon is psychology." His grin became broad and sinister. "Wherever the Orient Club opens up, as it does fairly frequently, you have some new and foolproof device for separating the gullible from their money. Paris and New York testify to that. Here you are more subtle; you've got a real jewel. It took me several days with a wet towel round my head to decide what it was."

"Oh?"

"Yes. Pocket-picking in Futurist style. Pocket-picking in which the guest doesn't even know he's been robbed."

As though casually, Colonel March went over and stared down at the body of Francine Rapport. He did not seem concerned with it. He went on speaking without looking at Caplin or the girl.

"Not ordinary pocket-picking," he assured them. "That's much too dangerous. All guests at night clubs have a drink; some have a tolerable number of drinks; still others (I think dom remembers exactly how much money he has got in his wallet. When he totals it up at the end of the evening, and finds three pounds or a fiver less than he expected, he simply assumes that he must have spent it himself. Just as we all do. Certainly he never thinks of his wallet being lifted; lifted and deftly returned, minus as much as the Orient Club thought he could spare without noticing it. The method is harmless and very nearly undetectable. But the takings at the end of the week must be enormous. Mr. Caplin, I congratulate you."

There was a pause. Jim Matthews could not read Caplin's face.

"He's gone off his head," Caplin said critically. "I don't think you can prove what you're saying."

Colonel March turned round from the dressing-table.

"I'm afraid not," he agreed. "Just when we were trying to prove it, this young lady butted in."

"So," said the girl in white, "you think I'm a pickpocket?"

"No," Colonel March said. "I think I know who you are now, though I don't blame Matthews for being taken in. Your name is probably Joan Forsythe. You live in Kensington, at an address I can't for the moment remember, and you have a brother named Thomas in the Diplomatic Service. I can also guess what you were doing with that wallet."

The girl sprang to her feet.

"You did not take it from anybody," he told her dryly. "On the contrary, you were trying to give it to somebody. To Mr. Caplin, in fact. Would you mind telling me, Matthews, exactly what happened here?"

His face was sardonic as Matthews explained. He took the wallet and held it up before the girl.

"Ah, yes. I see. This contains the blackmail money that Caplin and Rapport wanted from your brother for his affair with Miss Rapport. Gad, what a reminiscent note! You were

Caplin, in fact. Would you mind telling me, Matthews, exactly what happened here?"

His face was sardonic as Matthews explained. He took the wallet and held it up before the girl.

"Ah, yes. I see. This contains the blackmail money that Caplin and Rapport wanted from your brother for his affair with Miss Rapport. Gad, what a reminiscent note! You were instructed to hand the money to Caplin in public, in the presence of witnesses, in a wallet, and with the covering words: 'This is your wallet, isn't it?' You went to give it to him by the orchestra-platform; but at the last minute you lost your nerve and tried to fling it at Miss Rapport instead.

"That's another of their games," Colonel March added sadly. "The one they tried in Paris."

All Caplin's bounce and energy had come back to him. His eyes were still a little hysterical, like those of an actor who has played an exhausting part. But he did not seem to take offence; he only shook his head sceptically.

"You're going too fast, my friend," he suggested. "You could get into trouble, you know, talking like that. *I* don't know what you're talking about. But then you're telling me, aren't you?"

"Is he?" said the girl through her teeth.

For a second or two she did not seem to know whether to feel relief, or anger, or an even worse despair. But it was a slipping of the glazed determination, which showed a very human being underneath; human, and a little petulant.

"You've seen Tommy," she flared out at Colonel March.

"Not exactly, Miss Forsythe. He came to us last week; and then lost his nerve and refused to set a trap. There was nothing else we could do about it."

"Well, what else could I do? I had to get back those letters Tommy wrote her. It wouldn't have mattered twopence, don't you see, if Tommy hadn't been in the Diplomatic Service? But he's got a wonderful opportunity; he'll be sent to Paris or Rome if nothing happens. He won't help himself, and I—well, I—"

"Look here," muttered Jim Matthews. "I seem to have made an ass of myself again. Sorry, sir."

"Why should you be sorry?" asked Joan Forsythe. "You may not have caught a pickpocket. But how do you know you haven't caught a murderess? Look here. Look in her hand. Look at that piece of paper, signed by her adoring Tommy. That's torn off one of my brother's letters; and our wonderful Mr. Caplin knows it as well as I do."

"I don't know what Francine has been up to," said Caplin: "About letters, that is. If she wanted to sell some letters, that was her business. But if there were letters, where are they now?"

Colonel March took the question with great seriousness. Again he bent over to peer at the letter, unfolding the fingers so that he could look at the smooth, soft palm of the hand as well. The hand and arm seemed to interest him as much as the fragment of paper.

"Well, Miss Forsythe?" he asked over his shoulder. "Did you get the letters?"

"No, no, no! I've told you before—I told you," she appealed to Jim, "that she was dead when I got here. I was only here half a minute, anyway. I haven't got any letters; you can search me if you like. *He* had the letters. He probably still has them."

"I never had any letters," said Caplin.

Joan Forsythe pulled herself together. She studied Caplin in a curious way; and she spoke in a new, detached, wondering tone.

"You know," she said, "you really are a nasty bit of work."

"That may be," agreed Caplin frankly. "We're none of us

perfect, not even you. But you see, Miss So-and-So, you're in a jam. A bad jam. You ought to understand that, for your own good. And, honestly, you oughtn't to be so free with your accusations. Now, I'm not in a jam at all. I didn't kill that poor kid; I couldn't have killed her. The coppers themselves will tell you I never left that orchestra-platform at any time."

The girl appealed to Colonel March. "Is that true?"

"It is quite true, Miss Forsythe."

"You see?" said Caplin.

"No, I don't see," answered Joan Forsythe, in the same puzzled voice. She made a gesture. "What I can't get over is a kind of cheap meanness about the whole thing. It doesn't seem big or terrible or even tragic. It only seems grimy and mean. My brother isn't any persecuted figure who's guilty of a lot of high crimes. But just because he can't afford scandal, and goes out and makes a fool of himself over that woman, they're all ready and waiting to make money out of it. They're so used to helping themselves at other people's expense that they don't even see anything very strange in it. They only say to you, in a surprised kind of way, 'Well, of course you'll have to pay now for what we know, so pay up and let's have no more nonsense.'"

She drew a deep breath.

"Maybe they're right. I don't know. All I know is that it cost Tommy and me nearly everything we've got to scrape that money together. There must be lots of poor fools like us. I don't know whether you believe what this man tells you; but you seem to. Whatever you mean to do to me, there'll be a dreadful scandal at the end of it; and poor Tommy in the middle. The clever ones of this world have it all their own way, haven't they?"

"I think not, Miss Forsythe," said Colonel March.

And they all looked at him.

The abrupt stillness in the Orient Club, a sort of clang of stillness, reached farther than this dressing-room. The music of the orchestra, after wobbling, had stopped in the middle of the bar. The mutter of voices from the dance-floor, after rising abruptly, had died away; and Jim Matthews knew why. The crowd had seen police uniforms at the front door.

But Colonel March, his arms folded, did not seem to notice.

"You," he said sharply, turning his head towards the door. "Paula, I think your name is. The maid. Come in here, please."

Paula obeyed. She entered like a cat: not straight, but moving round the corner of the jamb. Though she did not seem nervous, there was defiance in her full-rounded eyes.

"Paula," Colonel March repeated. "Paula, Paula. Haven't I see you somewhere before?"

The reply was fired back quickly.

"Maybe happen you have. I was at the Tin-Hat Club two, three years. And at the Odalisque for six months."

"I have never been at the Tin-Hat Club. No: haven't I seen you more recently than that?"

Paula shrugged her shoulders.

"Well, we'll omit that," said Colonel March in a curious voice. "How many dressing-rooms are there here, can you tell me?"

"Two besides this, sir."

"Any other cabaret turns besides Miss Rapport's?"

"No."

"And the girls—I mean, the dance-hostesses: did they change in these rooms?"

Caplin was about to intervene; but Paula, keeping her eyes full and hypnotic, got in before him. "No. Other side. Miss Rapport wouldn't let them."

"When did you last see Miss Rapport alive?"

Paula snatched at this. "I passed her when she came off the floor, that's what. She gave me a message for Mr. Caplin."

"So you have an alibi, too. Just one other thing," observed Colonel March, with sudden politeness. "We came here to look for a very good pickpocket. So we may as well be thorough. Let me have a look at your hands, will you?"

"My hands?"

"Both hands."

She hesitated, flashing a look at Caplin; but she stretched them out.

"If," said Caplin, "you're saying Polly had anything to do with killing Francine, you're wrong. Fifty witnesses can prove it. She was out on the dance-floor the whole time. And if you're saying she's a pickpocket, you must be completely off your nut." Then he shouted: "What do you think you'll find on her hand, anyway? Beeswax?"

"No," said Colonel March. "Only oil. And you're quite right: she was out on the dance-floor the whole time."

Paula jerked away her hand as though she had burnt it. But Colonel March still had her gently by the other arm; and he did not let go.

"We've noticed several things about Francine Rapport," he went on. "She performed her Javanese dance in a blue spotlight, and with her face done into such a grotesque mask of paint that nobody could recognize it. But note the colour of her skin; and compare it with Paula's. Note her height and build; and compare them with Paula's. Yes, Paula was on the dance-floor, impersonating Francine in the temple dance, while Francine lay dead in this room. And, if you don't want to be accused of the murder yourself, young lady"—he swung a screaming Paula round to face him—"you had better admit that your friend Caplin stabbed Rapport with the scissors just before she was due to come out for her dance."

Tony Caplin tried to wrench her away from Colonel

March, and shake sense into her. But she was a bad accomplice. She had convicted both of them before the Divisional Detective-Inspector reached the room.

"The trick," Colonel March said to Joan Forsythe and Matthews afterwards, "was simple enough; and very easy to perform without a hitch. Our ingenious Mr. Caplin, who thought he deserved all the good things of life, was fed up with Francine. She was a nuisance. She was a nagger. She was ageing. She wanted too much money. So the partner had to be eliminated.

"It was easy to train Paula in the routine of the dance, as he had trained Francine. It was easy to manage the substitution: there were no other cabaret turns at the Orient Club, and nobody else came near those dressing-rooms. Paula could be seen, of course, only in her make-up, the headdress hiding her hair, and in that dim disguising blue spotlight. She could not be seen close at hand. When Francine had just finished changing into costume a few minutes before the dance, Caplin stabbed her while Paula was getting into a duplicate costume in an adjoining (empty) dressing-room.

"Paula came out, locked the door of Francine's room so that no one should discover the body too soon, took the key with her, and went out to dance. Afterwards she returned, unlocked the door, got into her ordinary clothes in the empty dressing-room, and was ready to appear in a very few minutes. All this time, of course, Caplin was preparing an impregnable alibi. That was the purpose of the whole scheme; and it entailed an alibi for Paula as well. Caplin was ready to swear to her presence near him should anyone question her.

"They did not particularly care who found the body. But I am certain they never intended *you* to find it, Miss Forsythe. On the contrary, Caplin must have been rather sick when you did not approach and hand him his thousand pounds. Afterwards, with the police there, he could hardly claim it when by an unfortunate mischance suspicion was plumped down on you. He never intended that scrap of paper to be found in the victim's fist. He asked for the letters from Francine, stabbed her as she was taking them out of that sandalwood box, and unfortunately tore them from her hand too quickly. So he had to attack you in order to protect himself."

Colonel March looked away musingly.

"Since we found the letters on Caplin, they won't be any trouble to your brother in the future. But I give you my word you were never in any great danger. It was plain from the first that there had been a substitution of identities—"

"From the first?" demanded Joan Forsythe. "But how?"

"That's what I should like to know, sir," agreed Jim Matthews, with a certain gloom. He looked at the girl, who laughed.

"They forgot the oil," said Colonel March. "You may have noticed the coating of oil put on all those large metal ornaments to give them the blurred, mysterious gleam in imitation of the real temple dance. The dance consisted of a series of evolutions with the dancer's hands and arms pressed flat against her body or brushing against it. We saw that. The palms of Francine's hands, and her arms, should have had a film of oil from brushing against the ornaments. They hadn't: we saw that too. Still, it was clear before then. Francine Rapport had been doing that dance for a long time. She could not have forgotten the quality called tempo. She finished her dance too soon, with the orchestra going wild. I did not know who the dancer was. But I hardly thought it could be Francine Rapport."

THE EMPTY FLAT

There it was, the confounded radio going again.

Chase put down his pen. For some minutes he had had a vague idea that there was a disturbance going on somewhere, and suddenly it broke into his thoughts with intolerable loudness from the flat below. A Study of the Royal Exchequer and its Custodians from 1660 to 1688 may not be a popular subject on which to be writing a thesis, but it requires concentration. Douglas Chase, Ph.D., F.R. Hist. S., poked his head out of a maze of books like a dazed turtle.

The simile is not altogether deserved. Douglas Chase was neither turtle nor worm, but an eminently serious-minded young man who had a job of work to do. This thesis—if he won the prize—meant a great deal to him. It meant a full professorship at an American university, and a salary amounting to nearly two thousand pounds a year. To an English scholar such a salary seemed incredible, and Chase wondered hazily what he would do with it if he got it; but there it was.

"I think your chances are very good," a colleague had told him that afternoon. "All the same, I wish we knew a bit more about K. G. Mills."

For the only serious competition seemed to come from a man named K. G. Mills. Chase had never met K. G. Mills, about whom, in fact, there was some element of mystery. But his attainments looked formidable; and among Chase's friends the very name of Mills had become a huge and legendary symbol of villainy. Now that concentration was most necessary to beat Mills, the tenant of the flat below had decided to let his radio run mad.

First of all Chase cursed the construction of modern flats. His own was a modest two-room affair on the first floor of a new block near Primrose Hill: a hive of raw red brick and white paint. Tenants had filled it like flies, for the rents were modest and Chase found modern conveniences very suitable to one who chronically forgot to light fires or put shillings in an electric meter. But the thinness of the walls was remarkable. Through those walls you could hear clocks strike and the pointed comments of your neighbour's wife when her husband came home late. And now it was radios, at an hour approaching midnight.

A fair-minded man, Chase tried to shut his ears against the noise. But the tenant of the ground-floor flat seemed to have a partiality for the shrillest dance bands that home or continental stations could provide, switched on at full volume. When at length he had read the same page three times without understanding a word, he decided that something would have to be done.

He got up, ran his hands through his hair with a vague idea of tidying himself, and started for the door. He was out in the corridor when the chilliness of the air reminded him that he had forgotten his coat. So he pulled on a sweater, and padded downstairs in his slippers.

Except for that radio, the whole building seemed unusually quiet. As a rule it was a shell of echoes, throwing back each gritty-sounding footstep or hum of the lift. He met nobody. Going down concrete stairs, where a faint mist had got into the bleakly lighted corridors, he turned into the passage which led to flat 10, directly below his own. And the passage was in darkness.

Trouble with the lights again, he supposed. He struck a match and groped his way down the passage. Flats 10 and 11, set side by side, occupied the end of the wing; and the music on the radio had now become a loud, confused mumble. Wondering who occupied number 10, he held the flame of the match up to the visiting-card stuck in its slot on the green-painted door. Then Douglas Chase struck another match in a hurry, and stared.

The card read: *K. G. Mills.*

Chase studied it incredulously. The thing was a coincidence, no doubt. It was impossible that this should be the legendary K. G. Mills. But it gave him a start to meet the name both on duty and off, and he almost turned away from the door. But the radio decided him. He rang the bell.

"Yes, yes, yes!" called a female voice—and he was conscious of a sudden suspicion. "Just a moment, please!"

The door was dragged open. In the little green-painted entrance hall he faced a woman who could not be more than twenty-three or twenty-four, a woman with a flurried manner and ink-stained fingers. The fact that her hair was drawn back into a bun did not lessen the attractiveness of a white complexion, a full-lipped but prim-looking mouth, and a pair of extraordinarily merry blue eyes. But they were not merry now. Irresolutely she drew the back of her hand across her forehead, leaving ink-smudges there.

"Yes, yes, yes?" she inquired.

"Oh, Lord," muttered Chase. He added, on a last hope, "May I speak to Mr. Mills?"

The girl's manner changed.

"I am Mr. Mills," she said with cold dignity. "That is, I mean," she frowned and drew herself up, "to speak with academic accuracy, my name is Kathleen Gerrard Mills and I am the only Mills present at the moment. Oh, you know what I mean; but I have some terribly important research work to do, and I have been driven to such annoyance by an insufferable radio in the flat above me, that I am hardly able to say what I mean."

Chase could hardly believe his ears.

"Madam," he said, "*I* am the tenant of the flat above. And

I do not own a radio. In fact, I came down here to protest about yours."

Kathleen Mills's eyes, rather bemused with study, now woke up.

"But I don't own one either," she said.

She was wearing, he noticed, a grey skirt and a tight-fitting grey jumper which outlined a small, sturdy figure. She folded her arms gravely, frowned, and assumed the argumentative posture known to all dons. In one so young and attractive it might have provoked amusement if she had not been so desperately in earnest.

"This is extraordinary," she declared. "That detestable cacophony is obviously coming from somewhere. Assuming the truth of your statement, Mr.—er—"

"Chase," he said half-guiltily. "Dr. Chase. That is, University College, you know."

"Oh, my *hat!*" said the girl, shocked into naturalness.

They stood and stared at each other. Then Kathleen Mills, her colour higher, spoke with great dignity.

"How do you do?" she said formally. "While I am very pleased to make your acquaintance, Dr. Chase, I am afraid that in fairness I must take this opportunity of saying to you that I believe your views on Episcopacy in Scotland to be the merest rubbish. Indeed, as I pointed out in the *Quarterly Survey*, you hardly even appear to have heard of Nottingham's Comprehension Bill." She added half annoyed, "And where is your beard? I thought you would have a beard."

"I must disagree with you," said Chase. "I do not refer to the beard, but to the earlier part of your remarks. And if you would do the honour of joining me in a coffee—or beer," he added doubtfully. "You drink beer?"

"Of course I drink beer," said the girl. "And I should love

to. But I was thinking about this intolerable noise. As I say, it must come from somewhere."

It did. They heard it all about them, more muffled but very insistent. In the quiet of the big building at past midnight it had an effect that verged on the eerie. And behind Kathleen Mills's manner Chase sensed some other emotion, something far from being at ease. His eyes wandered to the dark door of number 11 beside them.

"What about the flat next door?"

"I had thought of that," she admitted, rather too quickly. "My first idea was that it came from there. But that—well, it's an empty flat: the only empty flat in the building. And it seems unlikely that anybody would be operating a radio in an empty flat."

A stir of uncertainty touched Chase: the vision of a radio playing in a dark and empty flat was what he would have called an irrational one. The girl went on speaking.

"Superstition attaching to mere dead walls and plaster is foolish. We're rational beings, Dr. Chase; at least, I hope we are. Suppose a deed of violence is done in a certain house. Well! The house is torn down to make room for another— say a block of flats. Even suppose you do believe in emanations or influences, as I do not. Is there any reason why those influences should be present in a certain one flat on the ground floor, and not in any of the flats above? It is absurd."

"Look here," Chase asked quietly. "What are you talking about?"

"Well—that flat next door. It appears that dozens of people have looked at it, and all of them have refused to take it. I'm sure I can't imagine why. There is nothing wrong with it. It's just the same as twenty others: Mr. Hemphill, the letting-agent, swears it is. But an absurd rumour has gone round that something horrible moves into it at night, and doesn't leave until morning. I told my trustee. That's Arnot

Wilson, the barrister, you know; he's looked after things for me since my father died; and he was very much interested. He ridiculously tried to make jokes and frighten me about it. But after all, I do sleep on the other side of the wall."

Though she smiled, the whites of her eyes had acquired an odd kind of luminousness, and she spoke with a greater rapidity. Beside the door in the angle of the wall was the tiny door of the service-hatch—dumb-waiter—to flat 11. Chase pulled it open. The inner door of the box-like hatch was also open. And now there could be no doubt.

"Yes, the radio is in there," he said. "Hear it?"

"And—and what is to be done about it?"

"Why, I'll crawl through the service-hatch and shut it off," Chase said simply.

Being long and lean, he could just manage to worm through. It was not a dignified business, stuck there with legs in the air, but he did not concern himself with that. Before he dived through the service-hatch he had accidentally touched Kathleen Mills's hand; and the hand was cold.

The entrance hall of flat 11 was dark. It smelt of mist and raw paint, and it even felt unused. He was coming closer to the core of noise, the enigmatic wireless mumbling in the dark. It appeared to be in the living-room ahead. This was an ordinary flat like his own, though he wondered what had happened to the ground where he stood. The gritty floor creaked more than it should; and the farther he moved away from the door the more he felt like a man paying out a guide-line in a cave, uncertain of his footing.

A grey window moved out at him, then a glass-panelled door. He opened the door of the living-room, meeting the noise full-blast.

An edge of a street-lamp touched two misted windows. Down in the corner by the fireplace he saw a dim shape and a tiny glowing light. For such a volume of noise it was quite a small radio, one of those convenient affairs which can be carried about by hand. It was connected to a base-plug in the wall. He switched it off; and silence descended like an extinguisher-cap.

Afterwards there was nothing. No person, no movement, no sound beyond the creak of the floor when his heel pressed it—until a fierce ringing at the outer doorbell made him jump. Until then Douglas Chase did not realize how much the hide was off his nerves, or how deep into the nerves a sudden noise could strike. He hurried to the door, turned a knob of the spring-lock, and met Kathleen.

"You seemed to be gone for a long time," she told him. "Well?"

"I've turned it off," he said. "There is a radio in there, and nobody to play it or listen to it. There doesn't seem any rhyme or reason why it should be there. But there's nobody here now."

He was wrong.

It was perhaps just as well that they did not know it then. In the dim light of seven o'clock next morning, workmen constructing a boundary wall round the building passed the windows of flat number 11 on the ground floor. Through the living-room windows they saw nothing to interest them. But through the bedroom windows they saw a man huddled back into a corner as though he were trying to push himself through the wall. In appearance he was a short, stout, well-fed man, wearing an overcoat and a bowler hat. But he was dead; and they did not care to get too close to the expression on his face. James R. Hemphill, letting-agent of the flats, identified him as Mr. Arnot Wilson, barrister, of 56 Harrow Avenue, N.W.3, and the doctor in attendance said that he had died of cardiac and nervous shock caused by fright.

Two days later, when the doctor's verdict was confirmed at

a post-mortem by the Home Office Analyst, certain persons gathered in a room at New Scotland Yard.

The death of Mr. Arnot Wilson had caused a minor stir. In strictly limited circles Arnot Wilson was famous: as a "character," a persuasive lawyer, a rich after-dinner speaker, almost a public entertainer. His gentle wit had a scratch rather than a sting. He liked to collect walking-sticks and matchboxes once used by royalty. It could be said that he bounced through life. His round, guileless face; his spats and cravats; his brushed coat and glossy head; all this made a kind of india-rubber dandyism which carried him everywhere.

He lived alone, except for a cook and a man-servant, in a tall Victorian house in Harrow Avenue—not far from the block of flats where he was found dead. This house he kept too warm, with electric heaters blazing all day even in passages and in bathrooms; and almost too clean, for he was relentless to servants. Which made it all the more curious that he should be found dead of fright in an empty flat.

His body was found on Saturday morning. On Monday, Kathleen Mills and Douglas Chase were summoned to Scotland Yard. In a firelit room overlooking the Embankment they were met by a large, bland man with a speckled face, an amiable eye, and a cropped moustache. He introduced himself as Colonel March.

Colonel March's courtesy was as huge as himself.

"This," he said, "must be the dozenth time you have been troubled. But, as you understand, I must do it because my department is new to the case. I hope it does not upset you too much, Miss Mills?"

Kathleen bridled, as she always did at any hint of feminine weakness.

"I am not upset at all," she told him. "Mr. Wilson was one of my trustees. He managed the money my father left, what little there was of it. But I scarcely knew him. And—"

"You didn't like him?"

"I don't know," she replied, with an obvious struggle for honesty. "I've never been sure. All I know is that from the time I first knew him he never left off being facetious at my expense."

Suddenly she coloured, sensing an atmosphere, and broke out with violence:

"Oh, I'm being a prig and a fool! And you know it, don't you? But that's true. It was nothing but jokes, jokes, jokes; jokes about me, careers for women, our little scholar who has no boy-friends, never a pause, never a let-down in jokes. He was so tireless in it that sometimes he hardly seemed human."

Colonel March nodded gravely. Chase had not hitherto heard her speak with such frankness.

"Anyhow," she went on with a slight gesture, "there are some questions we—Dr. Chase and I—must get answered. Your people have questioned us for two days, and yet still we don't know anything. Chief Inspector—what's his name?— Chief Inspector Ames was too evasive. Will you answer four straight questions?"

"If I can," said Colonel March.

"Thank you. Well, here they are. What time did Mr. Wilson die? Did he really die of fright? Why was that radio playing? And what on earth was he doing there anyway? I happen to know he was horribly frightened of the dark."

Colonel March sat down behind a broad desk, lowering his seventeen stone with some difficulty. He looked at the desk, at the windows, at the fire, at Inspector Roberts, his second-in-command. Then he seemed to come to a decision.

"To your first two questions," he answered, clearing his throat, "I can reply. Mr. Wilson died about eleven o'clock on Friday. And it seems that he did die of fright."

Chase could not understand the brief look of uncertainty, almost of terror, on Kathleen's face. But she spoke.

"So he was actually in the bedroom, dead, when Dr. Chase and I were in that flat?"

"He was."

"And is it—well, is it medically correct to speak of death from fright?"

"It is," said Colonel March with abrupt vehemence. "You've hit it, Miss Mills. That is why it has been given over to me, to what we call here the Department of Queer Complaints. There never was a complaint queerer than this, for there are almost no precedents in law. Let's make a supposition. Let's suppose that this is murder."

It was a new and unpleasant word. Chase stirred, but Colonel March's eyes remained bland.

"I only say, let's suppose it. Suppose I find a way to frighten someone so that his heart and nervous-system are shattered as though by a blow from a gigantic hammer: that, in nontechnical language, is what the medical report means. I do not kill an invalid or a man with a weak heart, mind you. I choose a victim whose heart and nerves are sound, like Mr. Wilson. I do not touch him. But I expose to him, as though on a photographic plate, a mere sight so terrifying that his system cracks, and he dies."

Colonel March paused.

"Well, theoretically," he went on, "I am guilty of murder. That is the law. But could you get a jury to convict? I doubt it. I should say it would be impossible even to get a manslaughter verdict. Find a way to kill someone by fright, and you can commit murder almost with impunity."

Chase did not like this, because of its effect on Kathleen.

"As an interesting theory," he interposed, "it's all very well. But is there any suggestion of murder?"

"What's our alternative?" inquired Colonel March,

spreading out his hands. "That the empty flat is haunted? That we are beset by ghouls and hobgoblins? That a man dare not sleep at night for literal fear of his reason or his life? I can't believe it, my friend. The only other possibility—" He stopped, breathing rather heavily. Then he went on in his normal tone. "Miss Mills, Dr. Chase, it's only fair that you should hear the evidence. Inspector, will you ask Mr. Hemphill to come in?"

They waited. James Hemphill, the letting-agent, was not slow at coming in. He was a young, affable, harassed man who seemed to regard the affair less as a death than as a further bedevilment among all the complaints. Carefully dressed, with white hands and a black line of eyebrows, he sat down gingerly in the chair Colonel March indicated.

Colonel March seemed puzzled. "Mr. Hemphill, I should like to take you over certain points in the statement you've already given to the police. Now tell me. You knew that Mr. Arnot Wilson meant to spend several hours in flat number 11 on Friday night?"

(Chase felt rather than saw Kathleen sit up.)

"Yes, I did," said Hemphill, after clearing his throat several times like a nervous orator.

"In fact, you supplied him with the key he used to get in?"

"Yes, I did."

"And you saw to it that the light in the passage was extinguished so that he would not be seen when he did go in?"

"Yes, I did."

"Why did he want to spend some hours in that flat?"

Hemphill's bristly eyebrows seemed to stand out like antennae. "Oh, it was this crazy story about number 11 being—you know, something wrong with it. He was interested. He said he's always wanted to see a ghost."

"Had he any other reason, Mr. Hemphill?"

"Well," repeated Hemphill, after a swift, brief look at

Kathleen, "he seemed to have some idea that Miss Mills was—you know, leading a double life. He thought it was very funny; he went on and on about it. He said if he listened for a few hours in the next flat on Friday night, he could catch her red-handed with her—you know, her boy-friend." Hemphill's face seemed to swell with apology. "Look here, Miss Mills, I'm dashed sorry, and it was a rotten trick; but I didn't see any actual harm in it. That's why he didn't tell you he was there."

The very face and presence of the dead man seemed to peer into the room. Arnot Wilson had often said that he was "just interested" in things.

"Oh, no. No actual harm," said Kathleen through her teeth. "It's so absolutely characteristic of him that I'm not at all surprised."

"Then there it is," explained Hemphill, with white-faced relief. "He took that radio along with him. You see, those flat-walls aren't very thick. He was afraid someone in one of the other flats might hear him walking about, and might call the police. His idea was that the noise of the radio would cover him. It's very difficult to locate the direction of sound, as you probably know; and he thought that when the other tenants heard the radio they would never connect it with an empty flat."

"He was right," observed Douglas Chase. "And if for once I might violate the rule of *de mortuis*, I might add that he was a damned old he-gossip who deserved what he got."

"One moment," interrupted Colonel March, whose eyes never left the letting-agent. "Admitting that he brought the radio, can you explain why he put it on with such shattering loudness that it might have roused the whole building instead of concealing his movements?"

"No, I can't explain it."

"When did you last see him alive, Mr. Hemphill?"

"About eight o'clock on Friday night. He came round and fitted up the radio in the living-room. He got rather grubby doing it, and I asked him whether he would like to wash. He said no, he would go home and wash; then he would have some sandwiches and port there, and come back about eleven. Then he left at about eight-thirty."

Colonel March walked his fingers along the edge of the desk. He seemed even more heavily disturbed.

"Eight o'clock. Yes. It was dark then; and I think there are no lights in the flat?"

"No, there aren't any lights. But I had an electric torch."

"How did Mr. Wilson relish the prospect of a vigil in the flat alone?"

After a sort of internal struggle, as though he did not know whether to grin or stammer, Hemphill blurted it out.

"I think he was as scared as blazes, if you want the truth. He tried to hide it; it was all ha-ha, my lad, and pigeon-breasted walk; but he didn't like it one little bit. I *told* him there was nothing wrong with that flat! There isn't." Then the agent's grievances came pouring out. "My company says to me, 'Why did you let him do it?' I did it to show there was nothing wrong with that flat. Who's the loser by all this? I'll tell you: I am. I shall lose my job, just notice that. But I maintain I did my duty."

"And a man died. Thank you, Mr. Hemphill; that will be all for the moment. But don't go. There is just one more witness," Colonel March added to the others, "whom you ought to hear. Inspector, will you bring in Mr. Delafield, Maurice Delafield? Delafield has been Mr. Wilson's manservant for fifteen years."

Delafield looked it, Chase decided. He was a lean, powerful, large-knuckled man whose bodily vigour contrasted with a kind of shabbiness and tiredness in his face. His greyish hair was carefully brushed and parted. A stoop took away some of his height; and, more from a late physical illness than from fear, the large-knuckled hands had a tendency to twitch and shake.

Colonel March spoke to him almost gently.

"You were with Mr. Wilson a long time, I understand?"

"Yes, sir."

"You liked him?"

"Yes, sir," said Delafield. His voice had acquired a sort of thunderous hoarseness; for one bad moment Chase was afraid he would break down and weep. But he stared steadily back at Colonel March.

"Now, we have just heard from Mr. Hemphill that Mr. Wilson left him at about eight-thirty on Friday night, with the intention of going home. Did he go home?"

"Yes, sir."

"What did he do there?"

"You see, sir, he hadn't had any dinner, he was so excited about this ghost-hunting—if you see what I mean. He had a plate of sandwiches and three glasses of port. Then he had got himself mucked up in the dirt at the empty flat, so he said he would have a bath and change his clothes. He was always very particular about that. He"—the pinkish tinge had come back to Delafield's eyelids; his voice was hoarse again—"he had his bath. Then he read the evening papers, all jumpy-like, and about ten-thirty he told me to fetch round the car. He drove away alone."

"Tell me: you laid out the clothes he wore that night?"

"Yes, sir. I laid it out."

Selecting a paper from a pile on his desk, the colonel handed it across.

"Here we are. Here's a list of all the things found in Mr. Wilson's pockets when the body was discovered: or in the flat itself, for that matter. 'Address-book. Fountain-pen. Key-ring, six keys. Separate key to flat number 11. Watch and chain. Notecase with eight pounds in notes. Ten and nine-pence in silver and coppers.' Will you check this over care-fully and tell me whether it is everything he took with him?"

Though Delafield tried hard, his dry fingers rustled and shook on the paper. It slipped through his fingers, and he gave it a curious despairing look, like an angler who has lost a fish.

He said desperately:

"I'm very sorry, sir. I'm not scared. Honestly, I'm not. But I haven't been well. Mr. Wilson wouldn't even let me shave him recently; he would say, over and over, over and over, 'You will be cutting my throat one of these days; and then they will hang you, because I have remembered you in my will.'"

Delafield sat down again, after picking up the paper, hold-ing it in two hands, and putting it on Colonel March's desk. He continued to talk in the same vein until Kathleen cut him short gently.

"Does anybody doubt, please," she said, "the sort of man my esteemed Mr. Arnot Wilson really was? Or, as Dr. Chase says, whether he deserved what he got?"

"That's not true, miss! It's not!"

"True or not, it is hardly our point," interrupted Colonel March, in a tone he very seldom used. They all looked at him; his sandy eyebrows were drawn down, and his eyes were as fixed as though he were trying to draw the witness under hypnosis. "I have asked you a question, Mr. Delafield. Is that list correct?"

"Yes, sir."

"You're positive he took nothing else?"

"Positive, sir."

"I see. Then I am glad to inform you," observed Colonel March, "that this is not a supernatural crime nor a supernat-ural death."

There was a change in the atmosphere as palpable as a chilling or darkening of the room. Colonel March alone seemed unaffected by it. On the contrary, the blood had come back into his face and he was tuned up to a ferocious geniality. For the first time he picked up a fat-bowled pipe from his desk.

"It was murder," he went on, rapping the pipe on the edge of an ashtray. "The victim did not die of fright. He died from a cause commoner and better known. I said a while ago that there was another possibility. It remains to be seen whether I can prove this. We discarded the other possibility after the post-mortem, because circumstances seemed to rule it out. And yet there is just one other way in which a man can be killed with no other symptoms, external or internal, than that terrific hammer-blow to the heart and nervous system."

Hemphill spoke in a high voice. "If there aren't any symptoms, I don't see how you can prove it, though I hope to heaven you can. But how would you kill a man like that?"

"By passing a current of electricity through his bath-water," said Colonel March. He turned to Delafield. "Would you care to tell us how you killed him, or shall I?"

Inspector Roberts rose to his feet at the other side of the room, but it was not necessary. Delafield sat with his large-knuckled hands pressed together, nodding. Otherwise he did not move: but it was as though the shabbiness of his face increased.

"I'll tell you," he said simply. "If only you'll honest-to-God believe it was an accident."

"One moment," urged Colonel March. He hesitated; and his forehead was clouded. "I want you to understand that you are not obliged to answer—"

"Oh, that's all right," said Delafield, making an off-handed gesture. "I want these gentlemen and this lady to bear me out. I didn't mean to tell you unless you guessed it. But *I* didn't mean him any harm."

With the same air of toiling lucidity he unclasped his hands and held them up.

"These did it," he explained. "Maybe you know, sir, how warm Mr. Wilson liked to have the house? And how he had portable electric fires going everywhere all day, even in the passages and in the bathrooms?"

"Yes," said Colonel March quietly.

Delafield nodded. "I dropped one of the electric heaters into the bath," he said. "That's all. That's how bad and simple it all was. Mr. Wilson told me I might do it. Over and over he kept telling me how I might do it, not meaning to. It was a kind of a nightmare with me, thinking I might do it with these hands; and then he joggled my arm—

"You see, sir, Mr. Wilson read in the paper long ago how several people had got killed like that. At Bristol, I think it was. Accidents. It was a cold day, and they had propped them fires up on ledges by the bath. You wouldn't think people would be foolish enough to do that, but that's what they did. Mr. Wilson didn't do that, of course. But he liked lots of heat, and he liked to have the fire standing close to the bath.

"He was frightened of things like that. Over and over he said to me, 'Don't you do that to me, or they'll hang you for murder.' Like the shaving, you see, sir. It got so I couldn't look at an electric fire in the bathroom without being nervous. And he read up on the symptoms of being electrocuted like that, in a book called *Taylor's Medical Jurisprudence*, I think it was; him being a lawyer and all; and he was surprised at what the symptoms were.

"I expect I was off-guard on Friday night, with him talking so much about ghosts. He got into the bath. Then without thinking he called to me to move the heater closer to the bath. I picked it up in my hand, not thinking either. All of a sudden he shouted out to me, and said, 'Put it down, you damned doddering old fool!' and made a grab for my hand."

Again Delafield examined his hands. It was very quiet in the room. Kathleen rose and put a hand on his shoulder.

"It fell," he added.

"Afterwards I was afraid they would hang me, just like Mr. Wilson said, if they knew how it happened. I thought if I could pretend it happened some other way they wouldn't find out. It said in the book that the symptoms for this kind of electrocution were the same as the symptoms of death from fright; and poor Mr. Wilson had always been frightened of ghosts and the dark.

"So I moved him. First I dressed him: which wasn't hard, because that's what I've been doing for years. I carried him downstairs. That wasn't hard either, because I'm a pretty hefty specimen, as you can see; and he wasn't what you could call big. The car was at the door. I wasn't much afraid of being seen moving him, because the night was so misty.

"I had his key to the flat, and I knew what he was going to do. I knew the light would be out in the hall leading to the flat; and the service-door was near that. I put him down in the bedroom of the flat about eleven o'clock. Then I turned on the wireless and left. I put it on loud and strong so that somebody *should* find him soon; I didn't want him lying there all that time alone.

"That's all. Maybe he was difficult, but I've served him for fifteen years, and you sort of get used to people. He didn't die hard; just kind of a cry, and he fell back. All the same, I can't forget it, so I've been wanting to tell you. I suppose they'll hang me, but I swear I didn't mean any harm."

Kathleen tightened her grip on his shoulder. Chase, drawn by currents of sympathy as strong as electric currents, faced Colonel March.

"Sir," Chase said, "they surely won't—"

Colonel March shook his head. He studied Delafield with a long, thoughtful look.

"If he is telling the truth," said the head of Department D–3, "they assuredly won't. I question whether anything will be done to him at all. And somehow I suspect he is telling the truth. I shall turn in my report to that effect."

Kathleen blinked a little, and the more so when Chase's fingers closed round her hand.

"May I—er—apologize for what I was thinking of you?" she said to Colonel March. "Perhaps Arnot Wilson was right after all; perhaps I do think I know too much. But will you kindly, kindly enlighten a scientific curiosity on just one point? How on earth did you know what had happened?"

"Oh, that?" grunted Colonel March, blinking and suddenly chuckling at the vehemence with which she assailed him. "That wasn't difficult. The Queer Complaints Department had much more trouble with a doorbell-ringer at Hammersmith. It certainly wasn't difficult once you had grasped the crucial fact that Wilson had not died in the flat: he had been conveyed there after death.

"It seemed almost certain he had not walked there in life, because he had failed to take something he would never have gone there without. We did not find it either in his pockets or anywhere else in the flat. Everybody commented on Arnot Wilson's morbid fear of the dark. I could believe he might screw up enough courage to go there, particularly since he had the added incentive of spying on you. But I could not believe he would face the prospect of several hours alone in a supposedly haunted flat without taking along either an electric torch, a candle, or even a box of matches."

THE SILVER CURTAIN

The croupier's wrist moved with such fluent ease as to seem boneless. Over the green baize its snaky activity never hesitated, never wavered, never was still. His rake, like an enormous butter-pat, attracted the cards, flicked them up, juggled them, and slid them in a steady stream through the slot of the table.

No voice was raised in the Casino at La Bandelette. There was much casualness; hardly any laughter. The tall red curtains and the padded red floors closed in a sort of idle concentration at a dozen tables. And out of it, at table number six, the croupier's monotone droned on.

"*Six mille. Banco? Six mille. Banco? Banco?*"

"*Banco,*" said the young Englishman across the table. The cards, white and grey, slipped smoothly from the shoe. And the young man lost again.

The croupier hadn't time to notice much. The people round him, moving in hundreds through the season, were hardly human beings at all. There was a calculating machine inside his head; he heard its clicks, he watched the run of its numbers, and it was all he had time for. Yet so acutely were his senses developed that he could tell almost within a hundred francs how much money the players at his table still retained. The young man opposite was nearly broke.

(Best to be careful. This perhaps means trouble.)

Casually the croupier glanced round his table. There were five players, all English, as was to be expected. There was the fair-haired girl with the elderly man, obviously her father, who had a bald head and looked ill; he breathed behind his hand. There was the very heavy, military-looking man whom someone had addressed as Colonel March. There was the fat, sleek, swarthy young man with the twisty eyebrows (dubious English?), whose complacency had grown with his run of luck and whose wallet stuffed with *mille* notes lay at his elbow. Finally, there was the young man who lost so much.

The young man got up from his chair.

He had no poker face. The atmosphere about him was so desperately embarrassed that the fair-haired girl spoke.

"Leaving, Mr. Winton?" she asked.

"Er—yes," said Mr. Winton. He seemed grateful for that little help thrown into his disquiet. He seized at it; he smiled back at her. "No luck yet. Time to get a drink and offer up prayers for the next session."

(Look here, thought Jerry Winton, why stand here explaining? It's not serious. You'll get out of it, even if it does mean a nasty bit of trouble. They all know you're broke. Stop standing here laughing like a gawk, and get away from the table. He looked into the eyes of the fair-haired girl, and wished he hadn't been such an ass.)

"Get a drink," he repeated.

He strode away from the table with (imagined) laughter following him. The sleek young man had lifted a moon-face and merely looked at him in a way that roused Jerry Winton's wrath.

Curse La Bandelette and baccarat and everything else.

"There," reflected the croupier, "is a young man who will have trouble with his hotel. *Banco? Six mille. Banco?*"

In the bar, which adjoined the casino-rooms, Jerry Winton crawled up on one of the high stools, called for an Armagnac, and pushed his last hundred-franc note across the counter. His head was full of a row of figures written in the spidery style of France. His hotel-bill for a week would come to—what? Four, five, six thousand francs? It would be presented to-morrow, and all he had was his return ticket to London by plane.

In the big mirror behind the bar a new image emerged

from the crowd. It was that of the fat, sleek, oily-faced young man who had cleaned up such a packet at the table, and who was even now fingering his wallet lovingly before he put it away. He climbed up on a stool beside Jerry. He called for mineral water: how shrewd and finicky-crafty these expert gamblers were! He relighted the stump of a cigar in one corner of his mouth.

Then he spoke.

"Broke?" he inquired off-handedly.

Jerry Winton glared at his reflection in the mirror.

"I don't see," Jerry said, with a slow and murderous choosing of words, "that that's anybody's business except mine."

"Oh, that's all right," said the stranger, in the same unpleasantly off-handed tone. He took several puffs at his cigar; he drank a little mineral water. He added: "I expect it's pretty serious, though? Eh?"

"If the matter," said Jerry, turning round, "is of so much interest to you: no, it's not serious. I have plenty of money back home. The trouble is that this is Friday night, and I can't get in touch with the bank until Monday." Though this was quite true, he saw the other's fishy expression grow broader. "It's a damned nuisance, because they don't know me at the hotel. But a nuisance is all it is. If you think I'm liable to go out in the garden and shoot myself, stop thinking it."

The other smiled sadly and fishily, and shook his head.

"You don't say? I can't believe that, now can I?"

"I don't care what you believe."

"You should care," said his companion, unruffled. As Jerry slid down from the stool, he reached out and tapped Jerry on the arm. "Don't be in such a rush. You say you're a boy Croesus. All right: you're a boy Croesus. *I* won't argue with you. But tell me: how's your nerve?"

"My what?"

"Your nerve. Your courage," explained his companion, with something like a sneer.

Jerry Winton looked back at the bland, self-assured face poised above the mineral water. His companion's feet were entangled with the legs of the bar-stool; his short upper lip was lifted with acute self-confidence; and a blank eye jeered down.

"I thought I'd ask," he pursued. "My name is Davos, Ferdie Davos. Everybody knows me." He swept his hand towards the crowd. "How'd you like to make ten thousand francs?"

"I'd like it a whole lot. But I don't know whether I'd like to make it out of any business of yours."

Davos was unruffled. "It's no good trying to be on your dignity with me. It don't impress me and it won't help you. I still ask: how would you like to make ten thousand francs? That would more than cover what you owe or are likely to owe, wouldn't it? I thought so. Do you or don't you want to make ten thousand francs?

"Yes, I do," Jerry snarled back.

"All right. See a doctor."

"*What?*"

"See a doctor," Davos repeated coolly. "A nerve tonic is what you want: pills. No, I'm not wise-cracking." He looked at the clock, whose hands stood at five minutes to eleven. "Go to this address—listen carefully while I tell you—and there'll be ten thousand in it for you. Go to this address in about an hour. No sooner, no later. Do your job properly, and there may be even more than ten thousand in it for you. Number two, Square St. Jean, Avenue des Phares, in about an hour. We'll see how your nerve is then."

La Bandelette, "the fillet," that strip of silver beach along the channel, is full of flat-roofed and queerly painted houses which give it the look of a town in a Walt Disney film. But the town itself is of secondary consideration. The English colony, which is of a frantic fashionableness, lies among great trees behind. Close to the Casino de la Forêt are three great hotels, gay with awning and piling sham Gothic turrets into the sky. The air is aromatic; open carriages clop and jingle along broad avenues; and the art of extracting money from guests has become so perfected that we find our hands going to our pockets even in sleep.

This sleep is taken by day. By night, when La Bandelette is sealed up except for the Casino, the beam of the great island lighthouse sweeps the streets. It dazzles and then dies, once every twenty seconds. And, as Jerry Winton strode under the trees towards the Avenue of the Lighthouses, its beam was beginning to be blurred by rain.

Square St. Jean, Avenue des Phares. Where? And why?

If Davos had approached him in any other way, Jerry admitted to himself, he would have paid no attention to it. But he was annoyed and curious. Besides, unless there were a trick in it, he could use ten thousand francs. There was probably a trick in it. But who cared?

It was the rain that made him hesitate. He heard it patter in the trees, and deepen to a heavy rustling, as he saw the signboard pointing to the Avenue des Phares. He was without hat or coat. But by this time he meant to see the thing through.

Ahead of him was a street of fashionable villas, lighted by mere sparks of gas. An infernally dark street. Something queer, and more than queer, about this. Total strangers didn't ask you how strong your nerves were, and then offer you ten thousand francs on top of it, for any purpose that would pass the customs. Which was all the more reason why . . .

Then he saw Davos.

Davos did not see him. Davos was ahead of him, walking

fast and with little short steps along the dim street. The white beam of the lighthouse shone out overhead, turning the rain to silver; and Jerry could see the gleam of his polished black hair and the light tan topcoat he was now wearing. Pulling up the collar of his dinner-jacket, Jerry followed.

A few yards farther on Davos slackened his pace. He peered round and up. On his left was the entrance to a court-yard, evidently the Square St. Jean. But to call it a "square" was noble overstatement; it was only a cul-de-sac some twenty feet wide by forty feet deep.

Two of its three sides were merely tall, blank brick walls. The third side, on the right, was formed of a tall flat house all of whose windows were closely shuttered. But there was at least a sign of life about the house. Over its door burned a dim white globe, showing that there was a doctor's brass name-plate beside the door. A sedate house with blue-painted shutters in the bare cul-de-sac—and Davos was making for it.

All this Jerry saw at a glance. Then he moved back from the cul-de-sac. The rain was sluicing down on him, blurring the dim white globe with shadow and gleam. Davos had almost reached the doctor's door. He had paused as though to consider or look at something; and then . . .

Jerry Winton later swore that he had taken his eyes off Davos only for a second. This was true. Jerry, in fact, had glanced back along the Avenue des Phares behind him and was heartened to see the figure of a policeman some distance away. What made him look quickly back again was a noise from the cul-de-sac, a noise that was something between a cough and a scream, bubbling up horribly under the rain; and afterwards the thud of a body on asphalt.

One moment Davos had been on his feet. The next moment he was lying on his side on the pavement, and kicking.

Overhead the beam of the lighthouse wheeled again. Jerry, reaching Davos in a run of half a dozen long strides, saw the whole scene picked out by that momentary light. Davos's fingers still clutched, or tried to clutch, the well-filled wallet Jerry had last seen at the Casino. His tan topcoat was now dark with rain. His heels scraped on the pavement, for he had been stabbed through the back of the neck with a heavy knife whose polished-metal handle projected four inches. Then the wallet slipped out of his fingers, and splashed into a puddle, for the man died.

Jerry Winton looked, and did not believe his own eyes. Mechanically he reached down and picked up the wallet out of the puddle, shaking it. He backed away as he heard running footfalls pound into the cul-de-sac, and he saw the flying waterproof of a policeman.

"Halt there!" the law shouted in French. The policeman, a dim shape under the waterproof, pulled up short and stared. After seeing what was on the pavement, he made a noise like a man hit in the stomach.

Jerry pulled his wits together and conned over his French for the proper phrases.

"His—this wallet," said Jerry, extending it.

"So I see."

"He is dead."

"That would appear obvious," agreed the other, with a kind of snort. "Well! Give it to me. Quick, quick, quick! His wallet."

The policeman extended his hand, snapping the fingers. He added: "No stupidities, if you please! I am prepared for you."

"But I didn't kill him."

"That remains to be seen."

"Man, you don't think—?"

He broke off. The trouble was that it had happened too rapidly. Jerry's feeling was that of one who meets a super-salesman and under whirlwind tactics is persuaded to buy some huge and useless article before he realizes what the talk is all about.

For here was a minor miracle. He had seen the man Davos stabbed under his eyes. Davos had been stabbed by a straight blow from behind, the heavy knife entering in a straight line sloping a little upwards, as though the blow had been struck from the direction of the pavement. Yet at the same time Davos had been alone in an empty cul-de-sac as bare as a biscuit-box.

"It is not my business to think," said the policeman curtly. "I make my notes and I report to my commissaire. Now!" He withdrew into the shelter of the dim-lit doorway, his wary eye fixed on Jerry, and whipped out his notebook. "Let us have no nonsense. You killed this man and attempted to rob him. I saw you."

"No!"

"You were alone with him in this court. I saw as much myself."

"Yes, that is true."

"Good; he admits it! You saw no one else in the court?"

"No."

"*Justement.* Could any assassin have approached without being seen?"

Jerry, even as he saw the bleak eye grow bleaker, had to admit that this was impossible. On two sides were blank brick walls; on the third side was a house whose door or windows, he could swear, had not opened a crack. In the second's space of time while he looked away, no murderer could have approached, stabbed Davos, and got back to cover again. There was no cover. This was so apparent that Jerry could not even think of a reasonable lie. He merely stuttered.

"I do not know what happened," he insisted. "One minute he was there, and then he fell. I saw nobody." Then a light opened in his mind. "Wait! That knife there—it must have been thrown at him."

Rich and sardonic humour stared at him from the doorway. "Thrown, you say? Thrown from where?"

"I don't know," admitted Jerry. The light went out. Again he stared at blank brick walls, and at the house from whose sealed front no knife could have been thrown.

"Consider," pursued his companion, in an agony of logic, "the position of the knife. This gentleman was walking with his back to you?"

"Yes."

"Good; we progress." He pointed. "The knife enters the back of his neck in a straight line. It enters from the direction where you were standing. Could it have been thrown past you from the entrance to the court?"

"No. Impossible."

"No. That is evident," blared his companion. "I cannot listen to any more stupidities. I indulge you because you are English and we have orders to indulge the English. But this goes beyond reason! You will go with me to the Hôtel de Ville. Look at the note-case in his hand. Does he offer it to you and say: 'Monsieur, honour me by accepting my note-case'?"

"No. He had it in his own hand."

"He had it in his own hand, say you. Why?"

"I don't know."

Jerry broke off, both because the story of his losses at the Casino must now come out with deadly significance, and because they heard the rattle of a door being unlocked. The door of the doctor's house opened; and out stepped the fair-haired girl whom Jerry had last seen at the Casino.

Beside the door the brass name-plate read, "Dr. Edouard

Hébert," with consulting hours inscribed underneath, and an aggressive, "Speaks English." Behind the girl, craning his neck, stood a bristly middle-aged man of immense dignity. His truculent eyeglasses had a broad black ribbon which seemed to form a kind of electrical circuit with the ends of his brushed-up moustache.

But Jerry Winton was not looking at Dr. Hébert. He was looking at the girl. In addition to a light fur coat, she now wore a cream-coloured scarf drawn over her hair; she had in one hand a tiny box, wrapped in white paper. Her smooth, worried face, her long, pale-blue eyes, seemed to reflect the expression of the dead man staring back at her from the pavement. She jerked back, bumping into the policeman. She put her hand on Dr. Hébert's arm. With her other hand she pointed sharply to Davos.

"That's the man!" she cried.

M. Goron, prefect of Police, was a comfortable man, a round, cat-like amiable sort of man, famous for his manners. Crime, rare in La Bandelette, distressed him. But he was also an able man. At one o'clock in the morning he sat in his office at the town hall examining his finger-nails and creaking back and forth in a squeaky swivel chair whose noise had begun to get on Jerry Winton's nerves.

The girl, who for the tenth time had given her name as Eleanor Hood, was insistent.

"M. Goron!"

"Mademoiselle?" said the prefect politely, and seemed to wake out of a dream.

Eleanor Hood turned round and gave Jerry Winton a despairing look.

"I only wish to know," she urged, in excellent French, "why we are here, Dr. Hébert and I. And Mr. Winton too, if it comes to that." This time the look she gave Jerry was one of smiling companionship: a human sort of look, which warmed that miscreant. "But as for us—why? It is not as though we were witnesses. I have told you why I was at Dr. Hébert's house."

"Mademoiselle's father," murmured M. Goron.

"Yes. He is ill. Dr. Hébert has been treating him for several days, and he had another attack at the Casino to-night. Mr. Winton will confirm that."

Jerry nodded. The old boy at the table, he reflected, had certainly looked ill.

"I took my father back to our hotel, the Brittany, at half-past eleven," the girl went on, speaking with great intensity. "I tried to communicate with Dr. Hébert by telephone. I could not reach him. So I went to his house; it is only a short distance from the hotel. On the way I kept seeing that man— the man you call Davos. I thought he was following me. He seemed to be looking at me from behind every tree. That is why I said, 'That's the man,' when I saw him lying on the pavement with his eyes open. His eyes did not even blink when the rain struck them. It was a horrible sight. I was upset. Do you blame me?"

M. Goron made a sympathetic noise.

"I reached Dr. Hébert's house at perhaps twenty minutes to twelve. Dr. Hébert had retired, but he consented to go with me. I waited while he dressed. We went out, and on the doorstep we found—what you know. Please believe that is all I know about it."

She had a singularly expressive voice and personality. She was either all anxiety or all persuasiveness, fashioning the clipped syllables. When she turned her wrist, you saw Davos lying in the rain and the searchlight wheeling overhead. Then she added abruptly in English, looking at Jerry:

"He was a nasty little beast; but I don't for a moment believe you killed him."

"Thanks. But why?"

"I don't know," said Eleanor simply. "You just couldn't have."

"Now there is logic!" cried M. Goron, giving his desk an admiring whack.

M. Goron's swivel chair creaked with pleasure. There were many lights in his office, which smelt of creosote. On the desk in front of him lay Davos's sodden wallet and (curiously) the tiny round box, wrapped in a spill of paper, which Eleanor Hood had been carrying. M. Goron never spoke to Jerry, never looked at him; ignored him as completely and blandly as though he were not there.

"But," he continued, growing very sober again, "you will forgive me, mademoiselle, if I pursue this matter further. You say that Dr. Hébert has been treating your father?"

"Yes."

M. Goron pointed to the small box on the table.

"With pills, perhaps?"

"Ah, my God!" said Dr. Hébert, and slapped his forehead tragically.

For several minutes Jerry had been afraid that the good doctor would have an apoplectic stroke. Dr. Hébert had indicated his distinguished position in the community. He had pointed out that physicians do not go out in the middle of the night on errands of mercy, and then get dragged off to police stations; it is bad for business. His truculent eyeglasses and moustache bristling, he left off his stiff pacing of the room only to go and look the prefect in the eye.

"I *will* speak," he said coldly, from deep in his throat.

"As monsieur pleases."

"Well, it is as this lady says! Why are we here? Why? We are not witnesses." He broke off, and slapped at the shoulders of his coat as though to rid himself of insects. "This young man here tells us a story which may or may not be true. If it is true, I do not see why the man Davos should have given him *my* address. I do not see why Davos should have been knifed on my doorstep. I did not know the man Davos, except as a patient of mine."

"Ah!" said the prefect. "You gave him pills, perhaps?"

Dr. Hébert sat down.

"Are you mad on the subject of pills?" he inquired, with restraint. "Because this young man"—again he looked with disfavour at Jerry—"tells you that Davos made some drunken mention of 'pills' at the Casino to-night, is that why you pursue the subject?"

"It is possible."

"It is ridiculous," said Dr. Hébert. "Do you even question my pills on the desk there? They are for Miss Hood's father. They are ordinary tablets, with digitalin for the heart. Do you think they contain poison? If so, why not test them?"

"It is an idea," conceded M. Goron.

He picked up the box and removed the paper.

The box contained half a dozen sugar-coated pellets. With great seriousness M. Goron put one of the tablets into his mouth, tasted it, bit it, and finally appeared to swallow it.

"No poison?" asked the doctor.

"No poison," agreed M. Goron. The telephone on his desk rang. He picked it up, listened for a moment with a dreamy smile, and replaced it. "Now this is really excellent!" he beamed, rubbing his hands. "My good friend Colonel March, of the English police, has been making investigations. He was sent here when a certain form of activity in La Bandelette became intolerable both to the French and English authorities. You perhaps noticed him at the Casino to-night, all of you?"

"I remember," said Jerry suddenly. "Very large bloke, quiet as sin."

"An apt description," said the prefect.

"But—" began Dr. Hébert.

"I said 'all of you,' Dr. Hébert," repeated the prefect. "One small question is permitted? I thank you. When mademoiselle telephoned to your house at eleven-thirty to-night, you were not there. You were at the Casino, perhaps?"

Dr. Hébert stared at him.

"It is possible. But—"

"You saw M. Davos there, perhaps?"

"It is possible." Still Dr. Hébert stared at him with hideous perplexity. "But, Mr. Goron, will you have the goodness to explain this? You surely do not suspect either mademoiselle or myself of having any concern with this business? You do not think that either mademoiselle or I left the house at the time of the murder?"

"I am certain you did not."

"You do not think either mademoiselle or myself went near a door or window to get at this accursed Davos?"

"I am certain you did not," beamed the prefect.

"Well, then?"

"But there, you see," argued M. Goron, lifting one finger for emphasis, "we encounter a difficulty. We are among thorns. For this would mean that M. Winton must have committed the murder. And that," he added, looking at Jerry, "is absurd. We never for a moment believed that M. Winton had anything to do with this; and my friend Colonel March will tell you why."

Jerry sat back and studied the face of the prefect, wondering if he had heard aright. He felt like an emotional punching-bag. But with great gravity he returned the prefect's nod as a sergent de ville opened the door of the office.

"We will spik English," announced M. Goron, bouncing up. "This is my friend Colonel March."

"'Evening," said the colonel. His large, speckled face was

as bland as M. Goron's; his fists were on his hips. He looked first at Eleanor, then at Jerry, then at Dr. Hébert. "Sorry you were put to this inconvenience, Miss Hood. But I've seen your father, and it will be all right. As for you, Mr. Winton, I hope they have put you out of your misery?"

"Misery?"

"Told you you're not headed for Devil's Island, or anything of the sort? We had three very good reasons for believing you had nothing to do with this. Here is the first reason."

Reaching into the pocket of his dinner-jacket, he produced an article which he held out to them. It was a black leather note-case, exactly like the one already on M. Goron's desk. But whereas the first was stuffed with *mille* notes, this one had only a few hundred francs in it.

"We found this second note-case in Davos's pocket," said Colonel March.

He seemed to wait for a comment, but none came.

"Well, what about it?" Jerry demanded, after a pause.

"Oh, come! Two note-cases! Why was Davos carrying two note-cases? Why should any man carry two note-cases? That is my first reason. Here is my second."

From the inside pocket of his coat, with the air of a conjurer, he drew out the knife with which Davos had been stabbed.

A suggestive sight. Now cleansed of blood, it was a long, thin, heavy blade with a light metal handle and cross-piece. As Colonel March turned it round, glittering in the light, Jerry Winton felt that its glitter struck a chord of familiarity in his mind: that a scene from the past had almost come back to him: that, for a swift and tantalizing second, he had almost grasped the meaning of the whole problem.

"And now we come to my third reason," said Colonel March. "The third reason is Ferdie Davos. Ferdie was a hotel thief. A great deal too clever for us poor policemen. Eh,

Goron? Though I always told him he was a bad judge of men. At the height of the summer season, at hotels like the Brittany and the Donjon, he had rich pickings. He specialized in necklaces; particularly in pearl necklaces. Kindly note that."

A growing look of comprehension had come into Eleanor Hood's face. She opened her mouth to speak, and then checked herself.

"His problem," pursued Colonel March, "was how to smuggle the stolen stuff over to England, where he had a market for it. He couldn't carry it himself. In a little place like La Bandelette, Goron would have had him turned inside out if he had as much as taken a step towards Boulogne. So he had to have accomplices. I mean accomplices picked from among the hordes of unattached young men who come here every season. Find some young fool who's just dropped more than he can afford at the tables; and he may grab at the chance to earn a few thousand francs by a little harmless customs bilking. You follow me, Mr. Winton?"

"You mean that I was chosen—?"

"Yes."

"But, good lord, how? I couldn't smuggle a pearl necklace through the customs if my life depended on it."

"You could if you needed a tonic," Colonel March pointed out. "Davos told you so. The necklace would first be taken to pieces for you. Each pearl would be given a thick sugar-coating, forming a neat medicinal pill. They would then be poured into a neat bottle or box under the prescription of a well-known doctor. At the height of the tourist rush, the customs can't curry-comb everybody. They would be looking for a pearl-smuggler: not for an obviously respectable young tourist with stomach trouble."

Eleanor Hood, with sudden realization in her face, looked at the box of pills on M. Goron's desk.

"So *that* is why you tasted my pills!" she said to the prefect of police, who made deprecating noises. "And kept me here for so long. And—"

"Mademoiselle, I assure you! said M. Goron. "We were sure there was nothing wrong with those pills!" He somewhat spoiled the gallant effect of this by adding: "There are not enough of them, for one thing. But, since you received them from Dr. Hébert after office hours, you had to be investigated. The trick is neat, hein? I fear the firm of Hébert and Davos have been working it for some time."

They all turned to look at Dr. Hébert.

He was sitting bolt upright, his chin drawn into his collar as though he were going to sing. On his face was a look of what can only be called frightened scepticism. Even his mouth was half open with this effect, or with unuttered sounds of ridicule.

"We were also obliged to delay you all," pursued M. Goron, "until my men found Madame Fley's pearls, which were stolen a week ago, hidden in Dr. Hébert's surgery. I repeat: it was a neat trick. We might never have seen it if Davos had not incautiously hinted at it to M. Winton. But then Davos was getting a bit above himself." He added: "That, Colonel March thinks, is why Dr. Hébert decided to kill him."

Still Dr. Hébert said nothing.

It was, in fact, Jerry Winton who spoke. "Sir, I don't hold any brief for this fellow. I should think you were right. But how could he have killed Davos? He couldn't have!"

"You are forgetting," said Colonel March, as cheerfully as though the emotional temperature of the room had not gone up several degrees, "you are forgetting the two note-cases. Why was Davos carrying two note-cases?"

"Well?"

"He wasn't," said Colonel March, with his eye on Hébert.

"Our good doctor here was, of course, the brains of the partnership. He supplied the resources for Ferdie's noble front. When Ferdie played baccarat at the Casino, he was playing with Dr. Hébert's money. And, when Dr. Hébert saw Ferdie at the Casino to-night, he very prudently took away the large sum you saw in Ferdie's note-case at the tables. When Ferdie came to the doctor's house at midnight, he had only his few hundred francs commission in his own note-case, which was in his pocket.

"You see, Dr. Hébert needed that large sum of money in his plan to kill Ferdie. He knew what time Ferdie would call at his house. He knew Mr. Winton would be close behind Ferdie. Mr. Winton would, in fact, walk into the murder and get the blame. All Dr. Hébert had to do was take that packet of *mille* notes, stuff them into another note-case just like Ferdie Davos's, and use it as a trap."

"A trap?" repeated Eleanor.

"A trap," said Colonel March.

"Your presence, Miss Hood," he went on, "gave the doctor an unexpected alibi. He left you downstairs in his house. He went upstairs to 'get dressed.' A few minutes before Davos was due to arrive, he went quietly up to the roof of his house—a flat roof, like most of those in La Bandelette. He looked down over the parapet into that cul-de-sac, forty feet below. He saw his own doorstep with the lamp burning over it. He dropped that note-case over the parapet, so that it landed on the pavement before his own doorstep.

"Well?" continued Colonel March. "What would Davos do? What would *you* do, if you walked along a pavement and saw a note-case bulging with thousand-franc notes lying just in front of you?"

Again Jerry Winton saw that dim cul-de-sac. He heard the rain splashing; he saw it moving and gleaming past the door-lamp, and past the beam of the lighthouse overhead. He saw the jaunty figure of Davos stop short as though to look at something—

"I imagine," Jerry said, "that I'd bend over and pick up the note-case."

"Yes," said Colonel March. "That's the whole sad story. You would bend over so that your body was parallel with the ground. The back of your neck would be a plain target to anybody standing forty feet up above you, with a needle-sharp knife whose blade is much heavier than the handle. The murderer has merely to drop that knife: stretch out his fingers and drop it. Gravity will do the rest.

"My friend, you looked straight at that murder; and you never saw it. You never saw it because a shifting, gleaming wall of rain, a kind of silver curtain, fell across the door-lamp and the beam of the lighthouse. It hid the fall of a thin, long blade made of bright metal. Behind that curtain moved invisibly our ingenious friend Dr. Hébert, who, if he can be persuaded to speak—"

Dr. Hébert could not be persuaded to speak, even when they took him away. But Eleanor Hood and Jerry Winton walked home through the summer dawn, under a sky coloured with a less evil silver; and they had discovered any number of mutual acquaintances by the time they reached the hotel.

THE FOOTPRINT IN THE SKY

She awoke out of confused dreams; awoke with a start, and lay staring at the white ceiling of her bedroom for a minute or two before she could convince herself it was anything but a dream.

But it was a dream.

The cold, brittle sunlight poured in at the open window. The cold, brittle air, blowing the curtains, stirred a light coating of snow on the window-sill. It stirred briskly in that little, bare room; it should have set the blood racing, and Dorothy Brant breathed it deeply.

Everything was all right. She was at the country cottage, where she and Dad and Harry had come down for the skating on the frozen lake; possibly even a little mild skiing, if the snow came on according to the weather forecast. And the snow had fallen. She should have been glad of that, though for some reason the sight of it on the window-sill struck her with a kind of terror.

Shivering in the warm bed, clothes pulled up about her chin, she looked at the little clock on her bedside. Twenty minutes past nine. She had overslept; Dad and Harry would be wanting their breakfast. Again she told herself that everything was all right: though now, fully awake, she knew it was not. The unpleasantness of yesterday returned. Mrs. Topham next door—that old shrew and thief as well . . .

It was the only thing which could have marred this weekend. They had looked forward to the skating: the crisp blades thudding and ringing on the ice, the flight, the long scratching drag as you turned, the elm-trees black against a clear cold sky. But there was Mrs. Topham with her stolen watch and her malicious good manners, huddled up in the cottage next door and spoiling everything.

Put it out of your mind! No good brooding over it: put it out of your mind!

Dorothy Brant braced herself and got out of bed, reaching for her dressing-gown and slippers. But it was not her dressing-gown she found draped across the chair; it was her heavy fur coat. And there were a pair of soft-leather slippers. They were a pair of soft-leather moccasins, ornamented with bead-work, which Harry had brought her back from the States; but now the undersides were cold, damp, and stiff, almost frozen. That was when a subconscious fear struck at her, took possession, and would not leave.

Closing the window, she padded out to the bathroom. The small cottage, with its crisp white curtains and smell of old wood, was so quiet that she could hear voices talking downstairs. It was a mumble in which no words were distinguishable: Harry's quick tenor, her father's slower and heavier voice, and another she could not identify, but which was slowest and heaviest of all.

What was wrong? She hurried through her bath and through her dressing. Not only were they up but they must be getting their own breakfast, for she could smell coffee boiling. And she was very slow; in spite of nine hours' sleep she felt as edgy and washed-out as though she had been up all night.

Giving a last jerk of the comb through her brown bobbed hair, putting on no powder or lipstick, she ran downstairs. At the door of the living-room she stopped abruptly. Inside were her father, her cousin Harry, and the local Superintendent of Police.

"Good morning, miss," said the Superintendent.

She never forgot the look of that little room or the look on the faces of those in it. Sunlight poured into it, touching the bright-coloured rough-woven rugs, the rough stone fire-place. Through side windows she could see out across the snow-covered lawn to where—twenty yards away and separated from them only by a tall laurel hedge, with a gateway—was Mrs. Topham's white weather-boarded cottage.

But what struck her with a shock of alarm as she came into the room was the sense of a conversation suddenly cut off; the look she surprised on their faces when they glanced round, quick and sallow, as a camera might have surprised it.

"Good morning, miss," repeated Superintendent Mason, saluting.

Harry Ventnor intervened, in a kind of agony. His naturally high colour was higher still; even his large feet and bulky shoulders, his small sinewy hands, looked agitated.

"Don't say anything, Dolly!" he urged. "Don't say anything! They can't make you say anything. Wait until—"

"I certainly think—" began her father slowly. He looked down his nose, and then along the side of his pipe, everywhere except at Dorothy. "I certainly think," he went on, clearing his throat, "that it would be as well not to speak hastily until—"

"*If* you please, sir," said Superintendent Mason, clearing his own throat. "Now, miss, I'm afraid I must ask you some questions. But it is my duty to tell you that you need not answer my questions until you have seen your solicitor."

"Solicitor? But I don't want a solicitor. What on earth should I want with a solicitor?"

Superintendent Mason looked meaningly at her father and Harry Ventnor, as though bidding them to mark that.

"It's about Mrs. Topham, miss."

"Oh!"

"Why do you say 'Oh'?"

"Go on, please. What is it?"

"I understand, miss, that you and Mrs. Topham had 'words' yesterday? A bit of a dust-up, like?"

"Yes, you could certainly call it that."

"May I ask what about?"

"I'm sorry," said Dorothy; "I can't tell you that. It would only give the old cat an opportunity to say I had been slandering her. So that's it! What has she been telling you?"

"Why, miss," said Superintendent Mason, taking out a pencil and scratching the side of his jaw with it, "I'm afraid she's not exactly in a condition to tell us anything. She's in a nursing-home at Guildford, rather badly smashed up round the head. Just between ourselves, it's touch and go whether she'll recover."

First Dorothy could not feel her heart beating at all, and then it seemed to pound with enormous rhythm. The Superintendent was looking at her steadily. She forced herself to say:

"You mean she's had an accident?"

"Not exactly, miss. The doctor says she was hit three or four times with that big glass paper-weight you may have seen on the table at her cottage. Eh?"

"You don't mean—you don't mean somebody *did* it? Deliberately? But who did it?"

"Well, miss," said Superintendent Mason, looking at her still harder until he became a huge Puritan face with a small mole beside his nose. "I'm bound to tell you that by everything we can see so far, it looks as though you did it."

This wasn't happening. It couldn't be. She afterwards remembered, in a detached kind of way, studying all of them: the little lines round Harry's eyes in the sunlight, the hastily brushed light hair, the loose leather wind-jacket whose zip fastener was half undone. She remembered thinking that despite his athletic prowess he looked ineffectual and a little foolish. But then her own father was not of much use now.

She heard her own voice.

"But that's absurd!"

"I hope so, miss. I honestly hope so. Now tell me: were you out of this house last night?"

"When?"

"At any time."

"Yes. No. I don't know. Yes, I think I was."

"For God's sake, Dolly," said her father, "don't say anything more until we've got a lawyer here. I've telephoned to town; I didn't want to alarm you; I didn't even wake you: there's some explanation of this. There must be!"

It was not her own emotion; it was the wretchedness of his face which held her. Bulky, semi-bald, worried about business, worried about everything else in this world, that was John Brant. His crippled left arm and black glove were pressed against his side. He stood in the bright pool of sunlight, a face of misery.

"I've—seen her," he explained. "It wasn't pretty, that wasn't. Not that I haven't seen worse. In the war." He touched his arm. "But you're a little girl, Dolly; you're only a little girl. You couldn't have done that."

His plaintive tone asked for confirmation.

"Just one moment, sir," interposed Superintendent Mason. "Now, miss! You tell me you *were* outside the house last night?"

"Yes."

"In the snow?"

"Yes, yes, yes!"

"Do you remember the time?"

"No, I don't think so."

"Tell me, miss: what size shoes do you wear?"

"Four."

"That's a rather small size, isn't it?" When she nodded dumbly, Superintendent Mason shut up his notebook. "Now, if you'll just come with me?"

The cottage had a side door. Without putting his fingers on the knob, Mason twisted the spindle round and opened it. The overhang of the eaves had kept clear the two steps leading down; but beyond a thick coating of snow lay like a plaster over the world between here and the shuttered cottage across the way.

There were two strings of footprints in that snow. Dorothy knew whose they were. Hardened and sharp-printed, one set of prints moved out snakily from the steps, passed under the arch of the powdered laurel-hedge, and stopped at the steps to the side door of Mrs. Topham's house. Another set of the same tracks—a little blurred, spaced at longer intervals where the person had evidently been running desperately— came back from the cottage to these steps.

That mute sign of panic stirred Dorothy's memory. It wasn't a dream. She had done it. Subconsciously she had known all the time. She could remember other things: the fur coat clasped round her pyjamas, the sting of the snow to wet slippers, the blind rush in the dark.

"Yours, miss?" inquired Superintendent Mason.

"Yes. Oh, yes, they're mine."

"Easy, miss," muttered the Superintendent. "You're looking a bit white round the gills. Come in here and sit down; I won't hurt you." Then his own tone grew petulant. Or perhaps something in the heavy simplicity of the girl's manner penetrated his official bearing. "But why did you do it, miss? Lord, why did you do it? That's to say, breaking open that desk of hers to get a handful of trinkets not worth ten quid for the lot? And then not even taking the trouble to mess up your footprints afterwards!" He coughed, checking himself abruptly.

John Brant's voice was acid. "Good, my friend. Very good. The first sign of intelligence so far. I presume you don't suggest my daughter is insane?"

"No, sir. But they were her mother's trinkets, I hear."

"Where did you hear that? You, I suppose, Harry?"

Harry Ventnor pulled up the zip fastener of his wind-jacket as though girding himself. He seemed to suggest that he was the good fellow whom everybody was persecuting; that he wanted to be friends with the world, if they would only let him. Yet such sincerity blazed in his small features that it was difficult to doubt his good intentions.

"Now look here, Dad, old boy. I *had* to tell them, didn't I? It's not good trying to hide things like that. I know that, just from reading these stories—"

"Stories!"

"All right: say what you like. They always find out, and then they make it worse than it really was." He let this sink in. "I tell you, you're going about it in the wrong way. Suppose Dolly did have a row with the Topham about that jewellery? Suppose she *did* go over there last night? Suppose those are her footprints? Does that prove she bashed the Topham? Not that a public service wasn't done; but why couldn't it have been a burglar just as well?"

Superintendent Mason shook his head.

"Because it couldn't, sir."

"But why? I'm asking you, why?"

"There's no harm in telling you that, sir, if you'll just listen. You probably remember that it began to snow last night at a little past eleven o'clock."

"No, I don't. We were all in bed by then."

"Well, you can take my word for it," Mason told him patiently. "I was up half the night at the police station; and it did. It stopped snowing about midnight. You'll have to take my word for that too, but we can easily prove it. You see, sir, Mrs. Topham was alive and in very good health at well after midnight. I know that too, because she rang up the police station and said she was awake and nervous and thought there were burglars in the neighbourhood. Since the lady does that same thing," he explained with a certain grimness, "on the average of about three times a month, I don't stress *that*. What I am telling you is that her call came in at 12:10, at least ten minutes after the snow had stopped."

Harry hesitated, and the Superintendent went on with the same patient air:

"Don't you see it, sir? Mrs. Topham wasn't attacked until after the snow stopped. Round her cottage now there's twenty yards of clean, clear, unmarked snow in every direction. The only marks in that snow, the only marks of any kind at all, are the footprints Miss Brant admits she made herself."

Then he rose at them in exasperation.

"'Tisn't as though anybody else could have made the tracks. Even if Miss Brant didn't admit it herself, I'm absolutely certain nobody else did. You, Mr. Ventnor, wear size ten shoes. Mr. Brant wears size nine. Walk in size four tracks? Ayagh! And yet somebody did get into that cottage with a key, bashed the old lady pretty murderously, robbed her desk, and got away again. If there are no other tracks or marks of any kind in the snow, who did it? Who must have done it?"

Dorothy could consider it, now, in almost a detached way. She remembered the paper-weight with which Mrs. Topham had been struck. It lay on the table in Mrs. Topham's stuffy parlour, a heavy glass globe with a tiny landscape inside. When you shook the glass globe, a miniature snowstorm rose within—which seemed to make the attack more horrible.

She wondered if she had left any fingerprints on it. But over everything rose Renée Topham's face, Renée Topham, her mother's bosom friend.

"I hated her," said Dorothy; and, unexpectedly, she began to cry.

* * *

Dennis Jameson, of the law-firm of Morris, Farnsworth & Jameson, Lincoln's Inn Fields, shut up his brief-case with a snap. He was putting on his hat and coat when Billy Farnsworth looked into the office.

"Hullo!" said Farnsworth. "You off to Surrey over that Brant business?"

"Yes."

"H'm. Believe in miracles, do you?"

"No."

"That girl's guilty, my lad. You ought to know that."

"It's our business," said Jameson, "to do what we can for our clients."

Farnsworth looked at him shrewdly. "I see it in your ruddy cheek. Quixotry is alive again. Young idealist storms to relief of good-looker in distress, swearing to—"

"I've met her twice," said Jameson. "I like her, yes. But, merely using a small amount of intelligence on this, I can't see that they've got such a thundering good case against her."

"Oh, my lad!"

"Well, look at it. What do they say the girl did? This Mrs. Topham was struck several times with a glass paper-weight. There are no fingerprints on the paper-weight, which shows signs of having been wiped. But, after having the forethought to wipe her fingerprints carefully off the paper-weight, Dorothy Brant then walks back to her cottage and leaves behind two sets of footprints which could be seen by aerial observation a mile up. Is that reasonable?"

Farnsworth looked thoughtful.

"Maybe they would say she isn't reasonable," he pointed out. "Never mind the psychology. What you've got to get round are the physical facts. Here is the mysterious widow Topham entirely alone in the house; the only servant comes in by day. Here are one person's footprints. Only that girl could have made the tracks; and, in fact, admits she did. It's a physical impossibility for anybody else to have entered or left the house. How do you propose to get round that?"

"I don't know," said Jameson rather hopelessly. "But I want to hear her side of it first. The only thing nobody seems to have heard, or even to be curious about, is what she thinks herself."

Yet, when he met her at the cottage late that afternoon, she cut the ground from under his feet.

Twilight was coming down when he turned in at the gate, a bluish twilight in which the snow looked grey. Jameson stopped a moment at the gate, and stared across at the thin laurel-hedge dividing this property from Mrs. Topham's. There was nothing remarkable about this hedge, which was some six feet high and cut through by a gateway like a Gothic arch. But in front of the arch, peering up at the snow-coated side of the hedge just above it, stood a large figure in cap and waterproof. Somehow he looked familiar. At his elbows another man, evidently the local Superintendent of Police, was holding up a camera; and a flash-bulb glared against the sky. Though he was too far away to hear anything, Jameson had a queer impression that the large man was laughing uproariously.

Harry Ventnor, whom he knew slightly, met Jameson at the door.

"She's in there," Harry explained, nodding towards the front room. "Er—don't upset her, will you? Here, what the devil are they doing with that hedge?"

He stared across the lawn.

"Upset her?" said Jameson with some asperity. "I'm here, if possible, to help her. Won't you or Mr. Brant give some assistance? Do you honestly think that Miss Brant in her rational senses could have done what they say she did?"

"In her rational senses?" repeated Harry. After looking at Jameson in a curious way, he said no more; he turned abruptly and hurried off across the lawn.

Yet Dorothy, when Jameson met her, gave no impression of being out of her rational senses. It was her straightforwardness he had always liked, the straightforwardness which warmed him now. They sat in the homely, firelit room, by the fireplace over which were the silver cups to denote Harry's athletic and gymnastic prowess, and the trophies of John Brant's earlier days at St. Moritz. Dorothy herself was an outdoor girl.

"To advise me?" she said. "You mean, to advise me what to say when they arrest me?"

"Well, they haven't arrested you yet, Miss Brant."

She smiled at him. "And yet I'll bet that surprises you, doesn't it? Oh, I know how deeply I'm in! I suppose they're only poking about to get more evidence. And then there's a new man here, a man named March, from Scotland Yard. I feel almost flattered."

Jameson sat up. He knew now why that immense figure by the hedge had seemed familiar.

"Not Colonel March?"

"Yes. Rather a nice person, really," answered Dorothy, shading her eyes with her hand. Under her light tone he felt that her nerves were raw. "Then again, they've been all through my room. And they can't find the watch and the brooch and rings I'm supposed to have stolen from Aunt Renée Topham. Aunt Renée!"

"So I've heard. But that's the point: what are they getting at? A watch and a brooch and couple of rings! Why should you steal that from anybody, let alone her?"

"Because they weren't hers," said Dorothy, suddenly looking up with a white face, and speaking very fast. "They belonged to my mother."

"Steady."

"My mother is dead," said Dorothy. "I suppose it wasn't just the watch and the rings, really. That was the excuse, the breaking-point, the thing that brought it on. My mother was a great friend of Mrs. Topham. It was 'Aunt Renée' this and 'Aunt Renée' that, while my mother was alive to pamper her. But my mother wanted me to have those trinkets, such as they were. And Aunt Renée Topham coolly appropriated them, as she appropriates everything else she can. I never knew what had happened to them until yesterday.

"Do you know that kind of woman? Mrs. Topham is really charming, aristocratic and charming, with the cool charm that takes all it can get and expects to go on getting it. I know for a fact that she's really got a lot of money, though what she does with it I can't imagine: and the real reason why she buries herself in the country is that she's too mean to risk spending it in town. I never could endure her. Then, when my mother died and I didn't go on pampering Aunt Renée as she thought I should, it was a very different thing. How that woman loves to talk about us! Harry's debts, and my father's shaky business. And *me*."

She checked herself again, smiling at him. "I'm sorry to inflict all this on you."

"You're not inflicting anything on me."

"But it's rather ridiculous, isn't it?"

"Ridiculous," said Jameson grimly, "is not the word I should apply to it. So you had a row with her?"

"Oh, a glorious row. A beautiful row. The grandmother of all rows."

"When?"

"Yesterday. When I saw her wearing my mother's watch."

She looked at the fire, over which the silver cups glimmered.

"Maybe I said more than I should have," she went on. "But I got no support from my father or Harry. I don't blame Dad: he's so worried about business, and that bad arm of his troubles him so much sometimes, that all he wants is peace and quiet. As for Harry, *he* doesn't really like her; but she took rather a fancy to him, and that flatters him. He's a kind of male counterpart of Aunt Renée. Out of a job?—well, depend on somebody else. And I'm in the middle of all this. It's 'Dolly, do this,' and 'Dolly, do that,' and 'Good old Dolly; she won't mind.' But I do mind. When I saw that woman standing there wearing my mother's watch, and saying commiserating things about the fact that we couldn't afford a servant, I felt that something ought to be done about it. So I suppose I must have done something about it."

Jameson reached out and took her hands. "All right," he said. "Did you do it?"

"I don't know! That's just the trouble."

"But surely—"

"No. That was one of the things Mrs. Topham always had such sport with. You don't know much about anything when you walk in your sleep.

"Ridiculous, isn't it?" she went on, after another pause. "Utterly ludicrous. But not to me! Not a bit. Ever since I was a child, when I've been over-tired or nervously exhausted, it's happened. Once I came downstairs and built and lit a fire in the dining-room, and set the table for a meal. I admit it doesn't happen often, and never before with results like this." She tried to laugh. "But why do you think my father and Harry looked at me like that? That's the worst of it. I really don't know whether I'm a near-murderer or not."

This was bad.

Jameson admitted that to himself, even as his reason argued against it. He got up to prowl round the room, and her brown eyes never left him. He could not look away; he saw the tensity of her face in every corner.

"Look here," he said quietly; "this is nonsense."

"Oh, please. Don't you say that. It's not very original."

"But do you seriously think you went for that woman and still don't know anything about it now?"

"Would it be more difficult than building a fire?"

"I didn't ask you that. *Do* you think you did it?"

"No," said Dorothy.

That question did it. She trusted him now. There was understanding and sympathy between them, a mental force and communication that could be felt as palpably as the body gives out heat.

"Deep down inside me, no, I don't believe it. I think I should have waked up. And there was no—well, no blood on me, you know. But how are you going to get round the evidence?"

(The evidence. Always the evidence.)

"I did go across there. I can't deny that. I remember half waking up as I was coming back. I was standing in the middle of the lawn in the snow. I had on my fur coat over my pyjamas; I remember feeling snow on my face and my wet slippers under me. I was shivering. And I remember running back. That's all. If I didn't do it, how could anybody else have done it?"

"I bet your pardon," interposed a new voice. "Do you mind if, both figuratively and literally, I turn on the light?"

Dennis Jameson knew the owner of that voice. There was the noise of someone fumbling after an electric switch; then, in homely light, Colonel March beamed and basked. Colonel March's seventeen stone was swathed round in a water-proof as big as a tent. He wore a large tweed cap. Under this his speckled face glowed in the cold; and he was smoking, with gurgling relish, the large-bowled pipe which threatened to singe his sandy moustache.

"Ah, Jameson!" he said. He took the pipe out of his mouth and made a gesture with it. "So it *was* you. I thought I saw you come in. I don't want to intrude; but I think there are at least two things that Miss Brant ought to know."

Dorothy turned round quickly.

"First," pursued Colonel March, "that Mrs. Topham is out of danger. She is at least able, like an after-dinner speaker, to say a few words; though with about as much coherence. Second, that out on your lawn there is one of the queerest objects I ever saw in my life."

Jameson whistled.

"You've met this fellow?" he said to Dorothy. "He is the head of the Queer Complaints Department. When they come across something outlandish, which may be a hoax or a joke but, on the other hand, may be a serious crime, they shout for him. His mind is so obvious that he hits it every time. To my certain knowledge he has investigated a disappearing room, chased a walking corpse, and found an invisible piece of furniture. If he goes so far as to admit that a thing is a bit unusual, you can look out for squalls."

Colonel March nodded quite seriously.

"Yes," he said. "That is why I am here, you see. They thought we might be interested in that footprint."

"That footprint?" cried Dorothy. "You mean—?"

"No, no; not your footprint, Miss Brant. Another one. Let me explain. I want you, both of you, to look out of that window; I want you to take a look at the laurel-hedge between this cottage and the other. The light is almost gone, but study it."

Jameson went to the window and peered out.

"Well?" he demanded. "What about it? It's a hedge."

"As you so shrewdly note, it is a hedge. Now let me ask you a question. Do you think a person could walk along the top of that hedge?"

"Good lord, no!"

"No? Why not?"

"I don't see the joke," said Jameson, "but I'll make the proper replies. Because the hedge is only an inch or two thick. It wouldn't support a cat. If you tried to stand on it, you'd come through like a ton of bricks."

"Quite true. Then what would you say if I told you that someone weighing at least twelve stone must have climbed up the side of it?"

Nobody answered him; the thing was so obviously unreasonable that nobody could answer. Dorothy Brant and Dennis Jameson looked at each other.

"For," said Colonel March, "it would seem that somebody at least climbed up there. Look at the hedge again. You see the arch cut in it for a gate? Just above that, in the snow along the side of the hedge, there are traces of a footprint. It is a large footprint. I think it can be identified by the heel, though most of it is blurred and sketchy."

Walking quickly and heavily, Dorothy's father came into the room. He started to speak, but seemed to change his mind at the sight of Colonel March. He went over to Dorothy, who took his arm.

"Then," insisted Jameson, "somebody did climb up on the hedge?"

"I doubt it," said Colonel March. "How could he?"

Jameson pulled himself together.

"Look here, sir," he said quietly. "'How could he?' is correct. I never knew you to go on like this without good reason. I know it must have some bearing on the case. But I don't care if somebody climbed up on the hedge. I don't care if he danced the Big Apple on it. The hedge leads nowhere. It doesn't lead to Mrs. Topham's; it only divides the two properties. The point is, how did somebody manage to get from here to that other cottage—across sixty feet of unbroken snow—without leaving a trace on it? I ask you that because I'm certain you don't think Miss Brant is guilty."

Colonel March looked apologetic.

"I know she isn't," he answered.

In Dorothy Brant's mind was again that vision of the heavy globed paper-weight inside which, as you shook it, a miniature snowstorm arose. She felt that her own wits were being shaken and clouded in the same way.

"I knew Dolly didn't do it," said John Brant, suddenly putting his arm round his daughter's shoulder. "I knew that. I told them so. But—"

Colonel March silenced him.

"The real thief, Miss Brant, did not want your mother's watch and brooch and chain and rings. It may interest you to know what he did want. He wanted about fifteen hundred pounds in notes and gold sovereigns, tucked away in that same shabby desk. You seem to have wondered what Mrs. Topham did with her money. That is what she did with it. Mrs. Topham, by the first words she could get out in semi-consciousness, was merely a common or garden variety of miser. That dull-looking desk in her parlour was the last place any burglar would look for a hoard. Any burglar, that is, except one."

"Except one?" repeated John Brant, and his eyes seemed to turn inwards.

A sudden ugly suspicion came to Jameson.

"Except one who knew, yes. You, Miss Brant, had the blame deliberately put on you. There was no malice in it. It was simply the easiest way to avoid pain and trouble to the gentleman who did it.

"Now hear what you really did," said Colonel March, his face darkening. "You did go out into the snow last night. But you did not go over to Mrs. Topham's; and you did not make those two artistic sets of footprints in the snow. When you tell us in your own story that you felt snow sting on your face as well as underfoot, it requires no vast concentration, surely, to realize that the snow was still falling. You went out into it, like many sleep-walkers; you were shocked into semi-consciousness by the snow and the cold air; and you returned long before the end of the snowfall, which covered any real prints you may have made.

"The real thief—who was very much awake—heard you come back and tumble into bed. He saw a heaven-sent opportunity to blame you for a crime you might even think you had committed. He slipped in and took the slippers out of your room. And, when the snow had stopped, he went across to Mrs. Topham's. He did not mean to attack her. But she was awake and surprised him; and so, of course, Harry Ventnor struck her down."

"Harry—"

The word, which Dorothy had said almost at a scream, was checked. She looked round quickly at her father; she stared straight ahead; and then she began to laugh.

"Of course," said Colonel March. "As usual, he was letting his (what is it?) his 'good old Dolly' take the blame."

A great cloud seemed to have left John Brant; but the fussed and worried look had not left him. He blinked at Colonel March.

"Sir," he said, "I would give my good arm to prove what you say. That boy has caused me half the trouble I ever had. But are you raving mad?"

"No."

"I tell you he couldn't have done it! He's Emily's son, my sister's son. He may be a bad lot; but he's not a magician."

"You are forgetting," said Colonel March, "a certain large size-ten footprint. You are forgetting that interesting sight, a smeared and blurred size-ten footprint on the side of a hedge which would not have held up a cat. A remarkable footprint. A disembodied footprint."

"But that's the whole trouble," roared the other. "The two lines of tracks in the snow made by a size four shoe. Harry couldn't have made them, any more than I could. It's a physical impossibility. Harry wears size ten. You don't say he could get his feet into flat leather moccasins which would fit my daughter?"

"No," said Colonel March. "But he could get his hands into them."

There was a silence. The Colonel wore a dreamy look; almost a pleased look.

"And in this unusual but highly practical pair of gloves," he went on, "Harry Ventnor simply walked across to the other cottage on his hands. No more than that. For a trained gymnast (as those silver cups will indicate) it was nothing. For a rattle-brained gentleman who needed money it was ideal. He crossed in a thin coating of snow, which would show no difference in weight. Doorsteps cleared of snow by the overhanging roof, protected him at either end when he stood upright. He had endless opportunities to get a key to the side door. Unfortunately, there was that rather low archway in the hedge. Carrying himself on his hands, his feet were curved up and back over the arch of his body to balance him; he blundered, and smeared that disembodied footprint on the side of the hedge. To be quite frank, I am delighted with the device. It is crime upside down; it is leaving a footprint in the sky; it is—"

"A fair cop, sir," concluded Superintendent Mason, sticking his head in at the door. "They got him on the other side of Guildford. He must have smelled something wrong when he saw us taking photographs. But he had the stuff on him."

Dorothy Brant stood looking for a long time at the large, untidy blimp-like man who was still chuckling with pleasure. Then she joined in.

"I trust," observed Dennis Jameson politely, "that everybody is having a good time. For myself, I've had a couple of unpleasant shocks to-day; and just for a moment I was afraid I should have another one. For a moment I honestly thought you were going to pitch on Mr. Brant."

"So did I," agreed Dorothy, and beamed at her father. "That's why it's so funny now."

John Brant looked startled. But not half so startled as Colonel March.

"Now there," thee Colonel said, "I honestly do not understand you. I am the Department of Queer Complaints. If you have a ghost in your attic or a footprint on top of your hedge, ring me up. But a certain success has blessed us because, as Mr. Jameson says, I look for the obvious. And Lord love us! If you have decided that a crime was committed by a gentleman who could walk on his hands, I will hold under torture that you are not likely to succeed by suspecting the one person in the house who has a crippled arm."

WILLIAM WILSON'S RACKET

Colonel March, of the Department of Queer Complaints, has entertained many an odd sort of visitor in his office at New Scotland Yard. But it is seldom that he entertains a visitor so socially distinguished as Lady Patricia Mortlake, only daughter of the Earl of Cray.

She burst in like a whirlwind, that pleasant spring morning two or three years ago. She almost snorted through her aristocratic nose. And this despite the fact that Lady Patricia was normally one of those languid ladies, with a bored blank eye and a sullen underlip, who would have made an ideal heroine for Mr. Coward.

"She refuses to fill up an official form, sir," Colonel March was told. "And she's got a blasted Pekingese with her. But she showed me a note from the Commissioner himself—"

"Send her up," said Colonel March.

Lady Patricia subsided into a chair in a whirl and flop of furs, nursing the Pekingese. As a famous beauty, she perhaps photographed better than she looked. It was a highly enamelled sort of beauty, and her jaw looked as hard as porcelain.

She found herself facing a large, amiable man (weight seventeen stone) with a speckled face, a bland eye, and a cropped moustache. He was teetering before the fire, smoking a short pipe; and Inspector Roberts stood by with a notebook.

"I want you to find him," Lady Patricia said crisply.

"Find him?" repeated Colonel march. "Find whom?"

"Frankie, of course," said Lady Patricia, with some impatience. "My fiancé. Surely, you've heard of him?"

Light came to Colonel March. Any newspaper-reader will remember the political reputation which was being made at that time by the Right Hon. Francis Hale, youngest of the

Cabinet Ministers. Francis Hale was young. He was rich. He was intelligent. He had a great future ahead of him.

Anything that could be said against him was, so to speak, to his credit. Francis Hale always did the correct thing, even to becoming engaged to the impoverished daughter of an impoverished peer. He was a teetotaller, a nonsmoker, and a man of almost painfully straitlaced life. Colonel March privately considered him a good deal of a stuffed shirt.

"As far as I'm concerned," said Lady Patricia coolly, "I'm finished with him. We've done everything for that man. Everything! The right people, the right places, the right contacts. And I do hope I'm broadminded. But when he turned up to make a speech at that Corporation banquet, tight as a tick and practically blind to the world—!"

Now it has been stated before that nothing ever surprised Colonel March. This, however, came close to it.

"And," continued Lady Patricia, flirting her furs, "when it comes to that red-haired hussy—actually carrying on with her in public—well, really!"

Colonel March coughed.

In fact, he covered his happy smile only just in time. To any normal human being there is something heartening, something wholly satisfying about seeing any stuffed shirt go on the razzle-dazzle. The colonel was no exception to this rule. But he caught sight of her eye, and was silent. Lady Patricia Mortlake was no fool. Also, it struck him that she had rather a mean eye and jaw.

"I dare say you think this is all very funny?" she inquired.

"Not at all."

"And I dare say," she continued, opening her veiled eyes and cuddling the dog with dangerous quietness, "you wonder why this concerns the police?"

"Since you mention it—"

"But it *ould* interest the police, I hope, to hear that

Frankie has disappeared? Throwing his whole department into confusion at a critical time; to say nothing of the inconvenience to my parents and me? It *would* interest you to hear that he vanished out of that horrible office in Piccadilly, where heaven knows what has been happening?"

Colonel March regarded her grimly.

"Go on," he invited.

"He's been acting queerly," said Lady Patricia, "for over a month. Ever since he first saw this."

From under her coat she took out a copy of a famous literary weekly, of the conservative and highbrow order, and unfolded it. She turned to the advertisements. With the tip of a scarlet fingernail she indicated one advertisement printed in bold black type. It said simply:

*William and Wilhelmina Wilson, 250*A, *Piccadilly.* Nothing more.

"It's been appearing in only the best papers," the girl insisted. "And every time Frankie sees it, he seems to go off his head."

Colonel March frowned.

"What," he asked, "is the business of William and Wilhelmina Wilson?"

"That's just it! I don't know."

"But if they're in a legitimate business, they must be listed?"

"Well, they're not." Her upper lip lifted defiantly. "I know, because we've had a private detective after Frankie. The detective says they sell vacuum cleaners."

Though Inspector Roberts had ceased in despair to take notes, Colonel March betrayed only an expression of refreshed interest. He continued to teeter before the fire, and puff at his short pipe.

"It started," she went on, "one afternoon when I was waiting for him in the car outside the House of Commons. He stayed behind on the steps, talking interminably to that dreadful Labour man What's-his-name. He simply *wouldn't* come on, no matter how many gestures I made. When he did condescend to join me, he looked at me in a queer way, and asked the chauffeur to stop at the nearest news agent's. There he got out and bought a copy of that paper."

She pointed.

"I couldn't tell what he was looking at. But I knew there was something wrong with him. I asked him if he couldn't take *any* interest in what I was doing for him. Even in the concert of chamber music I'd arranged for that night, where Julio's Trio was to render selections from the modern masters. And he said—"

"Yes?" prompted Colonel March.

"He said 'Damn and blast the modern masters.' It was too utterly tiresome, when Julio is *all* the rage this season."

"Indeed?"

"Then I caught him cutting out that advertisement from the paper. That wouldn't have mattered, and I forgot all about it. But only a week ago I caught him cutting it out again, this time out of *The Times*. So," explained Lady Patricia, "I decided to find out who this 'William and Wilhelmina Wilson' really were. I paid them a visit yesterday."

Her eyes took on a shrewd, speculative look.

"Whoever they are," she said thoughtfully, "they've got pots of money. I expected to find the office some dreadful little place: you know. But it wasn't. My dear man, it's in a big new block of offices opposite the Green Park. So business-like: that's what I can't understand. You go up in a lift, and there's a big marble corridor and a ground-glass door with "William and Wilhelmina Wilson' on it."

Her expression was now one of active fury, which she tried to conceal. As though remembering to be maternal, she lifted the Pekingese, shook it in the air, and cooed to it with pouted lips. The dog sneezed the hair out of its eyes, and looked bored.

"I opened the door," she said, "and there was a big waiting-room. Empty. Some rather good bronzes and etchings, too. I called out. I rapped on the table. But nobody answered. Just when I was wondering what to do, Flopit here . . . izzums, precious! . . . Flopit found another door, and began to bark."

She drew a deep breath.

"I opened *that* door. It was a big office, like a secretary's office. In the middle was a big flat-topped desk, with a swivel-chair behind it. In the chair sat Frankie, my Frankie. And on his lap, with her arms round his neck, sat a horrible red-haired hussy, about nineteen years old."

This time it was a near thing.

Colonel March's cough was so prolonged and strangled that a blind man would have noticed something wrong. Lady Patricia's hard eye noted it, and hated it. But she had to speak now.

"Well, really! I mean to say! I hope I'm broadminded, but—! My dear man, I was boiling; positively boiling. I didn't say anything. I just picked up Flopit by his precious neck, and walked out, and slammed the door. I walked across the waiting-room and out into the hall.

"But I didn't go any farther. After all, I have Frankie's good at heart. And Frankie is awfully rich, and it didn't seem right that *she* should get his money, whereas I . . . I mean, when you've worked and slaved for a man, as I've worked and slaved for Frankie . . . well, it's rather thick.

"I waited in front of the door. Finally, I decided to go back and have it out with them. Back I marched into the waiting-room; and there I met somebody I hadn't seen before. A well-dressed elderly man. Rather distinguished-looking:

bald except for white hair at the back of his head, curling down nearly to his collar.

"He said, 'Yes, madam?'

"I said, 'Who are you?'

"He said, 'I am William Wilson. Have you an appointment?'

"I just froze him. I asked to see Mr. Hale. He had the nerve to raise his eyebrows and say that Frankie wasn't there: that he had never heard of any Mr. Hale and didn't know what I was talking about. I said I also supposed he didn't know anything about a red-haired girl either? He looked surprised and said he imagined I must mean Miss Wilhelmina Wilson, his niece and secretary—think of it!—but he still knew of no Mr. Hale.

"Well, really, that was too much! I just walked past him and opened the door to the office where I'd seen Frankie before. Frankie wasn't there; but the red-haired girl was. She was standing in front of another little door, which led to a kind of cloakroom, and looking disgustingly guilty. I simply pushed her out of the way, and looked in. But . . ."

Lady Patricia Mortlake gulped.

"Yes?" prompted Colonel March.

"Frankie wasn't there," she said.

"He wasn't in the cloakroom?"

"He wasn't *anywhere*," returned the girl, lifting her shoulders. "There was only one other room, a big private office overlooking Piccadilly, on the fourth floor. He wasn't hiding anywhere, because I looked. And there's no way out of any of the offices except through the door to the main corridor, where I'd been standing. Frankie wasn't there. But his clothes were."

"*What?*" demanded Colonel March.

"His clothes. The suit he'd been wearing: with his watch, and notecase, and papers, and key ring, and the fountain pen

I gave him for his birthday. They were hanging up in a locker in the cloakroom. Clothes, but no Frankie. And he hasn't been seen since. Now do you wonder why I'm here?"

Hitherto Colonel March had been listening with an indulgent air. Now his sandy eyebrows drew together.

"Let me understand this," he said in a sharp and rather sinister voice. "You mean he literally disappeared?"

"Yes!"

"He couldn't, for instance, have slipped out while you were examining the various offices?"

"Without his clothes?" asked Patricia unanswerably.

There was a silence.

"Frankie!" she almost wailed. "Of all people, Frankie! Of course I suppose he could have sneaked out. For that matter, he could have climbed out of a window and down the face of the building into Piccadilly. But in his underwear? Frankie?"

"Suppose he had another suit of clothes there?"

"Why?" asked Patricia, again unanswerably.

It is not often that Colonel March finds himself stumped, definitely left flat and up against it. This appeared to be one of the times.

"And what have you done since?"

"What could I do? He's not at his flat here, or at his place in the country. Not one of his friends, including his private secretary, seems to know where he is. I even tackled that dreadful Labour man he seems to have been so thick with recently; and I thought for a second he was going to burst out laughing. But even *he* swore he didn't know where Frankie was."

"H'm," said Colonel March.

"We can't make this public, you see. That would be dreadful. And so you're our last hope. Haven't you got any theory?"

"Oh, theories!" said Colonel March, waving a big arm irritably. "I can think of half a dozen theories. But they don't explain the main difficulty. Suppose any lurid theory you like. Suppose the mysterious William and Wilhelmina Wilson have murdered him and hidden his body. Suppose there is a sinister political conspiracy against him. Suppose Francis Hale has disguised himself and is masquerading as the distinguished-looking old gentleman with the white hair . . ."

Patricia sat up straight.

"A supposition," said the colonel grimly, "about as likely as any idea that he went walking about the streets in his underwear. But I repeat: suppose anything you like! It still won't explain what puzzles me most."

"Which is?"

"The profession of William and Wilhelmina Wilson," answered Colonel March. "Any ideas, Roberts?"

Inspector Roberts, shutting up his notebook, ruminated on this.

"Well, sir—" he began hesitantly.

"Yes, yes, go on!"

"Well, sir, the point seems to be this. Either Mr. Hale disappeared of his own free will, or else he didn't. It looks to me as though he didn't."

"Oh? Why not?"

"The personal effects," said Roberts. "The watch and the notecase and the rest of it. If you were going to do a bunk somewhere, wouldn't those be the very things you'd take with you? It isn't as though he were trying to stage a fake suicide, or anything like that. One minute he's comfortably in that office, with the young lady in his lap"—Roberts coughed, and looked swiftly away from their guest—"and the next he's gone. That's the part I don't like."

Colonel March grunted.

"And yet," pursued Roberts, "if that pair have managed to make away with him, I can't for the life of me see how or why. It's like something out of Edgar Allan Poe."

He broke off, for a curious expression crossed Colonel March's face: it was a though he had been hit across the back of the head with a club.

"Good lord!" he muttered, in a hollow voice like a ghost. "I wonder if that could be it?"

"If it could be what?" demanded Lady Patricia.

"The name," argued Colonel march, half to himself, "might be a coincidence. On the other hand, it might be most infernally apt: the seal of Wilson." He turned to Lady Patricia. "Tell me. Can Francis Hale hold his liquor?"

She stared back at him.

"I don't know what on earth you're talking about!"

"Yes, you do." The colonel was irritable. "You told me a while ago that Hale, in one of his fits of being fed up—ahem—in one of his more erratic moments, got tight at a Corporation banquet. What did he drink?"

His visitor set her jaw.

"Everything," she said. "Beginning with cocktails and going all the way through to brandy. He simply sloshed it down. My father was frantic."

"And how did it affect him? Hale, I mean?"

"They said he never made a better speech. He mixed up the pages in reading it; and to anybody who really knew what the speech was about, it sounded *horrible.* But nobody noticed anything. They even seemed to like it: which was a mercy, because—"

Colonel March rubbed his hands together. He was utterly pleased and absorbed, with a smile which threatened to dislodge the pipe from his mouth. Then he went over and patted his guest on the shoulder.

"Go home," he said. "Go home, take an aspirin, and stop

worrying. Inspector Roberts and I are going to call on the Wilsons. I have every reason to believe I see a way out of the difficulty. In fact, I think I can promise it, now that I am able to guess—"

"Guess what?" demanded Lady Patricia, lifting the dog and shaking it at him.

"The racket of William Wilson," said Colonel March.

A smooth-slipping lift took them up to the fourth floor of number 250A Piccadilly. A holy calm, as of a temple, pervaded these marble premises. The names *William and Wilhelmina Wilson* were printed on the ground-glass door in black lettering as discreet as a visiting-card. Motioning Inspector Roberts to precede him, Colonel March opened the door.

The waiting-room inside was softly lighted and carpeted. Magazines were scattered on a centre table for the convenience of those who waited; the point which racked Inspector Roberts's wits was what in blazes they were supposed to be waiting for. And behind the reception desk at the far end sat at a small, sleek, trim young lady with red hair. She was glancing through a copy of a fashionable weekly.

"Miss Wilson?" said Colonel March.

"Yes?" said Miss Wilson with polite briskness.

"I should like to see your uncle."

Colonel March laid his official card on the desk.

For a few seconds Miss Wilson looked at it gravely, and then raised her head. If the notoriously frigid Francis Hale had fallen for Miss Wilson, Inspector Roberts for one did not blame him; she had blue eyes of a deceptive demureness, and a mouth of the sort called generous.

But if Roberts expected to see any sign of guilt or even nervousness, he was disappointed. What flashed across her face was a smile of almost unholy glee, which she instantly corrected.

"My uncle has been rather expecting you," she admitted. "Will you walk into our parlour?"

She led them through the secretary's office—with its famous desk and swivel-chair—to a third office overlooking Piccadilly. Here, behind another flat-topped desk, sat a stout old gentleman with the manners of a cardinal. His glossy bald head was set off by a fringe of white hair which curved down to the back of his collar. He wore pince-nez, through which he was studying a pile of large photographs. He welcomed his visitors courteously.

"As my niece says," he told them, "I have been rather expecting you." His mouth tightened. "Please sit down. You had better remain too, Wilhelmina, my dear."

"In that case," said Colonel March, "I'll come straight to the point. Of course, your name isn't really Wilson?"

Mr. Wilson looked pained.

"Naturally not. It is a trade name. A"—he waved his hand—"a flight of poetic fancy, if you like."

"Yes," said Colonel march. "That's what I thought, as soon as I guessed what your racket was."

Now Mr. Wilson seemed more than pained; he seemed hurt.

"Racket!" he protested. "My dear sir! No, no, no, no! That is too much. Profession, if you like. Business, if you insist. Yes: say a business, and on a large scale. After all, I am a modern man who has simply seen a modern need for those who can afford it. I supply that need. And there you are."

"Aren't you afraid I'll give you away?"

Mr. Wilson permitted himself a slight smile.

"Hardly. If you were to look in there"—he indicated a row of filing cases along one wall—"and see the names of some of my more illustrious clients, I hardly think you would talk of exposure. There is one client, for instance . . .

but we must not be indiscreet." He returned to an old grievance. "Profession, yes. Business, yes. But racket? Really,
now! On the contrary, I flatter myself that I am something of
a public benefactor."

Inspector Roberts was a patient man. As Colonel March's
assistant, he had to be. But there are limits to the human
curiosity of even the best-trained subordinate.

"Sir," he suddenly cried, "I can't stand any more of this.
Before I go completely off my chump, will you tell me what
this is all about? What's going on here? What is the fellow's
racket? And why should he call himself Wilson?"

All three of them looked at him—Mr. Wilson with a
reproving cluck of the tongue, Miss Wilson with a smile, and
Colonel March with blandness.

"He calls himself William Wilson," replied Colonel
March, "After the story of the same name. That story was
written by Edgar Allan Poe, as you so helpfully suggested.
You don't remember the story?"

"No, sir, I can't say I do."

"William Wilson," said Colonel March, "met himself."

Roberts blinked.

"Met himself?"

"He met his own image," explained Colonel March, set-
tling back comfortably. "I rather admire Mr. Wilson here. He
is the proprietor of a unique Agency. He provides doubles for
eminent men and women in their unimportant public appearances, so that the real men can stop at home and get on with
their work."

Mr. Wilson leaned across the desk and spoke earnestly.

"You would be surprised," he said, "at the call there is for
our services. Consider the life of a public man! While he
should be at work, custom demands that he make endless
public appearances, none of them in the least an iota of
good. He makes interminable tours of inspection; he lays

cornerstones; he addresses mothers' meetings. Few if any of the people he meets have ever seen him before, or will ever see him again. And a good double—!"

Mr. Wilson drew a deep breath, rather sadly.

"I fear the idea is not mine," he went on. "It was tried out a few years ago by a very eminent American. He simply could not stand all the handshaking."

Wilhelmina Wilson intervened loyally.

"But you were the only one who saw its commercial possibilities," she cried, and sat down on the edge of his desk as though to defend him. She somewhat spoiled the effect of this by winking at Colonel March.

"Thank you, my dear," said Mr. Wilson. He turned back to his guests.

"Our fees, of course, are considerable," he added apologetically. "But you have no idea of the difficulties. Once I had to send all the way to South Africa to get a passable double for . . . well, well, again we mustn't be indiscreet!" He closed his eyes and smiled happily. "Then there is the question of elocution, voice-training, and so on. On the whole, I am proud of my handiwork. The next time you go to a cinema and see a newsreel, watch very closely! You may see something that will surprise you."

Inspector Roberts was getting his breath back.

"Then Mr. Hale—" he began.

"Ah, yes," murmured the proprietor of the Agency, brushing his dry palms together and frowning at Colonel March. "Mr. Hale! I imagine you saw a discrepancy when Mr. Hale's double, a promising young actor named Gabriel Fisk, got drunk at that banquet?"

"A discrepancy," said Colonel March; "but probably not the discrepancy you mean. Wasn't the rather rash of him, by the way?"

"Perhaps," admitted Mr. Wilson sadly. "But the lesser of

two evils. You see, we hadn't known that Mr. Hale's fiancée was to be present; otherwise we should not have risked it. So, in case Fisk made a bad slip of some kind, he had to have an excuse for making a slip. Mr. Hale is a notorious and genuine teetotaller. But then (I thought) even a teetotaller can change his mind."

Colonel March chuckled.

"He can change his mind," said the colonel. "What he can't change is his digestive system. He can't work his way through a huge wine list, from cocktails to brandy, without either becoming ill or going to sleep. In a man who has never taken a drink in his life, I submit that it's a physical impossibility. When I heard of that little performance, I said to myself: 'It is magnificent; but it isn't Hale.' And, speaking of his fiancée . . ."

Wilhelmina Wilson stiffened.

Throughout this conversation she had several times seemed on the point of speaking. She still sat on the edge of her uncle's desk, staring moodily at the toe of her slipper. When Colonel March spoke, she looked at her uncle as though with appeal.

But Mr. Wilson remained unruffled.

"Ah, yes!" he said. "That unfortunate affair yesterday morning!"

"What was unfortunate about it?" the girl demanded, with sudden passion.

"Tush!" said her uncle, raising a gentle but admonitory forefinger. He looked distressed. "Colonel March, my niece is—impulsive. Like her poor mother, my sister. And she is very fond of young Gabriel Fisk.

"You understand now what happened, I hope? That suit of clothes, with the notecase and watch and the rest of it, had nothing to do with the case. It's a supernumerary. Mr. Hale provided us with an exact duplicate of his possessions. I am an artist, sir, or I am nothing. Neither the suit nor its contents has been worn for a week. Fisk left it hanging there in the locker when he changed in that cloakroom after appearing at the Muswell Hill Flower Show last Tuesday week.

"Yesterday Fisk, in his ordinary clothes, came in for instructions. He and my niece—" Mr. Wilson coughed. "It was unfortunate that Lady Patricia Mortlake walked in when she did. Fisk, of course, simply slipped out when her back was turned. Unfortunately, Lady Patricia is a strong-minded person. She ransacked the place, found the suit, and suspected I hate to think what."

"And Hale?" asked Colonel March, without batting an eyelid. "The real Hale? Where is he now?"

Again Mr. Wilson was apologetic.

"At his country place, with his head under the bedclothes, until he can think up an excuse to explain his supposed conduct. Even if he tells the truth, I'm afraid Lady Patricia will not like it. And I shall probably—er—lose a client. Life," said Mr. Wilson, shaking his head, "is difficult."

"Yes."

"In any case, as I said before, you will respect our little secret? Our racket, as you prefer to call it?"

Colonel March got to his feet. Always an impressive figure, he now seemed to fill the room. He put on his soft hat at a more rakish angle than was seemly, and picked up his silver-headed stick. His speckled face was aglow.

"Candidly," he said, "I can't do anything else. You've got me. If I understand the situation, to show up this racket would be to wreck half the public reputations in England. We can't have that. The public demands to be deceived. By gad, it *shall* be deceived! So, if Miss Wilson vouches for the truth of this story—?"

"Yes," said the girl, with her eyes on the floor.

"Then there's nothing more to be said. Sir, good day to you!"

"And to you, Colonel March," beamed Mr. Wilson. "Wilhelmina, my dear, will you show these gentlemen out?"

Wilhelmina did show them out. Yet she did not appear to be happy about anything. For the first time her manner displayed a trace of nervousness. In the outer office she suddenly stopped, and whirled round on them.

"You old—" she began explosively, and then broke off to laugh; or cry—Colonel March was not sure which. "What are you thinking?"

"Thinking?" repeated Colonel March, with massive innocence.

"Yes, you were! You know you were! I could see it in your face. What's the matter? Don't you believe our story even now? I swear to you that that suit of clothes hasn't been touched for a week!"

"Oh, that?" said the colonel, as though enlightened. "I believe that."

"Then what is it? What were you thinking?"

"Well," said Colonel March, "since you ask, I was thinking about the dog."

"Dog?" she echoed blankly.

"Lady Patricia Mortlake's dog. An objectionable dog. But then I don't like Pekes." Colonel March reflected. "It had one quality, though, that I did notice. The dog Flopit took absolutely no interest in strangers. You could show it the whole personnel of Scotland Yard, and it never so much as opened an eye—let alone barking. It's the sort of dog which barks only when it scents or senses someone it knows very well. So, if it was Gabriel Fisk who was here with you yesterday, I only wondered why Flopit set up the clamour that drew Lady Patricia Mortlake's attention to you both."

While the blue eyes never left him, and an expression of

impish animation survived even the embarrassed colour of her face, Colonel March added a last word.

"Stick to him," he advised in an even lower voice. "You'll be much better for him than that high-born shrew who's got his life planned out to the last musicale and reception."

"I've been in love with Frank Hale for a long time," the girl confessed. "But I thought it might be better for him if we said—"

"There's no reason for you and your uncle to lie in order to please her," said Colonel March. "As for Hale, there are still a few gleams of humanity in him. Under you, please God, he may yet develop into a statesman. Good afternoon, Miss Wilson. Come, Roberts. We must go and find some more queer complaints."

AND OTHER STORIES

INTRODUCTION

The Christmas issues of glossy weekly magazines in Britain, including *The Illustrated London News*, *The Sketch*, and *The Tatler*, usually printed ghost stories to read by the fireside. Carr enjoyed writing what he called "terror tales" that had the possibility of both supernatural and material explanations, and, like the works of one of Carr's favorite authors, Montague Rhodes James, his Christmas stories are based on the fears produced when the commonplace goes awry. One of these tales, "Persons or Things Unknown," was published in *Fell and Foul Play*. Two others are included here. "Blind Man's Hood" is from the Christmas 1937 number of *The Sketch*, and it includes a possible explanation of a genuine unsolved murder, the Peasonhall case of 1902. "New Murders for Old," from the Christmas 1939 *Illustrated London News,* contains a situation that clearly fascinated Carr, for he used it in three other stories: "The Legend of the Cane in the Dark" in *The Haverfordian*, March 1927; "The Man Who Was Dead," published in *Dime Mystery*, May 1935 (and collected in *The Door to Doom*); and "The Man with Two Heads," a BBC radio play, November 6, 1945.

"The Diamond Pentacle" was published under the "Carter Dickson" pseudonym in the November 15, 1939 weekly edition of *The Times*. This fine locked-room story is reprinted here for the first time. Carr did not include "The Diamond Pentacle" in any of the short-story collections published during his own lifetime. The tale was then forgotten until Tony Medawar located a copy, and it is because of him that we can include it here.

"Strictly Diplomatic" and "The Clue of the Red Wig" were both published in *The Strand Magazine*. "Strictly Diplomatic," published in the December 1939 issue, uses one of nesses. "The Clue of the Red Wig," published in December 1940, is a lighthearted tale in which the problem is not to solve an impossible crime but to explain why a woman would have been found dead in a park, wearing only her underwear, with the rest of her clothes neatly folded beside her.

This book concludes with two more previously uncollected tales. "Lair of the Devil-Fish" is a radio script broadcast on the famous BBC program created by Carr, *Appointment with Fear.* Its date is December 21, 1944, but this Cuban mystery does not reflect the holiday season. Based on Carr's own trip to Cuba as a deckhand a number of years earlier, "Lair of the Devil-Fish" is an excellent example of his ability to upset the apple-cart when we least expect it. "Scotland Yard's Christmas" was published in *Weekend*, December 25/29, 1957, but the editor changed the title to the uninspired "Detective's Day Off." I have restored Carr's title. The story grew out of a situation that had intrigued Carr for almost thirty years. How can a person enter a telephone booth and completely disappear? He challenged his friend Clayton Rawson, also an author of impossible-crime stories, to solve the problem, and Rawson did so brilliantly in a story called "Off the Face of the Earth." (This story is most readily available in the anthology *Death Locked In*, edited by Robert Adey and me.) Carr's own solution to the problem is in "Scotland Yard's Christmas." No one would claim that it is one of his best stories, but I believe that the main reason that it has remained so little known is that the explanation for the vanishing is implied rather than stated. Either Carr neglected to explain fully, or (more likely) a key paragraph was removed by *Weekend*'s editor for reason of space. I have added my own explanation, set it off from the rest of the story with brackets.

BLIND MAN'S HOOD

I

Although one snowflake had already sifted past the lights, the great doors of the house stood open. It seemed less a snowflake than a shadow; for a bitter wind whipped after it, and the doors creaked. Inside, Rodney and Muriel Hunter could see a dingy, narrow hall paved in dull red tiles, with a Jacobean staircase at the rear. (At that time, of course, there was no dead woman lying inside.)

To find such a place in the loneliest part of the Weald of Kent—a seventeenth-century country house whose floors had grown humped and its beams scrubbed by the years—was what they had expected. Even to find electricity was not surprising. But Rodney Hunter thought he had seldom seen so many lights in one house, and Muriel had been wondering about it ever since their car turned the bend in the road. "Clearlawns" lived up to its name. It stood in the midst of a slope of flat grass, now wiry white with frost, and there was no tree or shrub within twenty yards of it. Those lights contrasted with a certain inhospitable and damp air about the house, as though the owner were compelled to keep them burning.

"But why is the front door *open*?" insisted Muriel.

In the drive-way, the engine of their car coughed and died. The house was now a secret blackness of gables, emitting light at every chink, and silhouetting the stalks of the wisteria vines which climbed it. On either side of the front door were little-paned windows whose curtains had not been drawn. Towards their left they could see into a low dining-room, with table and sideboard set for a cold supper; towards their right was a darkish library moving with the reflections of a bright fire.

The sight of the fire warmed Rodney Hunter, but it made

264

him feel guilty. They were very late. At five o'clock, without fail, he had promised Jack Bannister, they would be at Clearlawns to inaugurate the Christmas party.

Engine-trouble in leaving London was one thing; idling at a country pub along the way, drinking hot ale and listening to the wireless sing carols until a sort of Dickensian jollity stole into you, was something else. But both he and Muriel were young; they were very fond of each other and of things in general; and they had worked themselves into a glow of Christmas, which—as they stood before the creaking doors of Clearlawns—grew oddly cool.

There was no real reason, Rodney thought, to feel disquiet. He hoisted their luggage, including a big box of presents for Jack and Molly's children out of the rear of the car. That his footsteps should sound loud on the gravel was only natural. He put his head into the doorway and whistled. Then he began to bang the knocker. Its sound seemed to seek out every corner of the house and then come back like a questing dog; but there was no response.

"I'll tell you something else," he said. "There's nobody in the house."

Muriel ran up the three steps to stand beside him. She had drawn her fur coat close around her, and her face was bright with cold.

"But that's impossible!" she said. "I mean, even if they're out, the servants—! Molly told me she keeps a cook and two maids. Are you sure we've got the right place?"

"Yes. The name's on the gate, and there's no other house within a mile."

With the same impulse they craned their necks to look through the windows of the dining-room on the left. Cold fowl on the sideboard, a great bowl of chestnuts; and, now they could see it, another good fire, before which stood a chair with a piece of knitting put aside on it. Rodney tried the knocker again, vigorously, but the sound was all wrong. It was as though they were even more lonely in that core of light, with the east wind rushing across the Weald, and the door creaking again.

"I suppose we'd better go in," said Rodney. He added, with a lack of Christmas spirit: "Here, this is a devil of a trick! What do you think has happened? I'll swear that fire has been made up in the last fifteen minutes."

He stepped into the hall and set down the bags. As he was turning to close the door, Muriel put her hand on his arm.

"I say, Rod. Do you think you'd better close it?"

"Why not?"

"I—I don't know."

"The place is getting chilly enough as it is," he pointed out, unwilling to admit that the same thought had occurred to him. He closed both doors and shot their bar into place; and, at the same moment, a girl came out of the door to the library on the right.

She was such a pleasant-faced girl that they both felt a sense of relief. Why she had not answered the knocking had ceased to be a question; she filled a void. She was pretty, not more than twenty-one or two, and had an air of primness which made Rodney Hunter vaguely associate her with a governess or a secretary, though Jack Bannister had never mentioned any such person. She was plump, but with a curiously narrow waist; and she wore brown. Her brown hair was neatly parted, and her brown eyes—long eyes, which might have given a hint of secrecy or curious smiles if they had not been so placid—looked concerned. In one hand she carried what looked like a small white bag of linen or cotton. And she spoke with a dignity which did not match her years.

"I am most terribly sorry," she told them. "I *thought* I heard someone, but I was so busy that I could not be sure. Will you forgive me?"

She smiled. Hunter's private view was that his knocking had been loud enough to wake the dead; but he murmured conventional things. As though conscious of some faint incongruity about the white bag in her hand, she held it up.

"For Blind Man's Buff," she explained. "They do cheat so, I'm afraid, and not only the children. If one uses an ordinary handkerchief tied round the eyes, they always manage to get a corner loose. But if you take this, and you put it fully over a person's head, and you tie it round the neck"—a sudden gruesome image occurred to Rodney Hunter—"then it works so much better, don't you think?" Her eyes seemed to turn inward, and to grow absent. "But I must not keep you talking here. You are—?"

"My name is Hunter. This is my wife. I'm afraid we've arrived late, but I understood Mr. Bannister was expecting—"

"He did not tell you?" asked the girl in brown.

"Tell me what?"

"Everyone here, including the servants, is always out of the house at this hour on this particular date. It is the custom; I believe it has been the custom for more than sixty years. There is some sort of special church service."

Rodney Hunter's imagination had been devising all sorts of fantastic explanations: the first of them being that this demure lady had murdered the members of the household, and was engaged in disposing of the bodies. What put this nonsensical notion into his head he could not tell, unless it was his own profession of detective-story writing. But he felt relieved to hear a commonplace explanation. Then the woman spoke again.

"Of course, it is a pretext, really. The rector, that dear man, invented it all those years ago to save embarrassment. What happened here had nothing to do with the murder, since the dates were so different; and I suppose most people had forgotten now why the tenants *do* prefer to stay away during seven and eight o'clock on Christmas Eve. I doubt if Mrs. Bannister even knows the real reason, though I should imagine Mr. Bannister must know it. But what happens here cannot be very pleasant, and it wouldn't do to have the children see it—would it?"

Muriel spoke with such sudden directness that her husband knew she was afraid. "Who are you?" Muriel said. "And what on earth are you talking about?"

"I am quite sane, really," their hostess assured them, with a smile that was half-cheery and half-coy. "I dare say it must be all very confusing to you, poor dear. But I am forgetting my duties. Please come in and sit down before the fire, and let me offer you something to drink."

She took them into the library on the right, going ahead with a walk that was like a bounce, and looking over her shoulder out of those long eyes. The library was a long, low room with beams. The windows towards the road were uncurtained; but those in the side-wall, where a faded red-brick fireplace stood, were bay windows with draperies closed across them. As their hostess put them before the fire, Hunter could have sworn he saw one of the draperies move.

"You need not worry about it," she assured him, following his glance towards the bay. "Even if you looked in there, you might not see anything now. I believe some gentleman did try it once, a long time ago. He stayed in the house for a wager. But when he pulled the curtain back, he did not see anything in the bay—at least, anything quite. He felt some hair, and it moved. That is why they have so many lights nowadays."

Muriel had sat down on a sofa, and was lighting a cigarette: to the rather prim disapproval of their hostess, Hunter thought.

"May we have a hot drink?" Muriel asked crisply. "And then, if you don't mind, we might walk over and meet the Bannisters coming from church."

"Oh, please don't do that!" cried the other. She had been standing by the fireplace, her hands folded and turned outwards. Now she ran across to sit down beside Muriel; and the swiftness of her movement, no less than the touch of her hand on Muriel's arm, made the latter draw back.

Hunter was now completely convinced that their hostess was out of her head. Why she held such fascination for him, though, he could not understand. In her eagerness to keep them there, the girl had come upon a new idea. On a table behind the sofa, book-ends held a row of modern novels. Conspicuously displayed—probably due to Molly Bannister's tact—were two of Rodney Hunter's detective stories. The girl put a finger on them.

"May I ask if you wrote these?"

He admitted it.

"Then," she said with sudden composure, "it would probably interest you to hear about the murder. It was a most perplexing business, you know; the police could make nothing of it, and no one ever has been able to solve it." An arresting eye fixed on his. "It happened out in the hall there. A poor woman was killed where there was no one to kill her, and no one could have done it. But she was murdered."

Hunter started to get up from his chair; then he changed his mind, and sat down again. "Go on," he said.

II

"You must forgive me if I am a little uncertain about dates," she urged. "I think it was in the early eighteen-seventies, and I am sure it was in early February—because of the snow. It was a bad winter then; the farmers' livestock all died. My people have been bred up in the district for years, and I know that. The house here was much as it is now, except that there was none of this lighting (only paraffin lamps, poor girl!); and you were obliged to pump up what water you wanted; and people read the newspaper quite through, and discussed it for days.

"The people were a little different to look at, too. I am sure I do not understand why we think beards are so strange nowadays; they seem to think that men who had beards never had any emotions. But even young men wore them then, and looked handsome enough. There was a newly married couple living in this house at the time: at least, they had been married only the summer before. They were named Edward and Jane Waycross, and it was considered a good match everywhere.

"Edward Waycross did not have a beard, but he had bushy side-whiskers which he kept curled. He was not a handsome man, either, being somewhat dry and hard-favoured; but he was a religious man, and a good man, and an excellent man of business, they say: a manufacturer of agricultural implements at Hawkhurst. He had determined that Jane Anders (as she was) would make him a good wife, and I dare say she did. The girl had several suitors. Although Mr. Waycross was the best match, I know it surprised people a little when she accepted him, because she was thought to have been fond of another man—a more striking man, whom many of the young girls were after. This was Jeremy Wilkes: who came of a very good family, but was considered wicked. He was no younger than Mr. Waycross, but he had a great black beard, and wore white waistcoats with gold chains, and drove a gig. Of course, there had been gossip, but that was because Jane Anders was considered pretty."

Their hostess had bean sitting back against the sofa, quietly folding the little white bag with one hand, and speaking in a prim voice. Now she did something which turned her hearers cold.

You have probably seen the same thing done many times. She had been touching her cheek lightly with the fingers of the other hand. In doing so, she touched the flesh at the corner under her lower eyelid, and accidentally drew down the corner of that eyelid—which should have exposed the red part of the inner lid at the corner of the eye. It was not red. It was of a sickly pale colour.

"In the course of his business dealings," she went on, "Mr. Waycross had often to go to London, and usually he was obliged to remain overnight. But Jane Waycross was not afraid to remain alone in the house. She had a good servant, a staunch old woman, and a good dog. Even so, Mr. Waycross commended her for her courage."

The girl smiled. "On the night I wish to tell you of, in February, Mr. Waycross was absent. Unfortunately, too, the old servant was absent; she had been called away as a midwife to attend her cousin, and Jane Waycross had allowed her to go. This was known in the village, since all such affairs are well known, and some uneasiness was felt—this house being isolated, as you know. But she was not afraid.

"It was a very cold night, with a heavy fall of snow which had stopped about nine o'clock. You must know, beyond doubt, that poor Jane Waycross was alive after it had stopped snowing. It must have been nearly half-past nine when a Mr. Moody—a very good and sober man who lived in Hawkhurst—was driving home along the road past this house. As you know, it stands in the middle of a great bare stretch of lawn; and you can see the house clearly from the road. Mr. Moody saw poor Jane at the window of one of the upstairs bedrooms, with a candle in her hand, closing the shutters. But he was not the only witness who saw her alive.

"On that same evening, Mr. Wilkes (the handsome gentle-

man I spoke to you of a moment ago) had been at a tavern
in the village of Five Ashes with Dr. Sutton, the local doctor,
and a racing gentleman named Pawley. At about half-past
eleven they started to drive home in Mr. Wilkes's gig to
Cross-in-Hand. I am afraid they had been drinking, but they
were all in their sober senses. The landlord of the tavern
remembered the time because he had stood in the doorway
to watch the gig, which had fine yellow wheels, go spanking
away as though there were no snow; and Mr. Wilkes in one
of the new round hats with a curly brim.

"There was a bright moon. 'And no danger,' Dr. Sutton
always said afterwards; 'shadows of trees and fences as clear
as though a silhouette-cutter had made 'em for sixpence.'
But when they were passing this house Mr. Wilkes pulled up
sharp. There was a bright light in the window of one of the
downstairs rooms—this room, in fact. They sat out there
looking round the hood of the gig, and wondering.

"Mr. Wilkes spoke: 'I don't like this,' he said. 'You know,
gentlemen, that Waycross is still in London; and the lady in
question is in the habit of retiring early. I am going up there
to find out if anything is wrong.'

"With that he jumped out of the gig, his black beard jut-
ting out and his breath smoking. He said: 'And if it is a burglar, then, by Something, gentlemen'—I will not repeat the
word he used—'by Something, gentlemen, I'll settle him.'
He walked through the gate and up to the house—they could
follow every step he made—and looked into the windows of
this room here. Presently he returned looking relieved (they
could see him by the light of the gig lamps), but wiping the
moisture off his forehead.

"'It is all right,' he said to them; 'Waycross has come
home. But, by Something, gentlemen, he is growing thinner
these days, or it is shadows.'

"Then he told them what he had seen. If you look through

the front windows—there—you can look sideways and see out through the doorway into the main hall. He said he had seen Mrs. Waycross standing in the hall with her back to the staircase, wearing a blue dressing-wrap over her nightgown, and her hair down round her shoulders. Standing in front of her, with his back to Mr. Wilkes, was a tallish, thin man like Mr. Waycross, with a long greatcoat and a tall hat like Mr. Waycross's. *She* was carrying either a candle or a lamp; and he remembered how the tall hat seemed to wag back and forth, as though the man were talking to her or putting out his hands towards her. For he said he could not see the woman's face.

"Of course, it was not Mr. Waycross; but how were they to know that?

"At about seven o'clock next morning, Mrs. Randall, the old servant, returned. (A fine boy had been born to her cousin the night before.) Mrs. Randall came home through the white dawn and the white snow, and found the house all locked up. She could get no answer to her knocking. Being a woman of great resolution, she eventually broke a window and got in. But, when she saw what was in the front hall, she went out screaming for help.

"Poor Jane was past help. I know I should not speak of these things; but I must. She was lying on her face in the hall. From the waist down her body was much charred and—unclothed, you know, because fire had burnt away most of the nightgown and the dressing-wrap. The tiles of the hall were soaked with blood and paraffin oil, the oil having come from a broken lamp with a thick blue-silk shade which was lying a little distance away. Near it was a china candlestick with a candle. This fire had also charred a part of the panelling of the wall, and a part of the staircase. Fortunately, the floor is of brick tiles, and there had not been much paraffin left in the lamp, or the house would have been set afire.

"But she had not died from burns alone. Her throat had been cut with a deep slash from some very sharp blade. But she had been alive for a while to feel both things, for she had crawled forward on her hands while she was burning. It was a cruel death, a horrible death for a soft person like that."

There was a pause. The expression on the face of the narrator, the plump girl in the brown dress, altered slightly. So did the expression of her eyes. She was sitting beside Muriel; and moved a little closer.

"Of course, the police came. I do not understand such things, I am afraid, but they found that the house had not been robbed. They also noticed the odd thing I have mentioned, that there was both a lamp *and* a candle in a candlestick near her. The lamp came from Mr. and Mrs. Waycross's bedroom upstairs, and so did the candlestick: there were no other lamps or candles downstairs except the lamps waiting to be filled next morning in the back kitchen. But the police thought she would not have come downstairs carrying both the lamp *and* the candle as well.

"She must have brought the lamp, because that was broken. When the murderer took hold of her, they thought, she had dropped the lamp, and it went out; the paraffin spilled, but did not catch fire. Then this man in the tall hat, to finish his work after he had cut her throat, went upstairs, and got a candle, and set fire to the spilled oil. I am stupid at these things; but even I should have guessed that this must mean someone familiar with the house. Also, if she came downstairs, it must have been to let someone in at the front door; and that could not have been a burglar.

"You may be sure all the gossips were like police from the start, even when the police hemm'd and haw'd, because they knew Mrs. Waycross must have opened the door to a man who was not her husband. And immediately they found an indication of this, in the mess that the fire and blood had made in the hall. Some distance away from poor Jane's body there was a medicine-bottle, such as chemists use. I think it had been broken in two pieces; and on one intact piece they found sticking some fragments of a letter that had not been quite burned. It was in a man's handwriting, not her husband's, and they made out enough of it to understand. It was full of—expressions of love, you know, and it made an appointment to meet her there on that night."

Rodney Hunter, as the girl paused, felt impelled to ask a question.

"Did they know whose handwriting it was?"

"It was Jeremy Wilkes's," replied the other simply. "Though they never proved that, never more than slightly suspected it, and the circumstances did not bear it out. In fact, a knife stained with blood was actually found in Mr. Wilkes's possession. But the police never brought it to anything, poor souls. For, you see, not Mr. Wilkes—or anyone else in the world—could possibly have done the murder."

III

"I don't understand that," said Hunter, rather sharply.

"Forgive me if I am stupid about telling things," urged their hostess in a tone of apology. She seemed to be listening to the chimney growl under a cold sky, and listening with hard, placid eyes. "But even the village gossips could tell that. When Mrs. Randall came here to the house on that morning, both the front and the back doors were locked and securely bolted on the inside. All the windows were locked on the inside. If you will look at the fastenings in this dear place, you will know what that means.

"But, bless you, that was the least of it! I told you about

the snow. The snowfall had stopped at nine o'clock in the evening, hours and hours before Mrs. Waycross was murdered. When the police came, there were only two separate sets of footprints in the great unmarked half-acre of snow round the house. One set belonged to Mr. Wilkes, who had come up and looked in through the window the night before. The other belonged to Mrs. Randall. The police could follow and explain both sets of tracks; but there were no other tracks at all, and no one was hiding in the house.

"Of course, it was absurd to suspect Mr. Wilkes. It was not only that he told a perfectly straight story about the man in the tall hat; but both Dr. Sutton and Mr. Pawley, who drove back with him from Five Ashes, were there to swear he could not have done it. You understand, he came no closer to the house than the windows of this room. They could watch every step he made in the moonlight, and they did. Afterwards he drove home with Dr. Sutton, and slept there, or, I should say, they continued their terrible drinking until daylight. It is true that they found in his possession a knife with blood on it, but he explained that he had used the knife to gut a rabbit.

"It was the same with poor Mrs. Randall, who had been up all night about her midwife's duties, though naturally it was even more absurd to think of *her*. But there were no other footprints at all, either coming to or going from the house, in all that stretch of snow; and all the ways in or out were locked on the inside."

It was Muriel who spoke then, in a voice that tried to be crisp, but wavered in spite of her. "Are you telling us that all this is true?" she demanded.

"I am teasing you a little, my dear," said the other. "But, really and truly, it all did happen. Perhaps I will show you in a moment."

"I suppose it was really the husband who did it?" asked Muriel in a bored tone.

"Poor Mr. Waycross!" said their hostess tenderly. "He spent that night in a temperance hotel near Charing Cross Station, as he always did, and, of course, he never left it. When he learned about his wife's duplicity"—again Hunter thought she was going to pull down a corner of her eyelid—"it nearly drove him out of his mind, poor fellow. I think he gave up agricultural machinery and took to preaching, but I am not sure. I know he left the district soon afterwards, and before he left he insisted on burning the mattress of their bed. It was a dreadful scandal."

"But in that case," insisted Hunter, "who did kill her? And, if there were no footprints and all the doors were locked, how did the murderer come or go? Finally, if all this happened in February, what does it have to do with people being out of the house on Christmas Eve?"

"Ah, that is the real story. That is what I mean to tell you."

She grew very subdued.

"It must have been very interesting to watch the people alter and grow older, or find queer paths, in the years afterwards. For, of course, nothing did happen as yet. The police presently gave it all up; for decency's sake it was allowed to rest. There was a new pump built in the market square; and the news of the Prince of Wales's going to India in '75 to talk about; and presently a new family came to live at Clearlawns, and began to raise their children. The trees and the rains in summer were just the same, you know. It must have been seven or eight years before anything happened, for Jane Waycross was very patient.

"Several of the people had died in the meantime. Mrs. Randall had, in a fit of quinsy; and so had Dr. Sutton, but that was a great mercy, because he fell by the way when he was going out to perform an amputation with too much of the drink in him. But Mr. Pawley had prospered—and, above all, so had Mr. Wilkes. He had become an even finer figure of a man, they tell me, as he drew near middle age. When he married he gave up all his loose habits. Yes, he married; it was the Tinsley heiress, Miss Linshaw, whom he had been courting at the time of the murder; and I have heard that poor Jane Waycross, even after *she* was married to Mr. Waycross, used to bite her pillow at night because she was so horribly jealous of Miss Linshaw.

"Mr. Wilkes had always been tall, and now he was finely stout. He always wore frock-coats. Though he had lost most of his hair, his beard was full and curly; he had twinkling black eyes, and twinkling ruddy cheeks, and a bluff voice. All the children ran to him. They say he broke as many feminine hearts as before. At any wholesome entertainment he was always the first to lead the cotillion or applaud the fiddler, and I do not know what hostesses would have done without him.

"On Christmas Eve, then—remember, I am not sure of the date—the Fentons gave a Christmas party. The Fentons were the very nice family who had taken this house afterwards, you know. There was to be no dancing, but all the old games. Naturally, Mr. Wilkes was the first of all to be invited, and the first to accept; for everything was all smoothed away by time, like the wrinkles in last year's counterpane; and what's past *is* past, or so they say. They had decorated the house with holly and mistletoe, and guests began to arrive as early as two in the afternoon.

"I had all this from Mrs. Fenton's aunt (one of the Warwickshire Abbotts), who was actually staying here at the time. In spite of such a festal season, the preparations had not been going at all well that day, though such preparations usually did. Miss Abbott complained that there was a nasty earthy smell in the house. It was a dark and a raw day, and the chimneys did not seem to draw as well as they should. What is more, Mrs. Fenton cut her finger when she was carving the cold fowl, because she said one of the children had been hiding behind the window-curtains in here, and peeping out at her; she was very angry. But Mr. Fenton, who was going about the house in his carpet slippers before the arrival of the guests, called her 'Mother' and said that it was Christmas.

"It is certainly true that they forgot all about this when the fun of the games began. Such squealings you never heard!—or so I am told. Foremost of all at Bobbing for Apples or Nuts in May was Mr. Jeremy Wilkes. He stood, gravely paternal, in the midst of everything, with his ugly wife beside him, and stroked his beard. He saluted each of the ladies on the cheek under the mistletoe; there was also some scampering to salute him; and, though he *did* remain for longer than was necessary behind the window-curtains with the younger Miss Twigelow, his wife only smiled. There was only one unpleasant incident, soon forgotten. Towards dusk a great gusty wind began to come up, with the chimneys smoking worse than usual. It being nearly dark, Mr. Fenton said it was time to fetch in the Snapdragon Bowl, and watch it flame. You know the game? It is a great bowl of lighted spirit, and you must thrust in your hand and pluck out a raisin from the bottom without scorching your fingers. Mr. Fenton carried it in on a tray in the half-darkness; it was flickering with that bluish flame you have seen on Christmas puddings. Miss Abbott said that once, in carrying it, he started and turned round. She said that for a second she thought there was a face looking over his shoulder, and it wasn't a nice face.

"Later in the evening, when the children were sleepy and there was tissue-paper scattered all over the house, the grown-ups began their games in earnest. Someone sug-

gested Blind Man's Buff. They were mostly using the hall
and this room here, as having more space than the dining-
room. Various members of the party were blindfolded with
the men's handkerchiefs; but there was a dreadful amount of
cheating. Mr. Fenton grew quite annoyed about it, because
the ladies almost always caught Mr. Wilkes when they could;
Mr. Wilkes was laughing and perspiring heartily, and his
great cravat with the silver pin had almost come loose.

"To make it certain nobody could cheat, Mr. Fenton got a
little white linen bag—like this one. It was the pillow-cover
off the baby's cot, really; and he said nobody could look
through that if it were tied over the head.

"I should explain that they had been having some trouble
with the lamp in this room. Mr. Fenton said: 'Confound it,
mother, what is wrong with that lamp? Turn up the wick,
will you?' It was really quite a good lamp from Spence and
Minstead's, and should not have burned so dull as it did. In
the confusion, while Mrs. Fenton was trying to make the
light better, and he was looking over his shoulder at her, Mr.
Fenton had been rather absently fastening the bag on the
head of the last person caught. He has said since that he did
not notice who it was. No one else noticed, either, the light
being so dim and there being such a large number of people.
It seemed to be a girl in a broad bluish kind of dress, standing over near the door.

"Perhaps you know how people act when they have just
been blindfolded in this game. First they usually stand very
still, as though they were smelling or sensing in which direction to go. Sometimes they make a sudden jump, or sometimes they begin to shuffle gently forward. Everyone noticed
what an air of *purpose* there seemed to be about this person
whose face was covered; she went forward very slowly, and
seemed to crouch down a bit.

"It began to move towards Mr. Wilkes in very short but

quick little jerks, the white bag bobbing on its face. At this time Mr. Wilkes was sitting at the end of the table, laughing, with his face pink above the beard, and a glass of our Kentish cider in his hand. I want you to imagine this room as being very dim, and much more cluttered, what with all the tassels they had on the furniture then; and the high-piled hair of the ladies, too. The hooded person got to the edge of the table. It began to edge along towards Mr. Wilkes's chair; and then it jumped.

"Mr. Wilkes got up and skipped (yes, skipped) out of its way, laughing. It waited quietly, after which it went, in the same slow way, towards him again. It nearly got him again, by the edge of the potted plant. All this time it did not say anything, you understand, although everyone was applauding it and crying encouraging advice. It kept its head down. Miss Abbott says she began to notice an unpleasant faint smell of burnt cloth or something worse, which turned her half-ill. By the time the hooded person came stopping clear across the room, as certainly as though it could see him, Mr. Wilkes was not laughing any longer.

"In the corner by one bookcase, he said out loud: 'I'm tired of this silly, rotten game; go away, do you hear?' Nobody there had ever heard him speak like that, in such a loud, wild way, but they laughed and thought it must be the Kentish cider. 'Go away!' cried Mr. Wilkes again, and began to strike at it with his fist. All this time, Miss Abbott says, she had observed his face gradually changing. He dodged again, very pleasant and nimble for such a big man, but with the perspiration running down his face. Back across the room he went again, with it following him; and he cried out something that most naturally shocked them all inexpressibly.

"He screamed out: 'For God's sake, Fenton, take it off me!'"

"And for the last time the thing jumped.

"They were over near the curtains of that bay window, which were drawn as they are now. Miss Twigelow, who was nearest, says that Mr. Wilkes could not have seen anything, because the white bag was still drawn over the woman's head. The only thing she noticed was that at the lower part of the bag, where the face must have been, there was a curious kind of discoloration, a stain of some sort which had not been there before: something seemed to be seeping through. Mr. Wilkes fell back between the curtains, with the hooded person after him, and screamed again. There was a kind of thrashing noise in or behind the curtains; then they fell straight again, and everything grew quiet.

"Now, our Kentish cider is very strong, and for a moment Mr. Fenton did not know what to think. He tried to laugh at it, but the laugh did not sound well. Then he went over to the curtains, calling out gruffly to them to come out of there and not play the fool. But, after he had looked inside the curtains, he turned round very sharply and asked the rector to get the ladies out of the room. This was done, but Miss Abbott often said that she had one quick peep inside. Though the bay windows were locked on the inside, Mr. Wilkes was now alone on the window seat. She could see his beard sticking up, and the blood. He was dead, of course. But, since he had murdered Jane Waycross, I sincerely think that he deserved to die."

IV

For several seconds the two listeners did not move. She had all too successfully conjured up this room in the late 'seventies, whose stuffiness still seemed to pervade it now.

"But look here!" protested Hunter, when he could fight down an inclination to get out of the room quickly. "You say he killed her after all? And yet you told us he had an absolute alibi. You said he never went closer to the house than the windows. . . ."

"No more he did, my dear," said the other.

"He was courting the Linshaw heiress at the time," she resumed; "and Miss Linshaw was a very proper young lady who would have been horrified if she had heard about him and Jane Waycross. She would have broken off the match, naturally. But poor Jane Waycross meant her to hear. She was much in love with Mr. Wilkes, and she was going to tell the whole matter publicly: Mr. Wilkes had been trying to persuade her not to do so."

"But—"

"Oh, don't you see what happened?" cried the other in a pettish tone. "It is so dreadfully simple. I am not clever at these things, but I should have seen it in a moment: even if I did not already know. I told you everything so that you should be able to guess.

"When Mr. Wilkes and Dr. Sutton and Mr. Pawley drove past here in the gig that night, they saw a bright light burning in the windows of this room. I told you that. But the police never wondered, as anyone should, what caused that light. Jane Waycross never came into this room, as you know; she was out in the hall, carrying either a lamp or a candle. But that lamp in the thick blue-silk shade, held out there in the hall, would not have caused a bright light to shine through this room and illuminate it. Neither would a tiny candle; it is absurd. And I told you there were no other lamps in the house except some empty ones waiting to be filled in the back kitchen. There is only one thing they could have seen. They saw the great blaze of the paraffin oil round Jane Waycross's body.

"Didn't I tell you it was dreadfully simple? Poor Jane was upstairs waiting for her lover. From the upstairs window she saw Mr. Wilkes's gig drive along the road in the moonlight, and she did not know there were other men in it; she thought he was alone. She came downstairs—

"It is an awful thing that the police did not think more about that broken medicine-bottle lying in the hall, the large bottle that was broken in just two long pieces. She must have had a use for it; and, of course, she had. You knew that the oil in the lamp was almost exhausted, although there was a great blaze round the body. When poor Jane came downstairs, she was carrying the unlighted lamp in one hand; in the other hand she was carrying a lighted candle, and an old medicine-bottle containing paraffin oil. When she got downstairs, she meant to fill the lamp from the medicine-bottle, and then light it with the candle.

"But she was too eager to get downstairs, I am afraid. When she was more than half-way down, hurrying, that long nightgown tripped her. She pitched forward down the stairs on her face. The medicine-bottle broke on the tiles under her, and poured a lake of paraffin round her body. Of course, the lighted candle set the paraffin blazing when it fell; but that was not all. One intact side of that broken bottle, long and sharp and cleaner than any blade, cut into her throat when she fell on the smashed bottle. She was not quite stunned by the fall. When she felt herself burning, and the blood almost as hot, she tried to save herself. She tried to crawl forward on her hands, forward into the hall, away from the blood and oil and fire.

"That was what Mr. Wilkes really saw when he looked in through the window.

"You see, he had been unable to get rid of the two fuddled friends, who insisted on clinging to him and drinking with him. He had been obliged to drive them home. If he could not go to Clearlawns now, he wondered how at least he could leave a message; and the light in the window gave him an excuse.

"He saw pretty Jane propped up on her hands in the hall, looking out at him beseechingly while the blue flame ran up and turned yellow. You might have thought he would have pitied, for she loved him very much. Her wound was not really a deep wound. If he had broken into the house at that moment, he might have saved her life. But he preferred to let her die: because now she would make no public scandal and spoil his chances with the rich Miss Linshaw. That was why he returned to his friends and told a lie about a murderer in a tall hat. It is why, in heaven's truth, he murdered her himself. But when he returned to this friends, I do not wonder that they saw him mopping his forehead. You know now how Jane Waycross came back for him, presently."

There was another heavy silence.

The girl got to her feet, with a sort of bouncing motion which was as suggestive as it was vaguely familiar. It was as though she were about to run. She stood there, a trifle crouched, in her prim brown dress, so oddly narrow at the waist after an old-fashioned pattern; and in the play of light on her face Rodney Hunter fancied that its prettiness was only a shell.

"The same thing happened afterwards, on some Christmas Eves," she explained. "They played Blind Man's Bluff over again. That is why people who live here do not care to risk it nowadays. It happens at a quarter-past seven—"

Hunter stared at the curtains. "But it was a quarter-past seven when we got here!" he said. "It must now be—"

"Oh, yes," said the girl, and her eyes brimmed over. "You see, I told you you had nothing to fear; it was all over then. But that is not why I thank you. I begged you to stay, and you did. You have listened to me, as no one else would. And now I have told it at last, and now I think both of us can sleep."

Not a fold stirred or altered in the dark curtains that closed the window bay; yet, as though a blurred lens had come into focus, they now seemed innocent and devoid of harm. You could have put a Christmas-tree there. Rodney Hunter, with Muriel following his gaze, walked across and threw back the curtains. He saw a quiet window-seat covered with chintz, and the rising moon beyond the window. When he turned round, the girl in the old-fashioned dress was not there. But the front doors were open again, for he could feel a current of air blowing through the house.

With his arm round Muriel, who was white-faced, he went out into the hall. They did not look long at the scorched and beaded stains at the foot of the panelling, for even the scars of fire seemed gentle now. Instead, they stood in the doorway looking out, while the house threw its great blaze of light across the frosty Weald. It was a welcoming light. Over the rise of a hill, black dots trudging in the frost showed that Jack Bannister's party was returning; and they could hear the sound of voices carrying far. They heard one of the party carelessly singing a Christmas carol for glory and joy, and the laughter of children coming home.

NEW MURDERS FOR OLD

Hargreaves did not speak until he had turned on two lamps. Even then he did not remove his overcoat. The room, though cold, was stuffy, and held a faintly sweet odour. Outside the Venetian blinds, which were not quite closed, you saw the restless, shifting presence of snow past street-lights. For the first time, Hargreaves hesitated.

"The—the object," he explained, indicating the bed, "was there. *He* came in by this door, here. Perhaps you understand a little better now?"

Hargreaves' companion nodded.

"No," said Hargreaves, and smiled. "I'm not trying to invoke illusions. On the contrary, I am trying to dispel them. Shall we go downstairs?"

It was a tall, heavy house, where no clocks ticked. But the treads of the stairs creaked and cracked sharply, even under their padding of carpet. At the back, in a kind of small study, a gas-fire had been lighted. Its hissing could be heard from a distance; it roared up blue, like solid blue flames, into the white fretwork of the heater; but it did little to dispel the chill of the room. Hargreaves motioned his companion to a chair at the other side of the fire.

"I want to tell you about it," he went on. "Don't think I'm trying to be—" his wrist hesitated over a word, as though over a chesspiece—"highbrow. Don't think I'm trying to be highbrow if I tell it to you"—again his wrist hesitated— "objectively. As though you knew nothing about it. As though you weren't concerned in it. It's the only way you will understand the problem he had to face."

Hargreaves was very intent when he said this. He was bending forward, looking up from under his eyebrows; his heavy overcoat flopped over the sides of his knees, and his gloved hands, seldom still, either made a slight gesture or pressed flat on his knees.

"Take Tony Marvell, to begin with," he argued. "A good fellow, whom everybody liked. Not a good business man, perhaps: too generous to be a good business man; but as conscientious as the very devil, and with so fine a mathematical brain that he got over the practical difficulties.

"Tony was Senior Wrangler at Cambridge, and intended to go on with his mathematics. But then his uncle died, so he had to take over the business. You know what the business was then: three luxury hotels, built, equipped and run by Old Jim, the uncle, in Old Jim's most flamboyant style: all going to rack and ruin.

"Everybody said it was madness for Tony to push his shoulder up against the business world. His brother—that's Stephen Marvell, the former surgeon—said Tony would only bring Old Jim's card-houses down on everybody and swamp them all with more debts. But you know what happened. At twenty-five, Tony took over the business. At twenty-seven, he had the hotels on a paying basis. At thirty, they were hotels to which everybody went as a matter of course: blazing their sky-signs, humming with efficiency, piling up profits which startled even Tony.

"And all because he sneered at the idea that there could be any such thing as overwork. He never let up. You can imagine that dogged expression of his. 'Well, I don't like this work, but let's clean it up satisfactorily so that we can get on to more important things'—like his studies. He did it partly because he had promised Old Jim he would, and partly *because* (you see?) he thought the business so unimportant that he wanted to show how easy it was. But it wasn't easy. No man could stand that pace. London, Brighton, Eastbourne; he knew everything there was to know about the Marvell Hotels, down to the price of a pillow-case and the cost of grease for the lifts. At the end of the fifth year he collapsed one morning in his office. His brother Stephen told him what he had to do.

"'You're getting out of this,' Stephen said. 'You're going clear away. Round the world, anywhere; but for six or eight months at the shortest time. During that time, you're not even so much as to think of your work. Is that clear?'

"Tony told me the story himself last night. He says that the whole thing might never have happened if he had not been forbidden to write to anybody while he was away.

"'Not even so much as a postcard,' snapped Stephen, 'to anybody. If you do, it'll be more business; and then God help you.'

"'But Judith—' Tony protested.

"'Particularly to Judith,' said Stephen. 'If you insist on marrying your secretary, that's your affair. But you don't ruin your rest-cure by exchanging long letters about the hotels.'

"You can imagine Stephen's over-aristocratic, thin-nosed face towering over him, dull with anger. You can imagine Stephen in his black coat and striped trousers, standing up beside the polished desk of his office in Harley Street. Stephen Marvell (and, to a certain extent, Tony, too) had that over-bred air which Old Jim Marvell had always wanted and never achieved.

"Tony did not argue. He was willing enough, because he was tired. Even if he were forbidden to write to Judith, he could always think about her. In the middle of September, more than eight months ago, he sailed by the *Queen Anne* from Southampton. And on that night the terrors began."

Hargreaves paused. The gas-fire still hissed in the little, dim study. You would have known that this was a house in which death had occurred, and occurred recently, by the look on the face of Hargreaves' companion. He went on:

"The *Queen Anne* sailed at midnight. Tony saw her soaring up above the docks, as high as the sky. He saw the long decks, white and shiny like shoe-boxes, gleaming under skeins of lights; he saw the black dots of passengers moving along them; he heard the click rattle-rush of winches as great cranes swung over the crowd on the docks; and he felt the queer, pleasurable, restless feeling which stirs the nerves at the beginning of an ocean voyage.

"At first he was as excited as a schoolboy. Stephen Marvell and Judith Gates, Tony's fiancée, went down to Southampton with him. Afterwards he recalled talking to Judith; holding her arm, piloting her through the rubbery-smelling passages of the ship to show her how fine it was. They went to Tony's cabin, where his luggage had been piled together with a basket of fruit. Everybody agreed that it was a fine cabin.

"It was not until a few minutes before the 'all-ashore' gong that the first pang of loneliness struck him. Stephen and Judith had already gone ashore, for all of them disliked these awkward, last-minute leave-takings. They were standing on the dock, far below. By leaning over the rail of the ship he could just see them. Judith's face was tiny, remote and smiling; infinitely loved. She was waving to him. Round him surged the crowd; faces, hats, noise under naked lights, accentuating the break with home and the water that would widen between. Next he heard the gong begin to bang: hollow, quivering, pulsing to loudness over the cry: 'All ashore that's going ashore!'; and dying away into the ship. He did not want to go. There was still plenty of time. He could still gather up his luggage and get off.

"For a time he stood by the rail, with the breeze from Southampton Water in his face. Such a notion was foolish. He would stay. With a last wave to Judith and Stephen, he drew himself determinedly away. He would be sensible. He would go below and unpack his things. Feeling the unreality of that hollow night, he went down to his cabin on C Deck.

And his luggage was not there! He stared round the stuffy cabin with its neat curtains at the portholes. There had been a trunk and two suit-cases, gaudily labelled, to say nothing of the basket of fruit. Now the cabin was empty.

"Tony ran upstairs again to the purser's office. The purser, a harassed man behind a kind of ticket-window desk, was just getting rid of a clamouring crowd. In the intervals of striking a hand-bell and calling orders, he caught Tony's eye.

"'My luggage—' Tony said.

"'That's all right, Mr. Marvell,' said the harassed official. "It's being taken ashore. But you'd better hurry yourself.'

"Tony had here only a feeling of extreme stupidity. 'Taken ashore?' he said. 'But why? Who told you to send it ashore?'

"'Why, *you* did,' said the purser, looking up suddenly from a sheet of names and figures.

"Tony only looked at him.

"'You came here,' the purser went on, with sharply narrowing eyes, 'not ten minutes ago. You said you had decided not to take the trip, and asked for your luggage to be taken off. I told you that at this late date we could not, of course, refund the—'

"'Get it back!' said Tony. His own voice sounded wrong. 'I couldn't have told you that. Get it back!'

"'Just as you like, sir,' said the purser, smiting on the bell, '*if* there's time.'

"Overhead the hoarse blast of the whistle, that mournful-lest of all sounds at sea, beat out against Southampton Water. B Deck, between open doors, was cold and gusty.

"Now Tony Marvell had not the slightest recollection of having spoken to the purser before. That was what struck him between the eyes like a blow, and what, for the moment, almost drove him to run away from the *Queen Anne* before they should lift the gang-plank. It was the nightmare again. One of the worst features of his nervous breakdown had been the conviction, coming in flashes at night, that he was not real any longer; that his body and his inner self had moved apart, the first walking or talking in everyday life like an articulate dummy, while the brain remained in another place. It was as though he were dead, and seeing his body move. Dead.

"To steady his wits, he tried to concentrate on familiar human things. Judith, for instance; he recalled Judith's hazel eyes, the soft line of her cheek as she turned her head, the paper cuffs she wore at the office. Judith, his fiancée, his secretary, who would take care of things while he was away; whom he loved, and who was so maddeningly close even now. But he must not think of Judith. Instead, he pictured his brother Stephen, and Johnny Cleaver, and any other friends who occurred to him. He even thought of Old Jim Marvell, who was dead. And—so strong is the power of imaginative visualisation—at that moment, in the breezy lounge-room facing the purser's office, he thought he saw Old Jim looking at him round the corner of a potted palm.

"All this, you understand, went through Tony's mind in the brief second while he heard the ship's whistle hoot out over his head.

"He made some excuse to the purser, and went below. He was grateful for the chatter of noise, for the people passing up and down below decks. None of them paid any attention to him, but at least they were there. But, when he opened the door of his cabin, he stopped and stood very still in the doorway.

"The propellers had begun to churn. A throb, a heavy vibration, shook upwards through the ship; it made the tooth-glass tinkle in the rack, and sent a series of creaks through the bulkheads. The *Queen Anne* was moving. Tony Marvell took hold of the door as though that a movement had been a lurch, and he stared at the bed across the cabin. On the white bedspread, where it had not been before, lay an automatic pistol."

The gas-fire had heated its asbestos pillars to glowing red. Again there was a brief silence in the little study of the house in St. John's Wood. Hargreaves—Sir Charles Hargreaves, Assistant Commissioner of Police for the Criminal Investigation Department—leaned down and lowered the flame of the heater. Even the tone of his voice seemed to change when the gas ceased its loud hissing.

"Wait!" he said, lifting his hand. "I don't want you to get the wrong impression. Don't think that the fear, the slow approach of what was going to happen, pursued Tony all through his trip round the world. It didn't. That's the most curious part of the whole affair.

"Tony has told me that it was a brief, bad bout, lasting perhaps fifteen minutes in all, just before and just after the *Queen Anne* sailed. It was not alone the uncanny feeling that things had ceased to be real. It was a sensation of active malignancy—of hatred, of danger, of what you like—surrounding him and pressing on him. He could feel it like a weak current from a battery.

"But five minutes after the ship had headed out to open sea, every such notion fell away from him. It was as though he had emerged out of an evil fog. That hardly seems reasonable. Even supposing that there are evil emanations or evil spirits, it is difficult to think that they are confined to one country; that their tentacles are broken by half a mile's distance; that they cannot cross water. Yet there it was. One moment he was standing there with the automatic pistol in his hand, the noise of the engines beating in his ears and a horrible impulse joggling his elbow to put the muzzle of the pistol into his mouth and—

"Then—snap! Something broke: that is the only way he

can describe it. He stood upright. He felt like a man coming out of a fever, shaken and sweating, but back from behind the curtain into the real world again. He gulped deep breaths. He went to the porthole and opened it. From that time on, he says, he began to get well.

"How the automatic had got into his cabin he did not know. He knew he must have brought it himself, in one of those blind flashes. But he could not remember. He stared at it with new eyes, and new feeling of the beauty and sweetness of life. He felt as though he had been reprieved from execution.

"You might have thought that he would have flung the pistol overboard in sheer fear of touching it. But he didn't. To him it was the part of a puzzle. He stared much at it: a Browning .38, of Belgian manufacture, fully loaded. After the first few days, when he did keep it locked away out of sight in his trunk, he pondered over it. It represented the one piece of evidence he could carry back home with him, the one tangible reality in a nightmare.

"At the New York Customs-shed it seemed to excite no surprise. He carried it overland with him—Cleveland, Chicago, Salt Lake City—to San Francisco, in a fog, and then down the kindled sea to Honolulu. At Yokohama they were going to take it away from him; only a huge bribe retrieved it. Afterwards he carried it on his person, and was never searched. As the broken bones of his nerves knitted, as in the wash of the propellers, there was peace, it became a kind of mascot. It went with him through the blistering heat of the Indian Ocean, into the murky Red Sea, to the Mediterranean. To Port Said, to Cairo in early winter. To Naples and Marseilles and Gibraltar. It was tucked away in his hippocket on the bitter cold night, a little more than eight months after his departure, when Tony Marvell—a healed man again—landed back at Southampton in the S.S. *Chippenham Castle.*

"It was snowing that night, you remember? The boat-train roared through thickening snow. It was crowded, and the heat would not work.

"Tony knew that there could be nobody at Southampton to meet him. His itinerary had been laid out in advance, and he had stuck to the bitter letter of his instructions about not writing even so much as a postcard. But he had altered the itinerary, so as to take a ship that would get him home in time for Christmas; he would burst in on them a week early. For eight months he had lived in a void. In an hour or two he would be home. He would see Judith again.

"In the dimly-lighted compartment of the train, his fellow-passengers were not talkative. The long voyage had squeezed their conversation dry; they almost hated each other. Even the snow roused only a flicker of enthusiasm.

"'Real old-fashioned Christmas!' said one.

"'Hah!' said another appreciatively, scratching with his finger-nails at the frosted window.

"'Damn cold, *I* call it,' snarled a third. 'Can't they ever make the heat work in these trains? I'm damn well going to make a complaint!'

"After that, with a sympathetic grunt or mutter, each retired behind his newspaper; a white, blank wall which rustled occasionally, and behind which they drank up news of home.

"In other words (Tony remembers that he thought then), he was in England again. He was home. For himself, he only pretended to read. He leaned back in his seat, listening vaguely to the clackety-roar of the wheels, and the long blast of the whistle that was torn behind as the train gathered speed.

"He knew exactly what he would do. It would be barely ten

o'clock when they reached Waterloo. He would jump into a cab, and hurry home—to this house—for a wash and brush-up. Then he would pelt up to Judith's flat at Hampstead as hard as he could go. Yet this thought, which should have made him glow, left him curiously chilly round the heart. He fought the chill. He laughed at himself. Determinedly he opened the newspaper, distracting himself, turning from page to page, running his eye down each column. Then he stopped. Something familiar caught his eye, some familiar name. It was an obscure item on a middle page.

"He was reading in this paper the news of his own death. Just that.

"'Mr. Anthony Dean Marvell, of Upper Avenue Road, St. John's Wood, and owner of Marvell Hotels, Ltd., was found shot dead last night in his bedroom at home. A bullet had penetrated up through the roof of the mouth into the brain, and a small-calibre automatic was in his hand. The body was found by Mrs. Reach, Mr. Marvell's housekeeper, who . . .'

"A suicide!

"And once again, as suddenly as it had left him aboard ship, the grasp fell on him, shutting him off from the real world into the unreal. The compartment, as I told you, was very dimly lighted. So it was perhaps natural that he could only dimly see a blank wall of upheld newspapers facing him; as though there were no fellow-passengers there, as though they had deserted him in a body, leaving only the screen of papers that joggled a little with the rush of the train.

"Yes, he was alone.

"He got up blindly, dragging open the door of the compartment to get out into the corridor. The confined space seemed to be choking him. Holding his own newspaper up high so as to catch the light from the compartment, he read the item again.

"There could be no possibility of a mistake. The account was too detailed. It told all about him, his past and present . . .

"' . . . His brother, Mr. Stephen Marvell, the eminent Harley Street surgeon, was hurriedly summoned. . . . His fiancée, Miss Judith Gates . . . It is understood that in September Mr. Marvell suffered a nervous breakdown, from which even a long rest had not effected a cure. . . .'

"Tony looked at the date of the newspaper, afraid of what he might see. But it was the date of that day: the twenty-third of December. From this account, it appeared that he had shot himself forty-eight hours before.

"And the gun was in his hip-pocket now.

"Tony folded up the newspaper. The train moved under his feet with a dancing sway, jerking above the click of the wheels; and another thin blast of the whistle went by. It reminded him of the whistle aboard the *Queen Anne*. He glanced along the dusky corridor. It was empty except for someone, whom he supposed to be another passenger, leaning elbows on the rail past the windows and staring out at the flying snow.

"He remembers nothing else until the train reached Waterloo. But something—an impression, a subconscious memory—registered in his mind about that passenger he had seen in the corridor. First it had to do with the shape of the person's shoulders. Then Tony realized that this was because the person was wearing a greatcoat with an old-fashioned brown fur collar. He was jumping blindly out of the train at Waterloo when he remembered that Old Jim Marvell always used to wear such a collar.

"After that he seemed to see it everywhere.

"When he hurried up to the guard's van to claim his trunk and suitcases, the luggage-ticket in his hand, he was in such a crowd that he could not move his arms. But he thought he felt brown fur press the back of his shoulders.

"A porter got him a taxi. It was a relief to see a London cab again, in a coughing London terminus, and hear the bump of the trunk as it went up under the strap, and friendly voices again. He gave the address to the driver, tipped the porter, and jumped inside. Even so, the porter seemed to be holding open the door of the taxi longer than was necessary.

"'Close it, man!' Tony found himself shouting. 'Close it, quick!'

"'Yessir,' said the porter, jumping back. The door slammed. Afterwards, the porter stood and stared after the taxi. Tony, glancing out through the little back window, saw him still standing there.

"It was dark in the cab, and as close as though a photographer's black hood had been drawn over him. Tony could see little. But he carefully felt with his hands, all over the seat, all over the open space; and he found nothing."

At this point in the story Hargreaves broke off for a moment or two. He had been speaking with difficulty; not as though he expected to be doubted, but as though the right words were hard to find. His gloved fingers opened and closed on his knee.

For the first time his companion—Miss Judith Gates—interrupted him. Judith spoke from the shadow on the other side of the gas-fire.

"Wait!" she said. "Please!"

"Yes?" said Hargreaves.

"This person who was following Tony." She spoke also with difficulty. "You aren't telling me that it was—well, was—?"

"Was what?"

"Dead," said Judith.

"I don't know who it was," answered Hargreaves, looking at her steadily. "Except that it seemed to be somebody with a fur collar on his coat. I'm telling you Tony's story, which I believe."

Judith's hand shaded her eyes. "All the same," she insisted, and her pleasant voice went high, "even supposing it was! I mean, even supposing it was the person you think. *He* of all people, living or dead, wouldn't have tried to put any evil influence round Tony. Old Jim loved Tony. He left Tony every penny he owned, and not a farthing to Stephen. He always told Tony he'd look after him."

"And so he did," said Hargreaves.

"But—"

"You see," Hargreaves told her slowly. "You still don't understand the source of the evil influence. Tony didn't, himself. All he knew was that he was bowling along in a dark taxi, through slippery, snowy streets; and whatever might be following him, good or bad, he couldn't endure it.

"Even so, everything might have ended well if the taxi-driver had been careful. But he wasn't. That was the first snowfall of the year, and the drive miscalculated. When they were only two hundred yards from Upper Avenue Road, he tried to take a turn too fast. Tony felt the helpless swing of the skid; he saw the glass partition tilt, and a black tree-trunk rush up, huge at them until it exploded against the outer windscreen. They landed upright against the tree, with a buckled wheel.

"'I *'ad* to swerve,' the driver was crying. 'I *'ad* to! An old gent with a fur collar walked smack out in front of—'

"And so, you see, Tony had to walk home alone.

"He knew something was following him before he had taken half a dozen steps. Two hundred yards don't sound like a great distance. First right, first left, and you're home. But here it seemed to stretch out interminably, as such things do in dreams. He did not want to leave the taxi-driver. The driver thought this was because Tony doubted his honesty about bringing the luggage on when the wheel was repaired. But it was not that.

"For the first part of the way, Tony walked rapidly. The other thing walked at an equal pace behind him. By the light of a street-lamp Tony could see the wet fur collar on the coat, but nothing else. Afterwards he increased his pace to what was almost a run; and, though no difference could be seen in the gait of what was behind him, it was still there. Unlike you, Tony didn't wonder whether it might be good or evil. These nice differences don't occur to you when you're dealing with something that may be dead. All he knew was that he mustn't let it *identify* itself with him or he was done for.

"Then it began to gain on him, and he ran.

"The pavement was black, the snow dirty grey. He saw the familiar turning, where front gardens were built up above the low, stone walls; he saw the street sign fastened to one of those corners, white lettering on black; and, in sudden blind panic, he plunged for the steps that led up to his home.

"The house was dark. He got the cold keys out of his pocket, but the key-ring slipped round in his fingers, like soap in bath-water, and fell on the tiled floor of the vestibule. He groped after it in the dark—just as the thing turned in at the gate. In fact, Tony heard the gate creak. He found the keys, found the lock by a miracle, and opened the door.

"But he was too late, because the other thing was already coming up the front steps. Tony says that at close range, against a street-lamp, the fur collar looked more wet and moth-eaten; that is all he can describe. He was in a dark hall with the door open. Even familiar things had fled his wits and he could not remember the position of the light-switch.

"The other person walked in.

"In his hip-pocket, Tony remembered, he still had the weapon he had carried round the world. He fumbled under his overcoat to get the gun out of his pocket; but even that weak gesture was no good to him, for he dropped the gun on the carpet. Since the visitor was now within six feet of him, he did not stop. He bolted up the stairs.

"At the top of the stairs he risked a short glance down. The other thing had stopped. In faint bluish patches of light which came through the open front door, Tony could see that it was stooping down to pick up the automatic pistol from the carpet.

"Tony thinks—now—that he began to switch on lights in the upper hall. Also, he shouted something. He was standing before the door of his bedroom. He threw open this door, blundered in, and began to turn on more lamps. He had got two lamps lighted before he turned to look at the bed, which was occupied.

"The man on the bed did not, however, sit up at the coming of noise or lights. A sheet covered him from head to feet; and even under the outline of the sheet you could trace the line of the wasted, sunken features. Tony Marvell then did what was perhaps the most courageous act of his life. He had to know. He walked across and turned down the upper edge of the sheet, and looked down at his own face; a dead face, turned sightlessly up from the bed.

"Shock? Yes. But more terror? No. For this dead man was real, he was flesh and blood—as Tony was flesh and blood. He looked exactly like Tony. But it was now no question of a real world and an unreal world; it was no question of going mad. This man was real; and that meant fraud and imposture.

"A voice from across the room said: '*So you're alive!*' And Tony turned round, to find his brother Stephen looking at him from the doorway.

"Stephen wore a red dressing-gown, hastily pulled round him, and his hair was tousled. His face was one of collapse.

"'I didn't mean to do it!' Stephen was crying out at him. Even though Tony did not understand, he felt that the words were a confession of guilt; they were babbling words, words which made you pity the man who said them.

"'I never really meant to have you killed aboard that ship,' said Stephen. 'It was all a joke. You know I wouldn't have hurt you; you know that, don't you? Listen—'

"Now Stephen (as I said) was standing in the doorway, clutching his dressing-gown round him. What made him look round towards the hall behind, quickly, Tony did not know. Perhaps he heard a sound behind him. Perhaps he saw something out of the corner of his eye. But Stephen did look round, and he began to scream.

"Tony saw no more, for the light in the hall went out. The fear was back on him again, and he could not move. For he saw a hand. It was only, so to speak, the flicker of a hand. This hand darted in from the darkness out in the hall; it caught hold of the knob on the bedroom door, and closed the door. It turned a key on the outside, locking

Tony into the room. It kept Stephen outside in the dark hall—and Stephen was still screaming.

"A good thing, too, that Tony had been locked in the room. That saved trouble with the police afterwards.

"The rest of the testimony comes from Mrs. Reach, the housekeeper. Her room was next door to Stephen's bedroom, at the end of the upstairs hall. She was awakened by screams, by what seemed to be thrashing sounds, and the noise of hard breathing. These sounds passed her door towards Stephen's room.

"Just as she was getting out of her bed and putting on a dressing-gown, she heard Stephen's door close. Just as she went out into the hall, she heard, for the second time in forty-eight hours, the noise of a pistol-shot.

"Now, Mrs. Reach will testify in a coroner's court that nobody left, or could have left Stephen's room after the shot. She was looking at the door, though it was several minutes before she could screw up enough courage to open the door. When she did open it, all sounds had ceased. He had been shot through the right temple at close range; presumably by himself, since the weapon was discovered in a tangle of stained bed-clothing. There was nobody else in the room, and all the windows were locked on the inside. The only other thing Mrs. Reach noticed was an unpleasant, an intensely unpleasant smell of mildewed cloth and wet fur."

Again Hargreaves paused. It seemed that he had come to the end of the story. An outsider might have thought, too, that he had emphasized these horrors too much, for the girl across from him kept her hands pressed against her eyes. But Hargreaves knew his business.

"Well?" he said gently. "You see the explanation, don't you?"

Judith took her hands away from her eyes. "Explanation?"

"The natural explanation," repeated Hargreaves, spacing his words. "Tony Marvell is not going mad. He never had any brainstorms or 'blind flashes.' He only thought he had. The whole thing was a cruel and murderous fake, engineered by Stephen, and it went wrong. But if it had succeeded, Stephen Marvell would have committed a very nearly perfect murder."

The relief he saw flash across Judith's face, the sudden dazed catching at hope, went to Hargreaves' heart. But he did not show this.

"Let's go back eight months," he went on, "and take it from the beginning. Now, Tony is a very wealthy young man. The distinguished Stephen, on the other hand, was swamped with debts and always on the thin edge of bankruptcy. If Tony were to die, Stephen, the next of kin, would inherit the whole estate. So Stephen decided that Tony had to die.

"But Stephen, a medical man, knew the risks of murder. No matter how cleverly you plan it, there is always *some* suspicion; and Stephen was bound to be suspected. He was unwilling to risk those prying detectives, those awkward questions, those damning post-mortem reports— until, more than eight months ago, he suddenly saw how he could destroy Tony without the smallest suspicion attaching to himself.

"In St. Jude's Hospital, where he did some charity work, Stephen had found a broken-down ex-schoolmaster named Rupert Hayes. Every man in this world, they say, has his exact double. Hayes was Tony's double to the slightest feature. He was, in fact, so uncannily like Tony that the very sight of him made Stephen flinch. Now, Hayes was dying of tuberculosis. He had, at most, not

more than a year to live. He would be eager to listen to
any scheme which would allow him to spend the rest of
his life in luxury, and die of natural causes in a soft bed.
To him Stephen explained the trick.

"Tony should be ordered off—apparently—on a trip
round the world. On the night he was to sail, Tony should
be allowed to go aboard.

"Hayes should be waiting aboard that same ship, with a
gun in his pocket. After Stephen or any other friends had
left the ship conveniently early, Hayes should entice Tony
up to the dark boat-deck. Then he was to shoot Tony
through the head, and drop the body overboard.

"Haven't you ever realized that a giant ocean-liner, just
before it leaves port, is the ideal place to commit a murder? Not a soul will remember you afterwards. The passengers notice nothing; they are too excited. The crew
notice nothing; they are kept too busy. The confusion of
the crowd is intense. And what happens to your victim
after he goes overboard? He will be sucked under and
presently caught by the terrible propellers, to make him
unrecognizable. When a body is found—if it is found at
all—it will be presumed to be some dock-roysterer. Certainly it will never be connected with the ocean-liner,
because there will be nobody missing from the liner's passenger list.

"Missing from the passenger-list? Of course not! Hayes,
you see, was to go to the purser and order Tony's luggage
to be sent ashore. He was to say he was cancelling the
trip, and not going after all. After killing Tony he was
then to walk ashore as—"

The girl uttered an exclamation.

Hargreaves nodded. "You see it now. He was to walk
ashore *as Tony.* He was to say to his friends that he
couldn't face the journey after all; and everybody would

be happy. Why not? The real Tony was within an ace of doing just that.

"Then, Hayes, well coached, would simply settle down to play the part of Tony for the rest of his natural life. Mark that: his natural life; a year at most. He would be too ill to attend to the business, of course. He wouldn't even see you, his fiancée, too often. If ever he made any bad slips, that, of course, would be his bad nerves. He would be allowed to 'develop' lung trouble. At the end of a year, amid sorrowing friends . . .

"Stephen had planned brilliantly. 'Murder'? What do you mean, murder? Let the doctors examine as much as they like! Let the police ask what questions they like! Whatever steps are taken, Stephen Marvell is absolutely safe. For the poor devil in bed really has died a natural death.

"Only—well, it went wrong. Hayes wasn't cut out to be a murderer. I hadn't the favour of his acquaintance, but he must have been a decent sort. He promised to do this. But, when it came to the actual fact, he couldn't force himself to kill Tony: literally, physically couldn't. He threw away his pistol and ran. On the other hand, once off the ship, he couldn't confess to Stephen that Tony was still alive. He couldn't give up that year of sweet luxury, with all Tony's money at his disposal to soothe his aching lungs. So he pretended to Stephen that he had done the job, and Stephen danced for joy. But Hayes, as the months went on, did not dance. He knew Tony wasn't dead. He knew there would be a reckoning soon. And he couldn't let it end like that. A week before he thought Tony was coming home, after writing a letter to the police to explain everything, Hayes shot himself rather than face exposure."

There was a silence. "That, I think," Hargreaves said quietly, "explains everything about Tony."

Judith Gates bit her lips. Her pretty face was working; and she could not control the twitching of her capable hands. For a moment she seemed to be praying.

"Thank God!" she murmured. "I was afraid—"

"Yes," said Hargreaves; "I know."

"But it still doesn't explain everything. It—"

Hargreaves stopped her.

"I said," he pointed out, "that it explains everything about Tony. That's all you need worry about. Tony is free. You are free. As for Stephen Marvell's death, it was suicide. That is the official record."

"But that's absurd!" cried Judith. "I didn't like Stephen; I always knew he hated Tony; but he wasn't one to kill himself, even if he were exposed. Don't you see, you haven't explained the one real horror? I must know. I mean, I must know if you think what I think about it. Who was the man with the brown fur collar? Who followed Tony home that night? Who stuck close by him, to keep the evil influences off him? Who was his guardian? Who shot Stephen in revenge?"

Sir Charles Hargreaves looked down at the sputtering gas-fire. His face, inscrutable, was wrinkled in sharp lines from mouth to nostril. His brain held many secrets. He was ready to lock away this one, once he knew that they understood each other.

"You tell me," he said.

THE DIAMOND PENTACLE

I

He wouldn't dare, Sheila Lake thought. He might have had foolish notions before, but even Dick Mason wouldn't dare go through with this one.

Besides, he couldn't. This room—

Faintly through the open window she could hear the church clock in the village striking midnight. The grounds whispered with a conference of leaves; otherwise there was a heavy midsummer stillness over Broadlawns. The lamp in this room blazed with a naked glare of electricity, for she had removed the shade.

Sheila Lake looked round the room, ordinarily her aunt and uncle's bedroom, which had become hers during their absence. It was large, after the fashion of Broadlawns. Its windows were protected by ornamental iron grilles, after the French fashion of an earlier owner. In the mirror over the dressing-table Sheila caught sight of her own reflection—a blonde one, with very fair, smooth skin—and she wondered if it showed what she was thinking.

The little safe, of course, was built into the wall behind a picture not far from the dressing-table. That picture showed her Aunt Martha, handsome in a large hat and whalebone collar of some years ago, looking at her suspiciously. Sheila took down the picture and examined the wall-safe. It was the most modern pattern, ordered by her uncle Bart from America, and it opened to a letter-lock combination which she did not know. Not Dick Mason, not even Mephisto himself, could get into that safe.

All this talk about the diamond pentacle was ridiculous.

The beginning of the argument had been ridiculous as well. She remembered the scene that afternoon, in the drowsy sunlight over the tennis court. Major and Mrs. Prentice were playing an erratic set for the benefit of the major's figure, while she and Dick Mason lounged under a beach umbrella.

She even remembered the colours on the jacket of the book Dick had been waving at her. He had got hold of a biography of "Mephisto," the late celebrated escape-artist, whom no four walls could confine. With equal ease Mephisto had wormed his way out of locked rooms, locked safes, Russian prison-vans, and roped chests at the bottom of a river. Some of his feats were almost as startling as black magic.

"If a man like that had ever gone wrong," Dick had maintained, "he would have been the greatest criminal in the history of the world. I know the remark has been made before, but I can't help making it again. How would you keep the fellow out of your house? And how would you hold him in clink, even if you caught him?"

"A stage performer," said Sheila.

"There wasn't any stage," said Dick, "when that crowd from the foundry made an iron boiler for him, and shut him into it with their own bolts, and dropped him into the Thames. He was up again in one minute twenty seconds."

Sheila had been impatient.

"I tell you it's all nonsense," she insisted firmly. "Most of it, anyway. There was bound to have been funny business somewhere. I mean, nobody could *really* do all that."

"Are you sure?" asked Dick.

She felt uneasy. His ancient wrist-watch, with the decayed strap, seemed to have come loose again with excitement. At the same time he was wearing his "Cassius" expression: he looked too thoughtful; and that was a bad sign. It was one of the reasons why her aunt disliked him so much.

"Let us," Dick continued, "take a personal example for the sake of argument. Let's take your excellent uncle and aunt, Mr. and Mrs. Bartholomew Lake. Now, your uncle and I are great pals. But your Aunt Martha rather prefers the measles to me. Whatever her reasons may be, they are not the conventional ones. I am filthy with money, I am at home among the most complicated array of knives and spoons—"

Sheila almost wailed.

"It's because you get such wild ideas," she said. "Like that scheme of yours for robbing the Bank of England. Oh, and the one to give the Lord Chancellor an electric shock in the seat of the trousers when he sits down on the Woolsack."

"They are excellent ideas," he said with dignity. "And quite practical."

"Dick," she asked quietly, "what do you do for a living? I don't *mind*, you understand. But I've only known you a month, and you said you were going to tell me." She flushed. "I've been imagining the most horribly romantic things, like a detective or a Secret Service man—"

"No," said the other in the same quiet tone. "I can say with my hand on my heart that I am not connected with the law in any way. But let me come back to the point. You and I are semi-officially engaged to be married. What happens? Your aunt and uncle decide to go to Scotland. You refuse to go, because you have invited me down here. You are allowed to stay and entertain me, provided Major and Mrs. Prentice are here to chaperone us."

He glanced towards the tennis-court, and moved automatically as a ball whizzed past his head into the laurel-bushes. Major Prentice was serving. His first service usually went over the house or hit some spectator under the ear. The only reason why Major Prentice had never managed to break a window was that all the windows were covered with ornamental grilles.

"Well?" Sheila prompted.

"Well, I hope they enjoy themselves in Scotland. But I'll

tell you this: your aunt is damned well not going to walk off and leave you holding the baby."

"Holding the—Dick, I don't know what you mean!"

"I think you do know what I mean," said her *fiancé*, and the blood seemed to come up under his eyes. "There's a fortune in jewelry in that house, locked up in a wall safe in your aunt and uncle's bedroom. In particular there's that diamond pentacle, the one that's supposed to be a representation of the magical Pentacle of Solomon. Good old Uncle Bart liked it so much that he bought it for Aunt Martha. Of course, I know the old woman doesn't like jewelry. She's not human enough to like it—"

"Dick Mason, you have no right to talk like that."

"So, because she doesn't like it, she simply walks away and leaves all of it here. And none of it insured. 'Just sleep in my room, Sheila; then everything will be all right.'"

"And so it will."

"You think so? Suppose somebody got in and pinched any of those things, especially the diamond pentacle? Your Uncle Bart would be wild. And your Aunt Martha, the world's expert at dodging responsibility, would look at you reproachfully and say it was all your fault. Why don't you take that stuff out of the safe and leave it with the bank, where it belongs?"

"But I don't know the letter combination of the safe."

"I see," he observed, examining his tennis-racquet.

There were times, Sheila thought, when she did not know Dick at all. His expression retreated from her; she touched fog. He was bending forward examining the racquet as though he had never seen it before, and he wore a mechanical smile.

"Besides," she went on, "it's nonsense. That safe is burglar-proof. And a burglar couldn't even get into the room to begin with. Those windows have solid iron grilles that you can't even get your hands through. The door is nearly two inches thick, and has a bolt like a bank vault. Short of sawing through the bars—"

"Suppose," he said thoughtfully, "you had a super-burglar, someone like a Mephisto turned crook? Suppose you had someone who could slide through iron bars or a bolted door without leaving any trace, and open the safe in the same way? What would happen?"

"Oh, Dick, don't talk rubbish. There's nobody who could do that."

"Isn't there?" he said. "I'll bet you I could do it myself."

II

His words had come to her like the sharp *ping* of the racquet as Major Prentice drove.

"Sorry," he said. "I'm not trying to frighten you. But I'll just make you a little bet. I'll bet you that on two successive nights I can get into that room while you're asleep—"

"Dick!"

"I said while you were asleep, didn't I? Bolt your door, barricade the place in any way you like. My bet is that I can get in and out of there without leaving a trace, and without your knowing how I did it. Don't worry: I won't touch the safe. I'll only leave some sign so that you'll know I've been there. If after that night I prove to you it can be done, will you let me put that jewelry in a place where it's safe? If not, I'll come again the second night, and lift that diamond pentacle as clean as a whistle. Will you believe me then?"

"I dare you," said Sheila hotly.

There on the lawn in sunlight, among the familiar things of the day, it had seemed only another argument. Now, as the church clock was striking midnight and Sheila stood in her aunt's bedroom, she was not so sure.

The idea of her *fiancé* mysteriously getting into her room in the middle of the night was both disturbing and vaguely pleasant. On consideration, she found that she did not mind at all; but it stirred both a sense of adventure and a sense of the conventions outraged. Suppose a servant saw it? Suppose Mrs. Prentice came to hear of it?

Sheila Lake, blonde, blue-eyed, and unsuspicious, did not know which feeling of the two predominated. The suggestion of prudery she repudiated with indignation. But Mrs. Prentice? Sheila had a notion that the Major would chuckle all over his stomach and call the scheme sporting; but that his lady would dispatch a quick telegram to Aunt Martha, intimating the presence of Vice.

At dinner that evening, and afterwards, Sheila thought she had detected a curious look in Mrs. Prentice's eye. It may have been Dick's thoughtfulness, or her own guilty imagination. They had played bridge without great success. Dick had a habit of making wild calls, with a partiality for no-trumps; and Mrs. Prentice had a trick of saying "Double," in a tone which implied rich satisfaction.

The church clock struck the quarter hour after twelve. Sheila went across and bolted the door of the bedroom.

Of course, it was impossible to imagine that Dick could get in here. Nobody in the country ever bolted a door: the idea rather shocked Sheila; but she bolted this one with great care. And she was (correctly) certain that nobody could open it from outside.

In the wall to your right as you faced the door were the two windows. She shook the close-fitting iron grilles to test them, and was also (correctly) certain that nobody could get through those windows.

"Well!" Sheila said aloud.

She would go to bed, but she would *not* sleep. That she determined. What disturbed her, though she would not have admitted it, was uncertainty. She wanted to know whether he meant it, or whether it had been a joke.

After hurrying into her best night-dress, which she had brought upstairs secretly before dinner, she turned out the light. She would sit up in bed: that would be the most comfortable way.

It was difficult to settle comfortably, though. By twelve-thirty she was becoming a little nervous. Moonlight came through the curtains, which were not completely drawn. She did not like the swift, creeping rush of the wind in the trees outside, which made the moonlight writhe. She could hear the faint ticking of her wrist-watch on the table by the bed. Then the wind would rush again in the trees. She began to realize that this was all nonsense. Nobody could get into this room.

Suppose it was not Dick Mason, but somebody else?

This roused her with a shock of fear, until her strong common sense drove it out. By half-past one she admitted to herself that she was tired.

But she would *not* go to sleep. She would only settle back more comfortably.

The last thing she remembered was the church clock striking two.

Well, that vague idea of someone prowling in the room, and someone prowling near the wall-safe, was only a dream. Sheila Lake thought she realized this as soon as she opened her eyes on a warm and overcast morning.

It drove out a dream in which Richard Mason, to whom she was engaged, had figured as a criminal. But the dream was so vivid that she had to disentangle it from the ordinary affairs of morning. Then she began to laugh, for there had been no prowling footstep. Rather pleased with herself and annoyed with Dick Mason, she reached out for her wrist-watch on the bedside table.

But she sat up abruptly when she touched it. Then she held it up. It was not her wrist-watch. It was Dick Mason's.

She was very well acquainted with that ancient watch and its decaying strap. Even before she had hurried across and thrown open the curtains she realized that there had been a prowling footstep after all. Someone had come in here during the night, had taken away her watch, and had replaced it with—

Sheila stared round the room. First she looked at the wall-safe; a round, snub-nosed cylinder, its door still closed. But her Aunt Martha's picture had been removed from in front of the safe; and she found the picture tucked away in a drawer of the dressing table.

With the carefulness of shock and uneasiness she looked at the fastening of the room. The door was still securely bolted; the close-twined grilles of the windows were impenetrable; nobody could have got into this room. But someone had.

III

Major Bullivant Prentice, full of breakfast and well satisfied, was taking a third cup of coffee downstairs when Sheila came into the room.

Although he looked with gloom on the overcast day, Major Prentice was glad of an opportunity to relax. The young people, he thought, were always in a fuss and bother about something, from choosing a profession to playing a golf-stroke. Even his own wife seemed to be affected by it. He vaguely remembered that Agnes seemed to have been awake half the night, creaking in and out of the room. Then Agnes had gone off to the village this morning.

Well, damn it, why be so suspicious? All the same, he looked at Sheila narrowly as she came to the breakfast table.

"Good morning, major," said Sheila, and her voice was as abrupt as her smile. "Have you seen Dick Mason?"

"Went fishing," said Major Prentice, clearing his throat. "Before eight o'clock. *I've* got a bad foot," he explained apologetically.

All the same, he did not like her bright-eyed look as contrasted with her obvious nervousness. He was broad-minded: none broader; but if that fellow Mason had been making her unhappy, he'd wring his damned neck. But Major Prentice could not say this. He said:

"Have some breakfast."

"Er—no, thanks," smiled Sheila. "Fishing? That would be Green Acre Field way? Of course. See you soon."

A servant was clearing away the breakfast dishes, and Major Prentice was still looking unhappily at *The Times* in the big shadowy room, when Agnes Prentice returned. She sat down, drawing off her gloves. They looked at each other.

"Been out, my dear?" asked the major, somewhat unnecessarily.

"Yes," said his wife. "I've sent a telegram to Martha and Bartholomew to come back at once. They should be able to get here late to-night."

"Oh, hang it all," said the major, making a motion with his feet as though he were going to surge up out of the chair. He subsided. "I was afraid you had. But after all—"

Agnes Prentice smiled. She was the partner in a happy marriage; and Sheila Lake would have been surprised at her private views.

"No, my dear," she told him. "I wasn't thinking of the moral issues involved, though it's all very dreadful, no doubt. If I were ever alarmed at a little love-making, I should not consider myself quite grown-up, and I should certainly not be the person who has lived with you all these years."

Her forehead grew worried. "The trouble is that this Richard Mason is a criminal."

Major Prentice whistled.

"Steady, Agnes! Are you sure of that? How do you know it?"

"There was a letter for Bartholomew on the hall table yesterday afternoon. (Now don't scowl at me like that; we women have to do all the dirty work, and you only use it.) I didn't open it, naturally, but I saw the address on the envelope and read as much as I could when I held it up to the light. It's from a firm of private detectives in town. This Richard Mason isn't after Sheila. He's after a whacking great pile of jewelry in Martha's safe."

This time Major Prentice did get up—and he paced. Also he groaned.

"Agnes, I don't believe it. Can't believe it. The chap's flighty, but he's sound. I'd swear to it. I tell you I'd swear to it."

"Well, there it is."

Whereupon the major did swear to it. "Yes, but look here: what are we going to do?"

"I don't see that there is anything to do until Martha and Bartholomew get here. They'll probably wire."

It was one of the longest days Major Prentice could remember. Neither Sheila nor Mason came in to lunch. By the time he was becoming worried, and considered going out after them, they returned together in a subdued mood. Nothing was said. A telegram, skillfully smothered at the door by Mrs. Prentice, announced that Bartholomew Lake would arrive at the village station by the late train at 12:15. In the middle of the afternoon it began to rain.

And it was still raining when Major Prentice drove a battered car to the railway station that night. The downpour fell with dismal monotony, as though it were insisting on something he did not believe. A train, where carriage-windows seemed smeared with twenty years' grime, drew in at the station.

"Well?" demanded Bartholomew Lake.

Major Prentice did not relish this. Bartholomew was a little cynical, walnut-faced fellow, but he had a twinkle in his eye, and, when he once liked a person, it was difficult to shake that liking. The major was not so precise in his regard for Martha Lake. Martha, although Sheila worshipped her, tried to stay at once too young in her manners and too old in her remarks. Her large face was eager as Major Prentice bustled them into the car.

"Look here, Bart," he said. "Did you have a firm of private detectives after that chap Mason?"

The other nodded.

"I did. I was convinced nothing would come of it, but he wouldn't say anything about himself when I invited him down here, and he was making too many trips abroad to suit my taste. What's up?"

Major Prentice told him.

"I was wrong," Martha Lake admitted. "*I* thought he was a blackmailer."

"We don't know what he is," snapped her husband, opening and shutting his stubby fingers. "We don't even know if he's had a go at that safe. Presumably it's beaten him, or he wouldn't hang about the place after he'd got the stuff. But with Sheila in that room—my God, Prentice! You say Agnes thinks he was in Sheila's room last night? Then Sheila must have let him in. I told her to keep that door bolted. There's no crook alive who could get in or out of that room when the door's bolted, unless he broke in or somebody let him in. You say there weren't any signs of anybody breaking in?"

"None I could see," growled Major Prentice.

"Then he couldn't have got in or out without Sheila knowing it! There's no other way!"

"Maybe he's found one," said the major.

No light showed at Broadlawns when they drove up. Leaving the car under the *porte-cochere*, they entered by the side door, where Mrs. Prentice had now turned on the lights. She handed Bartholomew Lake a letter.

"I think," said Agnes Prentice, "that young man, or Sheila, or both must be completely out of their minds. I can't imagine what's going on here. They must have known we weren't in bed. They must have known my husband had gone out with the car. But I rather think he's up in her room with her now."

They stood looking at each other, four avenging adults, who now felt more confused than avenging. Aunt Martha began to cry out about honour and horsewhips, but Uncle Bartholomew told her to be quiet while he read the letter. All the same, his expression was no easier when he had finished.

"That settles it," he aid. "Shall we go upstairs?"

The upstairs passage was dark, and the door of the bedroom bolted on the inside. They could hear the insistent noise of the rain. Major Prentice muttered something about excusing his wife and himself, but there was no time to consider this after Bartholomew Lake's knock. The door was unbolted and opened by Dick Mason.

"By all means come in," he said through his teeth.

The table-lamp had been switched on. Mason, wearing dark clothes that were sodden with rain, was removing a pair of gloves; and his expression was curious. It seemed to hold no high guilt of any kind. If anything, it was sullen and rather embarrassed. After shaking himself like a dog, he threw the gloves on the table.

Behind him stood Sheila, in what her aunt's expert eye picked out as her best nightgown and *négligé*. And Sheila was in a cold, blue-eyed temper on one of the few occasions of her life.

"How very clever you are," she said from high in her throat. She was so furious that she had to articulate distinctly. "How very, very clever. Please do come in. Uncle Bart!"

Uncle Bartholomew said nothing. He went over to the wall-safe and began to riffle the small wheels of the letter-lock.

"It may interest you all to know," continued Sheila, quivering, "just what did happen here. Don't laugh when I tell you it's a joke: if you know what I mean. For it's more than a joke. Last night Dick showed me how easy it was to get in and out of a locked room without leaving a trace—"

"Ha! ha! ha!" said Aunt Martha sweetly. "Without leaving a trace, my dear. How very interesting."

Bartholomew Lake looked over his shoulder at Dick.

"Is that true?"

"Quite true," agreed Dick Mason, and there appeared in his eye a gleam of amusement which might or might not have been sinister.

"And to-night," stormed Sheila, "he proved how easy it was to steal the diamond pentacle out of your wall-safe, letter-lock and all. Bing! Just like that. If you don't believe me—"

"Is that true, young man?" asked the other. He had opened the safe-door and was peering inside. "The pentacle certainly isn't here now."

"No," said Dick. "It's here."

Small points of light shifted and winked under the lamp as he took the ornament from his pocket. The arabesque had five points, crossed with hieroglyphs of diamonds. It was arranged in the form of a pendant at the end of a thin platinum chain. It glittered in the air as Dick tossed it across to Bartholomew Lake, who caught it without comment.

"Yes," agreed the latter. "This is the diamond pentacle."

"Draw its sign," said Dick with gusto, "on a Wednesday at the hour of Mercury when the moon is in a sign of air or earth, and in the same degree as the sun. It will also help if you wear a false nose when you do this. Then you will learn all magical secrets, including how to get in and out of locked rooms."

"Look here, Bart, the fellow's laughing at us," growled Major Prentice uneasily. "Shall I—er—ring up the police?"

"He won't laugh much longer," said their host grimly. Putting the pentacle into the safe, he closed the door and spun the letter-wheels. "Now then, young man. Would you like to keep out of gaol?"

Dick became dull red.

"I said, would you like to keep out of gaol?"

"Naturally."

"Very well, then. Open that safe again. Didn't you hear me, young man?" insisted their little host, thrusting out his neck. "Open that safe for me. Then you won't go to gaol. That's short and sweet, isn't it?"

After a pause Dick spoke slowly.

"I've made a remarkable ass of myself," he said. "I've been the world's most whacking fool; but now, by thunder and Long John Silver, there are limits!"

"There are," agreed Uncle Bartholomew, and bristled up with a certain courtliness. "Yes, that'll be quite enough. So now let me beg your pardon and Sheila's." He indicated Aunt Martha. "My firm of private inquiry agents tells me what you seem to have known all along: that the person who really stole the pentacle was my wife."

Aunt Martha's blank and coy blue eyes moved round for

a moment as though uncomprehendingly. Then, in a kind of slow collapse, she sat down in a chair and began to cry.

IV

At just on daybreak, when the trees of Green Acre were outlined black against silver, three cigars seemed to hang in the air by an ornamental pond in the garden at Broadlawns. The cigars were not really disembodied, though they glowed and darkened in unison. They were being smoked, moodily, by Bartholomew Lake, Major Prentice, and Dick Mason.

It was Major Prentice who broke the line of cigars by taking his out of his mouth.

"But look here!" he protested. "How the blazes *did* you get in and out of that bedroom? That's what beats me. Sheila swears you did, and you don't seem to deny it yourself."

"Yes," said Lake. "I think, my lad, we'd better hear your side of it."

The glowing of Dick Mason's cigar seemed to express some doubt. "I don't suppose I can speak frankly?" he asked.

"You may," Lake told him with a certain grimness.

Dick shifted a little.

"You wanted to know who I am and what I do for a living. All right. I have the honour to have inherited from my old man the ownership of one of the largest and oldest established firms of diamond merchants in Hatton Garden. Vandervaal, Ltd., if you know it.

"There's no secret about that. There never was any secret about it. It's the reason for my frequent trips abroad, which seem to have bothered you. I intended to come down here and explain all this to you, with facts and figures to show I was capable of supporting Sheila. Only, unfortunately, something happened to prevent me from explaining it.

"It's like this, sir. Your wife pinched—I suppose I shouldn't say pinched, because in a sense you gave it to her—anyway, she lifted that pentacle over a week ago, before you left for Scotland. I was still in London, preparing to come down here. She came to town and sold it to a very shady dealer round the corner. I suppose she needed the money."

Bartholomew Lake was still more grim.

"She did," he said. "She always does."

"Well, I was already very much puzzled about several things. I'd only met her once or twice, but I knew she detested me. Then she wrote me a pleasant letter, inviting me to Broadlawns for a fortnight: that was all right, of course. But immediately on the heels of that came another letter, saying that you and she had suddenly been called to Scotland. However, she said that there was no need for me to postpone my visit; Sheila could stay behind and entertain me, provided we were chaperoned."

He grew somewhat violent.

"Excuse me, sir. Knowing her, seeing through her, knowing she would give an ear to see this match broken off, I simply couldn't believe she would deliberately throw Sheila and me together like that in her absence—unless she had a purpose, of course. On top of that, I couldn't understand her tireless references to her jewelry, especially the diamond pentacle you had bought her. She even wrote about them in letters. On top of *that*, I happened to know that she had just secretly sold the very pentacle she was talking about as still being in her wall-safe."

Major Prentice coughed. In the whitening daylight Bartholomew Lake was looking flushed and angry.

"I don't doubt you," the latter said quietly. "But do I understand what you're getting at? You mean she was going to take me to Scotland; to return and find the pentacle 'stolen' during our absence; and then throw the blame on you?"

"Not necessarily on me," muttered Dick. "Possibly on some poor devil of a maid. *Or on Sheila.* On anybody that came handy. With her particular talent for dodging responsibility, the easiest victim would be the best victim. She's a pretty selfish kind of person, sir.

"I suppose she thought that if she sold it to a crooked dealer, under hideous oaths of secrecy, nobody would ever know what had happened to it. And, if I hadn't been in the diamond trade myself, she might have been right. But we get to know these things—fortunately.

"Well, I bought the pentacle. Not for my firm, of course: we shouldn't have touched it: but for myself.

"I bought the pentacle. Whatever game she was up to. I meant to stop it: I had a full statement of its origin from the other dealer, naturally. And, once I had got it, I didn't know what to do with it. I came down here with the damned thing in my pocket, and I still didn't know what to do with it.

"Here's the plain fact. I thought she was a hypocrite and a twister. Something had to be done, because you two would come back from Scotland before long; and sooner or later you would discover the pentacle was gone—"

"The word is 'sooner,'" Lake told him dryly. "I am the jewel-fancier of the family. And the pentacle happens to be my favourite piece."

"All right. But when it came to the point of blowing the gaff, of telling Sheila, I found I couldn't. Literally, physically couldn't. It wasn't only that Sheila worshipped her. It was also, I thought, one fine sweet mess in which to begin married life. And when it came to the idea of telling you as well, I boggled completely. Knowing what I did in the days before I came down here, and before you left for Scotland. I couldn't even tell you what trade I was in. Out would have come the jewelry for my inspection, and started the hurricane with a bang.

"In other words, sir, I was more undecided than she will ever be. I thought the best course was to get the pentacle back into the safe, where it was supposed to be, and have it off my mind. If she ever tried to damage my marriage afterwards—well, I had my proof.

"But that was the difficulty. I couldn't get into the safe.

"In my business we have to know something about safes. To anything short of nitroglycerine or an acetylene drill that one was burglar-proof.

"Whereupon being an ingenious blighter"—he made a hideous and derisive grimace—"I conceived an ingenious scheme. I knew of a way of getting into the room undetectably, if not into the safe. If I could establish in Sheila's mind the belief that I had the talents of a Mephisto burglar to whom house-walls or safe-walls meant nothing, it would be easy.

"I meant to take two nights. On the first night I should get into the room, play a few *poltergeist* pranks to show I'd been there, and get out. That would establish me as Mephisto. On the second night I should let her see me fool about with the safe and 'produce' the diamond pentacle. I should decline to return it to the safe for the moment, and say I wanted to examine it.

"I could, then, thank the Lord, tell her who I really was; and prove it. I could end this messing about and giving evasive answers, which was the real point of the whole plan. It wouldn't matter, after that, if I kept the pentacle out of a safe I couldn't open. Only on the first night, curse the luck, the scheme worked too well. I scared her. And I couldn't stand that. So I promised to show her how it was done. I was in the middle of showing her how it was done when your party burst in. But I'm glad your private inquiry agents, in watching every sinister move I made, also got on the track of your wife. I shall not be surprised to hear you already had them on the track of your wife. For it simplified matters considerably when I was found in your room with the diamond pentacle in my pocket."

Bartholomew Lake chuckled dryly. "Then I wish you'd tell *me* how it was done," he suggested. "Getting into the room, I mean."

Dick stared at him.

"You mean you don't know?—Look here, sir. Imagine you're in that bedroom again. Now imagine you're facing the door. Got that?"

"Yes."

"What is in the wall to your right?"

"The two windows of course. Barred windows, mind."

"Barred windows, yes. But two windows. One of 'em, therefore, isn't an enormous distance—in a diagonal line— from the door. If you drew a diagonal line from the centre of the door to the centre of the nearer window, it wouldn't be much more than five feet, would it?"

"Well?"

"Finally, the bolt of the door is at the left side of the door as you face it. Good! I waited until I was sure Sheila was asleep. Then I propped a ladder against the wall and climbed to the window. In my hand I had an ordinary fishing-rod, the same rod with which I went fishing to-day. Only to the end of the rod was tightly tied with twine a hook larger than we use hereabouts.

"It was bright moonlight and the curtains were not drawn. It required very little dexterity to balance that rod through the window, catch the knob of the bolt with the hook, and draw the bolt back. I then went into the house in the proper way and opened the door. When I was ready to leave the bedroom I closed the door behind me, putting the bolt ready with its knob turned upwards. Out on the ladder again I put the fishing rod through the window; and, this time with the rounded end of the hook, I pushed the knob of the bolt along and locked it again.

"I had a bad time with it to-night, because there was no moonlight and I got sopping wet into the bargain. But I showed Sheila the secret. Good old Mephisto! Good old Aunt Martha!"

STRICTLY DIPLOMATIC

Now that he was nearly at the end of his rest-cure, Dermot had never felt so well in his life.

He leaned back in the wicker chair, flexing his muscles. He breathed deeply. Below him the flattish lands between France and Belgium sloped to the river: a slow Flemish river dark green with the reflection of its banks. Half a mile away he could see the houses of the town, with the great glass roof of the spa smoky in autumn sunshine. Behind him—at the end of the arbor—was the back of the hotel, now denuded of its awnings.

They had taken down the awnings; they were closing up many of the bedrooms. Only a few guests now pottered about the terrace. A crisp tang had come into the air: work, and the thunder of London again, now loomed up as a pleasant prospect. Once, hardly a month ago, it had been a nightmare of buses charging straight at you, like houses loose; a place where nerves snapped, and you started to run.

Even with that noise in his ears, he had not wanted to go away.

"But I can't take a holiday now!" he had told the doctor.

"Holiday?" snorted the doctor. "Do you call it a holiday? Your trouble is plain overwork, a complaint we don't often get nowadays. Why don't you relax? Not hard up, are you?"

"No, it isn't that."

"You're too conscientious," the doctor had said, rather enviously.

"No. It's not a virtue," said Dermot, as honestly as he could. "I can't help it. Every second I'm away from work, I'm worrying about it until I get back. I'm built like that. I can't relax. I can't even get drunk."

The doctor grunted.

"Ever try falling in love?"

"Not since I was nineteen. And, anyway, it's not something you can take down like a box of pills and dose yourself with. Or at least I can't."

"Well," said the doctor, surveying him, "I know a rising barrister who's going to come a cropper unless you get out of this. Now I warn you. You get off to the Continent this week. There's a spa I know—Ile St. Cathérine. The waters won't do you any harm; and the golf will do you good."

Here the doctor, who was an old friend of Andrew Dermot's, grinned raffishly.

"What you want," he added, "is adventure. In the grand manner. I hear there's a fenced-off area near Ile St. Cathérine, bayonets and all. The casino is probably full of beautiful slant-eyed spies with jade earrings. Forget you're turning into such a mossback. Pick up one of the beautiful slant-eyed spies, and go on the razzle-dazzle with her. It'll do you all the good in the world."

Alone on the lawn behind his hotel, Dermot laughed aloud. Old Foggy had been right, in a way. But he had gone one less or one better than that. He had fallen in love.

Anyone less like a slant-eyed spy than Betty Weatherill would be difficult to imagine. In fact even the tension which tautened nerves in the rest of Europe did not exist in Ile St. Cathérine. It was a fat, friendly, rather stodgy sort of place. Looking round the spa—where fountains fell, and people got very excited on the weighing-machines—Dermot wondered at old Foggy's notion of bayonets. He felt soothed, and free. Bicycle bells tinkled in the streets under once-gilded houses. At night, when you ordered thin wine by the glass, a band played beneath lights in the trees. A mild flutter in roulette at the casino caused excitement; and one Belgian burgher was caught bringing his supper in a paper packet.

Dermot first saw Betty Weatherill on the morning after his arrival.

It was at breakfast. There were not many guests at the hotel: a fat Dutchman eating cheese for breakfast, half a dozen English people, a foreign envoy, a subdued French couple. And, of course, the sturdy girl who sat alone at the sun-steeped table by the windows.

Dermot's nerves were still raw from the journey. When he first saw her he felt a twinge of what he thought was envy at her sheer health. It flashed out at him. He had an impression of a friendly mouth, a sun-tanned complexion; of eagerness, and even naïvéte. It disturbed him like the clattering coffee-cups. He kept looking round at her, and looking round again, though he did not understand why.

He played execrable golf that day.

He saw her again next morning. They ran into each other buying stamps at the cash desk. They both smiled slightly, and Dermot felt embarrassed. He had been trying to remember whether the color of her hair was fair or chestnut; it was, he saw, a light brown. That afternoon his golf was even worse. It was absurd that he, thirty-five years old, should seem as stale and crumpled as an old poster against a wall. He was a nerve-ridden fool. And he fell to thinking of her again.

On the following day they went so far as to say good morning. On the third day he took his nerve in both hands, and plumped down at the breakfast table next to hers.

"I *can't* do it," he heard her say, half-laughing.

The words gave him a start. Not a ladies' man, this move of his had struck him as distinctly daring. Yet he felt the communication between them, an uncomfortable awareness of each other's presence. He looked up, to find her eyes fixed on him.

"Do what?" he asked quickly.

"Manage Continental breakfasts," she answered, as though they were old friends discussing a problem of mutual importance. "I know I shouldn't, but every day I order bacon and eggs."

After that their acquaintance was off at a gallop.

Her name was Betty Weatherill. She was twenty-eight, and came from Brighton. She had been a schoolmistress (incongruous idea); but she had come into a small inheritance and, as she confessed, was blowing part of it. He had never met a girl who seemed so absolutely right: in what she said, in what she did, in her response to any given remark.

That afternoon they went to the fair and ate hot dogs and rode round and round on the wooden horses to the panting music of an electric piano. That night they dressed for the casino; and Andrew Dermot, shuffling roulette-counters, felt no end of an experienced gay-dog. And the knowledge came to him, with a kind of shock, "Good lord, I'm alive."

Betty was popular at the hotel. The proprietor, Monsieur Gant, knew her quite well and was fond of her. Even the fat Dr. Vanderver, of the Sylvanian Embassy, gave her a hoarse chuckle of appreciation whenever she went by. Not that she had no difficulties. There was, it appeared, some trouble about her passport. She had several times to go to the prefecture of police—from which she emerged flushed, and as near angry as it was possible for her to be.

As for Dermot, he was in love and he knew it. That was why he exulted when he sat by the tea-table on the lawn behind the hotel, at half-past five on that lazy, veiled autumn afternoon, waiting for Betty to join him. The lawn was dotted with little tables, but he was alone. The remains of tea and sandwiches were piled on a tray. Dermot was replete; no outside alarms troubled Ile St. Cathérine; no black emblems threw shadows.

This was just before he received the greatest shock of his life.

"Hello!" said Betty. "Sorry I'm late." She came hurrying out of the arbor, with the breathless smile she always wore when she was excited. She glanced quickly round the lawn, deserted except for a waitress slapping at crumbs. Dermot got up.

"You're not late," he told her. "But you swore to me you were going to have tea in town, so I went ahead." He looked at her suspiciously. "Did you?"

"Did I what?"

"Have tea."

"Yes, of course."

For no reason that he could analyze, a chill of uneasiness came to Dermot. His nightmares were cured. But it was as though an edge of the nightmare returned. Why? Only because the atmosphere suddenly seemed wrong, because the expression of her eyes was wrong. He drew out a chair for her.

"Sure you wouldn't like another cup? Or a sandwich?"

"Well—"

Now he thought he must be a fool reading huge meanings into trifles. But the impression persisted. He gave an order to the waitress, who removed the tea-tray and disappeared into the arbor. Betty had taken a cigarette out of her handbag; but, when he tried to light it for her, the cigarette slipped out of her fingers, and rolled on the table.

"Oh, damn," she whispered. Now he was looking into her eyes from a short distance away; they seemed the eyes of a slightly older, wiser woman. They were hazel eyes, the whites very clear against a sun-tanned face. The heavy lids blinked.

"I want to know what's wrong," Dermot said.

"There's nothing wrong," said Betty, shaking her head.

"Only—I wanted to talk to you. "I'm afraid I've got to leave here."

"When?"

"Tonight."

Dermot sat up. It seemed to him that there was a stranger sitting across from him, and that all his plans were toppling.

"If you must, you must," he said. "But I've got to go myself at the beginning of the week. I thought we were going to leave together."

"I can't. Very shortly"—she spoke with some intensity—"I hope I can explain to you what a beast I am. All I can tell you now is that it's not altogether safe for me to be here."

"Safe? In this place?"

Betty was not listening. She was wearing white, as he always remembered afterwards, with a white handbag. Again she had opened this handbag, and was going through it in something of a hurry.

"Derry." She spoke sharply. "You haven't seen my compact, have you? The white ivory one with the red band?" She looked round. "It didn't fall out when I opened my handbag before?"

"No, I don't think so. I didn't see it."

"I must have left it back in my room. Please excuse me. I'll be back in half a tick."

And she got to her feet, snapped shut the catch of the handbag.

Dermot also got up. It would not be fair to say that he exploded. He was a mild-mannered man who arrived at all emotions with difficulty. But in the past few minutes he felt that a door had opened on a world he could not understand.

"Look here, Betty," he said. "I don't know what's got into you; but I insist on knowing. If there's anything wrong, just tell me and we'll put it right. If—"

"I'll be back in a moment," she assured him.

And, disregarding the hand he put out, she hurried back through the arbor.

Dermot sat down heavily, and stared after her. A veiled sun had turned the sky to gray, making dingy the cloths of the little tables on the lawn. The cloths fluttered under a faint breeze.

He comtemplated the arbor, which was a very special sort of arbor. Monsieur Gant, the proprietor of the Hotel Suchard, had imported it from Italy and was very proud of it. Stretching back a full twenty yards to the rear terrace of the hotel, it made a sort of tunnel composed of tough inter-laced vines which in summer were heavy with purplish-pink blossom. A line of tables ran beside it, with lights from above. Inside the arbor, at night, Chinese lanterns hung from the roof. It was one of the romantic features of the hotel. But at the moment—cramped, unlighted, hooded with thick foliage—it was a tunnel which suggested unpleasant images.

"A good place for a murder," Betty had once laughed.

Andrew Dermot could hear his watch ticking. He wished she would come back.

He lit a cigarette and smoked it to a stump; but she had not returned. He got to his feet, stamping on the chilling grass. For the first time he glanced across the tea-table at Betty's empty chair. It was a wicker chair. And, lying on the seat in plain view, was a white ivory compact with a red band.

So that was it! She had been too much upset to notice the compact, of course. She was probably still searching her room for it.

He picked up the compact and went after her.

Inside the arbor it was almost dark, but chinks and glimmers of light flickered through interlaced vines and showed him an arched tunnel some ten feet high, with a floor of packed sand. There was a stagnant smell of dying blossom; the Judas tree, did they call it? Obscurely, he was relieved to find the gnat-stung arbor empty. He hurried along its length to the arch of light at the end, and emerged on a red-tiled terrace where there were more tables under the windows.

"Good eefening, Mr. Dermot," said an affable voice.

Dermot checked his rush.

He almost stumbled over Dr. Henrik Vanderver of the Sylvanian Embassy, who was sitting near the arbor, smoking a cigar with relish, and looking at him through thick-lensed spectacles.

"Ha, ha, ha!" said Dr. Vanderver, laughing uproariously and for no apparent reason, as was his custom.

"Good evening, Dr. Vanderver," said Dermot. His uneasiness had gone; he felt again a nerve-ridden fool. "Sorry to barge into you like that. Is Miss Weatherill down yet?"

Dr. Vanderver was proud of his English.

"Down?" he repeated, drawing down his eyebrows as though to illustrate.

"From her room, I mean."

"De young lady," said Vanderver, "iss with you. I have seen her go through dere"—he pointed to the arbor—"fifteen, twenty minutes ago."

"Yes, I know. But she came back here to get a compact."

Vanderver was now anxious about his English.

"Please?" he prompted, cupping his hand behind his ear.

"I said she came back here to get a compact. You know. This kind of thing." Dermot held it up. "She walked back through the arbor—"

"My friend," said Vanderver with sudden passion, "I do not know if I have understood you. Nobody has come back through this arbor while I am sitting here."

"But that's impossible."

"Please?"

Dermot thought he saw the explanation. "You mean you haven't been sitting here all the time?"

"My friend," said Vanderver, taking out a watch and shaking it, "I am sitting here one hour more—more!—where I sit always and smoke my cigar before I dress. Yes?"

"Well, Doctor?"

"I have seen the young lady go through, yes. But I have not seen her come back. I haf not seen nobody. In all dat time the only liffing soul I see on this terrace is the maid which gather up your tea-tray and bring it back here."

The terrace, always dark in the shadow of the arbor, was growing more dusky.

"Dr. Vanderver, listen to me." Dermot spoke coldly and sharply; he found Vanderver's thick-lensed spectacles turning on him with hypnotic effect. "That is not what I mean. I remember the maid going back through the arbor with the tray. But Miss Wetherill was with me then. I mean later. L-a-t-e-r, several minutes later. You saw Miss Weatherill come out through here about ten minutes ago, didn't you?"

"No."

"But you must have! I saw her go into the arbor on my side, and I never took my eyes off the entrance. She isn't in the arbor now; see for yourself. She must have come out here."

"So!" said Vanderver, tapping the table with magnificent dignity. "Now I tell *you* something. I do not know what you think has happened to the young lady. Perhaps de goblins ketch her, yes? Perhaps she dissolved to electrons, and bust, yes?" Dark blood suffused his face. "Now I will haf no more of this. I settle it. I tell you." He thrust out his thick neck. "Nobody," he said flatly, "hass come back through this arbor at all."

By nine o'clock that night, terror had come to the Hotel Suchard.

Until then Monsieur Gant, the manager, had refrained

from summoning the police. At first Monsieur Gant appeared to think that everybody was joking. He only began to gesticulate, and to run from room to room, when it became clear that Betty Weatherill was not to be found either in the hotel or in the grounds. If the testimony were to be believed—and neither Dermot nor Vanderver would retract one word—then Betty Weatherill had simply walked into the arbor, and there had vanished like a puff of smoke.

It was certain that she had not left the arbor by, say, getting out through the vines. The vines grew up from the ground in a matted tangle like a wire cage, so trained around their posts from floor to arch that it would be impossible to penetrate them without cutting. And nowhere were they disturbed in any way. There was not—as one romantic under-porter suggested—an underground passage out of the tunnel. It was equally certain that Betty could not have been hiding in the arbor when Dermot walked through it. There was no place there to hide in.

This became only too clear when the Chinese lanterns were lighted in the greenish tunnel, and Monsieur Gant stood on a stepladder to shake frantically at the vine-walls— with half the domestic twittering behind him. This was a family matter, in which everybody took part.

Alys Marchand, in fact, was the backstairs-heroine of the occasion. Alys was the plump waitress who had been sent to fetch fresh tea and sandwiches not fifteen minutes before Betty's disappearance, but who had not brought them back because of a disagreement with the cook as to what hours constituted feev-o'clock-tay.

Apart from Dermot, Alys had been the last person to see Betty Weatherill in the flesh. Alys had passed unscathed through the arbor. To Monsieur Gant she described, with a wealth of gesture, how she had taken the order for tea and sandwiches from Monsieur Dermot. She showed how she had picked up the big tray, whisking a cloth over its debris like a conjuror. A pink-checked brunette, very neat in her black frock and apron, she illustrated how she had walked back through the arbor towards the hotel.

Had she seen Dr. Vanderver on this occasion?

She had.

Where was he?

At the little table on the terrace. He was smoking a cigar, and sharpening a big horn-handled knife on a small whetstone block he carried in his pocket.

"That," interposed Vanderver, in excellent French, "is a damned lie."

It was very warm in the arbor, under the line of Chinese lanterns. Vanderver stood against the wall. He seemed less bovine when he spoke French. But a small bead of perspiration had appeared on his forehead, up by the large vein near the temple; and the expression of his eyes behind the thick spectacles turned Andrew Dermot cold.

"It is true as I tell you," shrieked Alys, turning round her dark eyes. "I told my sister Clothilde, and Gina and Odette too, when I went to the kitchen. He thrusts it into his pocket—quick, so!—when he sees me."

"There are many uses for knives," said Monsieur Gant, hastily and nervously. "At the same time, perhaps it would be as well to telephone the police. You are an advocate, Monsieur Dermot. You agree?"

Dermot did agree.

He had been keeping tight hold of his nerves. In fact, he found the cold reason of his profession returning to him; and it was he who directed matters. Instead of bringing back the nightmare, this practical situation steadied him. He saw the issue clearly now. It became even more clear when they arrived, amid a squad of plainclothes men, none other than Monsieur Lespinasse, the *juge d'instruction*.

After examining the arbor, M. Lespinasse faced them all in the manager's office. He was a long, lean, melancholy man with hollow cheeks, and the Legion of Honor in his buttonhole. He had hard uncomfortable eyes, which stared down at them.

"You understand," said Lespinasse, "we appear to have here a miracle. Now I am a realist. I do not believe in miracles."

"That is good," said Dermot grimly, in his careful French. "You have perhaps formed a theory?"

"A certainty," said Lespinasse.

The hard uncomfortable eyes turned on Dermot.

"From our examination," said Lespinasse, "it is certain that Mlle. Weatherill did not leave the arbor by any secret means. You, monsieur, tell one story." He looked at Vanderver. "You, monsieur, tell another." He looked back at Dermot. "It is therefore evident that one of you must be telling a lie."

Vanderver protested at this.

"I remind you," Vanderver growled, with a significant look, "that it will be unwise for you to make mistakes. As an acting representative of His Majesty the King of Sylvania, I enjoy immunities. I enjoy privileges—"

"Diplomatic privileges," said Monsieur Lespinasse. "That is no concern of mine. My concern is that you do not break the civil law."

"I have broken no law!" said Vanderver, purple in the face. "I have told no lie!"

The *juge d'instruction* held up his hand.

"And I tell you in return," he said sharply, "that either your story or Monsieur Dermot's must be untrue. Either the young lady never went into the arbor, in which case Monsieur Dermot is telling a falsehood. Or else she did go in, and for some reason you choose to deny that you saw her come out. In which case—" Again he held up his hand. "It is only fair to warn you, Dr. Vanderver, that Miss Weatherill told me you might try to kill her."

They could hear a clock ticking in the overcrowded room.

"Kill?" said Vanderver.

"That is what I said."

"But I did not know her!"

"Evidently she knew you," answered M. Lespinasse. His sallow face was alive with bitterness; he fingered the rosette in his buttonhole. Then he took a step forward. "Miss Weatherill several times came to me at the prefecture of police. She told me of your—murderous activities in the past. I did not choose to believe her. It was too much of a responsibility. Responsibility! Now this happens, and I must take the responsibility for it at least. One more question, if you please. What have you to say to the maid's story of the horn-handled knife?"

Vanderver's voice was hoarse. "I never owned such a knife. I never saw one. I call you a son of—"

"It will not be necessary to finish," said the *juge d'instruction*. "On the contrary, *we* shall finish." He snapped his fingers, and one of the plain-clothes men brought into the room an object wrapped in newspaper.

"Our search of the arbor," continued M. Lespinasse, "was perhaps more thorough than that of Monsieur Gant. This was found buried in the sand floor only a few feet away from where monsieur was sitting."

There were more than damp stains of sand on the bright, wafer-thin blade in the newspaper; there were others. Monsieur Lespinasse pointed to them.

"Human blood," he said.

At eleven o'clock Andrew Dermot was able to get out of the room.

They told him afterwards that he had made an admirable

witness; that his replies had been calm, curt, and to the point; and that he had even given sound advice on details of legal procedure, contrasting those of England with those of the present country.

He did not remember this. He knew only that he must get out into the air and stop himself from thinking of Betty.

He stood on the front terrace of the hotel, as far removed as possible from the arbor in whose floor the knife had been buried. Half a mile away the lights of the principal street in the town, the Promenade des Français, twinkled with deathly pallor. A cool wind swept the terrace.

They took Vanderver down the front steps and bundled him into a car. There was a chain round Vanderver's wrists; his legs shook so that they had to push him up into the car. The car roared away, with a puff of smoke from the exhaust—carbon monoxide, which meant death—and only the *juge d'instruction* remained behind searching Vanderver's room for some clue as to why a sudden meaningless murder had been done at dusk beside a commonplace hotel.

Andrew Dermot put his hands to his temples, pressing hard.

Well, that was that.

He sat down on the terrace. The little round tables had red tops, and the color did not please him, but he remained. He ordered brandy, which he could not taste. The brandy was brought to him by the same under-porter who had suggested an underground passage in the arbor, and who, agog, seemed to want to entertain him with speculations about motives for murder. Dermot chased him away.

But if Betty had to go—"go" was hardly the word for that—where was the sense in it? Why? Why? Vanderver was presumably not a homicidal maniac. Besides, all Dermot's legal instincts were bewildered by so clumsy a crime. If Vanderver were guilty, why had he from the first persisted in that unnecessary lie of saying Betty had never come out of the arbor? Why hadn't he simply faded away, never professing to have seen anything at all? Why thrust himself at that entrance as though determined to ensure suspicion for himself?

What Dermot had not permitted himself to wonder was where Betty herself might be.

But suppose Vanderver had been telling the truth?

Nonsense! Vanderver could not be telling the truth. People do not vanish like soap-bubbles out of guarded tunnels.

Presently they would be turning out the lights here on this windy, deserted terrace. The Hotel Suchard was ready, in any case, to close its doors for the winter; it would close its doors very early tonight. Behind him, in lighted windows, glowed the lounge, the smoking-room, the dining-room where he had first seen Betty. The head porter, his footsteps rapping on hardwood, darkened first the dining-room and then the lounge. Dermot would have to go upstairs to his room and try to sleep.

Getting to his feet, he walked through the thick-carpeted hall. But he could not help it. He must have one more look at the arbor.

It was a veritable tunnel now: a black shape inside which, for twenty yards, Chinese lanterns glowed against the roof. The sand was torn where the knife had been dug out. Near that patch two shovels had been propped against the wall in readiness for deeper excavations next morning. It was when he noted those preparations, and realized what they meant, that Dermot's mind turned black; he had reached his lowest depth.

He was so obsessed by it that he did not, at first, hear footfalls on the tiled terrace. He turned round. Two persons had come out to join him—but they came by different windows, and they stopped short and stared at each other as much as they stared at him.

One of these persons was M. Lespinasse, the *juge d'instruction*.

The other was Betty Weatherill.

"And now, mademoiselle," roared Lespinasse, "perhaps you will be good enough to explain the meaning of this ridiculous and indefensible trick?"

M. Lespinasse, his cheek-bones even more formidable, was carrying a briefcase and a valise. He let both fall to the floor.

"I had to do it," said Betty, addressing Dermot. "I *had* to do it, my dear."

She was not smiling at him. Dermot felt that presently, in the sheer relief of nerves, they would both be shouting with laughter. At the moment he only knew that she was there, and that he could touch her.

"One moment," said Lespinasse, coldly interrupting what was going on. "You do well, Monsieur Dermot, to demand an explanation—"

"But I don't. So long as she's—"

"—of this affair." The *juge d'instruction* raised his voice. "I can now tell you, in fact I came downstairs to tell you, *how* Miss Weatherill played this trick. What I do not know is why she did it."

Betty whirled round. "You know how?"

"I know, mademoiselle," snapped the other, "that you planned this foolishness and carried it out with the assistance of Alys Marchand, who deserves a formidable stroke of the boot behind for her part in the affair. When I found Alys ten minutes ago capering round her room waving a packet of thousand-franc notes, her behavior seemed to call for some explanation." He looked grim. "Alys was very shortly persuaded to give one."

Then he turned to Dermot.

"Let me indicate what happened, and you shall confirm it! Miss Weatherill asked you to meet her here, even specifying the table you were to occupy, and said she would arrive after tea?"

"Yes," said Dermot.

"At half-past five she came through the arbor—first making certain that Dr. Vanderver was on the terrace in the place he always occupied, every day, to smoke a cigar at that hour?"

"I—yes."

"Miss Weatherill was easily persuaded to have a fresh cup of tea?"

"Well, I asked her to."

"The waitress, Alys, was then pottering round for no apparent reason among otherwise deserted tables?"

"She was."

"You gave the order to Alys," said Monsieur Lespinasse grimly. "She picked up your tray—a big tray—whisking over it a large cloth to cover the dishes? Just as we later saw her do?"

"I admit it."

"Alys then walked away from you through the arbor. As she did so," leered Lespinasse, so intent that he made a face, "Miss Weatherill distracted your attention by getting a light for her cigarette. And kept your attention fixed on herself by dropping the cigarette, and pretending an agitation she did not feel."

Dermot gave a quick look at Betty. Whatever else this might be, it was not a hoax or a joke. Betty's face was white.

"Miss Weatherill held your attention," said Lespinasse, "so that Alys could slip back out of the arbor unnoticed. *Alys did not really go through at all!* Carrying the tray, she merely darted round the side of the arbor and returned unseen to the hotel by another way.

"Miss Weatherill was then ready to play the rest of the comedy. 'Discovering' the loss of her compact, *she* enters the arbor. Halfway up, in the darkness, is lying a stage-property these two have already left there. This is another tray: like the first, and covered with a cloth. But this cloth does not cover dishes. It covers—" Monsieur Lespinasse broke off.

He looked flustered and dishevelled, but in his wicked eye there was a gleam of admiration.

"Monsieur Dermot, I tell you a psychological truth. The one person in this world whose features nobody can remember are those of a waitress. You see her at close range; yet you do not see her. Should you doubt this, the next time in your abominable London you go into a Lyons or an A.B.C., try calling for your bill in a hurry and see if you can identify the particular young lady who served you with a cup of tea. I know it. So did Miss Weatherill.

"She was already wearing a thin black frock under her white one. The tray in the arbor contained the other properties by which a blonde is changed into a brunette, white stockings and shoes change to black, a tanned complexion is heightened to a vivid ruddiness. It was the clumsiest possible disguise because it needed to be no more. Dr. Vanderver never glanced twice at the black-clad figure in cap and apron who walked out of the arbor carrying a tray. He saw no black wig; he saw no false complexion; he saw nothing. In his mind there registered, 'waitress-has-passed': no more. Thus Miss Weatherill, inexpertly got up as Alys, passed safely through the dense shadow which the arbor casts on the terrace—carrying before her the tray whose cloth neatly hid the discarded white dress, stockings, and shoes."

The *juge d'instruction* drew a deep, whistling breath.

"Very well!" he said. "But what I wish to know is: *why?*"

* * *

"You don't see it even yet?" asked Betty.

"My deepest apologies," said Lespinasse, "if I am dense. But I do not see it. You cannot have liked cutting yourself so that you might get real blood to put on the knife you buried. But why? How does all this nonsense help us, when Dr. Vanderver has committed no crime?"

"Because he's Embassy," answered Betty simply.

"Mademoiselle?"

"He has diplomatic immunity," said Betty. "The government can't search him; can't even touch him. And so, you see, I had to get him arrested by the *civil* authorities so that his papers could be searched."

She turned to Dermot.

"Derry, I'm sorry," she went on. "That is, I'm sorry I'm not quite the candid-camera schoolmistress burbling to high heaven that I pretended to be. But I want to be just that. I want to enjoy myself. For the first time in all my life, I've enjoyed myself in the last month. What I mean is: I want to be with you, that's all. So, now that I'm chucking the beastly job—"

Monsieur Lespinasse swore softly. After remaining rigid for a moment, he picked up the briefcase and the valise he had dropped. Both were in green leather stamped in gold with the royal arms of Sylvania.

"—and of course," Betty was saying almost wildly, "the fellow's name wasn't 'Dr. Vanderver,' and he's no more a neutral than I am. Only he'd got that job on forged credentials, and he was safe. So I had to keep telling the *juge d'instruction* I suspected him of being a murderer. His real name is Karl Heinrich von Arnheim; and when Sir George—you know to whom I refer, Monsieur Lespinasse—asked me to go after him—"

Monsieur Lespinasse could not break the lock of the briefcase. So he opened a wicked-looking knife of his own to slit the leather; and so he found the secret.

"The English," he said, "are not bad." He waved the knife, which glittered against the light from the windows. "Dr. Vanderver will not, I think, leave the police station after all." He swept Betty Weatherill a profound bow. "The complete plans," he added, "of the underground fortifications whose fall would break the whole line of defense along this front."

THE CLUE OF THE RED WIG

They usually put the paper to press at 2 A.M. MacGrath, the news editor, who was not feeling well after the Christmas celebrations, went home early to his own bed and left things at the office to young Patterson. MacGrath was sleeping a shivering sleep when the telephone at his bedside rang.

MacGrath made unearthly noises, like a ghost roused before midnight. But he answered the phone.

"Hazel Loring?" he repeated. "What about her?"

"She's dead," answered Patterson. "Murdered, it's pretty certain. Do you know Victoria Square?"

"No."

"It's a quiet little residential square in Bayswater. Hazel Loring lived there. In the middle of the square there's a garden reserved for the use of residents. About eleven o'clock a policeman on his rounds found Hazel Loring dead in the garden with practically no clothes on—"

"What?" shouted MacGrath; and the sleep was struck from his eyes.

"Well, only a brassiere and a pair of step-ins. She was sitting on a bench, dead as Cleopatra, with the rest of her clothes folded up on the bench beside her."

"In *this* weather?"

"Yes. The policeman saw her go into the garden an hour before. Cause of death was a fractured skull, from several blows with a walking stick whose handle was loaded with lead. Signs of a struggle behind the bench."

"Right!" said MacGrath. "Splash it on the front page. Every woman in the land will want to know what happened to Hazel Loring!"

Everybody knew the name of Hazel Loring, the face of Hazel Loring, the opinions of Hazel Loring. "Smile and

Grow Fit" was the title of her weekly column in the *Daily Banner,* a deadly rival of MacGrath's own *Daily Record.* "Smile and Grow Fit" was also the title of the booklets, sold by the thousand, in which she explained to housewives how they might keep slim without anguish. She was no grim taskmistress of health. She did not sternly order them to eat a dry biscuit, and like it.

"I've devised these exercises on the advice of a doctor," she wrote. "Just three minutes each morning; and don't bother any more about it. If you like chocolates, in heaven's name eat chocolates. Only mind you do my exercises: and then eat what you like."

Her chatty, intimate manner warmed their hearts. She became more than an adviser on health. She counseled them about love and hats and husbands. Everybody had seen pictures of the strong, square, pleasant face, showing fine teeth in a smile, and with a dimple at each corner of the mouth. She was slim, with a good figure, and intensely active. She was well dressed, but not offensively so. Her brown hair was bobbed, her brown eyes grave. Her age might have been thirty-five. Thousands felt that they knew her personally, and wrote to tell her so.

Yet somebody killed her, half-dressed, in a public garden on a bitter December night.

If truth must be told, even in MacGrath, hard-boiled as he was, the first reaction was a twinge of pity. His wife was even more emphatic.

"Poor woman!" said Mrs. MacGrath from the opposite bed. "Poor woman!"

"Ho? Is that how it strikes you?" asked MacGrath, his news sense instantly on the alert.

"Of course it is. Of all the brutal, senseless—!"

"Then that's how we'll play the story. I think I'm getting an inspiration. But Hazel Loring. Oh Lord!"

The next day he carried his inspiration to Houston, the managing editor.

The offices of the *Daily Record* occupy a huge modernistic building, a sort of chromium-plated goldfish bowl. Fleet Street was buzzing with gossip. The murder of Hazel Loring, though they could not yet call it a murder, was considered so important that they held a conference in the managing editor's office. Here, in a cubist-designed room with bright curtains, the stately Houston sat behind a desk topped with black glass, and drew down the corners of his mouth.

"Impossible," Houston said. "We can't do it. Dignity."

"All right. *Be* dignified," said MacGrath. "But don't pass up a thing like this. Now see here, J. H. This is a woman's crime; it oozes feminine interest. It's good for a daily story. Our-Correspondent-Watches-Police; Developments-Day-By-Day. So, with half the women in England crying for news of their favorite, what do we do? Why, we put a woman to cover it."

Houston passed a hand over his thin, high forehead.

"A woman doing police reporting?"

"Why not? She can be dignified, can't she? Womanly and kind, with a touch of sadness? Man, they'll eat it up!"

Houston hunched up his shoulders. "She'd have to be tough," he pointed out. "Covering a war is one thing; covering a murder is another. I don't know who I could assign to it."

"What about that French girl? Jacqueline Dubois. Only been with us a week. Came over when things there went to blazes. But I'll tell you something, J. H. She had the reputation of being the smartest news hawk in Paris; Richart of *L'Oeil* recommended her in superlatives, and I think he's right."

"She speaks English?"

"She's half English. Her mother was a Cockney. She speaks English all right."

"And she will be—er—dignified?"

"Absolutely. I guarantee it, J. H."

"Get her," said Houston.

Nevertheless, he was uneasy until he actually set eyes on Jacqueline Dubois. Then he drew a breath of relief, and almost beamed.

MacGrath, on the other hand, was jarred. In recommending this girl MacGrath had been acting on a hunch; he knew little about her beyond Richart's word. And, at his first sight of Jacqueline, he had a panicky feeling that Richart must have been indulging in a deplorable Gallic sense of humor.

Jacqueline entered the office so timidly that Houston rose to draw out a chair for her. She was a golden blonde, small and plump, with one of those fair skins which flush easily, and those dark-blue eyes which are either wide open or modestly lowered. Her mouth expressed confusion, but anxiety to please. Her fur coat was good but unobtrusive; from her plain gray dress to her tan stockings and shoes she was trim and yet retiring. She kept her big eyes fixed on Houston except when he looked directly at her. In a soft, sweet voice she hesitantly asked what was wanted.

While MacGrath stood in despair, Houston told her.

"And that's the idea, Miss Dubois. Your purpose is to—"

"To pester the police," groaned MacGrath.

"To print," said Houston sternly, "all desirable news which will be of interest to our public. Would you like the assignment?"

Jacqueline raised her limpid blue eyes.

"Would I like it?" she breathed. "Hot ziggety damn!"

Houston sat back with a start. She was covered in confusion, modesty struggling with gratitude.

"I thank you on my knees," she went on, clasping her hands together. "Miss Loring. The poor lady who has so unfortunately kicked the ghost. I had wished to cover that story, yes; but, blimey, I never thought I should get it. Oh, you are a dear. Would you like me to kiss you?"

"Good heavens, no!" said Houston.

But Jacqueline was not listening. She was utterly absorbed. The toe of her shoe tapped the carpet. Her eyes were turned inward, a pucker of concentration between the brows; and, as she reflected, she nodded to herself.

"I am handicap," she confessed. "I am new to England and I do not know the ropes yet. If I get you a scoop, I must get it funny-ways. Who is the head of your whole police department?"

"The Assistant Commissioner for the Criminal Investigation Department," said MacGrath.

"Good!" said Jacqueline briskly. "I make love to him."

Houston gave her a long, slow look.

"No, no, no!" he said.

"Yes, yes, yes!" said Jacqueline, continuing to nod briskly.

"But you can't do that, Miss Dubois!"

"I do not understand," complained Jacqueline, breaking off to look at him with shy astonishment. "You do not wish me to do it? Why?"

"To explain that fully, Miss Dubois, might take a long time. I can sum up by saying that it would hardly be in accord with the policy of this newspaper. Besides, there are—er—practical considerations. In the first place, you'd never get near him. In the second place, even if you did you wouldn't get any story."

A twinkle appeared in Jacqueline's limpid eyes.

"Ha, ha, ha," she said. "That is what they tell me when I make eyes at Mornay, the *juge d'instruction*. He has whiskers this long"—her gesture indicated a beard of improbable dimensions—"but I get from him the official photographs of De La Rive shooting at all the gendarmes in the rue Jean Goujoun, and I scoop the town! Still, if you do not wish it?"

"Definitely not."

Jacqueline sighed. "Orright," she conceded. "Then I must find out the name of the policeman in charge of the case, and make love to *him*. Also, please, I should like a newspaper photographer to go with me all the time."

"A photographer? Why?"

"First because it is practical. I have got some fine pictures when I work for *L'Oeil*. Once I get a picture of the Comtesse de la Tour St. Sulpice, which is a kleptomaniac, pinching a necklace out of Paulier's in the rue de la Paix."

"Is that so?"

"Oo la la, what a sensation!" She gurgled delightedly. "Then too it is useful if you can get a picture of a police officer doing something he should not. You tell him you will publish the picture unless he gives you a story."

Houston had been listening under a kind of hypnosis. Jacqueline seemed to be surrounded by a rose-leaf cloud of innocence, like a figure on a valentine. He could not have been more startled if the Mona Lisa had suddenly leaned out of her frame and put out her tongue at him. He found his voice.

"We begin with vamping and pass on to blackmail," he said. "MacGrath, I can't do it. Young woman, you're fired! You'd ruin this paper in a week."

"If she's fired," roared MacGrath, "I resign. Splendor of saints, here's a newspaperman at last!"

"Do you want the Home Office to put us out business?"

"We've got subeditors to read her copy, haven't we? I tell you, J. H., if—"

"Then there is another thing," pursued Jacqueline timidly. "One of your photographers is called Henry Ashwin. He is a good fellow, though I think he drink too much visky-soda. He is the photographer I want, please."

"Ashwin? Why Ashwin?"

"I find out he is making the goo-goo eyes at Hazel Loring's maidservant. Yes! That is something the others pass up, eh? So I give him visky-soda and I talk to him. Already I get much information, you see."

"Before you were assigned to the story?"

Jacqueline raised her eyebrows.

"But yes, yes, yes! Of course. Listen! This Miss Loring, her age is thirty-five. In private life she is very bad-tempered. Henry Ashwin thinks she is what you call a phony, somehow, but he is not sure about what. Also she is good-goody, what you call a prude. Is she married? No! But she has a fiancé, a lawyer which is called Edward Hoyt; and he hang about her for five years and still it is no soap. Why does she not marry him, eh?"

"Well?"

"I find out," answered Jacqueline simply. "Now I tell you something the police have not told you."

"Go on," muttered Houston, still hypnotized.

"This is what her maid say to Henry Ashwin, and Henry Ashwin say to me. When Miss Loring is found sitting on the bench in that garden, wearing only the brassière and the step-ins and her shoes, the other clothes are folded up on the bench beside her."

MacGrath was instantly alert. "We know that. It's in all the papers."

"Yes! *But*," said Jacqueline, "there are other things too. Folded up in the clothes (so) there is a red wig and a pair of dark spectacles."

Houston and MacGrath stared at each other, wondering whether this might be some obscure French metaphor. But Jacqueline left them in no doubt.

"A red wig," she insisted, tapping her golden hair. "And the smoky spectacles you look through." She cupped her hands over her eyes in mimicry. "Why should Miss Loring have them, eh? Blimey, but that is not all! It is certain she undressed herself, and was not undressed by anybody. Her maid tells Henry Ashwin that Miss Loring has a special way of folding stockings, like . . . ah, zut! . . . Would you like me to take off mine and show you?"

"No, no!"

"Orright. I only ask. But it is special. Also the way of folding the dress. So she take her own dress off, and she have a wig and spectacles. Please, will you let me find out why?" Her big blue eyes turned reproachfully on Houston. "You say you will fire me, and that is not nice. I know I am a goofy little beasel; that is what they all say in Paris; but if you will please be a nice man and give me chance I will get you that story, cross my heart. Yes?"

Houston had the darkest misgivings. But he was a journalist.

"Hop to it," he said.

Inspector Adam Bell, Criminal Investigation Department, stood in the prim little front parlor of Number 22 Victoria Square. He looked alternately out of the window, toward the garden in the center, and then back to the white-faced man opposite him.

Sedate and dun-colored was Victoria Square, Bayswater, in the bleak winter afternoon. The house fronts were sealed up. In the garden, surrounded by teeth of spiked iron railings, the branches of trees showed black and knotted against a muddy twilight; its gravel paths wound between iron benches and skeleton bushes, on grass hard with frost.

Inspector Bell, in the white, antiseptic front parlor of the dead woman's house, faced Hazel Loring's fiancé. Inspector

Bell was a young and very serious-minded product of Hendon, but his sympathetic manner had already done much.

"And you can't tell me anything more, Mr. Hoyt?"

"Nothing!" said Edward Hoyt, and fingered his black tie. "I wanted to take her to a concert last night, but she refused, and I went alone. I—er—don't read the sensational press. So I knew nothing about this business until Hazel's secretary, Miss Alice Farmer, telephoned me this morning."

Inspector Bell shared Hoyt's views about the sensational press: the house was triple-guarded against reporters, though a hundred eyes came to stop and stare in the square.

Edward Hoyt suddenly sat down beside the small fire in the white grate. He was a long, lean, pleasant-faced man of just past forty, with big knuckly hands and a patient manner. He had certainly, Bell reflected, been a patient suitor. His eyes in the firelight were faintly bloodshot, and he turned them often toward a sofa on which lay a neat wig, a pair of dark spectacles, and a heavy black-thorn walking stick.

"It's fantastic and degrading," he went on, "and I still don't believe it. Can't *you* tell me anything, Inspector? Anything at all?"

Bell was noncommittal.

"You've heard the evidence, sir. Miss Farmer, her secretary, testifies that a few minutes before ten last night Miss Loring left the house, refusing to say where she was going." He paused. "It wasn't the first time Miss Loring had gone out like that: always about ten o'clock, and usually staying out two or three hours."

Hoyt did not comment.

"From here," said Bell, "she must have gone straight across to the garden—"

"But why, in heaven's name" Hoyt burst out, "the *garden?*"

Bell ignored this. "A policeman on his rounds heard

someone fumbling at the gate of the garden. He flashed his light, and saw Miss Loring opening the gate with a key. He questioned her, but she explained that she lived in the square and had a right to use the garden, even on a blacked-out December night.

"The constable let her go. But he was worried. About an hour later, his beat brought him round to the garden again. The gate was still open: he heard it creak. He went in, and found Miss Loring sitting on a bench . . . there . . . at the first turn of the gravel path, about fifteen feet from the gate.

Bell paused.

He visualized the scene, sharp in its loneliness. The gate squeaking in a raw wind; the brief, probing light on icy flesh and white silk underclothing; the head hanging down over the back of the bench; and the high-heeled shoes with button fastenings undone.

"The rest of her clothing—fur coat, dress, garter belt, and stockings—lay beside her: folded in such a way that her maid, Henrietta Simms, swears she took off the clothes herself. Her handbag was untouched. The key to the garden gate, with a large cardboard label attached, lay on the path."

Each time Bell made a statement, Edward Hoyt nodded at the fire.

Bell went over to the sofa and picked up the walking stick. It was top-heavy, because its nickel-plated head contained half a pound of lead.

"She'd been killed," Bell went on, "behind that bench. The ground was hard, but there were prints of those high heels of hers all over the place. There'd been a struggle: she wasn't any weakling."

"No," agreed Hoyt.

"Her skull was fractured over the left temple with this stick." Bell weighed it in his hand. "No doubt about this as the weapon. Microscopic traces of blood, and a hair, on the handle: though the wound hardly bled at all outwardly. Our laboratory identifies—"

He broke off apologetically.

"I beg your pardon, sir. I'm not trying to give you the third degree with this. I only brought it along to see whether anybody could identify it."

Hoyt spoke with old-fashioned courtesy.

"And I beg *your* pardon, Inspector. It is a pleasure to deal with a gentleman. He got to his feet, and drew the back of his hand across his mouth. "I'm glad there was no blood," he added. "I'm glad she wasn't—knocked about."

"Yes."

"But is that reasonable, Inspector? A fatal injury, with so little blood?"

"Oh yes. It's the rupture of brain tissues that counts. A friend of mine got concussion from being struck by the door of a railway carriage and never knew there was anything wrong with him until he collapsed." Bell's tone changed; he spoke sharply. "Now, sir, I've spoken my piece. Have you anything to tell me?"

"Nothing. Except—"

"Well?"

Hoyt hesitated. "I'd been a bit worried about her. She hadn't been looking at all well lately. I'm afraid she had a tendency to overeat." There was the ghost of a smile on his face, contradicted by the bloodshot eyes. "But she said, 'So long as I do my exercises every morning, as thousands of my followers are doing'—she was very proud of her position, Inspector—"

This was hardly what Bell wanted.

"I mean, do you know any reason why anybody should have wanted to kill her?"

"None. I swear!"

"Or why she should have undressed herself in order to get killed?"

Hoyt's mouth tightened. But he was prevented from answering by the entrance of a soft, quiet, but quick-moving woman in horn-trimmed spectacles. Miss Alice Farmer, the perfect secretary, resembled the old-time notion of a school-mistress. Her face, though not unattractive, was suggestive of a buttered bun; her brown hair was dressed untidily; she wore paper cuffs and flat-heeled shoes.

Miss Farmer had many times shown her devotion to Hazel Loring during six years' service. Now her eyelids looked pink and sanded, and occasionally she reached under the spectacles to dab at them with the tip of a handkerchief.

"Ghouls!" she said, gripping the handkerchief hard. "Ghouls! Inspector, I—I know poor Hazel's body has been taken away. But didn't you give orders that *none* of those horrible reporters were to be admitted to the square over there?"

"Yes, of course. Why?"

"Well," said Miss Farmer, putting out her chin bravely, "they're there now. You can see them from my window upstairs. Two of them. One is a man taking pictures; and the other, if you please, is a *woman*. How any *decent* woman could lower herself to write for the—" She stopped, and her face grew scarlet. "I mean *report*, of course; not write *nice* things; that's altogether different. Oh, dear. You do see what I mean, don't you?"

Inspector Bell saw only that his orders had been dis-obeyed. He stiffened.

"You're sure they're reporters?"

"Just *look* for yourself!"

Bell's pleasant face grew sinister. He drew a deep breath. He picked up his overcoat and his bowler hat from a chair.

"Excuse me just one moment," he said formally. "I'll attend to them."

* * *

By the time he left the house, Bell was running. The garden gate, on the west side of the square, was almost opposite Hazel Loring's house. The iron bench—once green, but now of a rust-color—itself faced due west, where the gravel path curved in front it.

Round it prowled a small golden-haired figure in a fur coat, and a large untidy figure with a mackintosh and a camera. Inspector Bell "Oi'd" at them; then he squared himself in front of them and began to talk.

Henry Ashwin, the photographer, took it stolidly. All he did was to pull his hat further on a pair of large projecting ears and shrug his shoulders in an apologetic way. But Jacqueline, between indignation and utter astonishment, was struck dumb. She sincerely felt that she was helping in the investigation, and she could not understand what this man was going on about.

"You must not be such a grimy camel!" she cried, reasoning with him kindly. "You do not understand at all. I am Dubois of the *Record*. This is Mr. Ashwin of the *Record.*"

"I know Mr. Ashwin, " said Bell grimly. "Now, for the last time, madam: will you get out of here, or must you be taken out by main force?"

"But you do not mean that!"

Bell stared at her.

"What makes you think so?"

"And you should not talk so to the Press. It is not nice and you get yourself into trouble. Henry, I do not like this man. Kick him out of here and then we get on with our work."

"Ashwin," said Bell, "is this girl completely off her head?"

Ashwin intervened in a protesting rumble. "Sorry, Inspector; I'll fix it. Look here, Jackie, things aren't the same here as they are in France. That's what I've been trying to tell you. In England, reporters aren't allowed to—"

"You will not do it?"

"I can't, Jackie!"

"Now I am mad," said Jackie, folding her arms with an air of cold grandeur. "Blimey, now I am good and mad; and just for that I do not tell you anything about the clue I have discovered."

"Clue?" said Bell sharply.

"Ha, *now* you are interested, eh?" cried Jacqueline, wagging her head. Her tone changed: it became timid and pleading. "Please, I like to be nice, and I like you to be nice too. I could help you if you would let me. I think I know what happen here last night. As soon as I hear about Miss Loring's shoes being unbuttoned, and hear about the wig and spectacles—"

Bell whirled round on her.

"How do you know her shoes were unbuttoned? And about any wig and spectacles? That wasn't given out to the Press!"

Twilight was deepening over the spiky trees of the garden. Not a gleam showed in Victoria Square except the hooded sidelights of a taxi, which circled the square with its engine clanking noisily. Jacqueline opened her handbag, and drew out a large oblong of glazed paper.

It was a photograph of Hazel Loring's body, taken from in front and some dozen feet away. The shadows were behind it, so that every detail showed with crude realism: the upright posture but limp arms, the head thrown back, the slim muscular legs and shoes whose open fastenings were visible at a glance.

"Where," Bell shouted, "did you get this?"

"*I* got it, Inspector," Ashwin admitted. "I climbed over the fence this morning, before they'd moved anything. If I'd used a flash bulb your men would have spotted me straight-away; but there was a good strong sun up to ten o'clock, so I just took a snap and hared off."

Ashwin's little eyes blinked out of the shadow of his shabby hat. It had grown so dark in the garden that little more could be seen of him except the shift and shine of his eyes, and the fact that he needed a shave. If ordinarily he might have been something of a swaggerer, he was subdued now. He also had found Jacqueline a handful.

"I wasn't even going to use the picture, I swear!" he went on, and stated his real grievance. "This girl pinched it from me, when I wasn't even going to show—"

"Shoes!" insisted Jacqueline.

Bell swung round again. "What about the shoes?"

"They is clues," said Jacqueline simply. "You must not ask me how I get my information. The wig and the spectacles I learn about from Miss Loring's maid, in a way. But I do not mind telling you what will solve your case for you, strike me pink."

Bell hesitated.

"If this is some sort of game," he snapped, "there's going to be a lot of trouble in store for certain people I could mention. Now, I warn you! But if you've got anything to tell me, let's hear it."

Jacqueline was complacent.

"You do not see that the shoes show what has happen here?"

"Frankly, I don't."

"Ah! That is why you need a woman to detect for you when a woman is murdered. Now I show you. You see in the picture that the shoes have very high heels. Yes?"

"Yes."

"And they fasten only with one strap and one button across the . . . the . . . ah, zut!"

"Instep?"

"I am spikking the English very well, thank you," said Jacqueline, drawing herself up coldly. "I do not need your help to be pure. And I have already think to say instep. But you still do not tumble? No?" She sidled closer. Coaxing and honeysweet, her voice caressed him out of the twilight. "If I tell you, then you do something for me? You will be a nice man and let me print what I like?"

"I most certainly will not."

"Orright. Then I will not tell you."

Adam Bell's wrath boiled clear to the top. Never in his career had he met anyone quite like this. It is true that his career had not been a long one; but then Jacqueline's could not have been so very long either. Now he meant to have no more nonsense. He would put her in her place, and with no uncertain adjectives.

He had opened his mouth to do this, when there was a flicker of a shrouded light across the square. The door of Number 22 opened and closed.

Bell had a sharp premonition of disaster as soon as he heard the flat-heeled footsteps rapping and ringing on frosty pavements. A squat little figure, coatless and with wisps of hair flying, hurried across the street into the garden.

When the figure came closer, Bell saw that tears were trickling down Miss Alice Farmer's face.

"It's all your fault," she said accusingly to Bell. "Oh dear, if only you hadn't left! If only you'd stayed with him!"

"Easy now. What is it? Steady, Miss Farmer!"

"Your sergeant's phoned for the ambulance; and he says they may pull him through, but oh dear, if they don't I don't know what I shall do. Oh dear, it's even more dreadful than—"

Then she pulled herself together.

"I'm sorry. It's poor Mr. Hoyt. He's taken poison. You'd better come over to the house at once."

* * *

Adam Bell was not able to interview Hoyt until the following day. That morning's edition of the *Daily Record* was in
Bell's pocket: he wondered what the Assistant Commissioner
would have to say about Jacqueline Dubois's story.

A nurse conducted him to a small private room, where
Edward Hoyt lay propped up among the pillows of a white
iron bed. Alice Farmer sat in a squeaky rocking chair by the
window, looking out at the snowflakes that had begun to
thicken over Kensington Gardens.

"Rather a foolish thing to do wasn't it, sir?" Bell asked
quietly.

"I recognize that, Inspector."

"Why did you do it?"

"Can't you guess?"

Hoyt even managed a sour smile. His hands, snake-
veined, lay listless on the coverlet; his gaze wandered over
the ceiling without curiosity. Yesterday he had seemed in his
middle forties: now he looked ten years older.

"The curious thing is," he went on, frowning, "that I had
no intention of doing it. That's a fact, Inspector. I hadn't
realized—by George, I hadn't!—how terrible and irresistible a mere *impulse* can be."

He paused, as though to get his breath.

"I went upstairs," he said, "to have a look at Hazel's room.
That's all. It honestly is all. I glanced into the bathroom. I
saw the medicine cabinet open, and a bottle of morphine tablets inside. Before I had any notion of what I meant, I had
filled a glass of water, and swallowed seven or eight of the
tablets as fast as I could get them down. At that time, I
admit, I didn't want to live any longer."

"No, sir?"

"No. But I have changed my mind now. I am sorry: it was,
as you say, a very foolish thing to do."

Always the gentleman, thought Inspector Bell.

From the direction of the window came a sharp, almost malignant squeak from the rocking chair. Alice Farmer glanced over her shoulder, and back again quickly. The snow shed shifting lights into the warm, close room.

"Of course I realize," Bell said awkwardly, "that as Miss Loring's fiancé—"

"It is not quite accurate to call me her fiancé," returned Hoyt, with detached calmness.

His tone made Inspector Bell sit up sharply.

"Meaning, sir?"

"Hazel never intended to get married, to me or anybody else."

"How do you know that?"

"She told me so. But I kept on patiently waiting. I have always had a fancy for the senseless role of the *preux chevalier.* God knows I'm cured of that now." Hoyt closed his eyes, and opened them again. "You see that I am being frank."

"You mean she didn't love you?"

Hoyt smiled faintly. "I doubt if Hazel was ever in love with anybody. No: I wasn't referring to that."

"Well?"

"I think she was married already. One moment!" The weak voice sharpened and grew firm. "I have absolutely no evidence for saying that. It's a guess. An impression. A—well, Inspector, I haven't known Hazel Loring for five years without learning something about her beyond those famous eyebrows and dimples. I knew her moods. And her heart. And her mind: which was, after all, a second-rate mind. Lord forgive me, what am I saying?"

He broke off, looking still more ill. There was another squeak from the rocking chair as Alice Farmer got up to pour him a glass of water from the bedside table.

Hoyt thanked her with a grateful nod; and she hardly glanced at him. But to Inspector Bell, watching every turn of lip or hand, that glance meant much. Bell thought to himself, with a rush of realization: if Hazel Loring wasn't in love with Edward Hoyt, I know who else is.

Miss Farmer fluttered back to her chair.

"I tell you that," pursued Hoyt, setting down the glass, "because I want to see this mess cleared up. If Hazel *had* a husband tucked away somewhere in secret, she could hardly divorce him. She had set herself up in too pious a position before the world."

Drawing up the collar of his overcoat, Bell went out of the nursing home into the falling snow. Jacqueline Dubois, wearing a fur coat and a hat with an outrageous veil, was waiting for him at the foot of the steps.

Inspector Bell took one look at her, and then began to run.

His excuse for this was a bus, which would set him down beside a hotel in a side street only a few yards away from Victoria Square. The bus was already some distance away, and lumbering fast. Bell sprinted hard after it, sprang aboard, and climbed up to a deserted top deck. He had no sooner settled back than Jacqueline, flushed and panting, was beside him.

The girl was almost in tears.

"You are not genteel!" she wailed. "I have twist my ankle. Would you like it that I should hurt myself bad?"

"Candidly," said Bell, "yes."

"You do not like me at *all?*"

"No. Remember, I've read your story in the *Record* this morning."

"You do not like it? But, *chéri*, I wrote it to please you!"

"In the course of that story," said Bell, "you four times described me as 'handsome.' How I'm going to dare show my face back at Scotland Yard again I don't know. What is more important, you headlined—"

"You are not angry?"

"Oh, no. Not at all."

"Besides, I have a clue."

Despite everything, Bell suddenly found himself chuckling. Rules were rules; but still, he reflected, he had been behaving like a good deal of a stuffed shirt. This girl need give him no trouble. And in her way Jacqueline was rather attractive.

"Not again?" he said.

"No, no, no! It is the same clue. You will not let me explain. You will not let me explain how I know that Miss Loring was not killed in the garden at all, but that the assassin kill her somewhere else and carry her to the garden afterward."

The bus lurched round a snow-rutted curve.

Bell, taking two tickets from the conductor, almost dropped both of them.

"Is this," he demanded, "another stunt?"

"It is the truth! I know it by the shoes. The shoes have very high heels, and their straps are not buttoned."

"Well?"

"She could not have walked in them. Yes, I tell you so! She could not have walked a step in them. It is impossible. Either the shoes fall off, or *she* fall off.

"Listen! You say to yourself, 'Miss Loring has entered the garden; she has started to undress herself.' So? Then why does she take off her stockings and put her shoes back on? You say, 'While she is like this, the assassin catch her; there is a struggle; she is hit; the assassin pick her up and put her on the bench.' I say, no, no, no! She could not have walk in those shoes. It is jolly sure she could not have *fight* in them.

They would just fall off, and then there would be marks on her feet. And there were no marks, eh?"

"Go on," said Bell, after a pause.

"It jumps to the eyes that the assassin has put the shoes on Miss Loring after she is dead."

"But—"

"Now I tell you something else. What is it that puzzle you so much, *chéri*? What is the big headache? It is the reason why Miss Loring should have undress herself in the open with the weather freezing zero. Yes? But she did not.

"She has gone first to the garden. Then she has left the garden, and gone somewhere else which is indoors; and there she has undressed herself. There the assassin catch her and kill her. Then he take her back to the garden in the blackout, to make you think she was killed there. He is just starting to dress her fully when he is interrupted, and has to run. Yes?"

Their bus had gone clanking up Gloucester Terrace, and was turning into Hargreaves Street, which led to Victoria Square. Already Bell could see the square ahead. Bell smote his hand against the top of the seat in front of them.

"By all the—" he burst out, and stopped. "I wonder if it could be?"

"I do not wonder," said Jacqueline. "I am sure it is true. For any woman to take off her clothes outdoors in such weather is not practical; and even if I am a goofy little beasel I see that straightaway, gorblimey!"

"Just a minute. What about the heel marks of the struggle in the earth behind the bench!"

"They is phony," returned Jacqueline calmly. "I do not think there be any marks with the ground so hard. The assassin has made them too."

Stopping with a jolt, the bus threw them against the bench ahead. They climbed down to the pavement beside the quiet hotel only a few steps from Victoria Square. Though Jacqueline was dancing round him, Bell would not be hurried either mentally or physically.

"It's nonsense," he decided.

"You are a nasty man and I do not like you. Why is it nonsense?"

"Well, where did the woman go? You say Miss Loring went somewhere and 'undressed.' Where? Apparently she didn't go back home. Where could any woman go at that hour of the night in order to undr—?"

He checked himself, and raised his eyes. A raw wind shouted down Hargreaves Street, whipping the snow to powder. The grimy red-brick building in front of them had two entrances. Across the top of one was blazoned in gilt letters the name of the hotel. On the glass doors of the other were smaller letters in white enamel, but they were letters which made Bell jump. They said: LADIES' AND GENTLEMEN'S TURKISH BATHS, OPEN DAY AND NIGHT.

The woman behind the counter was scandalized. When she first caught a glimpse of them, coming down in the automatic lift into the warm, dim basement foyer, she threw up the flap of the counter and ran out.

"You, sir!" she cried. "You can't come in here!"

"I am a police officer—" Bell began.

The woman hesitated only a second. "Sorry, sir, but you still aren't allowed here. This is Wednesday. It's Ladies' Day. Didn't you see the notice upstairs?"

"*I* can come in?" cooed Jacqueline.

"Yes, madam, of course."

"'Ow much?" asked Jacqueline, opening her handbag.

Taking hold of Jacqueline's arm in a grip that made her squeal, Bell drove the other woman before him until she retreated behind the counter. First he showed his warrant card. Then he drew out a large close-up photograph of Hazel Loring's face.

"Did you ever see this lady before?"

"I—I don't know. There are so many people here. What do you want?"

On the counter lay a tray of pens and pencils. With a colored pencil Bell drew on the photograph a crude representation of an auburn wig. To this he added a pair of dark spectacles.

"Did you ever see *this* lady before?"

"I did and all!" admitted the woman. "Of course I did. She was always coming here at night. If you'd just tell me what you—"

"Was she here on Monday night?"

The attendant, who seemed less frightened than anxious that Bell should not get beyond the doors at the left, admitted this too.

"Yes, she was. She came in about a quarter past ten, a little later than usual. I noticed because she looked awfully groggy; sicklike; and her hands were shaky and she didn't leave any valuables here at the desk."

"What time did she leave?"

"I don't know. I—I don't remember." A puzzled look, a kind of spasm, flickered across the attendant's face. "Here's Mrs. Bradford," she added. "She'll give you what-for if you don't get out of here!"

It was very warm and faintly damp in the tiled basement. A dim humming noise throbbed beyond it. Soft lights shone on the counter, on the wall of steel boxes behind it; and, toward the left, on leather-covered swing doors studded with brass nailheads.

One of these doors was pushed open. A stocky, medium-sized woman, with dark hair drawn behind her ears and eyebrows that met over the top of her nose, first jerked back as though for flight, and then stood solidly. Her face was impassive and rather sinister. She wore a white-duck coat and skirt; her bare feet were thrust into beach sandals.

"Mrs. Bradford—" the attendant began.

Mrs. Bradford gave the newcomers a long, slow look. Emotion, harsh and pressed to bursting, filled that foyer as thickly as the damp. Voices, faint laughter, made a ghostly background beyond.

"You'd better come in here," she told them. Opening a door which led into a small office, she nodded at them to precede her. When they were inside, she closed and locked the door. Then she flopped down in an office chair and presently began to cry.

"I knew I couldn't get away with it," she said.

"So that's it," Bell muttered ten minutes later. "Hoyt told me that Miss Loring was fond of overeating."

Mrs. Bradford uttered a contemptuous snort. She was sitting forward, her elbows carelessly on her knees; she seemed to feel better now that she had been given a cigarette.

"Overeating!" she growled. "She'd have been as big as a barrage balloon if she hadn't nearly killed herself with more Turkish baths than any human being ought to take. Yes, and keeping a medicine cabinet full of slimming drugs that were downright dangerous. I warned her. But, oh, no! She wouldn't listen. She was making too much money out of this slimming campaign of hers."

"You knew her?"

"I've known Hazel Loring for twenty years. We were kids together in the north. She was always the lady. Not like me. And she was clever: I give her that."

Bell was putting many facts together now.

"Then the simple-exercises-and-keep-fit campaign—?"

"It was all," said Mrs. Bradford, wagging her head and

blowing out smoke contemptuously, "a fake. Mind, her exercises maybe did do some people good. There's some women could hypnotize themselves into believing anything. And, if they thought it kept 'em slim, why, perhaps it did. But not little Hazel. That's why she had to sneak over here in a damn silly disguise, like a film star or something. She was desperately frightened somebody'd spot her."

"And yet," said Bell, "somebody murdered her. It was you, I suppose?"

The cigarette dropped out of Mrs. Bradford's hand.

"Murdered!" she whispered; and missed the cigarette altogether when she tried to stamp it out with her foot. Then her voice rose to a screech. "Man, what's the matter with you? Are you clean daft? Murdered?"

"Sh-h!"

"*Murdered?*" said Mrs. Bradford. "She fell down and died in the steam room. I had to get her out of here on the q.t., or the scandal would have ruined us."

"She died from concussion of the brain."

Mrs. Bradford's eyes seemed to turn inward,

"Ah? So that was it! I noticed she'd got a kind of red mark on her temple, half under the wig. I supposed she had hit her head on the edge of the marble bench when she collapsed—"

"No," said Bell. "She was beaten to death with a lead-loaded walking stick. The laboratory can prove that."

Distant fans whirred and hummed: the air was astir. Mrs. Bradford slid up from her chair, with a lithe motion for a woman so stocky, and began to back away.

"Don't you try to bluff a woman that's always been honest," she said, in a thin unnatural voice. "It was an accident, I tell you! Either heart failure, or hitting her head when she fell. It's happened before, when people can't stand the heat. And now you come and tell me—"

"Just a moment," said Bell quietly.

The tone of his voice made Mrs. Bradford pause, her hand half-lifted as though to take an oath.

"Now tell me," Bell continued, "did you see Miss Loring arrive here on Monday night?"

"Yes."

"How did she look? Ill, for instance?"

"Very ill. Lucy at the desk can tell you that. All shaky and funny. That's why I kept any eye on her."

"What happened then? No, I'm not accusing you of lying! Just tell me what happened."

Mrs. Bradford stared at him.

"Well . . . she went to one of the booths, and took off her clothes, wrapped herself up in that cotton robe they wear, and went on to the hot rooms. I'm manager here: I don't act as masseuse usually, but I did it for her so that nobody shouldn't discover about the wig. I was nervous because she looked so ill. Afterward I went up to the steam room, and there she was lying on the floor. Alone. Dead. I thought: Holy mother, I knew something would happen, and now—!"

"Go on."

"Well, what could I do? I couldn't carry her down to where her clothes were, because there were ten or a dozen other women here and they'd know what had happened."

"Go on."

"I had to get rid of her. I *had* to! I ran down and rolled her clothes and handbag up into a bundle and ran back up to the steam room. But I couldn't dress her there, because some-body might have walked in any minute. Don't you see?"

"Go on."

Mrs. Bradford moistened her lips. "Upstairs there's a door that leads out into an alley by the hotel. I slung her over my shoulder, and carried her out into the blackout wrapped in that cotton robe.

"I knew where to put her, too. Beside her handbag there'd

been a big key, with a cardboard label saying it was the key to the garden in Victoria Square. I got her into the garden and sat her down on the first bench I came to. Then I started to dress her properly so nobody shouldn't know she'd ever been at the baths. I'd just got the underclothes on, and slipped the shoes on her feet so they'd be handy, when I heard a noise. I slipped back a little; and it's a good thing I did, for there was a great big blazing light—"

"Did I not say it?" murmured Jacqueline softly. "Did I not say the policeman has come in and interrupted her?"

"So I hopped it," concluded Mrs. Bradford, wiping her eyes. "I still had the cotton robe in my hand; but I forgot the wig and spectacles." Her face grew harsh and ugly. "That's what I did. I admit it. But that's all I did. She wasn't murdered in these baths!"

"As a matter of fact," replied Bell calmly, "I don't think she was. For all practical purposes, I think she was dead before she got here."

It was not easy to frighten Jacqueline Dubois. Only her imagination could do this. Her imagination conjured up wild visions of a dead woman in a red wig, the face already bloodless, walking into the foyer and confronting the attendant with blind black spectacles. It unnerved her. Even the humming of the fans unnerved her.

She cried out at Bell, but he silenced her.

"Queer thing," Bell mused. "I was telling Mr. Hoyt yesterday about a friend of mine. He was struck by the door of a railway carriage. He got up, brushed himself, assured everybody he wasn't hurt, went home, and collapsed an hour later with concussion of the brain. Such cases are common enough. You'll find plenty of them in Taylor's *Medical Jurisprudence*. That's what happened to Hazel Loring, in my opinion."

"You mean . . ."

"Mind!" Bell held hard to his caution. "Mind, I don't promise anything. Whether they'll want to hold you as accessory after the fact, Mrs. Bradford, I can't say. But, just between ourselves, I don't think you've got a lot to worry about.

"As I read it, Hazel Loring met the murderer in the garden at ten o'clock. There was a fight. The murderer struck her down and left her for dead. She got to her feet, thought she was all right, and came over here to the baths. In the steam room she collapsed and died. And you, finding the key to the garden, carried her body straight back to the real scene of the crime."

Bell drew a deep breath and his forehead wrinkled in thought.

"Talk about the wheel revolving!" he added. "All we want now is the murderer."

Edward Hoyt, released from the nursing home on Friday morning, took a taxi to Victoria Square under a bright, watery sun which was turning the snow to slush.

The exposure of Hazel Loring's racket, appearing in Thursday's *Daily Record*, was both a revelation and a revolution. It was a real scoop for the paper.

MacGrath, the news editor, danced the saraband. Henry Ashwin, the photographer, swallowed three quick whiskies and went out to find Jacqueline. Sir Claude Champion, owner of the *Daily Banner*, swallowed aspirins and vowed vengeance. All over the country it made wives pause in the very act of the patent exercises. Yet nobody was satisfied. Through the excitement ran a bitter flavor: however much of a fake the dead woman might have been, still she was dead by a brutal attack and her murderer still walked and talked in the town.

Edward Hoyt's face seemed to express this as he went up

the steps of Number 22. The door was opened for him by Alice Farmer, whose face brightened with joy. And this performance was watched with interest by Jacqueline Dubois and Henry Ashwin, the photographer, lurking behind the railings in the garden opposite.

"The point is," insisted Ashwin, giving her a sideways glance, "what is Bell doing? He now seems to think you're a kind of mascot—"

Jacqueline was not without modest pride.

"He think I am pretty good," she admitted. "I just try to give him ideas, that is all. But between you and me and the pikestaff, I do not know *what* he is doing. He is very mysterious."

"Beaten, eh? Shame on you!"

Jacqueline's color went up like a flag.

"I am not beaten either! But maybe perhaps I am wrong about him. First I think he is only a stupid Englishman, all dumb and polite, and now I think his mind may work funnier than I expect. He keep talking about lights."

"Lights?"

"Big lights. Oi! Look!"

She pointed. There was another visitor for Number 22. Mrs. Eunice Bradford, almost unrecognizable in an oversmart outfit and a saucer hat, strode briskly along the street. The morning sun streamed full on the doorway; they saw Mrs. Bradford punching the doorbell with assurance. She was admitted by Miss Farmer.

"Got 'em taped," said the voice of Inspector Bell.

Jacqueline felt a shock. Bell, followed by Sergeant Rankin and a uniformed constable, was coming across the slush-marshy garden with the sun behind them.

"Don't sneak up like that, Inspector!" protested Ashwin. He nodded toward the house across the way. "So it's a gathering of the suspects, eh?"

"It is."

"And you're going to nab somebody over there?"

"I am."

Jacqueline began to shiver, though the air held an almost spring-like thaw. Bell's expression was guileless.

"You can come along, if you like," he said to Jacqueline. "In fact, I might say you've got to come along. A good deal of my evidence depends on you, though you may not know it. I'll give you some poetic justice too. You've spent half your time in this business worming things out of people or pinching things from people. I've taken the liberty of pinching something from you."

"You go away!" said Jacqueline. "Please, what is this? I do not understand."

Bell opened the brief case he was carrying. "You remember," he said, "how you solved your part of the problem by deducing something from the unbuttoned shoes in a photograph taken the morning after the murder?"

"Yes."

Bell drew a large glazed oblong of paper from the brief case. It was the picture they had all seen: Hazel Loring's body on the bench, every detail sharp etched with the shadows behind.

"Is this the same photograph?"

"Ah, zut! Of course it is."

Bell glanced inquiringly at Ashwin.

"You confirm that? This is the same photograph you took at about ten o'clock on Tuesday morning?"

Ashwin, with a face of hideous perplexity, merely nodded. Sergeant Rankin suddenly guffawed: a sharp sound which he covered up with a cough.

"Then it's very curious," said Bell. He held up the photograph. "It's the most curious thing we've come across yet. Look at it. Every shadow in this picture, as we see, falls straight behind bench and body. Yet the bench, as we've known from the start, faces due west and has its back to the east.

"Look at the bench now. See how the shadows fall in front of it along the path. In other words, this photograph couldn't possibly have been taken in the morning. It couldn't have been taken at any time during the day, because the sun was gone in the afternoon. That bright light and those dead-black shadows could have been made in only one way. The photograph must have been taken, after dark, by the glare of a flash bulb: which was the 'great big blazing light' Mrs. Bradford saw when she—"

Jacqueline screamed.

One face in the group altered and squeezed up as though it were crumpling like a wet paper mask. A pair of hands flung forward to grab the photograph from Bell and rend it in pieces; but Sergeant Rankin's arm was round the man's throat and the two of them went over backward in a crashing cartwheel on the path.

Bell's voice remained level.

"Henry Ashwin, I arrest you for the murder of your wife, Hazel Loring. I have to warn you that anything you say will be taken down in writing and may be used as evidence against you at your trial."

To Jacqueline, that night, Bell was a little more communicative.

"There's nothing much to tell," he said off-handedly. "Once I got Hoyt's tip, and we put the organization to work, it didn't take long to discover that one Hazel Ann Loring and one Henry Fielding Ashwin had been married at the Hampstead Registry Office in 1933." He grinned. "That's where the official police will always score over you amateurs."

Jacqueline was agog.

"He try the blackmail on her. Yes?"

"Yes, in a small way. A nasty bit of work is Ashwin. In the first place, he was a no-good who would take some explaining; in the second place, she couldn't afford to have the gaff blown about her racket. That was why Ashwin was pretending to make what you call goo-goo eyes at Hazel Loring's maid: he had to have some excuse for hanging round the house so constantly.

"But Hazel was getting fed up with it. She issued an ultimatum, and arranged to meet him in the garden. There was a wild, blind row: both of them, we know, had ugly tempers. Ashwin laid her out, and then ran. It wasn't a planned crime: he just ran.

"After he'd had a couple of drinks, he began to get scared. He'd left that stick behind. He didn't *think* they could trace it to him; but suppose they did? So he went back to the square—and must have thought he was losing his mind. For he saw Eunice Bradford bringing the body back.

"In any case, he thought it was a gift from heaven. If he could frame any evidence against her, Mrs. Bradford would swing for the crime as sure as eggs. He set his flash bulb and fired blindly for a picture. But in the dark his aim was bad; Mrs. Bradford had jumped back; and he didn't get her in the picture at all. He saw that when he developed the picture. Of course he'd never have shown that photograph to anyone. He'd have torn up the picture and destroyed the negative. Only—"

Jacqueline nodded radiantly.

"I pinch it from him," she declared, with pride. "And then he have to stew up some explanation for it."

"Yes. Of course, I saw that the dim, paper-covered torch of the policeman who discovered the body could never have produced that 'great big blazing light' described by Mrs. Bradford. Then, once you looked closely at the photograph and noticed the fall of the shadows, that tore it. I gathered the obvious suspects in one house to throw Ashwin off his guard; and got him to confirm his previous story before police witnesses. That's all."

He chuckled.

"There's one good result from it, anyway," he added. "Edward Hoyt and Alice Farmer should be extremely comfortable with each other."

But Jacqueline was not listening. Her eyes were shining and absorbed. She put her hand with innocent fervor on his arm.

"If I had not pinch the picture," she said, "and if I had not deduce those things, maybe you would not have solved the case. Eh?"

"Maybe not."

"You do not think I am such a goofy little beasel. No?"

"No."

"In fact, day by day in every way I am becoming indispensible to you. Yes?"

The hair froze on Bell's head. "Hold on! Take it easy! I didn't say that!"

"But *I* say it," declared Jacqueline, with fiery earnestness. "I think we go well together, yes? I pinch things for you; and if you like you can be my Conscience and go gobble-gobble at me, but you do not be too mad when I help you. Then each day I get an exclusive inter—inter—"

"Interview," suggested Bell.

"O.K., if you say so, though my knowledge of English is formidable and you do not have to tell me. If I like you very much and am a good girl, will you let me help with the detecting when I ask to?"

Bell looked down at the flushed, lovely face.

"I will," he said, "*ou je serai l'oncle d'un singe!* My knowledge of French is formidable, too."

LAIR OF THE DEVIL-FISH

The Characters:

Captain Forbes	Of the yacht *Venturer*
First Officer Browning	Of the yacht *Venturer*
Doc Trencher	Diver
Edmund Stanley	Treasure-hunter
Dick Lawrence	His son-in-law
Sally Lawrence	Stanley's daughter
Leon Romero	A landowner

Setting: A Cuban bay, May 1936.

NARRATOR: This is your storyteller, the Man in Black, here again to bring you another tale in our twilight series, *Appointment with Fear*.

The giant octopus, with its eight moving tentacles and its huge eyes unwinking in the green depths of the water: was it a myth, in that Cuban bay? Or was there something else—something worse—which lurked about the sunken wreck? And so, as we follow Edmund Stanley's adventure to its grim end, we trust we shall keep our promise to bring you . . . (*knife-chord*) an Appointment with Fear! (*Music up. The narrator speaks through.*)

Cuba, largest island of the West Indies, in the blazing heat of May some eight years ago. (*Slight pause*) The harsh green vegetation—dry, yet a-dazzle with sun—the brown hills, the white roads, all under a shimmer that makes the eyes ache. On the southeast coast of Cuba you will find many bays: large bays of deep water, secret beyond their channels, where palmetto trees shade dark green water. Into one of these bays, as dawn was breaking, crept the big motor yacht *Venturer*—fifteen hundred tons' burden—a yacht dazzling white under her single scarlet funnel. And, as she moved up the channel into the bay, echo-sounder switched on, you might have heard the Captain's eternal question from the bridge . . . .

(*Faint thudding of engines under the speaker's voices.* CAPTAIN FORBES *is middle-aged with a faint Scots accent.* FIRST OFFICER BROWNING *is young and enthusiastic.*)

FORBES: How much water now?

BROWNING: Twelve fathoms, sir.

FORBES: Plenty of depth, anyway. That'll do, Mr. Browning. Stop her.

(*Engine-room telegraph rings. The thudding dies away.*)

BROWNING: Engines stopped, sir.

FORBES: Let go starboard anchor.

BROWNING (*calling, away to fo'c'sle head*): Let go starboard anchor!

(*Long rattle of anchor-chain. Slight pause.*)

BROWNING: Ugly-looking place, isn't it? Like a jungle with a lake in the middle.

FORBES: That's none of our business, my lad. You might go below—

BROWNING: Yes, sir?

FORBES: —and wake up Mr. Stanley. Tell our good owner we've reached Devil-Fish Bay.

(*Music creeps in behind narration.*)

NARRATOR: That's how in the fiery afternoon certain preparations were made on the afterdeck. You see, in the knot of men, the seated figure in the suit of rubber and twill? The lead-soled boots? The helmet of tinned copper? The air-line from the helmet to the pumps—four men on those pumps—and the breast-rope that carries the telephone wire? That's Doc Trencher, Number One Diver of the Hoskins Company, New York. In front of him—a big man with an amiable blue eye—Mr.

Edmund Stanley, his employer; and Mr. Stanley's son-in-law, Dick Lawrence . . . .

(*Music comes out into a faint murmur of voices, which dies as* EDMUND STANLEY *speaks.*)

STANLEY: Trencher, all right inside that helmet?

(TRENCHER'S *voice comes with hollow and booming effect from inside the helmet. He is thirty-five or so; American; cheerful; tough.*)

TRENCHER: Absolutely okay, Mr. Stanley. Just as snug as a bug in a rug.

STANLEY: Half a minute, before you get on that ladder and put in your front glass. You're *sure* you've got the instructions straight?

TRENCHER (*wearily amused*): Now look, Mr. Stanley. We've been over those instructions till I'm cockeyed. I can't miss!

STANLEY (*hesitating*): You—don't mind the job?

TRENCHER: (*surprised*):Working in sixty feet of water? Cripes! I've worked at three hundred without much more'n a headache.

STANLEY: No, I meant this fable about the devil-fish. The giant squid or octopus.

TRENCHER (*earnestly*): Now look, Mr. Stanley—!

STANLEY: And it *is* a fable. I guarantee that.

TRENCHER: It's a hundred to one against findin' squids in open water. If we was working close in-shore, with rock caves and the rest of it: that's different. But we're not. And these instructions of yours . . .

(DICK LAWRENCE *intervenes. He is thirtyish and engaging.*)

DICK: Y-e-es. What *are* the instructions?

STANLEY (*sternly*):You keep out of this, Dick!

DICK: But listen, my good pop-in-law—!

STANLEY: And don't call me pop!

DICK: All right, governor. But what's all the mystery? Why

won't you tell Sally and me anything? What does Doc
Trencher expect to find down there, except the wreck of a
little boat?

TRENCHER (amused): Don't pay no attention to the kid, Mr.
Stanley. He's just sore because you won't let *him* do any
diving.

DICK: I certainly hoped you'd let me have a shot at it, governor. Diving's been my hobby for five years.

TRENCHER (grimly): Diving's not fun, kiddo.

DICK: I know that, Doc.

TRENCHER: Wait till you lose the shot-rope and can't find
your way back to the ship. Wait till you foul your airpipe.
Wait till you come up too quick, and get the bends so bad
that . . .

*(During this speech, a motorboat is heard faintly
approaching. A voice calls.)*

VOICE: Ola, amigo! Ola, amigo!

STANLEY: What the devil's that?

FORBES: Mr. Stanley.

STANLEY: Yes, Captain Forbes?

FORBES: There's a motorboat comin' up to port. And a little
old white-haired chap—brown as coffee—in a white
linen suit and a Panama hat, standing up at the wheel and
wavin' his arms like a windmill.

STANLEY (in explosive despair): My God, another official!

DICK: Take it easy, governor.

STANLEY: I've talked to every government official in Cuba.
It's taken me four months—four months!—to get this per-
mission. If I run into just one more tin-pot magistrate, trying to obstruct me . . . !

FORBES: Better see him, though. You never know.

STANLEY: All right, all right! Where is he?

FORBES: Boat's alongside, sir. He's comin' up the ladder now.

STANLEY: Red tape! Red tape!

DICK (*not loudly*): Here he is, governor. Better be polite.

STANLEY (*with an effort at heartiness*): Buenas afternoonas, señor. Buenas afternoonas. You spikka da Eenglish, no? (LEON ROMERO's *voice suggests a hale, hearty, elderly man, with hardly any accent.*)

ROMERO: I do indeed "spikka da Eenglish." And, I trust, in no uncultured accent.

DICK (*under his breath*): That's got you, governor.

STANLEY (*under his breath*): Be quiet, whelp!

ROMERO: I sweep off my hat—so. I make you the old-fashioned bow—so. I am Leon Romero: your servant.

STANLEY: I make *you* the old-fashioned bow, Mr. Romero. And I want to point out that I've got an order, signed by the Governor-General of Camaguey, authorizing me to conduct their diving operations in these waters. If you want to stop me—

ROMERO: Oh, but my dear sir! I don't wish to stop you. It is merely that I own the bay here . . .

STANLEY (*startled*): You own the bay?

ROMERO: Well, I own all the land hereabouts. My hacienda is a mile beyond the trees here. And—I am curious. You are American?

STANLEY: No. We're English.

ROMERO: English. I see. You have indeed come a long way. (*Sharply*) May I ask why?

STANLEY: Look here, Mr. Romero. You say you don't want to make trouble.

ROMERO (*sulkily*): Provided my curiosity is satisfied, no.

STANLEY: If I tell you the whole story—here and now—will you let me get on with it?

ROMERO: With all my heart. I promise.

STANLEY: Then—what about coming below to the cabin, and having a drink with us?

ROMERO: I shall be honored, señor.

FORBES: Better hurry up, Mr. Stanley. There's a storm comin'.

(*Music up. The Narrator speaks through.*)

NARRATOR: Below, in the main saloon—white-painted, with its brass-bound portholes and whirring fans—the heat pressed even more thickly between decks as . . .

STANLEY: By the way, Mr. Romero, let me introduce my daughter, Sally. She's married to Dick Lawrence here. Sally: Mr. Romero.

SALLY: How do you do?

ROMERO: I am enchanted, Mrs. Lawrence.

DICK: He makes you the old-fashioned bow, Sally. Don't you like it?

SALLY: I love it, Dick. I only wish others would be as gallant. Please sit down, Mr. Romero.

ROMERO: I thank you.

SALLY: You'll find cigarettes on the table. Dick, get something with ice in it, will you?

ROMERO: Your father, Mrs. Lawrence, promised to tell me why he comes to explore this bay.

SALLY: (*surprised*): He's promised to tell you? Then I wish he'd tell us! Dick?

DICK: Yes, angel-face?

SALLY: Never mind the drinks for a minute. Come and sit down.

STANLEY (*leisurely*): Tell me, Mr. Romero. You're a Cuban, of course?

ROMERO: No, I'm a Spaniard. I came here only eight, ten years ago.

STANLEY: Then *that's* why you haven't heard.

ROMERO: Heard—what?

STANLEY (*ignoring this*): It'll be no news to you, at least, that up to 1898 this island was owned by Spain? And in 1898 there was war with the United States?

ROMERO: With unhappy results for my country. Well?

STANLEY: Now look out of the porthole there. At the ruined landing-stage on the other side of the key.

ROMERO: Y-e-es, I know it well.

STANLEY: In the late nineties all the forest land for miles beyond was a sugar plantation. It was owned by a big man named Gonzales, but nobody called him anything except the Red Devil.

ROMERO (*slowly*): The Red Devil.

STANLEY: He was hated—loathed is a better word—by Spaniards and Yankees alike. It wasn't a plantation he kept; it was a slave colony. He'd flog men to death when they couldn't work. He'd crucify women to trees if they didn't please him. There were voodoo practices too: that's how the fable of the giant octopus got started.

SALLY: My father doesn't really believe all this nonsense, Mr. Romero. He's just being theatrical.

STANLEY (*sharply*): *Will* you be quiet, Sally—I'm stating facts.

SALLY: Sorry, Dad.

STANLEY: The Red Devil had one associate. An odd little card named Pedro, who'd knocked about all over the world. Pedro had been a sponge-diver in the Mediterranean. He'd run guns in Morocco. Mad as a hatter, in spite of his smooth manners, and very nearly a match for the Red Devil in torturing people. (*Slight pause*) That sort of thing couldn't go on forever, even with the whole island in a state of civil war. The Red Devil knew that sooner or later he'd have to get out in a hurry. So he and Pedro, with their own hands, built a big cabin cruiser.

ROMERO (*doubtful*): One moment, please. I do not quite . . . a "cabin cruiser"?

DICK: Sort of glorified motorboat, Mr. Romero. With living quarters and all.

STANLEY: They moored it to the landing-stage there. And they went on amassing a fortune—in American silver dollars. Ever see a silver dollar?

ROMERO: No, I don't think so.

STANLEY: They haven't been coined for years. But I've got one here. (*Rattle of large coin on table*) Heavy, isn't it? Like a silver cartwheel.

ROMERO (*worried*): My friend, you are trying to tell me something. Yes. But for the life of me, I can't think what.

DICK: That's just the point.

SALLY: Dad's only being mysterious.

DICK: I wonder.

STANLEY: Those two, the Red Devil and Pedro, got together a fortune and hid it. Where did they hide it?

ROMERO: Well? Did anyone try to find it?

STANLEY: Many people, in those upset times. A guerilla party even raided the plantation to get it. They searched the house: it wasn't there. They searched the grounds: it wasn't buried anywhere, or the peons would have known. They searched the cabin cruiser: still no result. Where *had* those two hidden the money?

ROMERO: Do *you* know, my friend?

STANLEY: Yes, I rather think I do.

DICK (*excitedly*): Look here, governor! That story about the Red Devil is old stuff. But this new bit, about a hidden fortune . . .

STANLEY (*politely*): Shall I go on, Mr. Romero?

ROMERO (*controlling excitement*): Yes, please do.

STANLEY: In the spring of '98, the civil troubles ended in war with the United States. The Red Devil could hear battleship guns from Santiago harbor. Infantry were landing; and there were a number of Yanks who'd sworn to get the Red Devil if they didn't do anything else. He decided to cut and run for it in that cabin cruiser . . .

ROMERO: With his friend Pedro?

STANLEY: No. Alone.

ROMERO: I see.

STANLEY: It was during a tropical thunderstorm, first black as pitch and then white with lightning followed by thunder . . .

(*Roll of thunder*)

SALLY: It's going to storm now. Look at that sky!

ROMERO: Storm? But this—surely—will interrupt your diving work?

DICK: In a land-locked bay? Not likely!

ROMERO: Go on, please, about the Red Devil.

STANLEY: He hadn't got away any too soon. As he ran for the jetty, people at his house could see the blue shirts of the Yankee riflemen coming through the wood. The two leading ones had a Gatling gun. Our Red Devil jumped into the boat, started the motor—it was a primitive affair in those days—and started out across the bay. In the next white lighting flash . . .

ROMERO: Well?

STANLEY: . . . they saw Pedro standing at the end of the pier.

ROMERO: Not to be left behind, eh?

STANLEY: Pedro made a flying leap—God knows how he did it—and landed on the deck. They saw him crawling below, after the Red Devil, with a knife in his teeth. The troops set up their Gatling gun and sprayed bullets after the boat, apparently without effect in that bad light. The boat was half way across the bay when . . . it happened.

ROMERO: What happened?

STANLEY: An old voodoo-woman later swore she saw a tentacle, a slimy tentacle . . .

SALLY: This is the part I hate.

STANLEY: . . . a slimy tentacle come up out of the water and fasten round the boat. Whether or not that was true, *some-*

thing happened. The boat didn't merely sink; it was pulled or dragged under. They heard the Red Devil screaming; they saw a thrashing in the water; the next second—nothing.

ROMERO: And—afterwards?

STANLEY (*coolly*): Sorry, old man. That's all.

ROMERO: All?

STANLEY: All until tonight. Until I can send Doc Trencher down and prove my theory. Have I satisfied your curiosity?

ROMERO: Satisfied it? *Madre de Dios!* I am worse than ever!

DICK: Why not stay and see the diving, Mr. Romero?

ROMERO: No, no, no, no! If it is going to rain, I return to my own boat. But—

STANLEY: But what? You're not going to make trouble for us?

ROMERO: No, no, no! I was thinking . . . both Pedro and the Red Devil died when *something* caught their boat?

STANLEY: Presumably. No trace of them was ever found.

ROMERO: I say no more, my friend. But—I am not easy. What is down under that bay?

(*Music up. The Narrator speaks through.*)

NARRATOR: On deck again, with the sky darkening and wind-blown palmetto trees outlined against lightning. Doc Trencher on the iron ladder, ready to go down. The yacht, the dark gray-green water heaving in a very gentle swell, as . . .

(*Crash of thunder*)

STANLEY: If my calculations are right, we ought to be just over the wreck of the cabin cruiser. Dick!

DICK: Yes, governor?

STANLEY (*indulgently satirical*): As the so-called diving expert, we'll let you take charge now—All right with you, Trencher?

TRENCHER (*muffled*): The kid knows his stuff, Mr. Stanley. It suits me.

STANLEY: The job's yours, Dick.

DICK (*calling*): Stand by the pumps!

BROWNING (*off*): Ready, sir!

DICK: Fasten on diver's back and breast weights. Easy. Not too tight a hitch—Okay, Doc?

TRENCHER: Okay, kid.

DICK: Start the pumps.

(*The pumps are heard in the background; then taken down so as to be nearly inaudible.*)

DICK: Fasten on the diver's face glass. Three turns to the right. Slow. That's got it. Down you go, Doc. (*Thudding footsteps are heard descending an iron ladder.*) We can't talk to him now except through the telephone. Will you take the telephone, governor, or shall I?

STANLEY: Let me have it. I want to direct him.

DICK: Here you are.

STANLEY: Hello, Trencher. Can you hear me?

(*Trencher's voice is now heard against air-noises inside the helmet.*)

TRENCHER: Sure. (*Formally*) Diver leaving ship.

DICK: Full speed the pumps! Diver leaving ship!

(*We hear the rush and bubbling as the waters close over Trencher.*)

SALLY: He's well under now. I wouldn't go down there for a thousand pounds!

STANLEY: Sally, what the devil are you doing here?

SALLY: I couldn't stay away! I've *got* to see it! What were those things he was carrying?

DICK: A diver's lamp and an oxy-hydrogen blowtorch.

SALLY: Oxy-hydrogen blowtorch?

DICK: For cutting wood or metal under water. Quiet now!

STANLEY: Hello, Trencher. Can you hear me? (*Slight pause*) Trencher! (*Roll of thunder*) Confound that thunder!

SALLY: You don't think anything's happened?

STANLEY: *Trencher!*

TRENCHER: (*against helmet noises*): Keep your shirt on, boss. Everything's under control. (*Formally*) Diver now on sea floor.

DICK (*calling*): What are your pumps making?

BROWNING: Twenty-five per minute, sir.

DICK: That'll do. Keep her steady.

STANLEY: Trencher, how are the conditions down there?

TRENCHER: Muddy as hell. Can't see a thing. Wait a second till it settles.

STANLEY: Any tide or swell?

TRENCHER: Practically none.

SALLY: The storm's going to break any minute. I know it can't affect him down there. But I wish it had been a clear day. I do wish it had been a clear day.

TRENCHER (*excited*): Mr. Stanley! You were right! It's here!

STANLEY: What is?

TRENCHER: The wreck of the cabin cruiser. Practically in front of me.

STANLEY: Got your light on?

TRENCHER: Sure, sure. I—(*Stops dead*)

STANLEY: *What's wrong?*

TRENCHER (*oddly*): Funny-looking shadow just went past me.

SALLY (*bursting out*): For God's sake, be careful!

STANLEY: Careful of what? He's safe as houses. In a few minutes we're going to learn the whole truth.

DICK (*exasperated*): Don't you think, governor, it's about time you explained this mystery?

STANLEY: A while ago, Dick, I asked you and Sally and Romero two questions. First, what dragged the boat under? Second, what happened to the Red Devil's fortune in silver dollars?

SALLY (*half-guessing*): You don't mean that—?

DICK: Wait a minute! You told us a guerilla party searched that boat without finding the money.

STANLEY: So they did. Because Pedro and the Red Devil had built it with double bulkheads.

SALLY: Double bulkheads?

STANLEY: Double walls, with the money packed inside. What the fools forgot was that all that cash in heavy silver dollars would weigh nearly half a ton. And the boat couldn't stand that weight. She was struck below the water line by Gatling gun bullets. So she simply cracked up and went down. *Now* do you understand?

DICK: Y-e-es. I think I do.

STANLEY: There's no devil-fish down there, my fatheads. But there *is* three-quarters of a million dollars for intelligent people to pick up.

TRENCHER: Mr. Stanley!

STANLEY: Quiet, everybody! Yes, Trencher?

TRENCHER: Somebody's been at this wreck.

STANLEY: How do you mean, *at* it?

TRENCHER: I mean the bulkheads are broke open. I mean—
(*The voice ends in a shrill scream, hollow inside the helmet.*)

STANLEY: Trencher! What's wrong?

TRENCHER (*screaming out*): It's got me! *God almighty, it's got me!*
(*The scream begins again, but is choked off as though water had poured into the helmet.*)

DICK: Governor! Give me that phone!

STANLEY: Well!

DICK: It's dead! The phone's dead!

BROWNING: Mr. Lawrence, the pumps aren't working right. Look at the gauge.

DICK: You mean his airpipe's fouled?

BROWNING: I think—I think his airpipe's out.

DICK: That's impossible! Haul him up by the breast-rope.

BROWNING: Richards gave it a tug, sir. And it came clean away through the water. The breast-rope's out too.

STANLEY (*not loudly*): Air-line out. Breast-rope out. What in Satan's name . . . ?

SALLY: Yes. What *is* it?

DICK: Listen, governor. You've got a spare set of diving gear, haven't you?

STANLEY: Yes. Why?

DICK: I'm going down there.

SALLY: You're not! I won't let you!

STANLEY: If his air-line's cut, son, that's the end of it. He's a goner.

DICK: Probably, yes. But in sixty feet of water there's still a chance.

STANLEY: And the thing that's down there? The thing that cuts airpipes and breast-ropes as though they were made out of paper?

DICK: I'll take along an oxy-hydrogen blowtorch with flame pressure enough to cut solid steel. And I'll blast it against anything that comes near me. Doesn't that satisfy you?

FORBES: Mr. Stanley?

STANLEY: Yes, Captain Forbes?

FORBES: There's no telephone attached to the other diving suit, that's all. If he goes down in that, he'll have to go down with no communication except rope signals.

SALLY: No! I won't allow it!

DICK: I tell you, governor, it's the only possible way of saving Doc Trencher's life. What do you say? Yes or no?

STANLEY: All right, son. Get into your gear.

(*Music up. The Narrator speaks through.*)

NARRATOR: Frantic seconds, frantic minutes. Time for other preparations to be made. Time for another diver to be dressed. Again the churning of the pumps, under a lightning-flecked sky and with the yacht still heaving uneasily. Again the thud of lead-soled boots on the ladder. Again the ominous bubbling rush of water as the big helmet sinks below the surface. Again, on the deck of the yacht *Venturer*, a white-faced group waiting, waiting, waiting . . .

(*The noise of the pumps rises as the music fades, and then goes out altogether.*)

SALLY: He's been down there for five minutes! Something's happened!

STANLEY (*fiercely*): Sally! Listen to me!

SALLY: Well, Dad?

STANLEY: He's been down exactly thirty seconds. Look at my watch.

SALLY: I *know* something's happened!

FORBES: The emergency signal, miss, is four pulls on the airpipe. And he hasn't given that signal.

STANLEY: The last one we got was one of the breast-rope for "all right."

FORBES: He'll never save Doc Trencher, though.

STANLEY: He'll have a ruddy good try, Captain Forbes! He—

SALLY: Dad! Look! The airpipe's moving!

STANLEY: I see it!

SALLY: One, two, three, f—

FORBES (*calling*): Emergency signal, Mr. Browning! Haul him up!

BROWNING (*off*): Aye, aye, sir!

STANLEY: Don't bring him up too fast. You mustn't do that. Doc Trencher says that's what gives divers the bends.

FORBES: He hasn't been down long enough for that, Mr.

Stanley. Anyway, we'll have to risk it—Mr. Browning, haul away!

BROWNING: Yes, sir.

FORBES: But not too fast, mind you. Easy does it. Easy, easy . . .

BROWNING: Heavy weight on this rope, sir.

SALLY: You don't mean something's got hold of him?

FORBES: More likely he's carrying Trencher's body. Easy does it. Easy. E-asy . . .

(There is a pause, after which we hear the bubbling rush of a diver surfacing).

STANLEY: There's his helmet! He's up safely! And he's got Trencher!

FORBES: Anderson! Young! Stand by to get Trencher aboard. Holmes! MacAndrew! Give Mr. Lawrence a hand. Easy does it now. E-asy . . .

(Music up to indicate the passage of a few minutes.)

STANLEY: There's your helmet off, son. Lean back against the bulkhead, now. How do you feel?

(Slight pause. Hard breathing from Dick.)

DICK: It's all right, governor. Got a drop of brandy?

FORBES: Get it for you in half a tick, Mr. Lawrence. You're lookin' a bit white.

DICK: Yes. How's Trencher?

FORBES: Can't tell yet. It's—a bad case.

DICK *(heavily)*: Yes, I was afraid of that.

SALLY *(tearful)*: Dick, you idiot! You scared us half to death! What happened?

DICK: I—met the devil-fish.

STANLEY: You—did what?

DICK: I met the devil-fish. And the devil-fish, if you want to call it that, is dead.

STANLEY *(quietly)*: Go on, Dick.

DICK: I had my lamp, but I didn't turn it on till I reached bottom, in case the glass should crack. Then I did turn it on. I found Doc lying in the mud and silt beside the wreck of the boat. And he was right about one thing, too. Somebody had been at it.

STANLEY: How do you mean?

DICK: Somebody had cracked open the bulkheads. Somebody, time after time, had been scooping loads of silver dollars out of that boat. And, while I was standing there wondering what in blazes it meant, *I* saw a shadow.

SALLY: You mean—?

DICK: I glanced up. And looking at me through the glass of my helmet was—

SALLY: Was what?

DICK: A human face.

(Knife-chord)

STANLEY: *What's that?*

DICK: Nothing supernatural, governor. Don't you remember what you told me about Pedro, the little partner of the Red Devil?

STANLEY: Well?

DICK: Pedro had been a sponge-diver. And that means . . .

STANLEY: It means these fellows who go down with only a knife and a loin-cloth, and can stay under water anything up to two minutes.

DICK: That's right, governor. Got it in one.

SALLY: Then Pedro didn't die when the boat was wrecked?

DICK: Drown a sponge-diver? What do *you* think?

STANLEY: But Pedro . . .

DICK: He's been haunting this place for years. Guarding the treasure. Getting money when he needed it. And when we arrived . . .

SALLY: Dick! What happened down there?

DICK: He took Trencher from behind with a razor-edged knife. But the fool swam straight in front of me with his white hair waving and a maniac's face if I ever saw one. I did the only thing I could do: I gave him a blast of the oxy-hydrogen gun straight through the stomach. (*Reaction from Sally*) I recognized him immediately, of course.

STANLEY: You recognized him? But you've never seen this fellow Pedro!

DICK: Oh, yes, I have. So have you.

STANLEY: *What's that?*

DICK: He must have slipped off his clothes, slid over the side of the motorboat, and waited for Trencher as he later waited for me. Don't you understand even yet, governor?

STANLEY (*suddenly realizing*): This Pedro was . . . ?

DICK: He was the man you just entertained aboard this yacht, the affable gentleman who called himself Señor Leon Romero. (*Slight pause*) There's his body floating to the surface now.

(*Music up*)

SCOTLAND YARD'S CHRISTMAS

With Christmas only three days away, men and women throughout London were celebrating the season of joy and goodwill by elbowing and pushing each other ferociously through every shop and department store.

And at Omnium's, the giant store in Oxford Street, it was worse than anywhere else.

Outside, past lanes of lighted windows, festive snowflakes sifted from a darkening sky. A loudspeaker van blared "Hark the Herald Angels Sing" to crowds struggling in slush.

Inside, frantic shoppers assailed the gift counters, and assaulted each other in the process.

Their noise was a shuffle and roar. Their aroma was a steam of wet overcoats.

And at the entrance to Toyland on the fifth floor stood a pretty, fair-haired girl. Her loving glance at the tall, handsome man beside her was clouded with annoyance. The little boy, clutching his hand, jumped up and down in a desperate attempt to break his far-away look of intense preoccupation.

The girl said, "For heaven's sake, Bob, what *is* the matter with you?"

Detective Superintendent Robert Pollard for a moment did not reply. Officially off duty, he was still thinking hard about the case he had left for others to solve at New Scotland Yard—so that he could take his fiancée, Elsa Rawson, shopping at Omnium's, and her six-year-old nephew, Tommy, to the toyfair.

"Bob," said the girl again, in exasperation, "do look as though you're enjoying yourself."

"I've just thought," said Bob, returning once again to the shopping battle. "When I left the office, I didn't ring the Duty Room to say where I was going."

"And that's all?" asked the astonished Elsa. "That's all you're worried about?"

"Elsa, everybody has to phone the Duty Room when he leaves Scotland Yard . . ."

Young Tommy, saucer-eyed, leaped high in the air.

"Scotland Yard!" he cried in ecstasy. "Scotland Yard . . . Yeepee!"

"Tommy, please do be quiet," said Elsa, "or Uncle Bob won't take you to see Father Christmas." Tommy writhed. Privately, he thought this Father Christmas business all a gag. But you couldn't be sure, and it was too close to Christmas to take any risks.

"Anyway, Bob, is it all that important?" she asked, searching his face closely for an endearing look.

From the moment they left for their shopping expedition, Elsa's suspicion grew—Bob did not have his mind on her. She wondered if perhaps Tommy's presence had annoyed him. Was he really more concerned about his precious crime work than pleasing her?

She couldn't restrain a petulant note when she asked:

"And how are all the little coppers at Scotland Yard? Are they having a happy Christmas?"

To Detective Superintendent Pollard this was the last straw. He raised his powerful voice above a din which included the whiz of toy trains and a radio loudly blaring "Hark the Herald Angels Sing."

"If anybody at the Yard started singing about herald angels," Pollard said, "I hate to think what would happen to him. Anyway, they've got something else to think about right now, Elsa. It's a really big case. And we're all in a flap about it."

"Is it a murder, Uncle Bob?" screamed Tommy.

"No, old chap, it's not a murder. And yet, in a way, it's worse."

"Crumbs," said Tommy, and jumped so high that he seemed to be levitated from Pollard's hand.

"Bob, stop it!" snapped Elsa. "You mustn't tease the child."

"I am not teasing. This case isn't a teasing matter. It's not every day that we hear about two people, at exactly the same moment, but in completely different parts of London, both disappearing like soap-bubbles before the eyes of police witnesses."

"Tommy, don't listen! He's joking!"

"Elsa, I'm not. A crook known as 'The Colonel' and another crook known as 'Shorty' both vanished off the face of the earth. Twenty thousand pounds' worth of uncut diamonds went with them. The point is *how did they vanish?*"

"Tommy, don't believe a word of this," cried Elsa, gripping Tommy's other hand so that he was tugged between them. "Uncle Bob never talks about police work. I can't make him talk about it!"

In fact, having just reached the howling centre of Toyland, Bob couldn't make himself heard.

Tommy was yanked away between his captors to a place of comparative quiet. There, behind his counter, the conjuror was exhibiting a large skull which first made whistling noises and then talked like Marshal Wyatt Earp.

Elsa was shivering with excitement.

"Why do they call him The Colonel?"

"Because he looks like a colonel in a comic paper. Middle-aged; military bearing; usually wears an eyeglass. Even when he doesn't wear an eyeglass, he has a gesture he can't help making. He keeps dragging down the side of his left eye. Like this!"

"Darling, for heaven's sake, don't *leer*. You look horrible."

"Well, so does The Colonel. But you can spot that gesture

a mile away, and you can spot him. As a rule, he's a confidence man."

"A confidence man? You mean he swindled somebody out of £20,000 worth of uncut diamonds?"

"No!" Pollard snapped. "It's worse. For the first time in his life, the fool used violence."

"Did he *murder* somebody?" shouted Elsa. "Cut some poor man's throat?"

Tommy, who had been trying vainly to scream gave it up and writhed in an agony of fascination. But Pollard only shook his head.

"Elsa, don't be so infernally bloodthirsty! *No*."

"Then what was it?"

"In Sykes Street, a little turning off Upper Regent Street, there's a diamond-merchant named Van Bele. For years, Van Bele's been carrying regularly a fortune in uncut stones in a little wash-leather bag in his pocket. Up to now he's got away with it; nobody's bothered him."

"And now?"

"On Tuesday, about 10:15 A.M., Van Bele had a phone-call asking him to visit some clients. It was a fake call; The Colonel sent it. Van Bele walked downstairs from his office. The Colonel, in his best Savile Row suit and overcoat, was waiting in the entry. He just walloped Van Bele on the jaw, knocked him out, took the little leather bag, and ran for it."

Elsa spluttered.

"But—my dear Bob! Wouldn't they have caught him straight away?"

"No. With all this Christmas rush, he could have got clean away. But he had bad luck. Two constables were coming along Sykes Street opposite the Regent Street end. They saw our friend grab the bag and run.

"The Colonel jumped aboard a bus crossing Oxford Circus and went along Oxford Street. One of the constables followed; the other phoned the Yard.

"Within a few minutes they had the whole area covered in a net. In just two minutes, one of the Sweeneys—sorry, I mean a Flying Squad car—pulled up beside the bus in Oxford Street. The Colonel was standing on the platform.

"He jumped down, and dodged across the street. Two of our men followed, keeping him in sight. The Colonel, believe it or not, ran into Omnium's. Our men still had him in sight when he ducked into a telephone box in the basement. And that's all."

"All? What do you mean?"

"The Colonel just vanished."

"In the telephone box?"

"Apparently, yes."

"But he can't have done!"

"I know it's impossible. But it happened."

Behind them, at the magician's counter, the talking skull left off gibbering and now loudly sang "Silent Night" in competition to the radio's version of "Silent Night." But Elsa, Tommy, and Pollard himself had forgotten the pandemonium of Toyland.

"Remember," Pollard insisted, "that these diamonds were uncut. That's to say: they were only greyish lumps, like pebbles, and of no use to The Colonel until they were cut and polished.

"What's the first thing he would do? He'd get in touch with his diamond-cutter, of course. Naturally, Criminal Records knew who it was."

"And this diamond-cutter was the other man you mentioned . . . Shorty?"

"Yes. Except that Shorty is a woman."

"A woman?" said Elsa, yanking Tommy forward.

"Yes; why not?" retorted Pollard, yanking Tommy back. "She's The Colonel's girlfriend. They live not far apart.

"After the first phone-call to the Yard, the division had orders to put a tail on Shorty. Not to arrest her—"

"Why ever not?"

"Dammit, Elsa, Shorty hadn't done anything—yet.

"But where was The Colonel meeting her to give her the diamonds? And how was he going to give her the diamonds? And when? That's what they had to know."

"So . . ."

"Two policewomen, in plain clothes, picked up Shorty outside her lodgings. Shorty was carrying a large parcel. She knew she was being followed. You'll have guessed she and The Colonel planned this before-hand, in case they were followed. Shorty's quite an attractive trick, by the way: brunette, smooth skin, in her early twenties. She walked faster. So did the policewomen. Shorty hurried into Ilkley's—that's that big women's dress shop not far from here. So did the policewomen. And in the shop, Shorty dodged into a telephone box . . ."

Here Pollard had to stop.

"You're not going to tell me," said Elsa, who still thought that her beloved was spinning a fairy story, "that she disappeared out of a 'phone box?"

"Apparently, yes. Parcel and all."

Elsa's pretty face coloured pink with anger. She turned away abruptly.

"I don't believe it," she said, violently jerking Tommy's left arm. "It's silly! Look at the crowd here now. Just look!"

"Very well," said Pollard, jerking Tommy's right arm. "I'm looking. What about it?"

"Crowds and crowds and crowds," said Elsa, "all moving. Could you be certain somebody's disappeared out of a 'phone box, even if you were only ten feet away?"

"You could be pretty certain that two different people couldn't vanish out of two different shops under the conditions the police established. As soon as The Colonel entered Omnium's, and Shorty entered Ilkley's, both places were surrounded. Every possible entrance or exit was guarded. Every nook and cranny was searched. Every customer was stopped and questioned."

"Wait! What about all the sales staff?"

"They were the first to be questioned. Both Omnium's and Ilkley's open at nine o'clock. The managers could tell from their time-sheets that every person was at his or her proper place. No employee could have been larking about with a pocket full of diamonds, or could have changed places afterwards with somebody who had. Face it, my dear! Shorty and The Colonel didn't leave the shops. And yet they weren't in the buildings either. They'd simply vanished."

Elsa marched forward, dragging the others like a string of sausages.

"Come along, Tommy," she said in exasperation. "It's not very nice of Uncle Bob to enrage you like this. He's insufferable, and I'll never speak to him again."

"Now wait a bit, Elsa!"

"This way, Tommy; mind where you're going. We'll take you to see Father Christmas."

They had pushed through to a long grotto, a kind of mysterious and softly lighted cavern, where even in Toyland voices were hushed.

Here children walked slowly.

At the grotto pay box, over which large red letters said that Father Christmas would be in attendance from 11A.M. to 6 P.M., Pollard bought three tickets.

The grotto was murmurous with "Oh's!" and "Ah's!" Brightly painted in cardboard or plaster, figures and backgrounds showed fairy stories. They were well along in the cavern when Pollard stopped. His mouth fell open. He stood rigid, staring straight ahead.

At the end of the cavern, on a platform festooned in holly where children could mount the two steps and whisper their wishes, sat Father Christmas himself.

At Father Christmas's right hand was a table piled with small gift-boxes wrapped in bright paper.

Even as Pollard stared, a little girl of possibly twelve years walked up the steps.

She was very dainty in white fur jacket and white cap. Her long yellow curls fell forward as she bent to whisper.

Father Christmas chuckled. He nodded. Selecting a gift-box from the table, he turned back in one vast beam to give this present to his small friend. And, as he did so, Father Christmas's large left eyebrow closed down as though he leered or held an eyeglass.

"*Uncle Bob!*" screamed Tommy. "Did you see it? The funny eyes. You remember. You said The Colonel . . ."

Detective Superintendent Pollard, Criminal Investigation Department, quickly turned to the boy and hushed him.

Then, in a flash, he charged.

He was a big man. He avoided the children, but parents scattered before him like skittles. There was a crash as he jumped up on the platform.

"I don't think you'd like that one, my dear," he said pleasantly to the little girl, and nodded towards the box held out in Father Christmas's hand.

In a low voice he added: "Better give me the diamonds, Colonel. As for you, Shorty . . ."

The little girl lifted sweet and innocent eyes.

"Coppers!" she whispered, showing her teeth. "He's a copper, Colonel; that's what the so-and-so is."

"When a man is called Shorty," said Pollard in the same

low tone, "it may not mean much. But when a woman is called that, as we ought to have realized, she must be almost a dwarf. I suppose your little-girl clothes, and the blonde wig, were in that parcel? And you changed in the dress-shop? Nobody would notice a twelve-year-old; the police weren't to blame for that mistake.

"But we were to be blamed about you, Colonel," he added. "Omnium's opens at nine; we thought everybody had to be on duty then. And yet, as you can see by a sign over the pay-box back there, this grotto doesn't open until eleven. You could slosh Van Bele and get back on time. [Both you and Shorty vanished by becoming someone else, someone whom the police would not suspect. The parcel Shorty was carrying contained her wig and clothes which made her look twelve years old, and when she ducked into a 'phone box she quickly changed clothes. You did something similar. I don't know whether you had the Father Christmas costume hidden in the 'phone box and were willing to take a chance that the box would be unoccupied when you needed it, or whether you were wearing it under your overcoat and Savile Row suit, but when you stepped out you were Father Christmas, not The Colonel. The police, trying to keep you in sight in the hordes of Christmas shoppers, did not suspect Father Christmas, whom they thought had been at work when the crime was committed].

In that paralyzed scene, the bright-coloured box was still held out in Father Christmas's hand. "Cut and run for it, Shorty!" he chuckled. "I hate to spoil the kids' Christmas, but I'll get this copper before they get me."

"Think so?" smiled Pollard. "You haven't a chance against me and you know it. I can't help you. But it's Christmas—and I can help Shorty get away. Fair?"

"Turn it up, copper!" sneered the sweet-faced girl—and yet an edge of hope appeared in her face.

"Give me the box," Pollard said. "If the diamonds are inside, she hasn't officially received them. She can go now and take her chance of being picked up later. Fair?"

Father Christmas looked warily at Pollard before exchanging a knowing glance with the girl.

Then, without a word, he handed over the box to Pollard.

As he did so, he noticeably sagged with relief behind his beard.

Then his rich, soothing, cultured voice rang out.

"Ladies and Gentlemen!" carolled Father Christmas. "This gentleman is particularly anxious to have this box. I hope he finds in it what he's looking for.

"Personally, I'd rather give the little girl another box. Here it is. Now hurry down the steps, and out of this store. Others are waiting."

At the sight of a monocled Father Christmas, a ripple of laughter spread out over the grotto, carrying with it the spirit of Christmas as children crowded forward.

Tommy, pushing forward, hardly noticed that Elsa was no longer watching Father Christmas.

She was looking at Pollard—and in her eyes shone admiration—and unconcealed adoration!

For Mal, because you always make me laugh.

1

There's a give and take to magic: if you craft a smart spell, the universe is supposed to help you out.

Apparently, magic didn't get the memo.

I glanced up at the two vampires and clenched my hand around the cards. Ethan gave me an encouraging smile, but Raquel was tapping her foot. I really needed this to work. There was a monster out there, preying on the people of Kurranderra, my adopted hometown. If my magic played ball, I could help find the rogue before it killed anyone else.

I laid the Three of Earth next to the Seven of Air in my circle, then added the Ace of Air over the top. Air was my weakest suit, but *this* time, surely? The Three represented Ethan, Raquel, and me working together. I smiled a little wistfully, hearing Mum's voice in my head saying, *Teamwork makes the dream work*. The Seven was the secret we wanted to steal, and the Ace would activate the spell.

"Aren't there supposed to be more cards in the deck?" Raquel asked, her red lip curled ever so slightly.

The blond vampire's bare arms were folded across her chest, and she was wearing a sleeveless top and a tight leather miniskirt. In September. In the Blue Mountains. Honestly, just *looking* at her made me break out in goosebumps.

I was rugged up like a bag lady in layers of clothes and I was *still* cold. The chill of the ground seeped through my jeans where I knelt in the grass, and the night air nipped at my face. September in the mountains was technically spring, but during the middle of the night, it was cold enough to freeze the balls off a brass monkey out here.

"Aren't vampires supposed to clean up their own messes?" Ariel sniped. "Shouldn't she at least *pretend* to be grateful that you're helping them find their stupid elder?"

Neither of the vampires reacted, of course. I cast Ariel a sideways glance. She stood beside them, her pale, silvery hair drifting around her head as if she were underwater. She was wearing the same T-shirt I was, neon pink with *Nap Queen* splashed across the front, though mine was covered by a jumper and a heavy jacket.

Ariel's bare arms didn't make me feel colder, though; she wasn't like the rest of us. She'd been my constant companion since I was six years old, but no one else could see or hear her—and I'd given up trying to convince people she existed long ago. Whatever she was made of, it wasn't flesh.

Calm your farm, I told her in my mind. *She'll come in handy when I find something. If I find something.*